# TALES OF HEROES, GODS & MONSTERS

# NORSE

# MYTHS & LEGENDS

FLAME TREE PUBLISHING
6 Melbray Mews, Fulham,
London SW6 3NS, United Kingdom
www.flametreepublishing.com

First published and copyright © 2022
Flame Tree Publishing Ltd

24 26 25 23
5 7 9 10 8 6 4

ISBN: 978-1-83964-886-1

Cover and pattern art was created by Flame Tree Studio, with elements courtesy of
Shutterstock.com/d1sk.

Judith John (Glossary) is a writer and editor specializing in literature and history. A former
secondary school English Language and Literature teacher, she has subsequently worked
as an editor on major educational projects, including *English A: Literature* for the Pearson
International Baccalaureate series. Judith's major research interests include Romantic and
Gothic literature, and Renaissance drama.

Other contributors, authors, editors and sources for this series include:
Loren Auerbach, Norman Bancroft-Hunt, E.M. Berens, Katharine Berry Judson, Laura
Bulbeck, Jeremiah Curtin, O.B. Duane, Dr Ray Dunning, W.W. Gibbings, H. A.
Guerber, Jake Jackson, Joseph Jacobs, Judith John, J.W. Mackail (translator of Virgil's
Aeneid) Chris McNab, Professor James Riordan, Rachel Storm, K.E. Sullivan.

A copy of the CIP data for this book is available
from the British Library.

Designed and created in the UK | Printed and bound in China

COLLECTOR'S EDITIONS

# TALES OF HEROES, GODS & MONSTERS

# NORSE

## MYTHS & LEGENDS

**Reading List & Glossary of Terms
with a New Introduction by
DR. LUKE JOHN MURPHY**

FLAME TREE PUBLISHING

# CONTENTS

# Legends of Odin and Frigga .......................... 61

# Legends of Loki ............................................. 104

# Legends of Thor ............................................ 124

# CONTENTS

# TALES OF HEROES, GODS & MONSTERS

# NORSE

# MYTHS & LEGENDS

# SERIES FOREWORD

**Stretching back** to the oral traditions of thousands of years ago, tales of heroes and disaster, creation and conquest have been told by many different civilizations in many different ways. Their impact sits deep within our culture even though the detail in the tales themselves are a loose mix of historical record, transformed narrative and the distortions of hundreds of storytellers.

Today the language of mythology lives with us: our mood is jovial, our countenance is saturnine, we are narcissistic and our modern life is hermetically sealed from others. The nuances of myths and legends form part of our daily routines and help us navigate the world around us, with its half truths and biased reported facts.

The nature of a myth is that its story is already known by most of those who hear it, or read it. Every generation brings a new emphasis, but the fundamentals remain the same: a desire to understand and describe the events and relationships of the world. Many of the great stories are archetypes that help us find our own place, equipping us with tools for self-understanding, both individually and as part of a broader culture.

For Western societies it is Greek mythology that speaks to us most clearly. It greatly influenced the mythological heritage of the ancient Roman civilization and is the lens through which we still see the Celts, the Norse and many of the other great peoples and religions. The Greeks themselves learned much from their neighbours, the Egyptians, an older culture that became weak with age and incestuous leadership.

It is important to understand that what we perceive now as mythology had its own origins in perceptions of the divine and the rituals of the sacred. The earliest civilizations, in the crucible of the Middle East, in the Sumer of the third millennium BC, are the source to which many of the mythic archetypes can be traced. As humankind collected together in cities for the first time, developed writing and industrial scale agriculture, started to irrigate the rivers and attempted to control rather than be at the mercy of its environment, humanity began to write down its tentative explanations of natural events, of floods and plagues, of disease.

Early stories tell of Gods (or god-like animals in the case of tribal societies such as African, Native American or Aboriginal cultures) who are crafty and use their wits to survive, and it is reasonable to suggest that these were the first rulers of the gathering peoples of the earth, later elevated to god-like status with the distance of time. Such tales became more political as cities vied with each other for supremacy, creating new Gods, new hierarchies for their pantheons. The older Gods took on primordial roles and became the preserve of creation and destruction, leaving the new gods to deal with more current, everyday affairs. Empires rose and fell, with Babylon assuming the mantle from Sumeria in the 1800s BC, then in turn to be swept away by the Assyrians of the 1200s BC; then the Assyrians and the

Egyptians were subjugated by the Greeks, the Greeks by the Romans and so on, leading to the spread and assimilation of common themes, ideas and stories throughout the world.

The survival of history is dependent on the telling of good tales, but each one must have the 'feeling' of truth, otherwise it will be ignored. Around the firesides, or embedded in a book or a computer, the myths and legends of the past are still the living materials of retold myth, not restricted to an exploration of origins. Now we have devices and global communications that give us unparalleled access to a diversity of traditions. We can find out about Native American, Indian, Chinese and tribal African mythology in a way that was denied to our ancestors, we can find connections, match the archaeology, religion and the mythologies of the world to build a comprehensive image of the human experience that is endlessly fascinating.

The stories in this book provide an introduction to the themes and concerns of the myths and legends of their respective cultures, with a short introduction to provide a linguistic, geographic and political context. This is where the myths have arrived today, but undoubtedly over the next millennia, they will transform again whilst retaining their essential truths and signs.

*Jake Jackson*
General Editor

# TALES OF HEROES, GODS & MONSTERS
# NORSE
# MYTHS & LEGENDS

# INTRODUCTION
## & FURTHER READING

# A NEW INTRODUCTION TO
# NORSE MYTHOLOGY

## DEEP-ROOTED STORYTELLING

**F**rom lonely islands and icy mountains to windswept seas and sprawling forests, the Scandinavian landscape has long inspired stories that have entertained, illuminated and fascinated audiences. Even today motifs borrowed from Nordic mythology and legends abound in storytelling – not only in historical fiction, but also in works of fantasy, science fiction and super-heroism. As you read this book, you might recognize scenes from that television show you love or characters from that video game that kept you up all night. I know that is one of the reasons I love Norse myths, sagas and legends. I might never sail a longboat to Iceland, embark on a blood feud with my neighbours over a missing sheep or have my hammer stolen by conniving *jǫtnar* ('giants' to you and me), but I have absolutely had to make a new start in a strange place, fallen out with people and once or twice been the target of not-very-funny pranks gone wrong. So despite the fact that these stories – or something like them – have been told for centuries, they continue to speak to me today. I hope that, through this book, they may speak to you too.

## WHAT IS THIS BOOK?
## NORSE MYTHS, SAGAS AND LEGENDS

While this book contains stories from a range of genres, retold by writers from a range of times and places, its focus is firmly on one of the most captivating aspects of the stories told in Old Norse: gods, goddesses, their supernatural foes and the humans with whom they interacted. These stories tend to fall into one of three types.

### Myths

These days we tend to throw around words such as 'myth' or 'legend' quite a lot, generally to mean something untrue. Someone might say 'Did you hear about Dave in Accounts? I heard he once–' only to be interrupted, 'Nah, that's a myth!' Maybe it is or maybe it is not: only Dave knows and he's not telling. However, the myths in this book are not quite like that. Of course, the events outlined here probably did not happen in quite the way the stories make out – assuming they ever happened at all. But that is not necessarily where their importance lies. Technically 'myth' is a term used by scholars to describe a story that explains how *something in the world came to be the way it is.*

Myths can be about big things: where the universe comes from, for instance, or what mountains are made out of. Myths in this book relate how Óðinn (Odin) and his family killed Ymir – the primeval being, and a not-so-distant relation of theirs – and constructed the world from his corpse (pages 46–49). Yet myths can also be about small things. Another story retold here recounts how salmon came to be, well, salmon-shaped. Loki, the shapeshifting troublemaker, was hiding out in the shape of a salmon when the proverbially strong Þórr (Thor) grabbed him by the tail. Thor seized him so hard that all salmon since have much narrower tails than other fish (page 117).

Given the power needed to literally shape the world, it is not surprising that most myths feature gods. People tell myths not only for their entertainment value, but also for their explanatory power: they help us understand the world around us. A collection of myths that fit more-or-less together and are told by more-or-less the same people is a called a mythology. Such a collection usually reflects the interests and priorities of those who tell them.

### Sagas

Another important word for a particular type of story – one that you will probably see used a lot in discussions of narratives told by or about Vikings – is *saga*. Unlike 'myth' and 'legend', which have been distinguished and defined by scholars such as my colleagues and I, the word 'saga' is an Old Norse word that simply means 'story', or even 'history'. (What is history, after all, but a series of stories that we tell each other about the past?) In particular, speakers of Old Norse – more on them in a moment – used the word 'saga' to mean *a longer story told in prose, not poetry*. There are genres of saga that feature Vikings and hardy settlers, heroes from the mists of time, even bishops.

### Legends

While most of the narratives in this book are technically myths, it also contains versions of two sagas. Both of them are *fornaldarsögur* (a genre of 'sagas about legendary times'), which simultaneously makes them both sagas and 'legends':

a term researchers use to designate *a story in which human action plays a key role and whose audience believes happened at some point in history*. Why include such human-focused stories in a book of Norse myths? The answer is that, unlike many mythologies around the world, Norse mythology is largely a human-free zone. That is not to say that there are no stories of Norse gods interacting with humans, of course – there absolutely are. However, those stories are rarely myths, which is why this book also contains legendary sagas where the gods cast a long shadow over human lives.

In an extract from *Vǫlsunga saga*, for example, we hear how the titular Vǫlsungar (Volsung) family were descended from Odin himself; the god also appears, disguised as an old man, to present the hero Sigmundr with a sword during his sister's wedding (pages 229–32). This gift sparks the jealousy and betrayal that drive much of the saga's plot. Similarly, in *Friðþjófs saga*, the brother kings Helgi (Helgé) and Hálfdan (Halfdan) refuse to grant the hand of their sister Ingibjǫrg (Ingeborg) in marriage to the eponymous Friðþjófr (Frithiof). They go so far as to imprison her in a temple of Baldr (Balder) in an effort to disrupt the budding romance – only for Frithiof to visit her there anyway (page 282). This gives the brothers the excuse they needed to banish him, thereby setting up the vengeance arc laid out in the rest of the story.

## NORSE, SCANDINAVIANS AND VIKINGS

We should probably talk about the 'Norse' in 'Norse Myths' (and 'Old Norse'). In a nutshell, the term is often used to designate a particular set of societies that shared something of a cultural and linguistic continuum in southern and coastal parts of the Nordic region during the 'Viking Age' – used by historians as a handy label for the years *c.* 750–1100. That said, 'Norse' may mean slightly different things to different people. The same issue plagues 'Viking' and 'Scandinavian', both commonly used as synonyms for 'Norse' when applied to 'myth', 'culture', 'society' and similar concepts, so let's try to unpick these three terms a little.

### Vikings

Let us start with 'Viking', which tends to be used in two distinct ways: firstly to refer to a particular type of raider-trader who travelled in groups from their Nordic homelands in order to secure wealth and fame during the ninth and tenth centuries AD. While their victims' Latin accounts often referred to these groups as *pirati* (literally 'pirates'), in their own language they called themselves *víkingar* – the origin of the English word 'Viking'. (The source of the Old Norse word itself remains something of a mystery.) What we should be very clear about, however, is that Vikings were *not* an ethnic, tribal or racial group. Being a Viking was rather like being a gap-year student: it was a temporary identity assumed by young people (usually men) who travelled around causing chaos for the locals, then headed home full of exaggerated stories to settle down and live a normal life. Which is why the second common use of 'Viking' today – designating the entire culture from which these raider-traders set out – is so problematic.

## Norse and Scandinavians

Given that 'Viking' is not an appropriate term for a whole society, what name should we use? 'Scandinavian' refers to inhabitants of the Scandinavian peninsula, which technically excludes Denmark. Even if we use it to mean 'from the region covered by the modern countries of Norway, Sweden and Denmark', it still includes other peninsular populations with very different cultures (such as the historically oppressed Sámi) while simultaneously excluding closely related populations with very similar cultures who lived in Iceland and parts of the eastern Baltic region. 'Norse' is also problematic. For centuries it was used to refer specifically to Norway, only recently gaining a more general meaning, so is best avoided to sidestep confusion.

How then did this society refer to itself? The short answer is that it did not. Until well into the Middle Ages (c. 1100–1600), most people living in Scandinavia would have probably identified themselves using local labels that referenced particular fjords, valleys or islands. Even the kingdoms of Denmark and Norway only came into being during the Viking Age, leaving us struggling to find a collective term.

## Old Norse

One thing that united the diverse peoples whom we might variously describe as 'Norse', 'Scandinavian' or 'Viking' in the Viking Age was their language. We refer to this as 'Old Norse' (they often used the name *norræna*, meaning something like 'northern'). Although not perfect, scholars often use 'Old Norse' to designate the literature, culture or mythology of southern Scandinavia and related regions during the Viking Age and Nordic Middle Ages.

So why is this book called 'Norse' Myths? This is simply because most of the narratives it contains are versions of myths whose oldest versions were written in Old Norse. Why not 'Old Norse' Myths? Well, the myths in this book aren't actually written in Old Norse. It probably wouldn't sell very well if they were. Instead, they're (mostly) versions of Old Norse myths in English.

## Reader Take Note: Old Norse Myths Retold

Some chapters in this book are relatively close translations of Old Norse texts. Others are freer, more creative retellings, and yet others are more academic examinations of particular characters or places in Norse myth. The text presented here as 'Geirrod and Agnar' (pages 80–84), for example, closely follows the eddic poem Grímnismál ('Grimnir's Words') in its account of the life and death of King Geirrod, although it does omit Odin's lengthy boasts of his own prowess as he is tortured by the hapless ruler. On the other hand, 'The Elves' (pages 222–26) consolidates what little we know of the Viking-Age álfar ('elves') with English and Irish folklore from much later periods in an ahistorical manner that most researchers would frown upon. It is true that offerings of dairy products were made to local landvættir ('land spirits') in medieval Scandinavia, but there is no Scandinavian tradition that links them to trees or plants such as Classical Dryads or the British Green Man.

Some of these retellings have an almost timeless quality, while in others the social mores and moral standards of their authors shine through. In 'The Origin of Poetry', for example, Odin makes his way to the underground cave where the giant-woman Gunnlǫð (Gunlod) guarded the precious mead from which poetry sprang. The English translation in this book then explains that 'won by his [Odin's] passionate wooing, Gunlod consented to become his wife', and produces the alcohol three days later (page 77). The original Old Norse text on which this is based, chapter two of *Skáldskaparmál* (part of a work called *Snorra Edda*), says only that Odin 'fór ... þar til sem Gunnlǫð var ok lá hjá henni þrjár nætr, ok þá lofaði hon honum at drekka af miðinum' ('went to the place where Gunlod was and lay with her for three nights, then she promised him he could drink some mead'). The addition of passionate wooing and marriage to this exchange may not seem like a big difference – perhaps it was a love match, perhaps something more violent – but it speaks to the reactionary attitudes of many translators before the twenty-first century, who saw it as their moral duty to reform what they saw as reprehensible behaviour. That Odin's deceit, lies and killing of slaves on the way to Gunlod's cave made it through uncensored says a lot about the primary concerns of such moral revisionism.

At the same time, the idea that *valkyrjur* ('Valkyries'), Odin's supernatural battlefield spirits who oversaw human warfare on his behalf, had to give up their professional careers and identities if they married – something you could be forgiven for thinking was a Victorian intervention (page 253) – genuinely appears in more than one medieval source, including the eddic poem *Sigrdrífumál* ('Sigrdrífa's Words') and *Vǫlsunga saga*. (Perhaps unsurprisingly, the active sexuality of the Valkyrie Sigrun, who attempted to seduce her undead, zombie-like husband in his grave when he was resurrected, appears in very few older translations of Norse legends.) Readers should thus be wary of chapters in this book that touch on issues of gender, class politics and notions of foreignness, as these are just as likely to represent the attitudes of post-medieval translators as their Old Norse sources.

The final section of this book, 'Greek and Northern Mythologies' (pages 319–45) is not based on a single mythological text, but is rather a reprint of part of H.A. Guerber's venerable 1895 study *Myths of Northern Lands*, reproduced here for further interest. While no longer regarded as cutting-edge scholarship, many of the parallels between Classical and Norse mythologies that Guerber notes are valid and continue to be investigated today.

## WHEN ARE THESE MYTHS FROM?

If these myths were around during the Viking Age, did they start there? And how did they survive to the present?

### Before the Viking Age

Some aspects of the myths as we know them may be even older than the Viking Age. A golden bracteate found near the Swedish city of Trollhättan and dated to the Migration Age (*c.* 375–550) seems to depict Týr's hand in the mouth of a wolf – events told here as 'How Tyr Lost His Hand' (pages 180–84). Even earlier, petroglyphs (rock carvings) on certain cliff faces near lakes and rivers in eastern Norway and central Sweden, dating from the Nordic Bronze Age (c. 1700–500 BC), appear to show the blessing of a marriage with a hammer – a motif that appears at the climax of the Old Norse poem Þrymskviða ('The Poem of Thrymr'), retold here as 'The Stealing of Thor's Hammer' (pages 145–49). Whether anything like the versions of those stories actually circulated before the Viking Age must, however, remain speculation.

## The Viking Age

It is probable that the myths as we know them took form largely during the Viking Age. The complex of ideas surrounding ragnarǫk (Ragnarok) and Balder's death (pages 299–317), for example, is likely to have been partially inspired by the Christian myth of Christ's crucifixion and resurrection, which became widespread in Scandinavia following the arrival of Christian missionaries. (The same may be true of Odin's sacrifice of 'himself to himself' while hanging suspended on the world tree Yggdrasil, spelt Yggdrasill in Old Norse, during his search for the runes, here pages 58–59.)

Nonetheless, we should acknowledge that the Viking Age was *prehistoric*. Literacy was extremely rare, with most stories circulating in what scholars call the 'oral milieu': people told them to one another again and again, spreading the ones they liked and forgetting those they did not. With each telling it was possible for details to change, as performers adapted their material to suit a particular agenda or simply to please their audiences. In Viking Age Scandinavia, as in any prehistoric society, no 'official' versions of any story existed – there was no master copy against which a version could be checked.

## The Middle Ages

That means that the mythological texts that have survived – mostly in Old Norse, but some in Latin – could not have been written down by people who believed in them. Instead, they were collected by their medieval, and therefore Christian, descendants. These medieval writers were interested in Norse myths for their entertainment value, as we are today, and as a historical legacy. Even so, the fact that medieval books had to be copied by hand meant that there was plenty of room for variation between different versions of 'the same' text. New influences could also be brought to bear. The social mores of Christianity, for example, meant that some pagan myths were 'cleaned up' to suit Christian tastes and moralities.

It was in the thirteenth century, when writing non-Latin texts about non-clerical subjects had been widely established, that some writers – overwhelmingly in Iceland – began to record Norse myths in earnest. We are incredibly fortunate that two of these works have survived: the *Prose Edda* (also called *Snorra Edda*, or *Snorri's Edda*) and the *Poetic Edda*. (Sadly scholars remain uncertain what the word *Edda* actually meant.) Neither work is particularly interested in Old Norse mythology for its own sake.

### The Prose Edda

The *Prose Edda* was compiled in the 1220s under the direction of scholar-statesman Snorri Sturluson – a chieftain with international political ambitions – as a handbook for complex 'skaldic' poetry. Snorri set out to explain the mythological allusions common in skaldic verse by retelling the pre-Christian myths in his own way, drawing on sources no longer available to us today. Despite this great knowledge, he also seems to have systematized away genuine inconsistencies in his sources; he papered over things that did not suit him and even went so far as to invent new goddesses as wives for the remaining male gods, enabling everyone to be neatly paired up. Perhaps because of this Christian attitude to pagan myth, Snorri's work was highly successful in the Middle Ages; multiple versions of it have survived over several centuries.

## The Poetic Edda

In contrast to Snorri's learned, highly Christian version of Norse mythology, the *Poetic Edda* offers us a more stark and raw vision of how things might have been. Preserved only in a single copy dating from around 1287, this *Edda* is an anonymous collection of poems in an 'eddic' style, far simpler than that found in skaldic poetry. The poems are largely narrative in nature, with the first half of the manuscript containing mythological stories and the second recounting legends about famous human heroes, particularly the Volsung family. It is hard to know how old these poems may be. Poetry is generally more resistant to casual variation and adaptation than prose stories due to the constraints of rhyme and metre, and on linguistic grounds some of the poems may well be dated to the Viking Age proper. However, the presence of short prose introductions to certain poems proves that the work as we have it is a medieval construction; some of the poems seem to be, too, for all that they retell pagan myths.

While some of the eddic poems are monologues spoken by a single voice, others are explicitly dialogues. In the latter, the identity of the speakers is indicated by their initials in the margins, much as in the script of a modern play. This led the folklorist Terry Gunnell to make the beguiling suggestion that some myths could have been acted out as a kind of 'ritual drama' during pagan times. This may have provided a way of bringing the gods physically into the human world, supplementing our traditional belief that such tales would have been told over the fire by a single speaker addressing an audience.

## Other Sources

Of course, there are other sources for Norse mythology as well as the Eddas. Runic inscriptions name particular gods, inscrutable kennings and iconographic carvings hint at lost stories, and medieval texts not written in Old Norse offer a foreigner's glimpse into the religious lives of pre-Christian Scandinavians. One work, the *Gesta Danorum* of the Danish monk Saxo Grammaticus, even offers a Latin version of some myths, where the gods have been transformed into human sorcerers deceiving their foolish worshippers. (Admittedly this is not too surprising: Saxo's clerical superiors would probably have been deeply unhappy with him had he produced versions of the myths portraying pagan gods as heroes.) Nonetheless, the two Eddas are the backbone of our modern understanding of Norse myth, and provide the direct inspiration of much of this book.

**Beyond the Middle Ages**

Even with the introduction of printed books from the fifteenth century, writers continued to pick and choose which myths they included in their work; they could thus shape them to suit the tastes and trends of their own times. As a result it is not possible to talk about an 'original' version of any of these myths. Works like this book are hybrids, products of the modern era as much as they are of the Viking and Middle Ages.

# WHEN, WHERE AND WHO?
# AN OVERVIEW OF NORSE MYTHOLOGY

So far I have written a lot about what these myths are, who told them and when different versions of them arose, but have not said much about what the myths themselves actually tell us. Of course, any attempt to summarize an entire mythology is bound to fall short in some ways and to reflect its author's own opinions and biases. You should thus take what I say here as a guide and be prepared to form your own opinions.

If you take away just one thing from this overview, I hope it will be that *it would be wrong to look for consistency in pagan myths*. The very nature of an oral society is that there are multiple versions of every story. People were clearly comfortable with, for example, Odin appearing as an obsessive wisdom-seeker determined to avert the end of the world in some texts (e.g. the eddic poem *Vafþrúðnismál* ('Vafthrudnir's Words'), here recounted as part of 'Mimir's Well', pages 70–72), and as a generous mentor to human champions in others (e.g. pages 80–84). A careful reader can find similar inconsistencies regarding the characters of major gods such as Thor and Loki, the number of worlds in the universe, even the ways in which the cosmos was created. I encourage you to embrace such tensions and contradictions as one of the charms of Norse mythology.

## When?

Reading mythology that explains how the world came to be as it is can be confusing – not least because myths will freely mix things that happened in the past, are happening in the 'now' of the story and will happen in the future. The best way to engage with this sort of temporality is to think in terms of a 'mythological present' that remains constant, even as human time advances in a linear fashion. Some events are easy to place on this mythological timeline: long ago Odin and his brothers were involved in the creation of both the world (although the details of how differ) and the first man and woman, Askr ('Ash') and Embla (probably 'Elm'); the story appears here as 'The First Humans' (pages 53–55). The climactic battle of Ragnarok lies in the future, although probably not far enough away for comfort. Other events are less clear cut. Loki is present in many myths, for example, but simultaneously lies bound and tortured under the earth, where his writhing causes earthquakes in the human realm (page 310).

## Where?

The cosmology (a technical term for 'mythological geography') of Norse mythology is complicated. Some aspects seem more or less fixed, such as the giant tree,

Yggdrasil, that supports various locations among its branches and roots (pages 57–59). Other details vary immensely. One popular belief today is that Norse mythology featured nine worlds. This concept finds backing in the eddic poems *Vǫluspá* ('The Seeress's Prophecy') and *Vafþrúðnismál*, but how widespread the idea was in the Viking Age, and precisely which worlds those were, remains unclear. Oft-mentioned mythological locations include *Ásgarðr* (Asgard, lit. 'god-yard' – in the sense of 'an enclosed space' – where the gods live), *Miðgarðr* (Midgard, lit. 'middle-yard', where humans live) and *Hel* (both an afterlife destination for some humans and the eponymous goddess of the place). Snorri, for example, probably invented *Ljósálfheimr* and *Svartálfheimr* ('light-' and 'dark-elf-world' respectively) as variations on the well-attested *Álfheimr* ('elf-world'), in order to support his binary division of the elves along the same lines as Christian angels and demons. In other cases, it is not clear whether the names of some worlds – such as *Niflheimr* ('mist-world'), *Niflhel* ('mist-Hel') and *Hel* – represent different places or are simply different labels for the same place. Similarly, travel between mythological locations is a vague exercise: sometimes gods walk, or ride on horseback; on other occasions they drive chariots. Sometimes bridges (such as Bifrǫst, the rainbow bridge) are needed, but at other times the gods wade through rivers or seas.

## Who?
### The Gods
The gods of Norse mythology are fascinating. Unlike the all-knowing, all-seeing, all-present God of the Abrahamic religions, these deities are strangely human. They repeatedly

act in selfish ways, make mistakes, are defeated and even die. Indeed, their social structure – that of a sprawling, loosely related family or clan featuring an unreliable patriarch (Odin), a bumbling heir apparent (Thor) and a disruptive source of drama (Loki) – resembles that of the Old Norse speakers in whose stories they live.

That said, recent scholarship has increasingly begun to reject the notion that the Norse gods were believed to coexist in some sort of otherworldly pantheon during the Viking Age. While some myths do give that impression, others – like the poem *Lokasenna* ('Loki's Quarrel'), here 'Loki's Last Crime' (pages 114–18) – suggest that the gods only gathered occasionally; the rest of the time they kept themselves to themselves. What we can puzzle out regarding worship of these gods during the Viking Age suggests this was probably a common view. Many pagans seem to have practised 'henotheism' – a belief system that acknowledges the existence of multiple gods, but focuses active worship on just one or two who fulfilled a broad range of functions. Such a practice is in contrast to 'polytheism' proper, in which an agreed pantheon of gods exists, with each worshipped according to their specific role in divine society.

## Thor

Although Thor is frequently depicted as subservient to Odin in our extant texts, data from the Viking Age suggests he may well have been the most widely worshipped pagan deity. His links to thunder and storms probably reflect an association with weather – an important concern of a society whose population is overwhelmingly directly engaged with, and dependent upon, the production of food through farming and fishing. Thor's combative relationship with giants and other threatening beings such as Jǫrmungandr (the World Serpent) also makes him a protective figure for humans – including the two human children that he adopts in 'Thor in the Hall of the Giants' (pages 136–45). This is a characteristic that most of the Norse deities lack.

## Odin

Dubbed *Alfǫðr* ('All-Father') and King of the Gods, Odin's dangerous quests for knowledge of the future, tactical genius, mentoring of human warriors and interest in poetry clearly reflects the interests of the Viking Age warrior elite. Worship of Odin was likely largely confined to kings and the tiny warrior class of society, whose medieval descendants would go on to write the mythological texts we have today. This accounts for Odin's prominence in Norse mythology as we know it.

## Freyr & Freyja (Frey & Freya)

These twin deities' names mean 'Lord' and 'Lady' respectively. This may reflect a taboo around the naming of powerful beings, not unlike the Christian use of 'God' for their supreme deity. Frey's original name was probably something like 'Ingvi', but that of Freya has been lost to time. They were traditionally viewed as members of the 'Vanir', a family, tribe or clan of beings distinct from the rest of the 'Æsir' gods (see pages 55–57). However, researchers have now grown sceptical of old-fashioned ideas that they (and their sometimes-father Njǫrðr or Niord) were a 'foreign' family of fertility deities. Instead we accept that gods were more popular in some places than others; the outsider status of these gods in Old Icelandic myths is likely rooted in the Swedish location of their main powerbase. Claims that Freyja was a goddess of sex and/or romantic love seem similarly informed more by modern cultural mores than by those of the Viking Age.

## Other Deities

It is difficult to give much detail regarding the other gods featured in Norse myth. If evidence from place-name research is to be believed, some – such as Ullr (Uller) and Týr (Tyr) – were widely worshipped, despite having little active role in myths recorded in medieval Iceland. At the other end of the scale, there is no evidence Loki was ever worshipped in the pre-Christian era. However, he seems to have been a staple of Norse myth for a long time, appearing in various guises as divine trickster, shifty sidekick and outright traitor to the gods.

Of the female gods we know frustratingly little, with the medieval versions of the myths available to us today firmly failing the Bechdel test (that is, no two female figures ever have a conversation with one another that does not revolve around a male figure). Many goddesses appear as little more than appendages of their husbands, although this probably stems from the male, martial focus of the extant mythology. Indeed, so little attention is paid to these deities that there remains uncertainty as to whether Frigga and Freya were two separate goddesses or two variations of the same figure. A similar debate continues as to the importance of priestesses in pagan times, as their role may have been obscured by the Christian tradition of a male-only clergy.

## The Giants

The giants appear to have been the personifications of the wild powers of the world against whom the forces of order and structure – gods and humans – had to struggle. Precisely what makes a giant a giant is somewhat unclear. They appear to have been the same size as humans and their deities, rather than literally gigantic, although some clearly had magical powers and supernatural knowledge outstripping that of the gods. An important book by Margaret Clunies Ross, *Prolonged Echoes*, observed that the giants are repeatedly portrayed as in possession of resources – wisdom, treasure, women – that the gods attempt to seize through trickery or violence. This sets the giants up as what John McKinnell termed a 'mythological *Other*', representing powers in the human world opposed to the dominant warrior-elite, including foreigners, rebels and women. (Note that such Others are not morally evil, as some of the retellings in this book – e.g. pages 46–49 – suggest. Evil, as opposed to good, is part of a Christian worldview, not a pagan one.) As such, the boundaries between the two groups are porous; some figures, such as Loki and Skaði (Skadi), appear to have switched from giganticness to godhood. With the arrival of Christianity, the giants gradually became demonized. They emerge in later folklore as stupid, avaricious *trǫll* ('trolls') who live underground.

## Other Supernatural Beings

The world of Norse myth is not restricted simply to gods, giants and humans. Other groups abound, sometimes blurring and overlapping with one another. The god Frey is sometimes called an elf (page 222), for example. Odin, on the other hand, is served by the *valkyjur* (valkyries, lit. 'choosers of the battle-slain'), who sometimes appear as terrifying battle-spirits manipulating the tides of combat to recruit human warriors to their patron's afterlife in Valhǫll (Valhalla), and sometimes as tragic human princesses, cursed by their romantic love for those same warriors (e.g. page 256). Indeed, the lines between various female spirits – Valkyries, *nornir* (fate-determining textile enthusiasts) and *dísir* (a collective of supernatural women of uncertain size and function) – are so blurred that it can be hard to distinguish between them. With the arrival of Christianity a similar consolidation played out between the elves, *dvergar* ('dwarves'), land spirits and even some trolls. Gradually these beings became the *nisser* ('elves'), *tomtar* ('fairies') and *huldufólk* (lit. 'hidden people') of Nordic folklore.

# FINAL WORDS

In sum, the myths in this book are retellings of retellings of retellings – stories adapted through the ages in response to the linguistic, cultural and aesthetic tastes of successive audiences. In this sense, the long life of these myths in all their different versions continues to help us understand the world around us. Evolving and dynamic, they do not belong just to Vikings or medieval Old Norse speakers, to their modern descendants or to scholarly experts. Their fierce zest for life, powerful tales of adventure and woe, and strangely relatable themes make Norse myths part of universal human heritage, and they belong to us all.

*Dr. Luke John Murphy, Aarhus, Denmark*

# FURTHER READING

If you enjoy the versions of the Norse myths presented here, I'd encourage you to seek out close translations of the extant medieval myths in *Snorra Edda* and the *Poetic Edda*. Two high-quality, affordable paperback translations are:

Snorri Sturluson, *Edda*, translated by Anthony Faulkes (Everyman, 1987)

*The Poetic Edda*, translated by Carolyne Larrington (Oxford University Press, 1996)

For more general guides to life, society and literature during the Viking and Nordic Middle Ages, I can recommend:

Richards, Julian D., *The Vikings: A Very Short Introduction* (Oxford University Press, 2005)

Brink, Stefan and Neil Price (editors), *The Viking World* (Routledge, 2008)

Jóhanna Katrín Friðriksdóttir, *Valkyrie: The Women of the Viking World* (Bloomsbury, 2020)

Handy reference guides to the many names, people and places in Norse mythology can be found in:

Simek, Rudy, *Dictionary of Northern Mythology* (D.S. Brewer, 1993)

Lindow, John, *Norse Mythology: A Guide to the Gods, Heroes, Rituals and Beliefs* (Oxford University Press, 2001) (Published in North America as *A Handbook of Norse Mythology* (ABC Clio, 2001))

**Influential scholarly works on mythology include:**

Motz, Lotte, 'Sister in the Cave: The Stature and the Function of the Female Figures of the Eddas', *Arkiv för nordisk filologi* 95 (1980), 168–82

Clunies Ross, Margaret, *Prolonged Echoes: Old Norse Myths in Medieval Northern Society* (Odense University Press, 1994)

Simek, Rudolf, 'The Vanir: An Obituary', *The Retrospective Methods Network Newsletter* 1 (2010), 10–19 (available online at www.helsinki.fi/en/networks/ retrospective-methods-network/archive)

McKinnell, John, *Meeting the Other in Norse Myth and Legend* (D.S. Brewer, 2005)

Ingunn Ásdísardóttir, 'Frigg and Freyja: One Great Goddess or Two?', published in *The Fantastic in Old Norse/Icelandic Literature: Preprint Papers of the Thirteenth International Saga Conference*, edited by John McKinnell, David Ashurst and Donata Kick (The Centre for Medieval and Renaissance Studies, 2006). (This short English report summarizes the contents of an important Icelandic-language book on the so-called 'great goddess' question: Ingunn Ásdísardóttir, *Frigg og Freyja: kvenleg goðmögn í heiðnum sið* (Hið íslenzka bókmenntafélag, 2007)

Taggart, Declan, *How Thor Lost His Thunder: The Changing Faces of an Old Norse God*, (Routledge, 2018)

A fascinating read on the post-medieval life of the god Thor can be found in:

Arnold, Martin, *Thor: Myth to Marvel* (Continuum, 2011)

Finally, if you're interested in the pre-Christian religion of the Nordic region, including and beyond mythology, a recent, once-in-a-generation publication collects a wide range of material. Although expensive for individual purchase, it should be accessible via university libraries:

Schjødt, Jens Peter, John Lindow and Anders Andrén (editors), *The Pre-Christian Religions of the North: History and Structures* (Brepols, 2020)

More generally, exciting works on pre-Christian Nordic religion include:

Gunnell, Terry, *The Origins of Drama in Scandinavia* (Boydell and Brewer, 1995)

Raudvere, Catharina and Jens Peter Schjødt (editors), *More than Mythology: Narratives, Ritual Practices and Regional Distribution in Pre-Christian Scandinavian Religions* (Nordic Academic Press, 2012)

Murphy, Luke John, 'Paganism at Home: Pre-Christian Private Praxis and Household Religion in the Iron-Age North', *Scripta Islandica* 69 (2018), 49–97 (Available online at http://urn.kb.se/resolve?urn=urn%3Anbn%3Ase%3Auu%3Adiva-371476)

Price, Neil S., *The Viking Way: Religion and War in Late Iron Age Scandinavia* (Oxbow Books, 2019)

**Dr. Luke John Murphy** is a researcher who works with pre-Christian religions in Europe. His publications and teaching cover Nordic mythology, early British religions, temples and religious objects, and the role of religion in past societies. He has held research posts at the University of Iceland, University of Leicester (UK), Stockholm University (Sweden) and Aarhus University (Denmark); as well as having studied in Denmark, Iceland, and the UK.

# THE CREATION MYTHS

*It was in distant times*
*When nothing was;*
*Neither sand nor sea*
*Nor chill waves;*
*No earth at all;*
*Nor the high heavens;*
*The great void only*
*And growth nowhere.*
**Matthew Arnold, Balder Dead**

The dramatic contradictions of the Viking landscape and the constant battle with the elements; the spectacular backdrop of perpetual darkness and then perpetual light provide a mythology of profound contrasts. The creation myths are no exception. It was believed that cold was malevolent, evil, and that heat was good and light; when the two meet – when fire meets ice – there comes into existence a cosmos from which the universe can be created. The myths are filled with frost and fire; they are allusive and incomplete; the images and events are impossible and unlinked. But the creation myths of the Viking people are supremely beautiful, and explain, in a way that only a people in a wilderness could conceive, how we came to be.

## THE CREATION OF THE UNIVERSE

*Under the armpit grew,*
*'Tis said of Hrim-thurs,*
*A girl and boy together;*
*Foot with foot begat,*
*Of that wise Jotun,*
*A six-headed son.*
**Benjamin Thorpe, Saemund's Edda**

In the beginning, before there was anything at all, there was a nothingness that stretched as far as there was space. There was no sand, nor sea, no waves nor earth nor heavens. And that space was a void that called to be filled, for its emptiness echoed with a deep and frozen silence. So it was that a land sprung up within that silence, and it took the place of half the universe. It was a land called Filheim, or land of fog, and where it ended sprung another land, where the air burned and blazed. This land was called Muspell. Where the regions met lay a great and profound void, called Ginnungagap, and here a peaceful river flowed, softly spreading into the frosty depths of the void where it froze, layer upon layer, until it formed a fundament. And it was here the heat from Muspell licked at the cold of Filheim until the energy they created spawned the great frost-giant Ymir. Ymir was the greatest and the first of all frost-giants, and his part in the creation of the universe led the frost-giants to believe that they should reign supreme on what he had made.

Filheim had existed for many ages, long before our own earth was created. In the centre was a mighty fountain and it was called Vergelmir, and from that great fountain all the rivers of the universe bubbled and stormed. There was another fountain called Elivagar (although some believe that it is the same fountain with a different name), and from this bubbled up a poisonous mass, which hardened into black ice. Elivagar is the beginning of evil, for goodness can never be black.

Muspell burned with eternal light and her heat was guarded by the flame giant, Surtr, who lashed at the air with his great sabre, filling it with glittering sparks of pure heat. Surtr was the fiercest of the fire giants who would one day make Muspell their home. The word Muspell means 'home of the destroyers of the world' and that description is both frightening and accurate because the fire giants were the most terrifying there were.

On the other side of the slowly filling chasm, Filheim lay in perpetual darkness, bathed in mists which circled and spun until all was masked. Here, between these stark contrasts, Ymir grew, the personification of the frozen ocean, the product of chaos. Fire and ice met here, and it was these profound contrasts that created a phenomenon like no other, and this was life itself. In the chasm another form was created by the frozen river, where the sparks of the Surtr's sabre caused the ice to drip, and to thaw, and then, when they rested, allowed it to freeze once again. This form was Audhumla, a cow who became known as the nourisher. Her udders were swollen with rich, pure milk, and Ymir drank greedily from the four rivers which formed from them.

Audhumla was a vast creature, spreading across the space where the fire met the ice. Her legs were columns, and they held up the corners of space.

Audhumla, the cow, also needed sustenance, and so she licked at the rime-stones which had formed from the crusted ice, and from these stones she drew salt from the depths of the earth. Audhumla licked continuously, and soon there appeared, under her thirsty tongue, the form of a god. On the first day there appeared hair, and on the second, a head. On the third day the whole god was freed from the ice and he stepped forth as Buri, also called the Producer. Buri was beautiful. He had taken the golden flames of the fire, which gave him a warm, gilded glow, and from the frost and ice he had drawn a purity, a freshness that could never be matched.

While Audhumla licked, Ymir slept, sated by the warmth of her milk. Under his arms the perspiration formed a son and a daughter, and his feet produced a giant called Thrudgemir, an evil frost-giant with six heads who went on to bear his own son, the giant Bergelmir. These were the first of the race of frost-giants.

Buri himself had produced a son, called Bor, which is another word for 'born', and as Buri and Bor became aware of the giants, an eternal battle was begun — one which is to this day waged on all parts of earth and heaven.

For giants represent evil in its many forms, and gods represent all that is good, and on that fateful day the fundamental conflict between them began – a cosmic battle which would create the world as we know it.

Buri and Bor fought against the giants, but by the close of each day a stalemate existed. And so it was that Bor married the giantess Bestla, who was the daughter of Bolthorn, or the thorn of evil. Bestla was to give him three fine, strong sons: Odin, Vili and Ve and with the combined forces of these brave boys, Bor was able to destroy the great Ymir. As they slayed him, a tremendous flood burst forth from his body, covering the earth and all the evil beings who inhabited it with his rich red blood.

## THE CREATION OF THE EARTH

*Of Ymir's flesh*
*Was earth created,*
*Of his blood the sea,*
*Of his bones the hills,*
*Of his hair trees and plants,*
*Of his skull the heavens,*
*And of his brows*
*The gentle powers*
*Formed Midgard for the sons of men;*
*But of his brain*
*The heavy clouds are*
*All created.*

**R.B. Anderson, Norse Mythology**

**Ymir's body was carried** by Odin and his brothers to Ginnungagap, where it was placed in the centre. His flesh became the earth, and his skeleton the rocky crags which dipped and soared. From the soil sprang dwarfs, spontaneously, and they would soon be put to work. Ymir's teeth and shards of broken bones became the rocks and pits covering the earth and his blood was cleared to become the seas and waters that flowed across the land. The three men worked hard on the body of Ymir; his vast size meant that even a day's work would alter the corpse only slightly.

Ymir's skull became the sky and at each cardinal point of the compass was placed a dwarf whose supreme job it was to support it. These dwarfs were Nordri, Sudri, Austri and Westri and it was from these brave and sturdy dwarfs that the terms North, South, East and West were born. Ymir's hair created trees and bushes.

The brow of Ymir became walls which would protect the gods from all evil creatures, and in the very centre of these brows was Midgard, or 'middle garden', where humans could live safely.

Now almost all of the giants had fallen with the death of Ymir, drowned by his surging blood – all, that is, except Bergelmir, who escaped in a boat with his wife and sought asylum at the edge of the world. Here he created a new world, Jotunheim, or the home of the giants, where he set about the creation of a whole new breed of giants who would carry on his evil deeds.

Odin and his brothers had not yet completed their work. As the earth took on its present form, they slaved at Ymir's corpse to create greater and finer things. Ymir's brains were thrust into the skies to become clouds, and in order to light this new world, they secured the sparks from Surtr's sabre and dotted them among the clouds. The finest sparks were put to one side and they studded the heavenly vault with them; they became like glittering stars in the darkness. The stars were given positions; some were told to pass forward, and then back again in the heavens. This provided seasons, which were duly recorded.

The brightest of the remaining stars were joined together to become the sun and the moon, and they were sent out into the darkness in gleaming gold chariots. The chariots were drawn by Arvakr (the early waker) and Alsvin (the rapid goer), two magnificent white horses under whom were placed balls of cool air which had been trapped in great skins. A shield was placed before the sun so that her rays would not harm the milky hides of the steeds as they travelled into the darkness.

Although the moon and the sun had now been created, and they were sent out on their chariots, there was still no distinction between day and night, and that is a story of its own.

## NIGHT AND DAY

*Forth from the east, up the ascent of heaven.*
*Day drove his courser with the shining mane.*
**Matthew Arnold, Balder Dead**

The chariots were ready, and the steeds were bursting at their harnesses to tend to the prestigious task of setting night and day in place. But who would guide them? The horses would need leadership of some sort, and so it was decided that the beautiful children of the giant Mundilfari – Mani (the moon) and Sol (the sun) would be given the direction of the steeds. And at once, they were launched into the heavens.

Next, Nott (night), who was daughter of one of the giants, Norvi, was provided with a rich black chariot which was drawn by a lustrous stallion called Hrim-faxi (frost mane). From his mane, the frost and dew were sent down to the earth in glimmering baubles. Nott was a goddess, and she had produced three children, each with a different father. From Naglfari, she had a son named Aud; Annar, her second husband, gave her Jord (earth), and with her third husband, the god Dellinger, a son was born and he was called Dag (day).

Dag was the most radiant of her children, and his beauty caused all who saw him to bend down in tears of rapture. He was given his own great chariot, drawn by a perfect white horse called Skin-faxi (shining mane), and as they travelled, wondrous beams of light shot out in every direction, brightening every dark corner of the world and providing much happiness to all.

Many believe that the chariots flew so quickly, and continued their journey round and round the world because they were pursued by wolves: Skoll (repulsion) and Hati (hatred). These evil wolves sought a way to create eternal darkness and like the perpetual battle of good and evil, there could be no end to their chase.

Mani brought along in his chariot Hiuki, who represented the waxing moon, and Bil, who was the waning moon. And so it was that Sun, Moon, Day and Night were in place, with Evening, Midnight, Morning, Forenoon, Noon and Afternoon sent to accompany them. Summer and Winter were rulers of all seasons: Summer was a popular and warm god, a descendant of Svasud. Winter, was an enemy for he represented all that contrasted with Summer, including the icy winds which blew cold and unhappiness over the earth. It was believed that the great frost-giant Hraesvelgr sat on the extreme north of the heavens and that he sent the frozen winds across the land, blighting all with their blasts of icy death.

## THE FIRST HUMANS

*There in the Temple, carved in wood,*
*The image of great Odin stood.*
**Henry Wadsworth Longfellow, Saga of King Olaf**

**O**din, **Allfather,** was king of all gods, and he travelled across the newly created earth with his brothers Vili and Ve. Vili was now known as Hoenir, and Ve had become Lothur, or Loki. One morning, the three brothers walked together on the shores of the ocean, looking around with pride at the new world around them. Ymir's body had been well distributed, and his blood now ran clear and pure as the ocean, with the fresh new air sparkling above it all. The winds blew padded clouds across a perfect blue sky, and there was happiness all around. But, and there was no mistaking it, there was silence.

The brothers looked at one another, and then looked out across the crisp sands. There lay on the shore two pieces of driftwood which had been flung onto the coast from the sea, and as their eyes caught sight of them, each brother shared the same thought. They raced towards the wood, and Hoenir stood over the first piece, so that his shadow lay across it and the wood appeared at once to have arms and legs. Loki did the same with the second piece of wood, but he moved rather more animatedly, so that the wood appeared to dance in the sunlight. And then Odin bent down and blew a great divine breath across the first piece of wood. There in front of them, the bark, the water-soaked edges of the log began to peel away, and there the body of a pale, naked woman appeared. She lay there, still and not breathing. Odin moved over to the next piece of wood, and he blew once more. Again, the wood curled back to reveal the body of a naked man. He lay as still as the woman.

Odin had given the gift of life to the man and woman, and they had become entities with a soul and a mind. It was now time for Loki to offer his own gifts. He stood at once over the woman and as he bent over her, he transferred the blush of youth, the power of comprehension, and the five senses of touch, smell, sight, hearing and taste. He was rewarded when the woman rose then and smiled unquestioningly at the three gods. She looked around in wonder, and then down at the lifeless body by her side. And Loki leaned across the body of man this time, and gave to him blood, which began to run through his veins. He too received the gifts of understanding, and of the five senses, and he was able to join woman as she stood on the beach.

Hoenir stepped forward then, and offered to both man and woman the power of speech. At this, the two human beings turned and walked together into the new world, their hands held tightly together.

'Stop,' said Odin, with great authority.

Turning, the two humans looked at him and nodded. 'You are Ash,' said Odin to the man, which represented the tree from which he had been created. 'And you are Elm,' he said to the woman. Then Odin leaned over and draped his cloak around the shoulders of the first human woman and sent her on her way, safe in the care of man, who would continue in that role until the end of time – or so the Vikings said.

## ASGARD

*From the hall of Heaven he rose away*
*To Lidskialf, and sate upon his throne,*
*The mount, from whence his eye surveys the world.*
*And far from Heaven he turned his shining orbs*
*To look on Midgard, and the earth, and men.*
**Matthew Arnold, Balder Dead**

Asgard is another word for 'enclosure of the gods'. It was a place of great peace, ruled by Odin and built by Odin and his sons on Yggdrasill, above the clouds, and centred over Midgard. Each of the palaces of Asgard was built for pleasure, and only things which were perfect in every way could become part of this wondrous land. The first palace built was Gladsheim, or Joyous home, and it was created to house the twelve thrones of the principal deities. Everything was cast from gold, and it shone in the heavens like the sun itself. A second palace was built for the goddesses, and it was called Vingof, or Friendly Floor. Here, too, everything was made from gold, which is the reason why Asgard's heyday became known as the golden years.

As Asgard was conceived, and built, a council was held, and the rules were set down for gods and goddesses alike. It was decreed at this time that there would be no blood shed within the limits of the realm, and that harmony would reign forever. A forge was built, and all of the weapons and tools required for the construction of the magnificent palaces were made there. The gods held their council at the foot of Yggdrasill, and in order to travel there, a bridge was erected – the rainbow bridge, or Bifrost as it became known. The bridge arched over Midgard, on either side of Filheim, and its colours were so spectacular that one could only gaze in awe upon seeing them for the first time.

The centre of Asgard displayed the plan of Idavale, with hills that dipped and soared with life. Here the great palaces were set in lush green grasses. One was Breibalik, or Broad Gleaming, and there was Glitnir, in which all was made gold and silver. There were palaces clustered in gems, polished and shimmering in the light of the new heavens. And that beauty of Asgard was reflected by the beauteous inhabitants – whose minds and spirits were pure and true. Asgard was the home of all the Aesir, and the setting for most of the legends told here. But there was another family of gods – and they were called the Vanir.

For many years the Vanir lived in their own land, Vanaheim, but the time came when a dispute arose between the two families of gods, and the Aesir waged war against the Vanir. In time, they learned that unity was the only way to move forward, and they put aside their differences and drew strength from their combined forces. In order to ratify their treaty, each side took hostages. So it was that Niord came to dwell in Asgard with Frey and Freyia, and Hoenir went to live in Vanaheim, the ultimate sacrifice by one of the brothers of creation.

## YGGDRASILL

*I know that I hung*
*On a wind-rocked tree*
*Nine whole nights,*
*With a spear wounded,*
*And to Odin offered*
*Myself to myself;*
*On that tree*
*Of which no one knows*
*From what root it springs.*
**Benjamin Thorpe, Odin's Rune Song**

**Yggdrasill is the world ash**, a tree that has been there for all time, and will always be there. Its branches overhang all nine worlds, and they are linked by the great tree. The roots of the Yggdrasill are tended by the Norns, three powerful sisters who are also called the fates. The roots are nourished by three wells. One root reaches into Asgard, the domain of the gods, and feeds from the well of Wyrd, which is the name of the eldest Norn. The second root leads to Jotunheim, the land of the frost-giants. The well at the end of this root is called Mimir, who was once a god. Only the head of Mimir has survived the creation of the world, and it drinks daily from the well and is kept alive by the magic herbs which are scattered in it. Mimir represents great wisdom, and even Odin chose to visit him there to find answers to the most profound questions that troubled his people.

The third root winds its way to Filheim, and the well here is the scum-filled fountain of black water called Vergelmir. Here, the root of the tree is poisoned, gnawed upon, and from it rises the scent of death and dying. In Vergelmir is a great winged dragon called Nithog, and he sits at the base of the root and inflicts damage that would have caused another tree to wither away.

And the magnificent tree stands, as it has always stood, as the foundation of each world, and a point of communication between all. The name Yggdrasill has many evil connotations, and translated it means 'Steed of Ygg' or, 'Steed of Odin'. There once was a time when Odin longed to know the secret of runes – the symbols which became writing, as we know it. The understanding of runes was a cherished one, and in order to acquire it, a terrible sacrifice must be undergone by the learner. Odin had longed for many years to have that knowledge, and the day came when he was prepared to make his sacrifice. Odin was told that he must hang himself by the neck from the bough of the World Ash, and he must remain there, swinging in the frozen anarchy of the dark winds, for nine days. The story has been told that Odin, the bravest of the gods, the father of all, screamed with such terror and pain that the gods held their hands to their ears for each of those nine wretched days.

But Odin's strength of character carried him through the tortuous ordeal and so it was that he was at once the master of the magic runes, the only bearer of the secret along the length of the great tree. His knowledge was shared amongst his friends and his wisdom became legendary.

Odin was at the helm of the nine worlds, which stretched from Asgard in the topmost branches, to the world of Hel down below, at the lowest root. In between were the worlds of the Vanir, called Vanaheim, Midgard, where humans lived, as well as the worlds of the light elves, the dark elves, the dwarfs, the frost and hill giants and, at last, the fire-giants of Muspell. The most magnificent, and the world we hear the most about was Asgard, and it is here that our story begins.

# LEGENDS OF ODIN AND FRIGGA

*Sokvabek Hight the fourth dwelling;*
*Over it flow the cool billows;*
*Glad drink there Odin and Saga*
*Every day from golden cups.*
**R.B. Anderson, Norse Mythology**

In the golden age of Asgard, Odin reigned at the head of the nine worlds of Yggdrasill. He was a fair man, well-liked by all, and his kingdom of Asgard was a magnificent place, where time stood still and youth and the pleasures of nature abounded. Odin was also called Allfather, for he was the father of all men and gods. He reigned high on his throne, overlooking each of the worlds, and when the impulse struck him, Odin disguised himself and went among the gods and people of the other worlds, seeking to understand their activities. Odin appeared in many forms, but he was often recognized for he had just one eye, and that eye could see all. Odin had many adventures, and before the war of the gods, before Odin began to prepare for Ragnarok, Frigga was Odin's wife and the Queen of Asgard. Asgard was a setting for many of them, as you will see. All of the gods have their stories, and some of the most exciting are recorded here.

## ODIN AND FRIGGA IN ASGARD

*Easily to be known is,*
*By those who to Odin come,*
*The mansion by its aspect.*
*Its roof with spears is laid,*
*Its hall with shields is decked,*
*With corselets are its benches strewed.*
**Benjamin Thorpe, Lay of Grimnir**

Odin was the son of Bor, and the brother of Vili and Ve. He was the most supreme god of the Northern races and he brought great wisdom to his place at the helm of all gods. He was called Allfather, for all gods were said to have descended from him, and his esteemed seat was Asgard itself. He held a throne there, one in an exalted and prestigious position, and it served as a fine watchtower from which he could look over men on earth, and the other gods in Asgard as they went about their daily business.

Odin was a tall, mighty warrior. While not having the brawn of many excellent men, he had wisdom which counted for much more. On his shoulders he carried two ravens, Hugin (thought) and Munin (Memory), and they perched there, as he sat on his throne, and recounted to him the activities in the great wide world. Hugin and Munin were Odin's eyes and his ears when he was in Asgard and he depended on their bright eyes and alert ears for news of everything that transpired down below. In his hand Odin carried a great spear, Gungnir, which had been forged by dwarfs, and which was so sacred that it could never be broken. On his finger Odin wore a ring, Draupnir, which represented fertility and fruitfulness and which was more valuable to him, and to his land, than anything in any other god's possession. At the foot of Odin's throne sat two wolves or hunting hounds, Geri and Freki, and these animals were sacred. If one happened upon them while hunting, success was assured.

Odin belonged to a mysterious region, somewhere between life and death. He was more subtle and more dangerous than any of the other gods, and his name in some dialects means 'wind', for he could be both forceful and gentle, and then elusive or absent. On the battlefield, Odin would dress as an old man – indeed, Odin had many disguises, for when things changed in Asgard, and became bad, he had reason to travel on the earth to uncover many secrets – attended by ravens, wolves and the Valkyrs, who were the 'choosers of the slain', the maidens who took the souls of fallen warriors to Valhalla.

Valhalla was Odin's palace at Asgard, and its grandeur was breathtaking. Valhalla means 'hall of the chosen slain', and it had five hundred great wooden doors, which were wide enough to allow eight hundred warriors to pass, breastplate to breastplate. The walls were made of glittering spears, polished until they gleamed like silver, and the roof was a sea of golden shields which shone like the sun itself. In Odin's great hall were huge banqueting tables, where the Einheriar, or warriors favoured by Odin, were served. The tables were laden with the finest horns of mead, and platters of roast boar. Like everything else in Asgard, Valhalla was enchanted. Even the boar was divine and Saehrimnir, as he was called, was slain daily by the cook, boiled and roasted and served each night in tender, succulent morsels, and then brought back to life again the following day, for the procedure to take place once again. After the meal, the warriors would retire to the palace forecourt where they would engage in unmatched feats of arms for all to see. Those who were injured would be healed instantly by the enchantment of Valhalla, and those who watched became even finer warriors.

Odin lived in Asgard with Frigga, who was the mother-goddess and his wife. Frigga was daughter of Fiogyn and sister of Jord, and she was greatly beloved on earth and in Asgard. She was goddess of the atmosphere and the clouds, and she wore garments that were as white as the snow-laden mountains that gently touched the land of Asgard. As mother of all, Frigga carried about her a heady scent of the earth – blossoming flowers, ripened fruit, and luscious greenery. There are many stories told about Frigga, as we will discover below.

Life in Asgard was one of profound comfort and grace. Each day dawned new and fresh for the passage of time had not been accorded to Asgard and nothing changed except to be renewed. The sun rose each day, never too hot, and the clouds gently cooled the air as the day waned. Each night the sky was lit with glistening stars, and the fresh, rich white moon rose in the sky and lit all with her milky light. There was no evil in Asgard and the good was as pure as the water, as the air, and as the thoughts of each god and goddess as he and she slept.

In the fields, cows grazed on verdant green grass and in the trees birds caught a melody and tossed it from branch to branch until the whole world sang with their splendid music. The wind wove its way through the trees, across the mountains, and under the sea-blue skies – kissing ripples into the streams and turning a leaf to best advantage. There was a peace and harmony that exists for that magical moment just before spring turns to summer, and it was that moment at which Asgard was suspended for all time.

And so it was that Odin and Frigga brought up their young family here, away from the darkness on the other side, far from the clutches of change and disharmony. There were nine worlds in Yggdrasill, the World Ash, which stretched out from Asgard as far as the eye could see. At the top there was Aesir, and in the bottom was the dead world of Hel, at the Tree's lowest roots. In between were the Vanir, the light elves, the dark elves, men, frost and hill giants, dwarfs and the giants of Muspell.

Frigga kept her own palace in Asgard, called Fensalir, and from his high throne Odin could see her there, hard at her work. Frigga's palace was called the hall of mists, and she sat with her spinning wheel, spinning golden threat or long webs of bright-coloured clouds with a marvellous, jewelled spinning wheel which could be seen as a constellation in the night's sky.

There was a story told once of Frigga, one in which her customary goodness and grace were compromised. Frigga was a slim and elegant goddess, and she took great pride in her appearance – something the later Christians would consider to be a sin, but which the Vikings understood, and indeed encouraged. She had long silky hair and she dressed herself in exquisite finery, and Odin showered her with gifts of gems and finely wrought precious metals. She lived contentedly, for her husband was generous, until the day came when she spied a splendid golden ornament which had been fastened to a statue of her husband. As the seamless darkness of Asgard fell one evening, she slipped out and snatched the ornament, entrusting it to dwarfs whom she asked to forge her the finest of necklaces. When the jewel was complete, it was the most beautiful decoration ever seen on any woman – goddess or humankind – and it made her more attractive to Odin so that he plied her with even more gifts, and more love than ever. Soon, however, he discovered that his decoration had been stolen, and he called together all of the dwarfs and with all the fury of a god demanded that this treacherous act be explained. Now Frigga was beloved both by god and dwarf, and although the dwarfs were at risk of death at the hand of Odin, they remained loyal to Frigga, and would not tell Allfather who had stolen the golden ornament.

Odin's anger knew no bounds. The silence of the dwarfs meant only one thing to him – treason – and he swore to find out the real thief by daybreak. And so it was that on that night Odin commanded that the statue be placed above the gates of the palace, and he began to devise runes which would enable it to talk, and to betray the thief. Frigga's blood turned cold when she heard this commandment, for Odin was a kind and generous god when he was happy and content, but when he was crossed, there was a blackness in his nature that put them all in danger. There was every possibility that Frigga would be cast out of Asgard if he were to know of her deceit, and it was at the expense of everything that she intended to keep it a secret.

Frigga called out to her favourite attendant, Fulla, and begged her to find some way to protect her from Odin. Fulla disappeared and several hours later returned with a dwarf, a hideous and frightening dwarf who insisted that he could prevent the secret from being uncovered, if Frigga would do him the honour of smiling kindly on him. Frigga agreed at once, and that night, instead of revealing all, the statue was smashed to pieces while the unwitting guards slept, drugged by the ugly dwarf.

Odin was so enraged by this new travesty that he left Asgard at once – disappearing into the night and taking with him all of the blessings he had laid upon Asgard. And in his absence, Asgard and the worlds around turned cold. Odin's brothers, it is said, stepped into his place, taking on his appearance in order to persuade the gods and men that all was well, but they had not his power or his great goodness and soon enough the frost-giants invaded the earth and cast across the land a white blanket of snow. The trees were stripped of their finery, the sun-kissed streams froze and forgot how to gurgle their happy song. Birds left the trees and cows huddled together in frosty paddocks. The clouds joined together and became an impenetrable mist and the wind howled and scowled through the barren rock.

For seven months Asgard stood frozen until the hearts of each man within it became frosted with unhappiness, and then Odin returned. When he saw the nature of the evil that had stood in his place, he placed the warmth of his blessings on the land once more, forcing the frost-giants to release them. He had missed Frigga, and he showered her once more with love and gifts, and as mother of all gods, once again she took her place beside him as his queen.

Asgard had many happy days before Frigga's necklace caused the earth to become cold. Frigga and Odin had many children, including Thor, their eldest son, who was the favourite of the gods and the people – a large and boisterous god with a zeal for life. He did everything with great passion, and spirit, and his red hair and red beard made him instantly identifiable, wherever he went. Thor lived in Asgard at Thruthvangar, in his castle hall Bilskirnir (lightning). He was often seen with a sheet of lightning, which he flashed across the land, ripening the harvest and ensuring good crops for all. With his forked lightning in another hand, he travelled to the edges of the kingdoms, fighting trolls and battling giants, the great guardian of Asgard and of men and gods.

Thruthvangar had five hundred and forty rooms, and it was the largest castle ever created. Here he lived with the beautiful Sif, an exquisite goddess with hair made of long, shining strands of gold. Sif was the goddess of the fields, and the mother of the earth, like Frigga. Her long, golden hair was said to represent the golden grass covering the harvest fields, and Thor was very proud of her.

Balder was the second son of Odin and Frigga at Asgard, and he was the fairest of all the gods – indeed, his purity and goodness shone like a moonbeam and he was so pale as to be translucent. Balder was beloved by all, and his innate kindness caused him to love everything around him – evil or good. He lived in Breidablik, with his wife Nanna.

The third son of Odin was Hodur, a blind but happy god who sat quietly, listening and enjoying the sensual experiences of the wind in his hair, the sun on his shoulders, the joyful cries of the birds on the air. While all was good in Asgar, Hodur was content, and although he represented darkness, and was the twin to Balder's light, that darkness had no real place and it was kept in check by the forces of goodness.

Odin's fourth son was Tyr, who was the most courageous and brave of the gods – the god of martial honour and one of the twelve gods of Asgard. He did not have his own palace, for he travelled widely, but he held a throne at Valhalla, and in the great council hall of Gladsheim. Tyr was also the god of the sword, and every sword had his rune carved into its handle. Although Odin was his father, Tyr's mother is said to have been a beautiful unknown giantess.

Heimdall also lived in Asgard, and he was called the white god, although he was not thought to be the son of Odin and Frigga at all. Some said he had been conceived by nine mysterious sisters, who had given birth to him together. His stronghold was a fort on the boundary of Asgard, next to the Bifrost bridge, and he slept there with one eye open, and both ears alert, for the sound of any enemy approaching.

There were many other gods in Asgard, and many who would one day come to live there. But in those early days of creation, the golden years of Asgard, life was simple, and its occupants few and wondrous. The gods and goddesses lived together in their palaces, many of them with children, about whom many stories can be told.

But even the golden years of Asgard held their secrets, and even the best of worlds must have its serpent. There was one inhabitant of Asgard who no one cared to discuss, the very spirit of evil. He was Loki, who some said was the brother of Odin, although there were others who swore he could not be related to Allfather. Loki was the very personification of trickery, and deceit, and his mischief led him into great trouble. But that is another story.

## MIMIR'S WELL

*"Through our whole lives we strive towards the sun;*
*That burning forehead is the eye of Odin.*
*His second eye, the moon, shines not so bright;*
*It has he placed in pledge in Mimer's fountain,*
*That he may fetch the healing waters thence,*
*Each morning, for the strengthening of this eye."*
**M. Howitt, Oehlenschläger**

To obtain the great wisdom for which he is so famous, Odin, in the morn of time, visited Mimir's (Memor, memory) spring, "the fountain of all wit and wisdom," in whose liquid depths even the future was clearly mirrored, and besought the old man who guarded it to let him have a draught. But Mimir, who well knew the value of such a favour (for his spring was considered the source or headwater of memory), refused the boon unless Odin would consent to give one of his eyes in exchange.

The god did not hesitate, so highly did he prize the draught, but immediately plucked out one of his eyes, which Mimir kept in pledge, sinking it deep down into his fountain, where it shone with mild lustre, leaving Odin with but one eye, which is considered emblematic of the sun.

Drinking deeply of Mimir's fount, Odin gained the knowledge he coveted, and he never regretted the sacrifice he had made, but as further memorial of that day broke off a branch of the sacred tree Yggdrasil, which overshadowed the spring, and fashioned from it his beloved spear Gungnir.

But although Odin was now all-wise, he was sad and oppressed, for he had gained an insight into futurity, and had become aware of the transitory nature of all things, and even of the fate of the gods, who were doomed to pass away. This knowledge so affected his spirits that he ever after wore a melancholy and contemplative expression.

To test the value of the wisdom he had thus obtained, Odin went to visit the most learned of all the giants, Vafthrudnir, and entered with him into a contest of wit, in which the stake was nothing less than the loser's head.

On this particular occasion Odin had disguised himself as a Wanderer, by Frigga's advice, and when asked his name declared it was Gangrad. The contest of wit immediately began, Vafthrudnir questioning his guest concerning the horses which carried Day and Night across the sky, the river Ifing separating Jötun-heim from Asgard, and also about Vigrid, the field where the last battle was to be fought.

All these questions were minutely answered by Odin, who, when Vafthrudnir had ended, began the interrogatory in his turn, and received equally explicit answers about the origin of heaven and earth, the creation of the gods, their quarrel with the Vanas, the occupations of the heroes in Valhalla, the offices of the Norns, and the rulers who were to replace the Aesir when they had all perished with the world they had created. But when, in conclusion, Odin bent near the giant and softly inquired what words Allfather whispered to his dead son Balder as he lay upon his funeral pyre, Vafthrudnir suddenly recognised his divine visitor. Starting back in dismay, he declared that no one but Odin himself could answer that question, and that it was now quite plain to him that he had madly striven in a contest of wisdom and wit with the king of the gods, and fully deserved the penalty of failure, the loss of his head.

As is the case with so many of the Northern myths, which are often fragmentary and obscure, this one ends here, and none of the scalds informs us whether Odin really slew his rival, nor what was the answer to his last question; but mythologists have hazarded the suggestion that the word whispered by Odin in Balder's ear, to console him for his untimely death, must have been "resurrection."

## THE ORIGIN OF POETRY

*And a draught obtained*
*Of the precious mead,*
*Drawn from Od-hroerir.*
**Benjamin Thorpe, Odin's Rune Song**

**B**esides being god of wisdom, Odin was god and inventor of runes, the earliest alphabet used by Northern nations, which characters, signifying mystery, were at first used for divination, although in later times they served for inscriptions and records. Just as wisdom could only be obtained at the cost of sacrifice, Odin himself relates that he hung nine days and nights from the sacred tree Yggdrasil, gazing down into the immeasurable depths of Nifl-heim, plunged in deep thought, and self-wounded with his spear, ere he won the knowledge he sought.

When he had fully mastered this knowledge, Odin cut magic runes upon his spear Gungnir, upon the teeth of his horse Sleipnir, upon the claws of the bear, and upon countless other animate and inanimate things. And because he had thus hung over the abyss for such a long space of time, he was ever after considered the patron divinity of all who were condemned to be hanged or who perished by the noose.

After obtaining the gift of wisdom and runes, which gave him power over all things, Odin also coveted the gift of eloquence and poetry.

At the time of the dispute between the Aesir and Vanas, when peace had been agreed upon, a vase was brought into the assembly into which both parties solemnly spat. From this saliva the gods created Kvasir, a being renowned for his wisdom and goodness, who went about the world answering all questions asked him, thus teaching and benefiting mankind. The dwarfs, hearing about Kvasir's great wisdom, coveted it, and finding him asleep one day, two of their number, Fialar and Galar, treacherously slew him, and drained every drop of his blood into three vessels – the kettle Od-hroerir (inspiration) and the bowls Son (expiation) and Boden (offering). After duly mixing this blood with honey, they manufactured from it a sort of beverage so inspiring that any one who tasted it immediately became a poet, and could sing with a charm which was certain to win all hearts.

Now, although the dwarfs had brewed this marvellous mead for their own consumption, they did not even taste it, but hid it away in a secret place, while they went in search of further adventures. They had not gone very far ere they found the giant Gilling also sound asleep, lying on a steep bank, and they maliciously rolled him into the water, where he perished. Then hastening to his dwelling, some climbed on the roof, carrying a huge millstone, while the others, entering, told the giantess that her husband was dead. This news caused the poor creature great grief, and she rushed out of the house to view Gilling's remains. As she passed through the door, the wicked dwarfs rolled the millstone down upon her head, and killed her. According to another account, the dwarfs invited the giant to go fishing with them, and succeeded in slaying him by sending him out in a leaky vessel, which sank beneath his weight.

The double crime thus committed did not long remain unpunished, for Gilling's brother, Suttung, quickly went in search of the dwarfs, determined to avenge him. Seizing them in his mighty grasp, the giant conveyed them to a shoal far out at sea, where they would surely have perished at the next high tide had they not succeeded in redeeming their lives by promising to deliver to the giant their recently brewed mead. As soon as Suttung set them ashore, they therefore gave him the precious compound, which he entrusted to his daughter Gunlod, bidding her guard it night and day, and allow neither gods nor mortals to have so much as a taste. The better to fulfil this command, Gunlod carried the three vessels into the hollow mountain, where she kept watch over them with the most scrupulous care, nor did she suspect that Odin had discovered their place of concealment, thanks to the sharp eyes of his ever-vigilant ravens Hugin and Munin.

As Odin had mastered the runic lore and had tasted the waters of Mimir's fountain, he was already the wisest of gods; but learning of the power of the draught of inspiration manufactured out of Kvasir's blood, he became very anxious to obtain possession of the magic fluid. With this purpose in view he therefore donned his broad-brimmed hat, wrapped himself in his cloud-hued cloak, and journeyed off to Jötunheim. On his way to the giant's dwelling he passed by a field where nine ugly thralls were busy making hay. Odin paused for a moment, watching them at their work, and noticing that their scythes seemed very dull indeed, he proposed to whet them, an offer which the thralls eagerly accepted.

Drawing a whetstone from his bosom, Odin proceeded to sharpen the nine scythes, skilfully giving them such a keen edge that the thralls, delighted, begged that they might have the stone. With good-humoured acquiescence, Odin tossed the whetstone over the wall; but as the nine thralls simultaneously sprang forward to catch it, they wounded one another with their keen scythes. In anger at their respective carelessness, they now began to fight, and did not pause until they were all either mortally wounded or dead.

Quite undismayed by this tragedy, Odin continued on his way, and shortly after came to the house of the giant Baugi, a brother of Suttung, who received him very hospitably. In the course of conversation, Baugi informed him that he was greatly embarrassed, as it was harvest time and all his workmen had just been found dead in the hayfield.

Odin, who on this occasion had given his name as Bolwerk (evil doer), promptly offered his services to the giant, promising to accomplish as much work as the nine thralls, and to labour diligently all the summer in exchange for one single draught of Suttung's magic mead when the busy season was ended. This bargain was immediately concluded, and Baugi's new servant, Bolwerk, worked incessantly all the summer long, more than fulfilling his contract, and safely garnering all the grain before the autumn rains began to fall. When the first days of winter came, Bolwerk presented himself before his master, claiming his reward. But Baugi hesitated and demurred, saying he dared not openly ask his brother Suttung for the draught of inspiration, but would try to obtain it by guile. Together, Bolwerk and Baugi then proceeded to the mountain where Gunlod dwelt, and as they could find no other mode of entering the secret cave, Odin produced his trusty auger, called Rati, and bade the giant bore with all his might to make a hole through which he might crawl into the interior.

Baugi silently obeyed, and after a few moments' work withdrew the tool, saying that he had pierced through the mountain, and that Odin would have no difficulty in slipping through. But the god, mistrusting this statement, merely blew into the hole, and when the dust and chips came flying into his face, he sternly bade Baugi resume his boring and not attempt to deceive him again. The giant did as he was told, and when he withdrew his tool again, Odin ascertained that the hole was really finished. Changing himself into a snake, he wriggled through with such remarkable rapidity that he managed to elude the sharp auger, which Baugi treacherously thrust into the hole after him, intending to kill him.

Having reached the interior of the mountain, Odin reassumed his usual godlike form and starry mantle, and then presented himself in the stalactite-hung cave before the beautiful Gunlod. He intended to win her love as a means of inducing her to grant him a sip from each of the vessels confided to her care.

Won by his passionate wooing, Gunlod consented to become his wife, and after he had spent three whole days with her in this retreat, she brought out the vessels from their secret hiding-place, and told him he might take a sip from each.

Odin made good use of this permission and drank so deeply that he completely drained all three vessels. Then, having obtained all that he wanted, he emerged from the cave and, donning his eagle plumes, rose high into the blue, and, after hovering for a moment over the mountain top, winged his flight towards Asgard.

He was still far from the gods' realm when he became aware of a pursuer, and, indeed, Suttung, having also assumed the form of an eagle, was coming rapidly after him with intent to compel him to surrender the stolen mead. Odin therefore flew faster and faster, straining every nerve to reach Asgard before the foe should overtake him, and as he drew near the gods anxiously watched the race.

Seeing that Odin would only with difficulty be able to escape, the Aesir hastily gathered all the combustible materials they could find, and as he flew over the ramparts of their dwelling, they set fire to the mass of fuel, so that the flames, rising high, singed the wings of Suttung, as he followed the god, and he fell into the very midst of the fire, where he was burned to death.

As for Odin, he flew to where the gods had prepared vessels for the stolen mead, and disgorged the draught of inspiration in such breathless haste that a few drops fell and were scattered over the earth. There they became the portion of rhymesters and poetasters, the gods reserving the main draught for their own consumption, and only occasionally vouchsafing a taste to some favoured mortal, who, immediately after, would win world-wide renown by his inspired songs.

As men and gods owed the priceless gift to Odin, they were ever ready to express to him their gratitude, and they not only called it by his name, but they worshipped him as patron of eloquence, poetry, and song, and of all scalds.

# BRAGI

*White-bearded bard, ag'd*
*Bragi, his gold harp*
*Sweeps – and yet softer*
*Stealeth the day.*
**R.B. Anderson, Viking Tales of the North**

**A**lthough Odin had thus won the gift of poetry, he seldom made use of it himself. It was reserved for his son Bragi, the child of Gunlod, to become the god of poetry and music, and to charm the world with his songs.

As soon as Bragi was born in the stalactite-hung cave where Odin had won Gunlod's affections, the dwarfs presented him with a magical golden harp, and, setting him on one of their own vessels, they sent him out into the wide world. As the boat gently passed out of subterranean darkness, and floated over the threshold of Nain, the realm of the dwarf of death, Bragi, the fair and immaculate young god, who until then had shown no signs of life, suddenly sat up, and, seizing the golden harp beside him, he began to sing the wondrous song of life, which rose at times to heaven, and then sank down to the dread realm of Hel, goddess of death.

While he played the vessel was wafted gently over sunlit waters, and soon touched the shore. Bragi then proceeded on foot, threading his way through the bare and silent forest, playing as he walked. At the sound of his tender music the trees began to bud and bloom, and the grass underfoot was gemmed with countless flowers.

Here he met Idun, daughter of Ivald, the fair goddess of immortal youth, whom the dwarfs allowed to visit the earth from time to time, when, at her approach, nature invariably assumed its loveliest and gentlest aspect.

It was only to be expected that two such beings should feel attracted to each other, and Bragi soon won this fair goddess for his wife. Together they hastened to Asgard, where both were warmly welcomed and where Odin, after tracing runes on Bragi's tongue, decreed that he should be the heavenly minstrel and composer of songs in honour of the gods and of the heroes whom he received in Valhalla.

As Bragi was god of poetry, eloquence, and song, the Northern races also called poetry by his name, and scalds of either sex were frequently designated as Braga-men or Braga-women. Bragi was greatly honoured by all the Northern races, and hence his health was always drunk on solemn or festive occasions, but especially at funeral feasts and at Yuletide celebrations.

When it was time to drink this toast, which was served in cups shaped like a ship, and was called the Bragaful, the sacred sign of the hammer was first made over it. Then the new ruler or head of the family solemnly pledged himself to some great deed of valour, which he was bound to execute within the year, unless he wished to be considered destitute of honour. Following his example, all the guests were then wont to make similar vows and declare what they would do; and as some of them, owing to previous potations, talked rather too freely of their intentions on these occasions, this custom seems to connect the god's name with the vulgar but very expressive English verb "to brag."

In art, Bragi is generally represented as an elderly man, with long white hair and beard, and holding the golden harp from which his fingers could draw such magic strains.

## GEIRROD AND AGNAR

*The fallen by the sword*
*Ygg shall now have;*
*Thy life is now run out:*
*Wroth with thee are the Dísir:*

*Odin thou now shalt see:*
*Draw near to me if thou canst*
**Benjamin Thorpe, Saemund's Edda**

**O**din, as has already been stated, took great interest in the affairs of mortals, and, we are told, was specially fond of watching King Hrauding's handsome little sons, Geirrod and Agnar, when they were about eight and ten years of age respectively. One day these little lads went fishing, and a storm suddenly arose which blew their boat far out to sea, where it finally stranded upon an island, upon which dwelt a seeming old couple, who in reality were Odin and Frigga in disguise. They had assumed these forms in order to indulge a sudden passion for the close society of their protégés. The lads were warmly welcomed and kindly treated, Odin choosing Geirrod as his favourite, and teaching him the use of arms, while Frigga petted and made much of little Agnar. The boys tarried on the island with their kind protectors during the long, cold winter season; but when spring came, and the skies were blue, and the sea calm, they embarked in a boat which Odin provided, and set out for their native shore. Favoured by gentle breezes, they were soon wafted thither; but as the boat neared the strand Geirrod quickly sprang out and pushed it far back into the water, bidding his brother sail away into the evil spirit's power. At that self-same moment the wind veered, and Agnar was indeed carried away, while his brother hastened to his father's palace with a lying tale as to what had happened to his brother. He was joyfully received as one from the dead, and in due time he succeeded his father upon the throne.

Years passed by, during which the attention of Odin had been claimed by other high considerations, when one day, while the divine couple were seated on the throne Hlidskialf, Odin suddenly remembered the winter's sojourn on the desert island, and he bade his wife notice how powerful his pupil had become, and taunted her because her favourite Agnar had married a giantess and had remained poor and of no consequence. Frigga quietly replied that it was better to be poor than hardhearted, and accused Geirrod of lack of hospitality – one of the most heinous crimes in the eyes of a Northman. She even went so far as to declare that in spite of all his wealth he often ill-treated his guests.

When Odin heard this accusation he declared that he would prove the falsity of the charge by assuming the guise of a Wanderer and testing Geirrod's generosity. Wrapped in his cloud-hued raiment, with slouch hat and pilgrim staff.

Odin immediately set out by a roundabout way, while Frigga, to outwit him, immediately despatched a swift messenger to warn Geirrod to beware of a man in wide mantle and broad-brimmed hat, as he was a wicked enchanter who would work him ill.

When, therefore, Odin presented himself before the king's palace he was dragged into Geirrod's presence and questioned roughly. He gave his name as Grimnir, but refused to tell whence he came or what he wanted, so as this reticence confirmed the suspicion suggested to the mind of Geirrod, he allowed his love of cruelty full play, and commanded that the stranger should be bound between two fires, in such wise that the flames played around him without quite touching him, and he remained thus eight days and nights, in obstinate silence, without food. Now Agnar had returned secretly to his brother's palace, where he occupied a menial position, and one night when all was still, in pity for the suffering of the unfortunate captive, he conveyed to his lips a horn of ale. But for this Odin would have had nothing to drink – the most serious of all trials to the god.

At the end of the eighth day, while Geirrod, seated upon his throne, was gloating over his prisoner's sufferings, Odin began to sing – softly at first, then louder and louder, until the hall re-echoed with his triumphant notes – a prophecy that the king, who had so long enjoyed the god's favour, would soon perish by his own sword.

As the last notes died away the chains dropped from his hands, the flames flickered and went out, and Odin stood in the midst of the hall, no longer in human form, but in all the power and beauty of a god.

On hearing the ominous prophecy Geirrod hastily drew his sword, intending to slay the insolent singer; but when he beheld the sudden transformation he started in dismay, tripped, fell upon the sharp blade, and perished as Odin had just foretold. Turning to Agnar, who, according to some accounts, was the king's son, and not his brother, for these old stories are often strangely confused, Odin bade him ascend the throne in reward for his humanity, and, further to repay him for the timely draught of ale, he promised to bless him with all manner of prosperity.

On another occasion Odin wandered to earth, and was absent so long that the gods began to think that they would not see him in Asgard again. This encouraged his brothers Vili and Ve, who by some mythologists are considered as other personifications of himself, to usurp his power and his throne, and even, we are told, to espouse his wife Frigga.

## THE VALKYRS

*There through some battlefield, where men fall fast,*
*Their horses fetlock-deep in blood, they ride,*
*And pick the bravest warriors out for death,*
*Whom they bring back with them at night to Heaven*
*To glad the gods and feast in Odin's hall*
**Matthew Arnold, Balder Dead**

Odin's special attendants, the Valkyrs, or battle maidens, were either his daughters, like Brunhild, or the offspring of mortal kings, maidens who were privileged to remain immortal and invulnerable as long as they implicitly obeyed the god and remained virgins. They and their steeds were the personification of the clouds, their glittering weapons being the lightning flashes. The ancients imagined that they swept down to earth at Valfather's command, to choose among the slain in battle heroes worthy to taste the joys of Valhalla, and brave enough to lend aid to the gods when the great battle should be fought.

These maidens were pictured as young and beautiful, with dazzling white arms and flowing golden hair. They wore helmets of silver or gold, and blood-red corselets, and with spears and shields glittering, they boldly charged through the fray on their mettlesome white steeds. These horses galloped through the realms of air and over the quivering Bifrost, bearing not only their fair riders, but the heroes slain, who after having received the Valkyrs' kiss of death, were thus immediately transported to Valhalla.

As the Valkyrs' steeds were personifications of the clouds, it was natural to fancy that the hoar frost and dew dropped down upon earth from their glittering manes as they rapidly dashed to and fro through the air. They were therefore held in high honour and regard, for the people ascribed to their beneficent influence much of the fruitfulness of the earth, the sweetness of dale and mountain-slope, the glory of the pines, and the nourishment of the meadow-land.

The mission of the Valkyrs was not only to battlefields upon earth, but they often rode over the sea, snatching the dying Vikings from their sinking dragon-ships. Sometimes they stood upon the strand to beckon them thither, an infallible warning that the coming struggle would be their last, and one which every Northland hero received with joy.

The numbers of the Valkyrs differ greatly according to various mythologists, ranging from three to sixteen, most authorities, however, naming only nine. The Valkyrs were considered as divinities of the air. It was said that Freyia and Skuld led them on to the fray.

The Valkyrs had important duties in Valhalla, when, their bloody weapons laid aside, they poured out the heavenly mead for the Einheriar. This beverage delighted the souls of the new-comers, and they welcomed the fair maidens as warmly as when they had first seen them on the battlefield and realised that they had come to transport them where they fain would be.

## VÖLUND AND THE VALKYRS

"There they stayed
Seven winters through;
But all the eighth
Were with longing seized;
And in the ninth
Fate parted them.
The maidens yearned
For the murky wood,
The young Alvit,
Fate to fulfil."

**Benjamin Thorpe, Lay of Völund**

The Valkyrs were supposed to take frequent flights to earth in swan plumage, which they would throw off when they came to a secluded stream, that they might indulge in a bath. Any mortal surprising them thus, and securing their plumage, could prevent them from leaving the earth, and could even force these proud maidens to mate with him if such were his pleasure.

It is related that three of the Valkyrs, Olrun, Alvit, and Svanhvit, were once sporting in the waters, when suddenly the three brothers Egil, Slagfinn, and Völund, or Wayland the smith, came upon them, and securing their swan plumage, the young men forced them to remain upon earth and become their wives. The Valkyrs, thus detained, remained with their husbands nine years, but at the end of that time, recovering their plumage, or the spell being broken in some other way, they effected their escape.

The brothers felt the loss of their wives extremely, and two of them, Egil and Slagfinn, putting on their snow shoes, went in search of their loved ones, disappearing in the cold and foggy regions of the North. The third brother, Völund, however, remained at home, knowing all search would be of no avail, and he found solace in the contemplation of a ring which Alvit had given him as a love-token, and he indulged the constant hope that she would return. As he was a very clever smith, and could manufacture the most dainty ornaments of silver and gold, as well as magic weapons which no blow could break, he now employed his leisure in making seven hundred rings exactly like the one which his wife had given him. These, when finished, he bound together; but one night, on coming home from the hunt, he found that some one had carried away one ring, leaving the others behind, and his hopes received fresh inspiration, for he told himself that his wife had been there and would soon return for good.

That selfsame night, however, he was surprised in his sleep, and bound and made prisoner by Nidud, King of Sweden, who took possession of his sword, a choice weapon invested with magic powers, which he reserved for his own use, and of the love ring made of pure Rhine gold, which latter he gave to his only daughter, Bodvild. As for the unhappy Völund himself, he was led captive to a neighbouring island, where, after being hamstrung, in order that he should not escape, the king put him to the incessant task of forging weapons and ornaments for his use. He also compelled him to build an intricate labyrinth, and to this day a maze in Iceland is known as "Völund's house."

Völund's rage and despair increased with every new insult offered him by Nidud, and night and day he thought upon how he might obtain revenge. Nor did he forget to provide for his escape, and during the pauses of his labour he fashioned a pair of wings similar to those his wife had used as a Valkyr, which he intended to don as soon as his vengeance had been accomplished. One day the king came to visit his captive, and brought him the stolen sword that he might repair it; but Völund cleverly substituted another weapon so exactly like the magic sword as to deceive the king when he came again to claim it. A few days later, Völund enticed the king's sons into his smithy and slew them, after which he cunningly fashioned drinking vessels out of their skulls, and jewels out of their eyes and teeth, bestowing these upon their parents and sister.

The royal family did not suspect whence they came; and so these gifts were joyfully accepted. As for the poor youths, it was believed that they had drifted out to sea and had been drowned.

Some time after this, Bodvild, wishing to have her ring repaired, also visited the smith's hut, where, while waiting, she unsuspectingly partook of a magic drug, which sent her to sleep and left her in Völund's power. His last act of vengeance accomplished, Völund immediately donned the wings which he had made in readiness for this day, and grasping his sword and ring he rose slowly in the air. Directing his flight to the palace, he perched there out of reach, and proclaimed his crimes to Nidud. The king, beside himself with rage, summoned Egil, Völund's brother, who had also fallen into his power, and bade him use his marvellous skill as an archer to bring down the impudent bird. Obeying a signal from Völund, Egil aimed for a protuberance under his wing where a bladder full of the young princes' blood was concealed, and the smith flew triumphantly away without hurt, declaring that Odin would give his sword to Sigmund – a prediction which was duly fulfilled.

Völund then went to Alf-heim, where, if the legend is to be believed, he found his beloved wife, and lived happily again with her until the twilight of the gods.

But, even in Alf-heim, this clever smith continued to ply his craft, and various suits of impenetrable armour, which he is said to have fashioned, are described in later heroic poems. Besides Balmung and Joyeuse, Sigmund's and Charlemagne's celebrated swords, he is reported to have fashioned Miming for his son Heime, and many other remarkable blades.

There are countless other tales of swan maidens or Valkyrs, who are said to have consorted with mortals; but the most popular of all is that of Brunhild, the wife of Sigurd, a descendant of Sigmund and the most renowned of Northern heroes.

William Morris, in "The Land East of the Sun and West of the Moon," gives a fascinating version of another of these Norse legends. The story is amongst the most charming of the collection in "The Earthly Paradise."

The story of Brunhild is to be found in many forms. Some versions describe the heroine as the daughter of a king taken by Odin to serve in his Valkyr band, others as chief of the Valkyrs and daughter of Odin himself. In Richard Wagner's story, "The Ring of the Nibelung," the great musician presents a particularly attractive, albeit a more modern conception of the chief Battle-Maiden, and her disobedience to the command of Odin when sent to summon the youthful Siegmund from the side of his beloved Sieglinde to the Halls of the Blessed.

## FRIGGA'S ATTENDANTS

*My lily tall, from her saddle bearing,*
*I led then forth through the temple, faring*
*To th' altar-circle where, priests among,*
*Lofn's vows she took with unfalt'ring tongue.*
**R.B. Anderson, Viking Tales of the North**

**F**rigga had, as her own special attendants, a number of beautiful maidens, among whom were Fulla (Volla), her sister, according to some authorities, to whom she entrusted her jewel casket. Fulla always presided over her mistress's toilet, was privileged to put on her golden shoes, attended her everywhere, was her confidante, and often advised her how best to help the mortals who implored her aid. Fulla was very beautiful indeed, and had long golden hair, which she wore flowing loose over her shoulders, restrained only by a golden circlet or snood. As her hair was emblematic of the golden grain, this circlet represented the binding of the sheaf. Fulla was also known as Abundia, or Abundantia, in some parts of Germany, where she was considered the symbol of the fulness of the earth.

Hlin, Frigga's second attendant, was the goddess of consolation, sent out to kiss away the tears of mourners and pour balm into hearts wrung by grief. She also listened with ever-open ears to the prayers of mortals, carrying them to her mistress, and advising her at times how best to answer them and give the desired relief.

Gna was Frigga's swift messenger. Mounted upon her fleet steed Hofvarpnir (hoof-thrower), she would travel with marvellous rapidity through fire and air, over land and sea, and was therefore considered the personification of the refreshing breeze. Darting thus to and fro, Gna saw all that was happening upon earth, and told her mistress all she knew. On one occasion, as she was passing over Hunaland, she saw King Rerir, a lineal descendant of Odin, sitting mournfully by the shore, bewailing his childlessness. The queen of heaven, who was also goddess of childbirth, upon hearing this took an apple (the emblem of fruitfulness) from her private store, gave it to Gna, and bade her carry it to the king. With the rapidity of the element she personified, Gna darted away, and as she passed over Rerir's head, she dropped her apple into his lap with a radiant smile.

The king pondered for a moment upon the meaning of this sudden apparition and gift, and then hurried home, his heart beating high with hope, and gave the apple to his wife to eat. In due season, to his intense joy, she bore him a son, Volsung, the great Northern hero, who became so famous that he gave his name to all his race.

Besides the three above mentioned, Frigga had other attendants in her train. There was the mild and gracious maiden Lofn (praise or love), whose duty it was to remove all obstacles from the path of lovers.

Vjofn's duty was to incline obdurate hearts to love, to maintain peace and concord among mankind, and to reconcile quarrelling husbands and wives. Syn (truth) guarded the door of Frigga's palace, refusing to open it to those who were not allowed to come in. When she had once shut the door upon a would-be intruder no appeal would avail to change her decision. She therefore presided over all tribunals and trials, and whenever a thing was to be vetoed the usual formula was to declare that Syn was against it.

Gefjon was also one of the maidens in Frigga's palace, and to her were entrusted all those who died unwedded, whom she received and made happy for ever.

According to some authorities, Gefjon did not remain a virgin herself, but married one of the giants, by whom she had four sons. This same tradition goes on to declare that Odin sent her before him to visit Gylfi, King of Sweden, and to beg for some land which she might call her own. The king, amused at her request, promised her as much land as she could plough around in one day and night. Gefjon, nothing daunted, changed her four sons into oxen, harnessed them to a plough, and began to cut a furrow so wide and deep that the king and his courtiers were amazed. But Gefjon continued her work without showing any signs of fatigue, and when she had ploughed all around a large piece of land forcibly wrenched it away, and made her oxen drag it down into the sea, where she made it fast and called it Seeland.

As for the hollow she left behind her, it was quickly filled with water and formed a lake, at first called Logrum (the sea), but now known as Mälar, whose every indentation corresponds with the headlands of Seeland. Gefjon then married Skiold, one of Odin's sons, and became the ancestress of the royal Danish race of Skioldungs, dwelling in the city of Hleidra or Lethra, which she founded, and which became the principal place of sacrifice for the heathen Danes.

Eira, also Frigga's attendant, was considered a most skilful physician. She gathered simples all over the earth to cure both wounds and diseases, and it was her province to teach the science to women, who were the only ones to practise medicine among the ancient nations of the North.

Vara heard all oaths and punished perjurers, while she rewarded those who faithfully kept their word. Then there were also Vör (faith), who knew all that was to occur throughout the world, and Snotra, goddess of virtue, who had mastered all knowledge.

With such a galaxy of attendants it is little wonder that Frigga was considered a powerful deity; but in spite of the prominent place she occupied in Northern religion, she had no special temple nor shrine, and was but little worshipped except in company with Odin.

## THE DISCOVERY OF FLAX

There was once a peasant who daily left his wife and children in the valley to take his sheep up the mountain to pasture; and as he watched his flock grazing on the mountain-side, he often had opportunity to use his cross-bow and bring down a chamois, whose flesh would furnish his larder with food for many a day.

While pursuing a fine animal one day he saw it disappear behind a boulder, and when he came to the spot, he was amazed to see a doorway in the neighbouring glacier, for in the excitement of the pursuit he had climbed higher and higher, until he was now on top of the mountain, where glittered the everlasting snow.

The shepherd boldly passed through the open door, and soon found himself in a wonderful jewelled cave hung with stalactites, in the centre of which stood a beautiful woman, clad in silvery robes, and attended by a host of lovely maidens crowned with Alpine roses. In his surprise, the shepherd sank to his knees, and as in a dream heard the queenly central figure bid him choose anything he saw to carry away with him. Although dazzled by the glow of the precious stones around him, the shepherd's eyes constantly reverted to a little nosegay of blue flowers which the gracious apparition held in her hand, and he now timidly proffered a request that it might become his. Smiling with pleasure, Holda, for it was she, gave it to him, telling him he had chosen wisely and would live as long as the flowers did not droop and fade. Then, giving the shepherd a measure of seed which she told him to sow in his field, the goddess bade him begone; and as the thunder pealed and the earth shook, the poor man found himself out upon the mountain-side once more, and slowly wended his way home to his wife, to whom he told his adventure and showed the lovely blue flowers and the measure of seed.

The woman reproached her husband bitterly for not having brought some of the precious stones which he so glowingly described, instead of the blossoms and seed; nevertheless the man proceeded to sow the latter, and he found to his surprise that the measure supplied seed enough for several acres.

Soon the little green shoots began to appear, and one moonlight night, while the peasant was gazing upon them, as was his wont, for he felt a curious attraction to the field which he had sown, and often lingered there wondering what kind of grain would be produced, he saw a misty form hover above the field, with hands outstretched as if in blessing. At last the field blossomed, and countless little blue flowers opened their calyxes to the golden sun. When the flowers had withered and the seed was ripe, Holda came once more to teach the peasant and his wife how to harvest the flax – for such it was – and from it to spin, weave, and bleach linen. As the people of the neighbourhood willingly purchased both linen and flax-seed, the peasant and his wife soon grew very rich indeed, and while he ploughed, sowed, and harvested, she spun, wove, and bleached the linen. The man lived to a good old age, and saw his grandchildren and great-grandchildren grow up around him. All this time his carefully treasured bouquet had remained fresh as when he first brought it home, but one day he saw that during the night the flowers had drooped and were dying.

Knowing what this portended, and that he too must die, the peasant climbed the mountain once more to the glacier, and found again the doorway for which he had often vainly searched. He entered the icy portal, and was never seen or heard of again, for, according to the legend, the goddess took him under her care, and bade him live in her cave, where his every wish was gratified.

## IDUNN AND THE APPLES

*Bright Iduna, Maid immortal!*
*Standing at Valhalla's portal,*
*In her casket has rich store*
*Of rare apples gilded o'er;*
*Those rare apples, not of Earth,*
*Ageing Aesir give fresh birth.*
**J.C. Jones, Valhalla**

One fine day, Odin, Loki and Hoenir wandered throughout the worlds on one of their regular missions to see that all was well. As they travelled, they grew hungry, and finally stopped in order to cook an ox to give them sustenance to carry on. A fine ox was chosen from a herd in a field, and it was duly slain and placed on a spit over roaring flames. After several hours, the ox was removed from the fire, and the three wanderers licked their lips and they prepared for their meal. Hoenir cut into the beef, and stopped. Under the crisp exterior, the beef was raw through and through. Fresh blood dripped on to the fire. Hoenir looked puzzled, but he placed the beef back on the spit and motioned to his friends that they could not eat just yet.

The fire was built up once more and the three men waited for another hour or so before removing the beef from

LEGENDS OF ODIN AND FRIGGA

the spit once more. This time Odin cut into the meat, but again it was uncooked – it appeared that the fire had had no effect whatsoever.

Suddenly there was a movement in the trees, and a rush of wings. There, at the top of the tree overlooking their fire sat a great eagle. He sat looking down at them with great satisfaction.

'Our meat is uncooked,' Odin said helplessly, pointing to the fire.

'The meat will remain uncooked,' said the eagle, 'until I ordain it to be cooked.'

The three travellers looked at the eagle with interest. It was not often that gods were challenged, and they waited to hear the reason.

'All right, then,' said Odin fairly, 'please could you allow our meat to cook.'

'I shall do so,' said the eagle, 'if I can eat my fill before you partake from the ox.'

Odin nodded and agreed, for he was famished by hunger now and he was determined to have some of this fine piece of ox. Within five minutes the beef was cooked, and with a flurry of feathers, the eagle landed by the fire and stirring up a great cloud of ashes, began to eat. Moments later there was silence. The eagle had returned to the tree, and the spit was empty.

Now Loki in particular was enraged by this act. He was accustomed to being the trickster, and was not used to having tricks played on him – whatever the reason. 'Who are you,' he called out angrily, to which the eagle only laughed and shrugged.

Loki grabbed a burning log from the fire, and made towards the eagle, who only ducked and dove at Loki until he was quite reddened with fury. Finally, the eagle swooped down and took in his talons the log which Loki held, drawing it up into the air as he flew. Loki struggled to let go of the wood, but he was unable to free himself. His fingers clutched the branch and nothing he could do would loosen them.

'Let me down,' he cried, angrily kicking his feet and shouting. But the eagle flew higher and higher, turning and soaring through the air and terrifying Loki so that he closed his eyes in fear. When at last the eagle sensed that his prisoner could take no more, he spoke.

'I am Thiazzi, the great giant. I will let you loose only if you swear to deliver the goddess Idunn to me. You must lure her beyond the walls of Asgard where I can catch her, and she must bring with her the basket of apples.'

Loki considered this for a moment, and then agreed. Far below him Odin and Hoenir watched, never imagining the treachery of which Loki was capable. In a moment, Loki was set safely on the ground, and for a moment he sat there, stunned. Odin and Hoenir reached his side, and asked him what had passed with the eagle, but Loki told them nothing. The three men returned to Asgard.

Loki knew that the promise he had made to Thiazzi was the worst he could possibly have made, for without the golden apples of Idunn, the ravages of time would take their toll on the occupants of Asgard and he, Loki, alone would be responsible for the ageing and eventual death of each and every one of them.

He paced and paced the gardens where Idunn worked happily, her sweet ways bringing a nuance of spring to all she touched. But as much as Loki realized the trouble he would cause by luring Idunn from Asgard, he knew there would be much more trouble if he did not satisfy his solemn oath to Thiazzi. And so it was on that fateful day that Loki approached Idunn, who was curled up by a bed of flowers.

Idunn smiled innocently at Loki, and began to explain how the flowers responded to her love, and how all growing things could benefit from praise and care.

Loki smiled briefly and interrupted.

'Come, Idunn,' he said carelessly. 'Did you know that yesterday when I walked with Odin and Hoenir I saw a tree bearing enchanted apples just like your own.'

Idunn laughed. 'Why that's not possible,' she said brightly, knowing that her own golden apples were unique. They did not come from any tree, but appeared magically in her basket. When one was eaten, another quickly took its place so that there was an eternal supply of youth.

But Loki talked and talked to Idunn, and he managed to convince her that another source of apples would be a fine thing, for what should transpire if something were to happen to Idunn's basket?

'Bring your basket,' he said slyly, 'and you'll see that the apples are much the same.'

Idunn finally agreed to travel with Loki to see the tree, and they set out for the walls of Asgard. No sooner had Idunn stepped outside when Thiazzi swept down and clutching her in his talons, carried her away. With her went her basket of apples.

Loki skulked back inside the walls of Asgard, and mentioned nothing of what had happened. Soon it was discovered that Idunn was missing, and the Aesir became greatly distressed. Within a few days wrinkles appeared on their youthful cheeks, and their backs became hunched with age. They hardly recognized one another and as the bloom of youth disappeared, so did their happiness. Asgard was a changed place, and everyone called out for the return of Idunn.

Heimdall admitted that he had seen Idunn with Loki, on the fateful day of her disappearance, and at once Odin and his men set out to find the trickster. Loki admitted what had happened and the rage of Odin was so great that Loki volunteered to see about the return of Idunn himself.

Loki sat alone, deeply concerned by the task that lay ahead of him. For how was he to travel to the skies where Thiazzi lived as an eagle? Loki could take many forms when the need arose, but he had not yet mastered the art of flying, and he found himself in a quandary which even his quick wits could not find a way out of. Suddenly it came to him – Freyia's coat! Freyia's coat of feathers!

Freyia agreed at once to the loan of her hawk coat, for she was frightened by the wrinkles which cut deeply into her face and without her legendary beauty she would never be able to attract the souls of the warriors to her domain. And so Loki set out wearing Freyia's coat, and he flew at once over the walls of Asgard until he found the giant's castle.

There, in a pen, sat Idunn, and she was alone. Thiazzi's daughter Skadi had been watching the goddess, but because she was so serene and presented no threat of escape, Skadi had gone off for a walk, leaving Idunn to sit quietly, clutching her basket of apples.

Loki swooped down and spoke quietly to Idunn. 'Idunn, it's me, Loki,' he said quickly. 'Listen carefully: I am here to rescue you. In a moment you must hold your basket to you and I will turn you into a hazelnut and lift you into the sky and back to Asgard.'

Ever trusting, Idunn nodded her head and soon found herself high in the air with Loki the hawk. Just at that moment, Skadi returned and it took her no time at all to realize what had happened. She called out to her father, who was fishing several miles away, and he returned at once, rowing like a crazed person in order to reach his daughter. At once he saw Loki carrying away the nut, and he transformed himself into the giant eagle in order to give chase.

Loki was within reach of the gates of Asgard when the eagle approached. From Asgard the gods watched with horror, and Freyia cried out, 'My hawk will never outfly an eagle.'

And so the gods got to work, and directed by Tyr they put together a great pile of wood shavings which they set alight. Tyr held up the burning shavings and as the eagle flew across, he touched it to him, and the giant bird burst into flames, his feather coat melting off until the giant fell helplessly to the ground, where he was burnt in a rush of flames. There beside him stood Loki, trembling and frightened, but complete, and there was Idunn, mercifully unharmed by the chase, and by the blast of flames. She carefully handed each of the Aesir an apple, and youth was once more restored.

Just as the gods began to settle back into their daily routines, there came a shriek from the walls. There stood

Skadi, crying out for her father who was nothing more than two burning embers. She cried out for vengeance, but Odin approached her and settled her down, pointing out that it had been her father who had begun this unhappy episode. It was finally agreed that Skadi would choose a god as her husband, in order that she would have a man to take care of her. She was to choose the one she wanted by looking at his feet.

So a screen was erected and each man in Asgard was bidden to walk past the screen so that she could see their feet. Choosing those that were the cleanest, and purest white, Skadi looked smug, sure that she had picked Balder, for no one else could have such clean white feet.

But when the screen was removed, there was Niord, god of the sea, whose feet were washed clean on the sands of the ocean each day. And so it was that the girl of the mountains married the god of the sea, and the two came together for all eternity. Thiazzi's embers were carried to the sky by Loki in Freyia's coat, and there they sit today, the twin stars of Thiazzi which bear his name and appear each night in the Northern skies.

# LEGENDS OF LOKI

*Odin! dost thou remember*
*When we in early days*
*Blended our blood together?*
*When to taste beer*
*Thou did'st constantly refuse*
*Unless to both 'twas offered*
**Benjamin Thorpe, Saemund's Edda**

Besides the hideous giant Utgard-Loki, the personification of mischief and evil, whom Thor and his companions visited in Jötun-heim, the ancient Northern nations had another type of sin, whom they called Loki also, and whom we have already seen under many different aspects.

In the beginning, Loki was merely the personification of the hearth fire and of the spirit of life. At first a god, he gradually becomes "god and devil combined," and ends in being held in general detestation as an exact counterpart of the mediaeval Lucifer, the prince of lies, "the originator of deceit, and the back-biter" of the Aesir.

By some authorities Loki was said to be the brother of Odin, but others assert that the two were not related, but had merely gone through the form of swearing blood brotherhood common in the North.

## LOKI'S CHARACTER

*Loki begat the wolf*
*With Angur-boda.*
**Benjamin Thorpe, Saemund's Edda**

**While Thor is the embodiment** of Northern activity, Loki represents recreation, and the close companionship early established between these two gods shows very plainly how soon our ancestors realised that both were necessary to the welfare of mankind. Thor is ever busy and ever in earnest, but Loki makes fun of everything, until at last his love of mischief leads him entirely astray, and he loses all love for goodness and becomes utterly selfish and malevolent.

He represents evil in the seductive and seemingly beautiful form in which it parades through the world. Because of this deceptive appearance the gods did not at first avoid him, but treated him as one of themselves in all good-fellowship, taking him with them wherever they went, and admitting him not only to their merry-makings, but also to their council hall, where, unfortunately, they too often listened to his advice.

As we have already seen, Loki played a prominent part in the creation of man, endowing him with the power of motion, and causing the blood to circulate freely through his veins, whereby he was inspired with passions. As personification of fire as well as of mischief, Loki (lightning) is often seen with Thor (thunder), whom he accompanies to Jötun-heim to recover his hammer, to Utgard-Loki's castle, and to Geirrod's house. It is he who steals Freyia's necklace and Sif's hair, and betrays Idunn into the power of Thiassi; and although he sometimes gives the gods good advice and affords them real help, it is only to extricate them from some predicament into which he has rashly inveigled them.

Some authorities declare that, instead of making part of the creative trilogy (Odin, Hoenir, and Lodur or Loki), this god originally belonged to a pre-Odinic race of deities, and was the son of the great giant Fornjotnr (Ymir), his brothers being Kari (air) and Hler (water), and his sister Ran, the terrible goddess of the sea. Other mythologists, however, make him the son of the giant Farbauti, who has been identified with Bergelmir, the sole survivor of the deluge, and of Laufeia (leafy isle) or Nal (vessel), his mother, thus stating that his connection with Odin was only that of the Northern oath of good-fellowship.

Loki (fire) first married Glut (glow), who bore him two daughters, Eisa (embers) and Einmyria (ashes); it is therefore very evident that Norsemen considered him emblematic of the hearth-fire, and when the flaming wood crackles on the hearth the goodwives in the North are still wont to say that Loki is beating his children. Besides this wife, Loki is also said to have wedded the giantess Angur-boda (the anguish-boding), who dwelt in Jötun-heim, and who, as we have already seen, bore him the three monsters: Hel, goddess of death, the Midgard snake Iörmungandr, and the grim wolf Fenris.

Loki's third marriage was with Sigyn, who proved a most loving and devoted wife, and bore him two sons, Narve and Vali, the latter a namesake of the god who avenged Balder. Sigyn was always faithful to her husband, and did not forsake him even after he had definitely been cast out of Asgard and confined in the bowels of the earth.

As Loki was the embodiment of evil in the minds of the Northern races, they entertained nothing but fear of him, built no temples to his honour, offered no sacrifices to him, and designated the most noxious weeds by his name. The quivering, overheated atmosphere of summer was supposed to betoken his presence, for the people were then wont to remark that Loki was sowing his wild oats, and when the sun appeared to be drawing water they said Loki was drinking.

The story of Loki is so inextricably woven with that of the other gods that most of the myths relating to him have already been told, and there remain but two episodes of his life to relate, one showing his better side before he had degenerated into the arch deceiver, and the other illustrating how he finally induced the gods to defile their peace-steads by wilful murder.

## LOKI AND THE NECKLACE

*Out of the morning land,*
*Over the snowdrifts,*
*Beautiful Freya came*
**Charles Kingsley, The Longbeards' Saga**

**O**ne evening, when Freyia had become part of Asgard, Loki spied her marvellous necklace, a golden symbol of the fruitfulness of the earth which she wore about her slender neck at all times. Loki coveted this necklace, and he found he could not sleep until he had it in his possession. So it was that he crept one night into her chamber and bent over as if to remove it. Finding that her position in sleep made this feat impossible, he turned himself into a small flea, and springing under the bedclothes, he bit the lovely goddess so that she turned in her sleep. Loki returned to his shape and undid the clasp of the necklace, which he removed without rousing Freyia.

Not far from Freyia's palace, Heimdall had heard the sound of Loki becoming a flea – a sound so slight that only the great watchman of the gods could have heard it – and he travelled immediately to the palace to investigate. He saw Loki leaving with the necklace, and soon caught up with him, drawing his sword in order to remove the thief's head. Loki immediately changed himself into a thin blue flame, but quick as a flash, Heimdall became a cloud and sent down a sheath of rain in order to douse the flame. Loki quickly became a polar bear and opened his jaws to swallow the water, whereupon Heimdall turned himself into bear and attacked the hapless trickster. In haste, Loki became a seal, and then, once again, Heimdall transformed himself in the same form as Loki and the two fought for many hours, before Heimdall showed his worth and won the necklace from Loki.

## SKRYMSLI AND THE PEASANT'S CHILD

*Many a time has he exposed the gods to very great perils,*
*and often extricated them again by his artifices.*
**I.A. Blackwell, The Prose Edda**

**A giant and a peasant** were playing a game together one day (probably a game of chess, which was a favourite winter pastime with the Northern vikings). They of course had determined to play for certain stakes, and the giant, being victorious, won the peasant's only son, whom he said he would come and claim on the morrow unless the parents could hide him so cleverly that he could not be found.

Knowing that such a feat would be impossible for them to perform, the parents fervently prayed to Odin to help them, and in answer to their entreaties the god came down to earth, and changed the boy into a tiny grain of wheat, which he hid in an ear of grain in the midst of a large field, declaring that the giant would not be able to find him. The giant Skrymsli, however, possessed wisdom far beyond what Odin imagined, and, failing to find the child at home, he strode off immediately to the field with his scythe, and mowing the wheat he selected the particular ear where the boy was hidden. Counting over the grains of wheat he was about to lay his hand upon the right one when Odin, hearing the child's cry of distress, snatched the kernel out of the giant's hand, and restored the boy to his parents, telling them that he had done all in his power to help them. But as the giant vowed he had been cheated, and would again claim the boy on the morrow unless the parents could outwit him, the unfortunate peasants now turned to Hoenir for aid. The god heard them graciously and changed the boy into a fluff of down, which he hid in the breast of a swan swimming in a pond close by. Now when, a few minutes later, Skrymsli came up, he guessed what had occurred, and seizing the swan, he bit off its neck, and would have swallowed the down had not Hoenir wafted it away from his lips and out of reach, restoring the boy safe and sound to his parents, but telling them that he could not further aid them.

Skrymsli warned the parents that he would make a third attempt to secure the child, whereupon they applied in their despair to Loki, who carried the boy out to sea, and concealed him, as a tiny egg, in the roe of a flounder. Returning from his expedition, Loki encountered the giant near the shore, and seeing that he was bent upon a fishing excursion, he insisted upon accompanying him. He felt somewhat uneasy lest the terrible giant should have seen through his device, and therefore thought it would be well for him to be on the spot in case of need. Skrymsli baited his hook, and was more or less successful in his angling, when suddenly he drew up the identical flounder in which Loki had concealed his little charge. Opening the fish upon his knee, the giant proceeded to minutely examine the roe, until he found the egg which he was seeking.

The plight of the boy was certainly perilous, but Loki, watching his chance, snatched the egg out of the giant's grasp, and transforming it again into the child, he instructed him secretly to run home, passing through the boathouse on his way and closing the door behind him. The terrified boy did as he was told immediately he found himself on land, and the giant, quick to observe his flight, dashed after him into the boathouse. Now Loki had cunningly placed a sharp spike in such a position that the great head of the giant ran full tilt against it, and he sank to the ground with a groan, whereupon Loki, seeing him helpless, cut off one of his legs. Imagine the god's dismay, however, when he saw the pieces join and immediately knit together. But Loki was a master of guile, and recognising this as the work of magic, he cut off the other leg, promptly throwing flint and steel between the severed limb and trunk, and thereby hindering any further sorcery. The peasants were immensely relieved to find that their enemy was slain, and ever after they considered Loki the mightiest of all the heavenly council, for he had delivered them effectually from their foe, while the other gods had lent only temporary aid.

## THE GIANT ARCHITECT

> To Asgard came an architect,
> And castle offered to erect,
> A castle high
> Which should defy
> Deep Jotun guile and giant raid;
> And this most wily compact made:
> Fair Freya, with the Moon and Sun,
> As price the fortress being done.
> **J.C. Jones, Valhalla**

**N**otwithstanding their wonderful bridge Bifrost, the tremulous way, and the watchfulness of Heimdall, the gods could not feel entirely secure in Asgard, and were often fearful lest the frost giants should make their way into Asgard. To obviate this possibility, they finally decided to build an impregnable fortress; and while they were planning how this could be done, an unknown architect came with an offer to undertake the construction, provided the gods would give him sun, moon, and Freyia, goddess of youth and beauty, as reward. The gods were wroth at so presumptuous an offer, but when they would have indignantly driven the stranger from their presence, Loki urged them to make a bargain which it would be impossible for the stranger to keep, and so they finally told the architect that the guerdon should be his, provided the fortress were finished in the course of a single winter, and that he accomplished the work with no other assistance than that of his horse Svadilfare.

The unknown architect agreed to these seemingly impossible conditions, and immediately set to work, hauling ponderous blocks of stone by night, building during the day, and progressing so rapidly that the gods began to feel somewhat anxious. Ere long they noticed that more than half the labour was accomplished by the wonderful steed Svadilfare, and when they saw, near the end of winter, that the work was finished save only one portal, which they knew the architect could easily erect during the night:

Terrified lest they should be called upon to part, not only with the sun and moon, but also with Freyia, the personification of the youth and beauty of the world, the gods turned upon Loki, and threatened to kill him unless he devised some means of hindering the architect from finishing the work within the specified time.

Loki's cunning proved once more equal to the situation. He waited until nightfall of the final day, when, as Svadilfare passed the fringe of a forest, painfully dragging one of the great blocks of stone required for the termination of the work, he rushed out from a dark glade in the guise of a mare, and neighed so invitingly that, in a trice, the horse kicked himself free of his harness and ran after the mare, closely pursued by his angry master. The mare galloped swiftly on, artfully luring horse and master deeper and deeper into the forest shades, until the night was nearly gone, and it was no longer possible to finish the work. The architect was none other than a redoubtable Hrim-thurs, in disguise, and he now returned to Asgard in a towering rage at the fraud which had been practised upon him. Assuming his wonted proportions, he would have annihilated the gods had not Thor suddenly returned from a journey and slain him with his magic hammer Miolnir, which he hurled with terrific force full in his face.

The gods had saved themselves on this occasion only by fraud and by the violent deed of Thor, and these were destined to bring great sorrow upon them, and eventually to secure their downfall, and to hasten the coming of Ragnarok. Loki, however, felt no remorse for his part, and in due time, it is said, he became the parent of an eight-footed steed called Sleipnir, which, as we have seen, was Odin's favourite mount.

Loki performed so many evil deeds during his career that he richly deserved the title of "arch deceiver" which was given him. He was generally hated for his subtle malicious ways, and for an inveterate habit of prevarication which won for him also the title of "prince of lies."

## LOKI'S LAST CRIME

*Now, to assuage the high gods' grief*
*And bring their mourning some relief,*
*From coral caves*
*'Neath ocean waves,*
*Mighty King Aegir*
*Invited the Aesir*
*To festival*
*In Hlesey's hall;*
*That, tho' for Baldur every guest*
*Was grieving yet,*
*He might forget*
*Awhile his woe in friendly feast*
**J.C. Jones, Valhalla**

**L**oki's last crime, and the one which filled his measure of iniquity, was to induce Hodur to throw the fatal mistletoe at Balder, whom he hated merely on account of his immaculate purity. Perhaps even this crime might have been condoned had it not been for his obduracy when, in the disguise of the old woman Thok, he was called upon to shed a tear for Balder. His action on this occasion convinced the gods that nothing but evil remained within him, and they pronounced unanimously upon him the sentence of perpetual banishment from Asgard.

To divert the gods' sadness and make them, for a short time, forget the treachery of Loki and the loss of Balder, Aegir, god of the sea, invited them to partake of a banquet in his coral caves at the bottom of the sea.

The gods gladly accepted the invitation, and clad in their richest garb, and with festive smiles, they appeared in the coral caves at the appointed time. None were absent save the radiant Balder, for whom many a regretful sigh was heaved, and the evil Loki, whom none could regret. In the course of the feast, however, this last-named god appeared in their midst like a dark shadow, and when bidden to depart, he gave vent to his evil passions in a torrent of invective against the gods.

Then, jealous of the praises which Funfeng, Aegir's servant, had won for the dexterity with which he waited upon his master's guests, Loki suddenly turned upon him and slew him. At this wanton crime, the gods in fierce wrath drove Loki away once more, threatening him with dire punishment should he ever appear before them again.

Scarcely had the Aesir recovered from this disagreeable interruption to their feast, and resumed their places at the board, when Loki came creeping in once more, resuming his slanders with venomous tongue, and taunting the gods with their weaknesses or shortcomings, dwelling maliciously upon their physical imperfections, and deriding them for their mistakes. In vain the gods tried to stem his abuse; his voice rose louder and louder, and he was just giving utterance to some base slander about Sif, when he was suddenly cut short by the sight of Thor's hammer, angrily brandished by an arm whose power he knew full well, and he fled incontinently.

Knowing that he could now have no hope of being admitted into Asgard again, and that sooner or later the gods, seeing the effect of his evil deeds, would regret having permitted him to roam the world, and would try either to bind or slay him, Loki withdrew to the mountains, where he built himself a hut, with four doors which he always left wide open to permit of a hasty escape. Carefully laying his plans, he decided that if the gods should come in search of him he would rush down to the neighbouring cataract, according to tradition the Fraananger force or stream, and, changing himself into a salmon, would thus evade his pursuers. He reasoned, however, that although he could easily avoid any hook, it might be difficult for him to effect his escape if the gods should fashion a net like that of the sea-goddess Ran.

Haunted by this fear, he decided to test the possibility of making such a mesh, and started to make one out of twine. He was still engaged upon the task when Odin, Kvasir, and Thor suddenly appeared in the distance; and knowing that they had discovered his retreat, Loki threw his half-finished net into the fire, and, rushing through one of his ever-open doors, he leaped into the waterfall, where, in the shape of a salmon, he hid among some stones in the bed of the stream.

The gods, finding the hut empty, were about to depart, when Kvasir perceived the remains of the burnt net on the hearth. After some thought an inspiration came to him, and he advised the gods to weave a similar implement and use it in searching for their foe in the neighbouring stream, since it would be like Loki to choose such a method of baffling their pursuit. This advice seemed good and was immediately followed, and, the net finished, the gods proceeded to drag the stream. Loki eluded the net at its first cast by hiding at the bottom of the river between two stones; and when the gods weighted the mesh and tried a second time, he effected his escape by jumping up stream. A third attempt to secure him proved successful, however, for, as he once more tried to get away by a sudden leap, Thor caught him in mid-air and held him so fast, that he could not escape. The salmon, whose slipperiness is proverbial in the North, is noted for its remarkably slim tail, and Norsemen attribute this to Thor's tight grasp upon his foe.

Loki now sullenly resumed his wonted shape, and his captors dragged him down into a cavern, where they made him fast, using as bonds the entrails of his son Narve, who had been torn to pieces by Vali, his brother, whom the gods had changed into a wolf for the purpose. One of these fetters was passed under Loki's shoulders, and one under his loins, thereby securing him firmly hand and foot; but the gods, not feeling quite satisfied that the strips, tough and enduring though they were, would not give way, changed them into adamant or iron.

Skadi, the giantess, a personification of the cold mountain stream, who had joyfully watched the fettering of her foe (subterranean fire), now fastened a serpent directly over his head, so that its venom would fall, drop by drop, upon his upturned face. But Sigyn, Loki's faithful wife, hurried with a cup to his side, and until the day of Ragnarok she remained by him, catching the drops as they fell, and never leaving her post except when her vessel was full, and she was obliged to empty it. Only during her short absences could the drops of venom fall upon Loki's face, and then they caused such intense pain that he writhed with anguish, his efforts to get free shaking the earth and producing the earthquakes which so frighten mortals.

In this painful position Loki was destined to remain until the twilight of the gods, when his bonds would be loosed, and he would take part in the fatal conflict on the battlefield of Vigrid, falling at last by the hand of Heimdall, who would be slain at the same time.

As we have seen, the venom-dropping snake in this myth is the cold mountain stream, whose waters, falling from time to time upon subterranean fire, evaporate in steam, which escapes through fissures, and causes earthquakes and geysers, phenomena with which the inhabitants of Iceland, for instance, were very familiar.

# HEL

*Now Loki comes, cause of all ill!*
*Men and Aesir curse him still.*
*Long shall the gods deplore,*
*Even till Time be o'er,*
*His base fraud on Asgard's hill.*
*While, deep in Jotunheim, most fell,*
*Are Fenrir, Serpent, and Dread Hel,*
*Pain, Sin, and Death, his children three,*
*Brought up and cherished; thro' them he*
*Tormentor of the world shall be.*
**J.C. Jones, Valhalla**

**H**el, **goddess of death**, was the daughter of Loki, god of evil, and of the giantess Angurboda, the portender of ill. She came into the world in a dark cave in Jötun-heim together with the serpent Iörmungandr and the terrible Fenris wolf, the trio being considered as the emblems of pain, sin, and death.

In due time Odin became aware of the terrible brood which Loki was cherishing, and resolved, as we have already seen, to banish them from the face of the earth. The serpent was therefore cast into the sea, where his writhing was supposed to cause the most terrible tempests; the wolf Fenris was secured in chains, thanks to the dauntless Tyr; and Hel or Hela, the goddess of death, was hurled into the depths of Nifl-heim, where Odin gave her power over nine worlds.

This realm, which was supposed to be situated under the earth, could only be entered after a painful journey over the roughest roads in the cold, dark regions of the extreme North. The gate was so far from all human abode that even Hermod the swift, mounted upon Sleipnir, had to journey nine long nights ere he reached the river Giöll. This formed the boundary of Nifl-heim, over which was thrown a bridge of crystal arched with gold, hung on a single hair, and constantly guarded by the grim skeleton Mödgud, who made every spirit pay a toll of blood ere she would allow it to pass.

The spirits generally rode or drove across this bridge on the horses or in the waggons which had been burned upon the funeral pyre with the dead to serve that purpose, and the Northern races were very careful to bind upon the feet of the departed a specially strong pair of shoes, called Hel-shoes, that they might not suffer during the long journey over rough roads. Soon after the Giallar bridge was passed, the spirit reached the Ironwood, where stood none but bare and iron-leafed trees, and, passing through it, reached Hel-gate, beside which the fierce, blood-stained dog Garm kept watch, cowering in a dark hole known as the Gnipa cave. This monster's rage could only be appeased by the offering of a Hel-cake, which never failed those who had ever given bread to the needy.

Within the gate, amid the intense cold and impenetrable darkness, was heard the seething of the great cauldron Hvergelmir, the rolling of the glaciers in the Elivagar and other streams of Hel, among which were the Leipter, by which solemn oaths were sworn, and the Slid, in whose turbid waters naked swords continually rolled.

Further on in this gruesome place was Elvidner (misery), the hall of the goddess Hel, whose dish was Hunger. Her knife was Greed. "Idleness was the name of her man, Sloth of her maid, Ruin of her threshold, Sorrow of her bed, and Conflagration of her curtains."

This goddess had many different abodes for the guests who daily came to her, for she received not only perjurers and criminals of all kinds, but also those who were unfortunate enough to die without shedding blood. To her realm also were consigned those who died of old age or disease – a mode of decease which was contemptuously called "straw death," as the beds of the people were generally of that material.

Although the innocent were treated kindly by Hel, and enjoyed a state of negative bliss, it is no wonder that the inhabitants of the North shrank from the thought of visiting her cheerless abode. And while the men preferred to mark themselves with the spear point, to hurl themselves down from a precipice, or to be burned ere life was quite extinct, the women did not shrink from equally heroic measures. In the extremity of their sorrow, they did not hesitate to fling themselves down a mountain side, or fall upon the swords which were given them at their marriage, so that their bodies might be burned with those whom they loved, and their spirits released to join them in the bright home of the gods.

Further horrors, however, awaited those whose lives had been criminal or impure, these spirits being banished to Nastrond, the strand of corpses, where they waded in ice-cold streams of venom, through a cave made of wattled serpents, whose poisonous fangs were turned towards them. After suffering untold agonies there, they were washed down into the cauldron Hvergelmir, where the serpent Nidhug ceased for a moment gnawing the root of the tree Yggdrasil to feed upon their bones.

Hel herself was supposed occasionally to leave her dismal abode to range the earth upon her three-legged white horse, and in times of pestilence or famine, if a part of the inhabitants of a district escaped, she was said to use a rake, and when whole villages and provinces were depopulated, as in the case of the historical epidemic of the Black Death, it was said that she had ridden with a broom.

The Northern races further fancied that the spirits of the dead were sometimes allowed to revisit the earth and appear to their relatives, whose sorrow or joy affected them even after death, as is related in the Danish ballad of Aager and Else, where a dead lover bids his sweetheart smile, so that his coffin may be filled with roses instead of the clotted blood drops produced by her tears.

# LEGENDS OF THOR

*I am the Thunderer!*
*Here in my Northland,*
*My fastness and fortress,*
*Reign I forever!*
**Henry Wadsworth Longfellow,**
**Saga of King Olaf**

Thor was one of the twelve principal deities of Asgard, and he lived in the splendid realm of Thrudvang, where he built a palace called Bilskirnir. Here he lived as god of thunder, and his name was invoked more than any other in the age of the Vikings. For Thor was the protector of the land, a fine figure of a man with glowing eyes, firm muscles, and a red beard that made him instantly recognizable. He became known across the worlds for his great hammer, Miolnir (the crusher), which had been forged by the dark elves. This hammer, together with Thor's strength and his terrible temper, made him the fiercest god of Asgard, and the personification of brute force. Thor was also god of might and war, and because of his popularity, he soon grew to embody the forces of agriculture, and became a symbol of the earth itself. He is remembered throughout the world on the fourth day of every week – Thursday, or Thor's day.

## HOW THOR GOT HIS HAMMER

*First, Thor with the bent brow,*
*In red beard muttering low,*
*Darting fierce lightnings from eyeballs that blow,*
*Comes, while each chariot wheel*
*Echoes in thunder peal,*
*As his dread hammer shock*
*Makes Earth and Heaven rock,*
*Clouds rifting above, while Earth quakes below.*
**J.C. Jones, Valhalla**

**T**hor was married to Sif, whose long golden hair was her one great pride. It fell to her feet like a ray of sunlight, and it was the colour of ripe cornsilk in the summer fields. As she brushed it, it glinted in the light and became a symbol of great beauty across Asgard. One day, the glistening cascade of hair caught the eye of Loki, and he wondered then how he ever could have imagined living without it. He thought about that hair all day, and all through the night. And then, just as the moon reached her pinnacle in the midnight sky, Loki leapt to his feet and made for Sif's bedchamber, where he knew he would find her sleeping. The moon cast long shadows into the sleeping goddess's delicately furnished room, and it was easy for the fleet-footed Loki to steal in and set to work.

Loki crept to the side of Sif's bed and very gently, so that he did not disturb her, he withdrew a pair of great shears from his cloak and cut her long veil of hair from her head.

Winding the tresses around his arm, he darted from the room once again, and there was silence. Until, that is, Sif awoke to discover the travesty that had occurred.

Her shrieks brought everyone in the kingdom running to her side, and Thor howled with such outrage that the entire kingdom of Asgard shook. It was not long before Loki was ferreted out and brought before the irate god. Thunder boomed in the sky as the shaking trickster fell to his knees before Thor.

'I beg you, Thor,' he cried, 'let me free and I will find a new head of hair for Sif – one that is even more beautiful than the one she has now. I'll go to the dark elves. They'll fashion one!' Loki's head bobbed up and down with fright and eventually Thor gave in.

'You have twenty hours to come forward with the tresses, and if you fail, Loki, you will be removed from Asgard forever.' Thor banged down a thunderbolt at Loki's feet, and the traitor scampered hastily away, hardly daring to breathe at his good fortune.

Loki travelled at once to the centre of the earth, down into the Svart-alfa-heim, where the wily dwarf Dvalin had his home. He threw himself on the mercy of the dwarf, and requested as well two gifts with which he could win the favour of Odin and Frey, who were bound to hear of the news and wish to punish him themselves.

Dvalin worked over the heat of his forge for many hours, and as he worked he chanted the words which would make all he forged the finest there was – for there are no arms as powerful nor as invincible as those fashioned by dwarfs. First he finished the spear Gungnir, which would always hit its mark. Next, he formed the ship Skiblanir, which would always find wind, on even the most silent of seas, and which could sail through the air as well as on water. The ship was folded carefully and placed in a tiny compass. Loki's eyes shone at its undoubted worth.

Finally Dvalin spun the most graceful of golden threads, and these he wove into a head of hair so lustrous and shining that all the dark elves gasped at its beauty. Dvalin handed it carefully to Loki, wrapped in the softest of tissues, and said, 'As soon as this touches your princess's head, it shall grow there and become as her own.'

Loki took all the gifts from Dvalin, who he thanked profusely, and feeling very pleased with himself he set off for Asgard with a skip in his step. His jauntiness attracted the attention of two dwarfs who sat by the side of a small cottage.

'Why do you smile so?' asked the first – for Loki's reputation had preceded him and the dwarfs were certain that his happiness could have no virtuous cause.

'Dvaldi,' boasted Loki, 'is the most clever of smiths – both here and in all the nine worlds.' And with that he held up his prizes for the dwarfs to examine.

'Pish,' said the first dwarf, who was called Brokki, 'my brother Sindri can fashion gifts that are far more beautiful than those – and sturdier too.' He paused, and then continued, leaning towards Loki who began to look rather put out. 'Our gifts would hold the magic of the very centre of the earth,' he whispered.

Loki choked, and then, recovering himself, immediately challenged the dwarf to prove his words. So confident was he of the gifts he held now that he placed a wager on his own head.

And so it was that Brokki and Sindri made their way into their smithy and began work on the hottest of forges. Sindri agreed to fashion the goods, on the condition that Brokki blew the bellows – a task which would prove difficult over the great heat that was necessary for Sindri to win the wager.

Sindri at once threw some gold into the fire, and left the room, eager to invoke the powers which would be invested in a great wild boar, which he had decided upon for Frey. Alone with the roaring fire, Brokki worked hard at the bellows, never pausing despite the tremendous heat. Loki watched from the window and as he observed the determination and strength of the dwarf he began to grow uneasy. At once, he decided that he must intervene and as quick as a flash of light he turned himself into a gadfly and alighted on the hand of Brokki, where he set in a stinger so deep that a rush of blood rose to the surface immediately.

Brokki cried out in pain, but he continued the bellowing, never missing a beat. Sindri returned to the room and drew from the fire an enormous boar, who they called Gulinbursti for its radiant gold bristles. This boar would have the strength of all other boars there were, but he would have the additional ability to shine a rich and powerful light into any part of the world in which he travelled. He was the perfect gift for the sungod Frey and nothing could match the brilliance of its light but the sungod himself.

So Sindri flung more gold into the fire, and instructed Brokki to continue to blow. Once again, he left the room to seek the necessary enchantment, and once again Loki took on the form of a gadfly. In an instant he had landed on Brokki's cheek and stung through the weathered skin until Brokki cried out and turned white with pain. But still he worked on, pumping the bellows until Sindri returned once more. And triumphant, Sindri drew from the fire a ring which he called Draupnir, which would become the very symbol of fertility – for on every ninth night, eight identical rings would drop from Draupnir, with powers to match.

The final gift was yet to be prepared, and this time Sindri threw iron on to the fire, leaving Brokki hard at work as he left to call upon the final spirits. Brokki's strength was beginning to flag, but his will was as strong as ever. He pumped away as the fire burned brighter and brighter until, suddenly, a horsefly lit on his neck and stung him with a ferocity that caused him to leap into the air, but still he did not miss even one pump of the bellows. Loki was becoming desperate. He arranged himself on the forehead of the hapless dwarf and he stung straight into a vein on his forehead that throbbed with effort. He was rewarded by a gush of blood that streamed out into the fire and into the Brokki's eyes. The dwarf raised his hand for a split second to wipe aside the blood, but that moment caused damage that could not be erased. When Sindri returned and drew out the great hammer, its handle was short and ungainly.

Brokki hung his head in disappointment, but Sindri pointed out that the powers of the great hammer would more than make up for its small size. Indeed, he thought it might be an advantage, in that it could be neatly hidden in a man's tunic.

So Brokki gathered up the gifts and carried them outside to Loki, who accompanied the dwarf back to Asgard with his booty. Odin was given the ring Draupnir, Frey was given the boar Gulinbursti, and Thor was given the hammer, which they had named Miolnir – meaning invincible power.

Loki then presented Sif with her golden hair, and when she placed it upon her shorn head it latched itself there and began to grow in swirls and waves until it reached her feet once more – a shining veil of hair that shone more brightly than ever. Gungnir, the spear, was given to Odin, and the ship Skidbladnir to Frey. Each god was delighted with his gift, and there was much camaraderie as they slapped the backs of the dwarfs and the redeemed Loki. It was Brokki who put a stop to the celebrations when he stepped forward and explained the wager that had been made by Loki.

The gods looked at one another, and eyed their magnificent gifts. Although it was agreed that Sif's hair could not be more lustrous, or more beautiful, the gods announced that Brokki's gifts were the finest and the most magical – for the sole reason that Thor's great hammer was of such a magnificent size that it could be hidden away and used against the frost-giants at a moment's notice.

Loki's games had backfired, and he turned on his heels and fled before Brokki could undertake his part of the bargain and behead him! Brokki started in outrage and implored Thor to come to his rescue in catching Loki who was making away at all speed. Still smarting from Sif's agony, Thor threw out a lightning bolt and caught Loki by the ankles, returning him to face his fate at the hands of Brokki and his brother.

But when Loki was delivered to the dwarfs, Thor took pity on Loki and insisted to Brokki that he could have Loki's head but that he must not touch his neck – for the neck of Loki belonged to him, Thor. Of course there was no way to remove a head without touching the adjoining neck, and Brokki stomped around in fury before he came up with a plan which would serve him equally. Gathering his brother's great awl for the purpose, he punched holes along Loki's lips and stitched them together with an unbreakable cord.

It was many days before Loki's howls of pain ceased, and many more before he was able to unstitch the cord. Loki did not speak for almost one hundred days, as his torn lips were so painful he could not bear to move them. In time, however, Loki was able to speak once again causing Thor – and everyone in Asgard – to rue the day that the wager was broken.

## THOR GOES FISHING

*On the dark bottom of the great salt lake,*
*Imprisoned lay the giant snake,*
*With naught his sullen sleep to break.*
**Henry Wadsworth Longfellow, Poets of the North**

**T**hor **was a great traveller**, and it was in his capacity of war god that he took it upon himself to keep an eye on the activities of the occupants of the other worlds. One day, bored of his battles against the giants, he decided to take on a more dangerous opponent – the world serpent, Jormungander. How he longed to have the horns and head of the great beast on the walls of his palace hall.

And so it was that Thor dressed himself one morning in the attire of a human, trimming and curling his magnificent red beard until he looked the picture of elegance and gentility. He left Midgard and sailed across the sea until he reached Jotunheim. He anchored his ship and with his belongings tied upon his massive back, he set off across the sandy shores. A day or two later, he reached the cabin of the giant Hymir, who was not pleased to see the unexpected visitor.

Hymir knew that customs called for him to welcome the seafarer, but he had lived alone for many years and he disliked company.

'There's no point in resting your head in this household,' he said curtly to Thor, 'for I am up at the crack of the early light to go fishing, and then for the remainder of the day I've to see to my herd.' Hymir was the owner of a magnificent herd of steer, and he tended them zealously, allowing no one to interrupt his duties. He hoped that he would put off the unexpected visitor by being too busy to entertain him, or to provide him with a comfortable bed, but Thor was not to be dissuaded.

Continuing to allow the giant to believe that he was nothing more than a travelling man, Thor laughed and said that he would enjoy very much accompanying the giant on his fishing expedition, in the hopes that he would learn something from his skills. And so it was that Hymir grudgingly allowed Thor into his hut and showed him a room where he could lay his head.

The first light of morning found Hymir preparing to set out for the river, which roared along the bottom of his property towards the sea. He moved quietly so as not to waken the traveller – he had no interest in or intention of taking him fishing and he wanted to be gone before Thor wakened. Slipping silently from the cottage, he moved towards the cattle, which he planned to milk before setting out in his boat. He was dismayed to find Thor waiting for him, patiently stroking one of the cattle.

'You'll be fishing next, I imagine,' said Thor with a wide grin.

'I fish alone,' said Hymir curtly.

'I'd like to join you,' said Thor.

'No room for passengers,' said Hymir again, moving to work on the first cow.

'Not as a passenger,' said Thor with a smile, 'as a fisherman. I'll help you with the rowing.'

Hymir could see that Thor was intent upon joining him and so he nodded grudgingly and pointed towards the manure heap. 'Find yourself some bait then,' he said with a grunt.

Now Thor had seen the giant gesticulating towards the cattle, who lounged over the manure heap. With a mighty blow of his sword, he beheaded one of the finest steer and held it up to show Hymir, blood dripping down his arm. The giant could hardly control his rage – he had intended Thor to dig for grubs, not behead one of his sacred cattle – but he said nothing. I'll lose him at sea, he thought to himself.

Eventually the two men set out in the boat and they began to row. Hymir had noticed Thor's carefully curled beard and assumed he was not the most manly of men, perhaps unaccustomed to the rigours of fishing and farming. He was greatly surprised when Thor took the oars and rowed with splendid ease for hours without showing any sign of fatigue. At last Hymir begged him to stop, pointing out that the best fishing spots were around them.

But Thor carried on rowing, intent on reaching the place where the Jormungander lived. He rowed for an hour, and then Hymir leaned forward and put a hand on his oar. 'You must stop here,' he said, 'for we have reached the waters where the Jormungander swims. Any further and we will attract his attention and be his first meal of the day.'

Thor brightened at this news, and rowed steadily until he was certain they were in the waters of the evil serpent. Then he carefully chose the strongest of Hymir's rods and reels, and placing a line as thick as his forearm on the rod, he placed his tackle on the great hook and let it fall into the water. It was only moments before there was a stirring of the water, and Thor felt his rod being pulled from his grasp.

In the dark reaches of the sea, Jormungander had spied the head of the slain cattle, and taken it in one bite. Now the sturdy hook was trapped in his throat and he thrashed and shrieked as he tried to dislodge it.

Thor stood firmly in the boat, his determination making him strong. He called upon the divine powers that made him godly, and drew in the writhing beast as if it were no more than a fish on a simple rod. Hymir sat back aghast – he knew now that his passenger could be no man. He had never seen such strength, such resolve, and when the serpent was drawn forth from the water, spitting poison and snarling, he turned yellow and fell into a deep faint. For the Jormungander was a frightening sight to behold – with massive teeth, huge, bulging eyes, and a deathly odour that spoke of all who had fallen at his will. Thor held tightly to his rod, muscles groaning with effort. The huge body of the serpent lashed the water into a frenzied current and the boat tossed and tipped, water filling the bottom, and then emptying once again with each terrible wave that passed.

Hymir came to and could take no more. Swiftly he leant forward and grabbed his sharp knife, sawing through Thor's line with all the force he could muster. And then there was silence. The Jormungander slipped silently into the black depths of the sea and disappeared.

Thor's roar was heard far away in Asgard, and his fury caused a great storm to erupt. He had been just about to draw the beast into the ship when robbed of his quarry. The serpent would not be such easy prey from now on and this trip had been wasted. He snarled at the giant and withdrawing his hammer, gave him a blow that sent him flying into the icy waters, never to be seen again.

Some say it was a blessing that Thor did not catch the world serpent on that day, for a prophecy had been made that if ever the Jormungander's tail were removed from his mouth, the perpetrator would suffer a curse that would hang over him until the rest of his days. Thor rowed steadily until he reached the shore, and within a day he was back in Asgard. He did not speak of the fishing expedition again.

## THOR IN THE HALL OF THE GIANTS

*The strong-armed Thor*
*Full oft against Jotunheim did wend,*
*But spite his belt celestial, spite his gauntlets,*
*Utgard-Loki still his throne retains;*
*Evil, itself a force, to force yields never.*
**R.B. Anderson, Viking Tales of the North**

**T**hor had planned one of his regular trips to Jotunheim, and he set out on this occasion with Loki. It had not been many months since Loki had shorn Sif's hair and Thor decided that it was safer for all if Loki was under his own keen eye. So it was that they set out in Thor's chariot, and as night fell, they came upon the hut of a peasant, where they requested a bed for the night.

The peasant lived in a small hut with his wife and two children, and although they did not have much food to spare, they offered it all to Thor, who ate greedily. It soon became clear that there was not anywhere near enough food for all, so Thor took his two goats from the stable where he'd put them for the night, and slew them, roasting them over the coals of the peasant's hearth until the succulent meat slipped from the bones. He threw down his cloak on the floor and requested that the bones be placed there.

The peasant and his family were in ecstasy, for it had been many months since they had tasted fresh meat. And so carried away was the peasant himself that when Thor looked away from his meal, he slyly cut into the bone of the goat leg he was eating and tasted the marrow. When the meal was finished, Thor wrapped up the bones and placed them outside the door, and the two gods settled down for the night.

When morning came, Thor opened the door, and pulling aside his cloak, set free the two goats which had been reborn. He noticed, however, that one of his goats was rather lame, and that his front right leg appeared to be damaged in some way so that he found it difficult to walk. Thor was furious that his commands had been so rashly disregarded, and he realized that he would have to leave the goat behind, for it was too lame to travel. He thrust his great hammer into the air and was about to slaughter the entire family, when the peasant crept forward and confessed that he had been the one to eat the bone. He begged Thor to show clemency to his family, and grudgingly Thor agreed to take his two children Thialfi, a strong young boy, and Roskva, a pretty girl, to be his lifelong servants, as repayment.

So the peasant was left with the goats, and the four set out on foot, the chariot left behind until the crippled goat could walk again. The countryside was cold and sparse; what water they could find to drink was tainted by the smell of giants, and Thor became ill-tempered. Eventually, night began to fall and they were forced to find a place in which to sleep. Ahead of them was a great hall, and they approached it thankfully, curling up in its centre to spend the night. They had not been sleeping for long when there was a great banging and the earth began to rock and shake. The peasant's two children moaned with fear, but Thor pressed his hands over their mouths and bid them to follow him into an alcove which lead off to the side of the hall. There they huddled, and at last slept.

When morning dawned, the four weary travellers made their way from the hall and stopped with a start. For there lay sleeping a giant bigger than any they had seen before. His snores laid flat the sparse vegetation, and the peasant's children hurled themselves behind Thor in fright. Eventually the giant opened one sleepy eye and caught sight of Thor and his party. He snorted and then sat up, speaking in a loud rumbling voice, 'So you are the ones who dared to make your camp in my mitten.'

Thor looked around in surprise, and his eyes settled on the great hall in which they had managed to find shelter. The hall was none other than the giant's mitten – the alcove had been the thumb! Thor stepped forward and identified himself, and in return the giant said his name was Vasti. Vasti seemed a friendly giant and he suggested that the two parties put together their provisions and travel on together. Thor agreed, for it would do them no harm to have the additional assistance of a giant should they encounter trouble on their travels. And so they set off, Thor, Loki and the children scuttling along in the giant's footsteps.

The day was long and difficult. Even the great Thor struggled to keep up with the immense strides of the giant, and when it came time to eat, and to rest, he was as grateful as the others. Vasti opened his sack and removed a large piece of meat, which he consumed in a few moments. He grunted and passed the sack to Thor, and then turned on his side and fell into a deep sleep, his noisy snores disrupting the landscape once again.

Thor reached greedily for the bag. They had had no sustenance all day and all four of them were weak with hunger. He struggled with the cord, and stamped and shouted, but despite his greatest efforts he was unable to unfasten the knots tied by Vasti. Loki then took the opportunity to weave his own magic on the knots, but they remained tightly fastened. Loki and the children settled down to sleep, too cold and hungry to bother any further, but Thor was irate. The giant's snoring made it impossible to sleep, and he was more hungry than he'd been since the day of his conception. Finally, he lifted up his great hammer and banged it down with all the force he could muster, on the giant's head.

Vasti turned, and muttered, and called out in his sleep that the leaf which had dropped on to him was a nuisance, and then he fell back into a deep sleep and left Thor to gaze at him in astonishment. A few moments later, he tried again, this time invoking a series of enchantments to make his blow even more supremely powerful, and he hit Vasti upon the brow – deep enough that the hammer was imbedded in the giant's skull. Thor dragged it out and waited for the inevitable shriek of pain, but Vasti only turned again in his sleep, and complained about a bit of bark that must have fallen from the trees overhead.

Thor had never been so infuriated. Everyone knew that he was invincible, that his powers were stronger than any on earth, and yet, with his fine hammer, he was unable to make the slightest dent on the sleeping giant. He tried one last time, and when Vasti started only slightly, and suggested that perhaps an acorn had fallen upon his head, Thor gave up, and tried to settle down to sleep.

He slept not a wink that night, and when Vasti rose, early on the morrow, he was in a fiery mood. Vasti had gone as far as he could with Thor and his men, and he would be travelling on to his own home across the icy mountains. He carefully pointed out the way to the castle of Utgard-loki, King of the Giants. But before he left, Vasti spoke quietly to the travellers and told them that they would find giants even larger than he was at the palace. Perhaps they should turn back now, he suggested, for he could not guarantee them any safety if they went on alone ...

But Thor was too fractious to listen to his warnings, and they went on towards the palace. In a few short hours they had arrived. The tiny size of the gods meant that it was easy for them to slip between the bars of the fence surrounding the castle, and soon enough they had made their way to the inner chambers, the sanctuary of Utgard-loki himself.

The king of the gods was, as Vasti had promised, larger than all giants and fierce of countenance and expression. He laughed uproariously when he saw Thor.

'We have heard tales of you, Thor,' he said, 'and we know who you are by that red beard of yours. We didn't expect you to be ... so ... so ... small.' And with that, he broke out into laughter again, sending Thor into spasms of anger.

'My size is of no importance,' he said stoutly, 'for I am capable of feats that men of all sizes would find impossible.' Loki, who had also suffered enough on their journey leapt forward in Thor's defence.

'We challenge you to beat our many talents,' he shouted. 'And to begin with, I challenge you to find someone in your ranks who can eat a meal more quickly than I can.' Now

Loki was more than confident of winning such a feat for he had an appetite that was keener than most gods at the best of times – here he was virtually starving after two days without food.

The king nodded his head in assent, and signalled to his cook Logi to join them. The table was laden with platters of bones, gravy and huge slices of dripping meat. At the sound of the horn, Logi and Loki began to eat. Loki ate ravenously, devouring meat and gravy with gusto enhanced by the powers he had called down to help him. At the sound of the horn he stopped and looked around. The king pointed to the other end of the table, and Loki stopped in his tracks. For not only had Logi eaten all the meat and gravy at his side of the table, but he had eaten the bones, the platters and the table as well. Utgard-loki smiled contemptuously and with a wave of his hand dismissed Loki, who hung his head in shame.

Thor stepped forward next, and held up his hand for silence. 'I hereby challenge any man or giant to drink a greater draught than me – anyone at all,' he shouted.

A horn was dragged before Thor and Utgard-loki smiled once again. 'Your challenge, Thor, shall be met,' he said. 'You'll see before you a horn which can, by our champion, be drunk in one or two great swallows. Let us see you match that.'

So Thor placed his mouth around the great vessel, which stretched the entire length of the room, and drawing in a deep breath, he began to drink. He sucked in the liquid and after many moments without breathing, he stopped, and crept along the length of the horn to see how deeply he had drunk. The horn was full. The level of the drink had not moved by even the tiniest percentage. Thor shook his head in amazement. He knew his capacity for drinking was greater than anyone's and yet he could not make any real dent in the contents of the horn. He swallowed again, and then spat on the floor. 'Salty,' he muttered to himself, and sat down.

Utgard-loki just nodded his head and said quietly, 'One would have expected more from Thor, would they not?'

Thialfi had enough of the taunting; he had grown to love Thor in the days they had been together and he leapt quickly to his defence, volunteering himself for a race with the quickest of the giants. So Utgard-loki put forward his quickest man, a young giant called Hugi. The two boys lined up, and the race began. It seemed that the first race had been a draw, for both men appeared to reach the finish line at the same moment. And so another race was called, and they lined up once again. As the bell went, and as Thialfi lifted his foot to set off in the direction of the finish, Hugi raced to the line and back. The race was over and this time there was no question of who had won.

'Well, well, well,' said Utgard-loki, roaring with laughter. 'There are not many tricks to your trade, are there Thor?' to which the angry god trembled, but said nothing.

'What do you say,' shouted Utgard-loki, winking furiously at the crowd of giants who had arrived to witness the spectacle, 'you try to raise our pretty kitty.' He pointed to a giant cat who reclined gracefully in the corner of the hall.

Thor's pride had taken a beating and he was determined to prove himself. Surely it could not be difficult to lift a cat? He strode purposefully towards the cat, who yawned and licked her paw before sitting up. He tightened his belt Megingiord, which made him stronger, and then he tugged and pulled at the cat with all his might. But only one paw was lifted from the ground, and despite his every effort he could not move her. The cat batted him playfully with the paw he'd managed to lift, and laid back once again, her tail flicking to and fro in the sunlight.

Thor looked towards Utgard-loki and asked for one final challenge.

'Hmmm,' said the king, 'there is one person in my household who may be suitable to wrestle with you. May I introduce you to my nurse, the hundred-year-old Elli.' There was great laughter amongst the crowd as Elli crept forth, hardly able to hold herself upright.

Thor moved quickly towards her, and pulled and shoved until Utgard-loki called for him to stop.

Thor swallowed with difficulty. He was bewildered and he was furious; he stared at Utgard-loki and said quietly, 'I have been beaten. Until this day I thought there was no one greater than I. You have shown me my place, and for that I must respect you.' Thor signalled to Thialfi and Roskva, and with Loki on one arm, they made to leave the hall, defeated and humiliated.

But Utgard-loki called out in a voice that was at once humane and conciliatory. 'You have come here today against my will,' he said proudly. 'This is our home and you are not welcome here. Your show of strength is not welcome here. I was forced to do something to keep you away forever.'

At that the giant transformed and in an instant he was Vasti. 'Do you recognize me?' he said. 'When I lay sleeping just last night, I took the precaution of placing a mountain over my head – one which was invisible to you, Thor. And it is just as well, for it seems that when you were unable to open the magic cord of my sac, you took it upon yourself to hit the mountain.' There he paused, and casting open a curtain, gesticulated out the window at a series of valleys surrounding the mountain on the horizon. 'Those valleys,' he said solemnly, 'are the blows you aimed to my head.'

Thor gasped, but said nothing, waiting for the king to continue. And continue he did. Loki's opponent had been none other than wildfire, and Thialfi's racing partner had been the king's thoughts – and there could be none as swift as these. Thor's drinking horn had been dipped at one end into the ocean, and no matter how deeply he had drunk, the ocean would have remained undrinkable. Utgard-loki commented that the tides of the ocean had been altered by Thor's great swallows, but then he hurriedly went on.

The cat was in reality Jormungander, the world serpent, and had Thor not heard the gasp of terror when it seemed as though Thor may be responsible for removing the serpent's tail from its mouth? Everyone there knew what chaos would exist when such an occurrence would happen, for it had been prophesied that the end of the world would be nigh.

Elli was old age itself, and he had nearly unseated her. In all, Thor had been successful in many ways.

'You may hold your head high,' said Utgard-loki proudly. 'But please, Thor, do not return to our shores.'

Thor was only slightly placated by the king's explanations, and he lifted his powerful hammer to bring to an end the sedate lifestyle of Utgard-loki and his men. But as quickly as he could lift his hammer, the castle was enveloped in a sea of mist, and he could see nothing. The world of the giants was completely enshrouded and Thor had no recourse but to return home to Asgard. His mission was incomplete, and Thor had been branded a puny weakling in the eyes of the giant, but he had faced many of nature's most formidable enemies and had left his mark. And for that the god of war could stand tall once again.

## THE STEALING OF THOR'S HAMMER

*Wrath waxed Thor, when his sleep was flown,*
*And he found his trusty hammer gone;*
*He smote his brow, his beard he shook,*
*The son of earth 'gan round him look;*
*And this the first word that he spoke:*
*'Now listen what I tell thee, Loke;*
*Which neither on earth below is known,*
*Nor in heaven above: my hammer's gone.'*
**William Herbert, Thrym's Quida**

**T**hor's hammer became a symbol of his energy and power, and the mere mention of its name, Miolnir, was enough to send the giants of Jotunheim trembling. Its neat compact size allowed it to be hidden easily on Thor's person, and he never was without it – except on those nights that he shared his marriage bed with Sif. On one such occasion, after a long and happy night, Thor woke, and stretching out a lazy hand, reached for Miolnir. It had vanished.

His cry of anger soon had all of the palace attendants at his side, and many fruitless hours were spent searching for the missing weapon.

Loki was summoned, for matters involving theft – particularly in Thor's household – tended to have his hand in them, but his innocence was undoubted on this occasion, and he pledged to help Thor find the real thief.

Loki asked to borrow Freyia's hawk's coat, and after collecting it from Folkvang, he set off for Jotunheim, travelling across sea and barren stretches of land until he found what he was looking for – a giant was sitting alone on a crag. Now this giant's name was Thrym, and as prince of the frost-giants, he had cause to dislike and indeed fear Thor, who had made massive losses in their numbers with his great hammer. Loki settled himself beside the giant, and mustering up all of his wile, set about asking him questions. At last the truth was divulged – Thrym had stolen the hammer and had buried it in a secret location. He would not return it to Thor, unless ... and here the great giant paused ... unless Freyia was presented to him as his bride.

Loki let out a great guffaw! Freyia was the most beautiful of all goddesses – a prize sought after by gods, men and all other creatures alike. It was certainly unlikely that she would agree to marry this prince of giants. Loki told Thrym these things, but Thrym stood firm. He would return the hammer when Freyia was made his bride – this was his sole condition.

Loki thought hard for a moment, and then made a quick

decision. He'd promise Thrym what he wanted, and then leave the matters in the hands of Thor, who would surely find a way round it all. With a smile he rose and indicated that Thrym's conditions had been accepted. The giant's smile was greedy, and he rubbed his hands together in glee as Loki disappeared into the morning sky.

Now Loki's journey took long enough for him to realize that Freyia was not going to be happy about the bargain he had just arranged, and he immediately regretted his hasty acceptance of the giant's proposal. Surely a man of greater wit could have concocted something more practical, he lamented as he flew. When he arrived, he cornered Freyia and spoke as quickly as he could, begging her to consider the proposal – for wasn't Thor's hammer important to all of them? Wasn't the very safety of Asgard at risk if he was unable to fight off the attacks of the frost-giants?

But Freyia was outraged at the suggestion that she marry a mere giant, and give up all the splendours of her home. She commanded Loki to leave her, and she shut the door smartly behind him. Loki returned to Thor with his head bowed low in shame. Thor listened carefully to his explanation, and patted the surprised Loki on the shoulder.

'You've done the best thing, ' he said gently, much to Loki's astonishment. 'My hammer is the most important thing here.'

And so it was that Loki and Thor set out to beg Freyia to reconsider. They had underestimated the passion of her feelings, for she commenced a tantrum that lasted for one whole day and night _ one so fierce that the necklace about her neck was splintered in to pieces that flew from one end to the other of Asgard. Thor and Loki realized that their attempts were useless, and returned back to Thrudvang.

There they sat and ruminated for many hours, eventually calling upon Heimdall to provide them with advice. His suggestions were met with outrage as profound as Freyia's own anger – for he believed that the very best way for Thor to retrieve his hammer was to dress himself in Freyia's necklace and wedding garments, and present himself as Freyia herself. Thor refused to consider such a plan, until it became quite clear that there were no alternatives. Grudgingly he agreed to don her clothes, and the necklace was secured from the many parts of Asgard and rebuilt to fit his own brawny neck.

Thor travelled with Loki to Jotunheim and with his eyes averted, and a veil covering the coarse red beard and hair, he was presented to Thrym. Thrym welcomed them at the palace door, and his anticipation of having the lovely Freyia as his bride caused him to lick his lips, and made his eyes water so that his eyesight was compromised. He looked slightly astonished by Freyia's size, but he accepted that gods were larger than humans, and that they were much closer to giants in that respect. He led Loki and Thor to the banqueting hall, where the women of the bridal party were taking a meal.

Thor sat down at the end of the table, and reached greedily for the platters of meat and bread. Within a few moments, he had eaten an ox, eight great salmon, and all of the sweet cakes and viands which had been prepared for the women. And this great meal was washed down with two full barrels of mead. Thrym gaped at the spectacle, and could only be comforted when Loki explained that the lovely Freyia had been unable to eat for nearly eight days in anticipation of their meeting.

Thrym gazed with great admiration at such an appetite, for such things were commended in those times, and caught Freyia's eyes. He started back at once, for there was there such burning fury that he felt as if he had been struck by a bolt of Thor's own lightning. He turned with dismay to Loki, but he was soon soothed by Loki's assurance that Freyia was so deeply in love with him that her passion had consumed her, and her look was one of intense longing.

Thrym gathered together the men and women in his party and called for the great hammer to be brought forth – a symbol of the sacred vows which were to commence. He took Freyia's hand, and was slightly disconcerted to discover that on its back were thick, curling red hairs. As he looked into his loved one's eyes, Thor struck. He grabbed his hammer and with one great burst of energy, he slew every giant in the room, and left the palace in ruins. And then, turning to the destruction, he called out a proclamation which caused Loki to stop in his tracks. Thor claimed the land as his own, and from every corner tender green shoots of grass and greenery began to grow. The barren wasteland was fertile; their journey had been a success.

So Thor removed Freyia's clothing, and returned to present the goddess of love with her necklace. The Aesir rejoiced at the return of Thor's hammer, and all was happy again in Asgard.

## THOR AND HRUNGNIR

*Thou now remindest me*
*How I with Hrungnir fought,*
*That stout-hearted Jotun,*
*Whose head was all of stone;*
*Yet I made him fall*
*And sink before me.*

**Benjamin Thorpe, Saemund's Edda**

**O**din himself was once dashing through the air on his eight-footed steed Sleipnir, when he attracted the attention of the giant Hrungnir, who proposed a race, declaring that Gullfaxi, his steed, could rival Sleipnir in speed. In the heat of the race, Hrungnir did not notice the direction in which they were going, until, in the vain hope of overtaking Odin, he urged his steed to the very gates of Valhalla. Discovering then where he was, the giant grew pale with fear, for he knew he had jeopardised his life by venturing into the stronghold of the gods, his hereditary foes.

The Aesir, however, were too honourable to take even an enemy at a disadvantage, and, instead of doing him harm, they asked him into their banqueting-halls, where he proceeded to indulge in liberal potations of the heavenly mead set before him. He soon grew so excited that he began to boast of his power, declaring he would come some day and take possession of Asgard, which he would destroy, together with the gods, save only Freyia and Sif, upon whom he gazed with an admiring leer.

The gods, knowing he was not responsible, let him talk unmolested; but Thor, coming home just then from one of his journeys, and hearing his threat to carry away the beloved Sif, flew into a terrible rage. He furiously brandished his hammer, with intent to annihilate the boaster. This the gods would not permit, however, and they quickly threw themselves between the irate Thunderer and their guest, imploring Thor to respect the sacred rights of hospitality, and not to desecrate their peace-stead by shedding blood.

Thor was at last induced to bridle his wrath, but he demanded that Hrungnir should appoint a time and place for a holmgang, as a Northern duel was generally called. Thus challenged, Hrungnir promised to meet Thor at Griottunagard, the confines of his realm, three days later, and departed somewhat sobered by the fright he had experienced. When his fellow giants heard how rash he had been, they chided him sorely; but they took counsel together in order to make the best of a bad situation. Hrungnir told them that he was to have the privilege of being accompanied by a squire, whom Thialfi would engage in fight, wherefore they proceeded to construct a creature of clay, nine miles long, and proportionately wide, whom they called Mokerkialfi (mist wader). As they could find no human heart big enough to put in this monster's breast, they secured that of a mare, which, however, kept fluttering and quivering with apprehension. The day of the duel arrived. Hrungnir and his squire were on the ground awaiting the arrival of their respective opponents. The giant had not only a flint heart and skull, but also a shield and club of the same substance, and therefore deemed himself well-nigh invincible. Thialfi came before his master and soon after there was a terrible rumbling and shaking which made the giant apprehensive that his enemy would come up through the ground and attack him from underneath. He therefore followed a hint from Thialfi and stood upon his shield.

A moment later, however, he saw his mistake, for, while Thialfi attacked Mokerkialfi with a spade, Thor came with a rush upon the scene and flung his hammer full at his opponent's head. Hrungnir, to ward off the blow, interposed his stone club, which was shivered into pieces that flew all over the earth, supplying all the flint stones thereafter to be found, and one fragment sank deep into Thor's forehead. As the god dropped fainting to the ground, his hammer crashed against the head of Hrungnir, who fell dead beside him, in such a position that one of his ponderous legs was thrown over the recumbent god.

Thialfi, who, in the meanwhile, had disposed of the great clay giant with its cowardly mare's heart, now rushed to his master's assistance, but his efforts were unavailing, nor could the other gods, whom he quickly summoned, raise the pinioning leg. While they were standing there, helplessly wondering what they should do next, Thor's little son Magni came up. According to varying accounts, he was then only three days or three years old, but he quickly seized the giant's foot, and, unaided, set his father free, declaring that had he only been summoned sooner he would easily have disposed of both giant and squire. This exhibition of strength made the gods marvel greatly, and helped them to recognise the truth of the various predictions, which one and all declared that their descendants would be mightier than they, would survive them, and would rule in their turn over the new heaven and earth.

To reward his son for his timely aid, Thor gave him the steed Gullfaxi (golden-maned), to which he had fallen heir by right of conquest, and Magni ever after rode this marvellous horse, which almost equalled the renowned Sleipnir in speed and endurance.

After vainly trying to remove the stone splinter from his forehead, Thor sadly returned home to Thrud-vang, where Sif's loving efforts were equally unsuccessful. She therefore resolved to send for Groa (green-making), a sorceress, noted for her skill in medicine and for the efficacy of her spells and incantations. Groa immediately signified her readiness to render every service in her power to the god who had so often benefited her, and solemnly began to recite powerful runes, under whose influence Thor felt the stone grow looser and looser. His delight at the prospect of a speedy deliverance made Thor wish to reward the enchantress forthwith, and knowing that nothing could give greater pleasure to a mother than the prospect of seeing a long-lost child, he proceeded to tell her that he had recently crossed the Elivagar, or ice streams, to rescue her little son Orvandil (germ) from the frost giants' cruel power, and had succeeded in carrying him off in a basket. But, as the little rogue would persist in sticking one of his bare toes through a hole in the basket, it had been frost-bitten, and Thor, accidentally breaking it off, had flung it up into the sky, to shine as a star, known in the North as "Orvandil's Toe."

Delighted with these tidings, the prophetess paused in her incantations to express her joy, but, having forgotten just where she left off, she was unable to continue her spell, and the flint stone remained embedded in Thor's forehead, whence it could never be dislodged.

Of course, as Thor's hammer always did him such good service, it was the most prized of all his possessions, and his dismay was very great when he awoke one morning and found it gone. His cry of anger and disappointment soon brought Loki to his side, and to him Thor confided the secret of his loss, declaring that were the giants to hear of it, they would soon attempt to storm Asgard and destroy the gods.

## THOR AND GEIRROD

*Once I employed*
*My asa-might*
*In the realm of giants,*
*When Gialp and Greip,*
*Geirrod's daughters,*
*Wanted to lift me to heaven.*
**R.B. Anderson, Norse Mythology**

**L**oki once borrowed Freyia's falcon-garb and flew off in search of adventures to another part of Jötun-heim, where he perched on top of the gables of Geirrod's house. He soon attracted the attention of this giant, who bade one of his servants catch the bird. Amused at the fellow's clumsy attempts to secure him, Loki flitted about from place to place, only moving just as the giant was about to lay hands upon him, when, miscalculating his distance, he suddenly found himself a captive.

Attracted by the bird's bright eyes, Geirrod looked closely at it and concluded that it was a god in disguise, and finding that he could not force him to speak, he locked him in a cage, where he kept him for three whole months without food or drink. Conquered at last by hunger and thirst, Loki revealed his identity, and obtained his release by promising that he would induce Thor to visit Geirrod without his hammer, belt, or magic gauntlet. Loki then flew back to Asgard, and told Thor that he had been royally entertained, and that his host had expressed a strong desire to see the powerful thunder-god, of whom he had heard such wonderful tales. Flattered by this artful speech, Thor was induced to consent to a friendly journey to Jötun-heim, and the two gods set out, leaving the three marvellous weapons at home. They had not gone far, however, ere they came to the house of the giantess Grid, one of Odin's many wives. Seeing Thor unarmed, she warned him to beware of treachery and lent him her own girdle, staff, and glove. Some time after leaving her, Thor and Loki came to the river Veimer, which the Thunderer, accustomed to wading, prepared to ford, bidding Loki and Thialfi cling fast to his belt.

In the middle of the stream, however, a sudden cloud-burst and freshet overtook them; the waters began to rise and roar, and although Thor leaned heavily upon his staff, he was almost swept away by the force of the raging current.

Thor now became aware of the presence, up stream, of Geirrod's daughter Gialp, and rightly suspecting that she was the cause of the storm, he picked up a huge boulder and flung it at her, muttering that the best place to dam a river was at its source. The missile had the desired effect, for the giantess fled, the waters abated, and Thor, exhausted but safe, pulled himself up on the opposite bank by a little shrub, the mountain-ash or sorb. This has since been known as "Thor's salvation," and occult powers have been attributed to it. After resting awhile Thor and his companions resumed their journey; but upon arriving at Geirrod's house the god was so exhausted that he sank wearily upon the only chair in sight. To his surprise, however, he felt it rising beneath him, and fearful lest he should be crushed against the rafters, he pushed the borrowed staff against the ceiling and forced the chair downward with all his might. Then followed a terrible cracking, sudden cries, and moans of pain; and when Thor came to investigate, it appeared that the giant's daughters, Gialp and Greip, had slipped under his chair with intent treacherously to slay him, and they had reaped a righteous retribution and both lay crushed to death.

Geirrod now appeared and challenged Thor to a test of strength and skill, but without waiting for a preconcerted signal, he flung a red-hot wedge at him. Thor, quick of eye and a practised catcher, caught the missile with the giantess's iron glove, and hurled it back at his opponent. Such was the force of the god, that the missile passed, not only through the pillar behind which the giant had taken refuge, but through him and the wall of the house, and buried itself deep in the earth without.

Thor then strode up to the giant's corpse, which at the blow from his weapon had been petrified into stone, and set it up in a conspicuous place, as a monument of his strength and of the victory he had won over his redoubtable foes, the mountain giants.

# FREYIA AND OTHER GODS

*Freyia, thin robed, about her ankles slim*
*The grey cats playing.*
**William Morris, The Lovers of Gudrun**

**F**reyia came to Asgard from Vanaheim, and before long she
was as beloved as if she had been born one of the Aesir. She
married well, and brought forth many fine children. She was
known particularly for her fine feathered coat, which allowed
her – and those she permitted to borrow it – to soar through
the air as a hawk. Freyia's story touches on those of many of
the other gods, and there are other myths and legends which
must be recorded in order to understand how the golden age
of Asgard became what it was, how evil entered, and how it
eventually fell. There is Niord, who came with Freyia to bring
summer, once the seasons had fallen into place. And Tyr, the
god of war, who showed bravery which far surpassed any shown
by man or god in the heyday of Asgard. And in the stories that
follow we meet the elves, and learn why they abandoned their
happy existence deep in the bowels of the earth. For every
tale leads towards a single inevitable event – Ragnarok, and
it hovers at the edge of all, just as it did in those early days
of sunlight, when darkness had not yet touched the world of
Asgard, and the gods lived a life of splendour...

## FREYIA AND ODUR

*And Freyia next came nigh, with golden tears;*
*The loveliest Goddess she in Heaven, by all*
*Most honour'd after Frea, Odin's wife.*
**Matthew Arnold, Balder Dead**

**F**reyia was the Northern goddess of beauty and of love, a maiden so fair and graceful that the gods honoured her with the realm of Folkvang and the great hall Sessrymnir, where she would, in eternity, surround herself with all of those who loved her. Like many Viking goddesses, Freyia was fierce and fiery, her cool demeanour masking a passion which lay burning beneath. She was clever, and masterful in battle, and as Valfreyia, she often led the Valkyrs to the battlefields where she would claim many of the slain heroes. She wore a simple, flowing garment, held firmly in place on her torso and arms with the finest shining armour, a helmet and shield.

Slain heroes were taken to Folkvang, where they lived a life such as they had never experienced on earth. Their wives and lovers came to join them and Freyia's reputation spread far and wide among the dead and the living. So luxurious was Folkvang, so exquisite were Freyia's charms that lovers and wives of the slain would often take their own lives in order to meet with their loved ones sooner, and to experience the splendour of her land.

And so it was that Freyia, gold of hair and blue of eyes, came to be a symbol of love and courtship, and through that, the earth – which, of course, represents fecundity and new life. She married Odur who symbolized the sun, and together they had two daughters, Hnoss and Gersemi, beautiful maidens who had inherited their mother's beauty, and their father's charisma and charm. But Odur was a man of wandering eyes, and one who appreciated the inner music of women – and not just that of his wife. He grew tired of her song, and her absorption with their daughters, and he grew restless and reckless. And after many months and then years of growing weary of the smiling face of his lovely wife, he left Freyia and his daughters and set off on travels which would take him to the ends of the earth, and around it.

Freyia sank into a despair that cast a shadow across the earth. Her tears ran across cheeks that no longer bloomed, and as they touched the earth they became golden nuggets, sinking deep into the soil. Even the rocks were softened by her tears which flowed without ceasing as she made her decision. And it was decided by Freyia that she could not live without Odur. As well as being the symbol of the summer sun, Odur represented passion and ardour. Without him, Freyia could no longer find it in her heart to bring love and affection to those around her, and she could not fulfil her duties as goddess of love. It was decided that she should travel to find him, so across the lands she passed, leaving behind her tears which glistened and hardened into the purest gold. She travelled far and wide, and took on disguises as she moved, careful to leave no clue as to her identity in the event that he should hear word of her coming and not wish to see her. She was known as Syr and Skialf, Thrung and Horn, and it was not until she reached the deepest south, where summer clung to the land, that she found Odur.

Her husband lay under the myrtle trees that lined the sunny banks of a stream. Reunited, they lay together there, warm in one another's arms and dusted with the glow of true love. And as the passion drew colour into the cheeks of his wife, Odur knew he had to look no further to find his heart's content. The trees above them cast their scent across this happy couple, endowing them with good fortune. They rose together then, and Odur and Freyia made their way towards their home, and their exquisite daughters. As they walked, the earth rose up to meet them, casting bouquets of fragrant flowers in their path, drawing down the boughs of the flowering trees so they kissed the heads of the lovers. The air was filled with the rosy glow of their love, and everything living joined a chorus of cheers with followed their path. Spring and summer warmed the frozen land which had stood desolate and empty when Odur left.

The loveliest of the new flowers which bloomed were named 'Freyia's hair', and 'Freyia's eyedew' and to this day brides wear myrtle in their hair – a symbol of good fortune and true love.

## OTTAR AND ANGANTYR

*A duty 'tis to act*
*So that the young prince*
*His paternal heritage may have*
*After his kindred.*
**Benjamin Thorpe, Saemund's Edda**

**The Northern people** were wont to invoke Freyia not only for success in love, prosperity, and increase, but also, at times, for aid and protection. This she vouchsafed to all who served her truly, as appeared in the story of Ottar and Angantyr, two men who, after disputing for some time concerning their rights to a certain piece of property, laid their quarrel before the Thing. That popular assembly decreed that the man who could prove that he had the longest line of noble ancestors should be declared the winner, and a special day was appointed to investigate the genealogy of each claimant.

Ottar, unable to remember the names of more than a few of his progenitors, offered sacrifices to Freyia, entreating her aid. The goddess graciously heard his prayer, and appearing before him, she changed him into a boar, and rode off upon his back to the dwelling of the sorceress Hyndla, a most renowned witch. By threats and entreaties, Freyia compelled the old woman to trace Ottar's genealogy back to Odin, and to name every individual in turn, with a synopsis of his achievements. Then, fearing lest her votary's memory should be unable to retain so many details, Freyia further compelled Hyndla to brew a potion of remembrance, which she gave him to drink.

Thus prepared, Ottar presented himself before the Thing on the appointed day, and glibly reciting his pedigree, he named so many more ancestors than Angantyr could recollect, that he was easily awarded possession of the property he coveted.

# FREY

*There was Frey, and sat*
*On the gold-bristled boar, who first, they say,*

*Plowed the brown earth, and made it green for Frey.*
**William Morris, The Lovers of Gudrun**

**F**rey, or Fro, as he was called in Germany, was the son of Niörd and Nerthus, or of Niörd and Skadi, and was born in Vana-heim. He therefore belonged to the race of the Vanas, the divinities of water and air, but was warmly welcomed in Asgard when he came thither as hostage with his father. As it was customary among the Northern nations to bestow some valuable gift upon a child when he cut his first tooth, the Aesir gave the infant Frey the beautiful realm of Alf-heim or Fairyland, the home of the Light Elves.

Here Frey, the god of the golden sunshine and the warm summer showers, took up his abode, charmed with the society of the elves and fairies, who implicitly obeyed his every order, and at a sign from him flitted to and fro, doing all the good in their power, for they were pre-eminently beneficent spirits.

Frey also received from the gods a marvellous sword (an emblem of the sunbeams), which had the power of fighting successfully, and of its own accord, as soon as it was drawn from its sheath. Frey wielded this principally against the frost giants, whom he hated almost as much as did Thor, and because he carried this glittering weapon, he has sometimes been confounded with the sword-god Tyr or Saxnot.

The dwarfs from Svart-alfa-heim gave Frey the golden-bristled boar Gullin-bursti (the golden-bristled), a personification of the sun. The radiant bristles of this animal were considered symbolical either of the solar rays, of the golden grain, which at his bidding waved over the harvest fields of Midgard, or of agriculture; for the boar (by tearing up the ground with his sharp tusk) was supposed to have first taught mankind how to plough.

Frey sometimes rode astride of this marvellous boar, whose speed was very great, and at other times harnessed him to his golden chariot, which was said to contain the fruits and flowers which he lavishly scattered abroad over the face of the earth.

Frey was, moreover, the proud possessor not only of the dauntless steed Blodug-hofi, which would dash through fire and water at his command, but also of the magic ship Skidbladnir, a personification of the clouds. This vessel, sailing over land and sea, was always wafted along by favourable winds, and was so elastic that, while it could assume large enough proportions to carry the gods, their steeds, and all their equipments, it could also be folded up like a napkin and thrust into a pocket.

It is related in one of the lays of the Edda that Frey once ventured to ascend Odin's throne Hlidskialf, from which exalted seat his gaze ranged over the wide earth. Looking towards the frozen North, he saw a beautiful young maiden enter the house of the frost giant Gymir, and as she raised her hand to lift the latch her radiant beauty illuminated sea and sky.

A moment later, this lovely creature, whose name was Gerda, and who is considered as a personification of the flashing Northern lights, vanished within her father's house, and Frey pensively wended his way back to Alf-heim, his heart oppressed with longing to make this fair maiden his wife. Being deeply in love, he was melancholy and absent-minded in the extreme, and began to behave so strangely that his father, Niörd, became greatly alarmed about his health, and bade his favourite servant, Skirnir, discover the cause of this sudden change. After much persuasion, Skirnir finally won from Frey an account of his ascent of Hlidskialf, and of the fair vision he had seen. He confessed his love and also his utter despair, for as Gerda was the daughter of Gymir and Angur-boda, and a relative of the murdered giant Thiassi, he feared she would never view his suit with favour.

Skirnir, however, replied consolingly that he could see no reason why his master should take a despondent view of the case, and he offered to go and woo the maiden in his name, providing Frey would lend him his steed for the journey, and give him his glittering sword for reward.

Overjoyed at the prospect of winning the beautiful Gerda, Frey willingly handed Skirnir the flashing sword, and gave him permission to use his horse. But he quickly relapsed into the state of reverie which had become usual with him since falling in love, and thus he did not notice that Skirnir was still hovering near him, nor did he perceive him cunningly steal the reflection of his face from the surface of the brook near which he was seated, and imprison it in his drinking horn, with intent "to pour it out in Gerda's cup, and by its beauty win the heart of the giantess for the lord" for whom he was about to go a-wooing. Provided with this portrait, with eleven golden apples, and with the magic ring Draupnir, Skirnir now rode off to Jötun-heim, to fulfil his embassy. As he came near Gymir's dwelling he heard the loud and persistent howling of his watch-dogs, which were personifications of the wintry winds. A shepherd, guarding his flock in the vicinity, told him, in answer to his inquiry, that it would be impossible to approach the house, on account of the flaming barrier which surrounded it; but Skirnir, knowing that Blodug-hofi would dash through any fire, merely set spurs to his steed, and, riding up unscathed to the giant's door, was soon ushered into the presence of the lovely Gerda.

To induce the fair maiden to lend a favourable ear to his master's proposals, Skirnir showed her the stolen portrait, and proffered the golden apples and magic ring, which, however, she haughtily refused to accept, declaring that her father had gold enough and to spare.

Indignant at her scorn, Skirnir now threatened to decapitate her with his magic sword, but as this did not in the least frighten the maiden, and she calmly defied him, he had recourse to magic arts. Cutting runes in his stick, he told her that unless she yielded ere the spell was ended, she would be condemned either to eternal celibacy, or to marry some aged frost giant whom she could never love.

Terrified into submission by the frightful description of her cheerless future in case she persisted in her refusal, Gerda finally consented to become Frey's wife, and dismissed Skirnir, promising to meet her future spouse on the ninth night, in the land of Buri, the green grove, where she would dispel his sadness and make him happy.

Delighted with his success, Skirnir hurried back to Alfheim, where Frey came eagerly to learn the result of his journey. When he learned that Gerda had consented to become his wife, his face grew radiant with joy; but when

Skirnir informed him that he would have to wait nine nights ere he could behold his promised bride, he turned sadly away, declaring the time would appear interminable.

In spite of this loverlike despondency, however, the time of waiting came to an end, and Frey joyfully hastened to the green grove, where, true to her appointment, he found Gerda, and she became his happy wife, and proudly sat upon his throne beside him.

According to some mythologists, Gerda is not a personification of the aurora borealis, but of the earth, which, hard, cold, and unyielding, resists the spring-god's proffers of adornment and fruitfulness (the apples and ring), defies the flashing sunbeams (Frey's sword), and only consents to receive his kiss when it learns that it will else be doomed to perpetual barrenness, or given over entirely into the power of the giants (ice and snow). The nine nights of waiting are typical of the nine winter months, at the end of which the earth becomes the bride of the sun, in the groves where the trees are budding forth into leaf and blossom.

Frey and Gerda, we are told, became the parents of a son called Fiolnir, whose birth consoled Gerda for the loss of her brother Beli. The latter had attacked Frey and had been slain by him, although the sun-god, deprived of his matchless sword, had been obliged to defend himself with a stag horn which he hastily snatched from the wall of his dwelling.

Besides the faithful Skirnir, Frey had two other attendants, a married couple, Beyggvir and Beyla, the personifications of mill refuse and manure, which two ingredients, being used in agriculture for fertilising purposes, were therefore considered Frey's faithful servants, in spite of their unpleasant qualities.

# NIORD

*Niord, the god of storms, whom fishers know;*
*Not born in Heaven – he was in Vanheim rear'd,*
*With men, but lives a hostage with the gods;*
*He knows each frith, and every rocky creek*
*Fringed with dark pines, and sands where sea-fowl scream.*
**Matthew Arnold, Balder Dead**

When the war between the Aesir and the Vanir was concluded, and hostages were taken by each side, Niord, with his children, Freyia and Frey, went to live in Asgard. There Niord was made the ruler of the winds and of the sea near the shore, and he was presented with a lush palace on the shores of Asgard, which he called Noatun. Here he took up the role of protecting the Aesir from Aegir, the god of the sea, who had a fiery temper, and who could, at a moment's notice, send waves crashing upon the unprotected shores of Asgard.

Niord was a popular god, and he was as handsome as his children. On his head he wore a circle of shells, and his dress was adorned with fresh, lustrous green seaweed. Niord was the very embodiment of summer, and each spring he was called upon to still the winds and move the clouds so that the sun's bright rays could touch the earth and encourage all to grow.

Niord had been married to Mother Earth, Nerthus, but she had been forced to stay behind when Niord was summoned to become a hostage for the Vanir, so he lived alone in Niord, an arrangement which he did not mind in the least. For from Noatun he could breathe in the fresh salt air, and revel in the flight of the gulls and other seabirds that made their home on the banks. The crashing waves lulled him into a state of serenity, and with the gentle seals, he basked in the sunlight of his new home.

All was well, until Skadi arrived. Skadi had chosen Niord as her husband, because of his clean feet, and he had grudgingly agreed to marry her. There could not have been two more different beings, for Skadi was now goddess of winter, and she dressed in pure white, glittering garments, embroidered with icicles and the fur of the white wolf. Skadi was beautiful, and her skin was like alabaster; her eyes were stormy, and told of a deep passion which burned within her. Niord was happy to take her as his wife, although he longed for the days of solitude that his unmarried days had accorded.

And so it was that Skadi moved her belongings to Noatun, and settled in there. The first night spoke of the nights to come, for from that first instant, Skadi was unable to sleep a wink. The sounds of the waves echoed deep in her head, and the cries of the gulls wakened her every time she drifted into the first ebbs of sleep. So Skadi announced to all that she could not live with Niord in Noatun – he would have to return with her to Thrymheim. Niord was deeply saddened by this arrangement, for the sea was a part of him – food for his soul. He finally agreed to travel with Skadi to Thrymheim, where he would live with her for nine out of every twelve months.

It was many days before Skadi and Niord reached her home, high in the frozen mountains, where frost clung to every surface and the air was filled with the vapour of their breath. The wind howled through the trees, sending showers of ice to the ground below, where it cracked and broke into tiny, glistening shards. The waterfalls roared in the background, sending up spray that glistened in the sunlight. At night the wolves joined the fracas, howling at the icy moon. Niord was quite unable to sleep even one wink.

So an agreement was finally forged between the two – for nine months of the year, Niord would make his home with Skadi in the kingdom of winter. For the other three months they would return to Noatun, where he would invoke summer for everyone in Asgard. This arrangement worked well for many years, but both Niord and Skadi felt saddened by having to vacate their homes for months on end. Finally, despite their affection for one another, it was decided that they should part.

Skadi threw herself into hunting, honing her skills so that she became the finest marksman in the land. She married the historical Odin, and she bore him a son called Saeming. Eventually, she married Uller, the god of winter and the perfect companion for the frigid goddess.

Niord returned to his palace by the sea, and frolicked there with the seals, who basked in the summer sun.

## HEIMDALL IN MIDGARD

*To battle the gods are called*
*By the ancient*
*Gjaller-horn.*

*Loud blows Heimdall,*
*His sound is in the air.*
**Benjamin Thorpe, Saemund's Edd**a

Heimdall was called the watchman of the gods, and he was distinguished by his role at the Bifrost bridge, which he had constructed from fire, air and water which glowed as a rainbow in the sky. The Bifrost bridge was also called the Rainbow bridge, and it connected heaven with earth, ending just under the great tree Yggdrasill.

The golden age of Asgard was one of such happiness that there was never any threat to the peace of the land, and so it was that its watchman became bored. Heimdall was easily spotted, so he could not travel far without being recognized and commended for his fine work. He carried over his shoulder a great bugle, Giallarhorn, the blasts of which could summon help from all nine worlds. One fine day, Odin noticed that Heimdall had been hard at work without any respite for many many years. Odin himself would occasionally slip into a disguise in order to go out into the worlds beneath them, and he decided then that Heimdall should have the same opportunity – after all, Asgard was hardly in need of defence when all was quiet.

Heimdall was delighted, for he had been longing to visit Midgard and to get to know the people there. He carefully laid his bugle and his sword to one side, and dressed in the garb of the people of Midgard, he slipped across the bridge and reached a deserted shore. The first people he clapped eyes upon were Edda and Ai, a poor couple who lived on the bare beaches of

Midgard, eking a meagre living from the sands. They lived in a tumble-down shack and had little in their possession, but what they did have they offered gladly to Heimdall. Their shack was sparsely furnished, with only a seaweed bed on which to lay, but it was agreed that Heimdall could sleep there with them, and at night he laid himself between the couple and slept well.

After three nights, Heimdall summoned Ai and Edda as they gathered snails and cockles from the seashore. He had put together several pieces of driftwood, and as they watched, he fashioned a pointed stick from one, and cut out a hole in another. The pointed stick was placed inside the hole, and he turned it quickly, so that sparks, and then a slender stream of smoke was produced. And then there was fire. Ai and Edda flew back against the walls of the shack, astonished by this magical feat. It was then that Heimdall took his leave from them.

Ai and Edda's lives were transformed by fire. Their water was heated; the most inedible nuggets from the beach were softened into tender morsels of food. And most of all, they had warmth. Nine months later a second gift appeared to Edda, for she gave birth to a son who she called Thrall. Thrall was an ugly, wretched-looking boy, with a knotted body and a twisted back, but he was kind and he worked hard. When he came of age, he married one like him – a deformed young woman called Serf. Together they had many children, all of whom worked about the house or on the land with the same diligence as their father and mother. These were the ancestors of the thralls.

Heimdall had left the home of Ai and Edda and travelled on. Soon enough he came to a lovely little house occupied by an older couple Amma and Afi. As he arrived, Afi was hard at work, whittling away at beams with which to improve their house. Heimdall set down his belongings and began to work with Afi. Soon they had built together a wonderful loom, which they presented to Amma, who was seated happily by the fire with her spinning wheel. Heimdall ate well that evening, and when the time came for sleep, he was offered a place between them in the only bed. For three nights Heimdall stayed with Afi and Amma, and then he left them. Sure enough, nine months later, and to the astonishment of the elderly couple, Amma gave birth to a son, who they called Karl the Yeoman. Karl was a thick-set, beautiful boy, with sparkling eyes and cheeks of roses. He loved the land and the fresh air was almost food enough for him, he drew so much goodness from it. When he became of age, he married a whirlwind of a woman who saw to it that their household ran as smoothly as a well-oiled rig, and that their children, their oxen and all the other animals on their farm, were fed and comfortable. They grew very successful, and they are the first of the ancestors of the yeoman farmer.

The third visit in Midgard was to a wealthy couple who lived in a fine castle. The man of the household spent many hours honing his hunting bow and spears, and his wife sat prettily by his side, well-dressed and flushed by the heat of the fire in the hearth. They offered him rich and delicious food, and at night he was given a place between them in their luxurious and comfortable bed. Heimdall stayed there for three nights, although he would happily have stayed there forever, after which time he returned to his post at the

Bifrost bridge. And so it was, nine months later, that a son was born to that couple in the castle, and they called him Jarl the Earl. His father taught him well the skills of hunting and living off the land, and his mother passed on her refinement and breeding, so that Jarl became known as 'Regal'. When Regal was but a boy, Heimdall returned again to Midgard, and claimed him as his son. Regal remained in Midgard, but his fine pedigree was soon known about the land and he grew to become a great ruler there. He married Erna, who bore him many sons, one of whom was the ancestor of a line of Kings who would rule the land forever.

Heimdall took up his place once more in Asgard, but he was prone to wandering, as all gods are, and there are many more stories of his travels.

## TYR'S SWORD

*The god Tyr sent*
*Gondul and Skogul*
*To choose a king*
*Of the race of Ingve,*
*To dwell with Odin*
*In roomy Valhal.*
**R.B. Anderson, Norse Mythology**

**Tyr, Tiu, or Ziu** was the son of Odin, and, according to different mythologists, his mother was Frigga, queen of the gods, or a beautiful giantess whose name is unknown, but who was a personification of the raging sea. He is the god of martial honour, and one of the twelve principal deities of Asgard. Although he appears to have had no special dwelling there, he was always welcome to Vingolf or Valhalla, and occupied one of the twelve thrones in the great council hall of Glads-heim.

As the God of courage and of war, Tyr was frequently invoked by the various nations of the North, who cried to him, as well as to Odin, to obtain victory. That he ranked next to Odin and Thor is proved by his name, Tiu, having been given to one of the days of the week, Tiu's day, which in modern English has become Tuesday. Under the name of Ziu, Tyr was the principal divinity of the Suabians, who originally called their capital, the modern Augsburg, Ziusburg. This people, venerating the god as they did, were wont to worship him under the emblem of a sword, his distinctive attribute, and in his honour held great sword dances, where various figures were performed. Sometimes the participants forming two long lines, crossed their swords, point upward, and challenged the boldest among their number to take a flying leap over them. At other times the warriors joined their sword points closely together in the shape of a rose or wheel, and when this figure was complete invited their chief to stand on the navel thus formed of flat, shining steel blades, and then they bore him upon it through the camp in triumph. The sword point was further considered so sacred that it became customary to register oaths upon it.

A distinctive feature of the worship of this god among the Franks and some other Northern nations was that the priests called Druids or Godi offered up human sacrifices upon his altars, generally cutting the bloody- or spread-eagle upon their victims, that is to say, making a deep incision on either side of the back-bone, turning the ribs thus loosened inside out, and tearing out the viscera through the opening thus made. Of course only prisoners of war were treated thus, and it was considered a point of honour with north European races to endure this torture without a moan. These sacrifices were made upon rude stone altars called dolmens, which can still be seen in Northern Europe. As Tyr was considered the patron god of the sword, it was deemed indispensable to engrave the sign or rune representing him upon the blade of every sword – an observance which the Edda enjoined upon all those who were desirous of obtaining victory.

Tyr was identical with the Saxon god Saxnot (from sax, a sword), and with Er, Heru, or Cheru, the chief divinity of the Cheruski, who also considered him god of the sun, and deemed his shining sword blade an emblem of its rays.

According to an ancient legend, Cheru's sword, which had been fashioned by the same dwarfs, sons of Ivald, who had also made Odin's spear, was held very sacred by his people, to whose care he had entrusted it, declaring that those who possessed it were sure to have the victory over their foes. But although carefully guarded in the temple, where it was hung so that it reflected the first beams of the morning sun, it suddenly and mysteriously disappeared one night. A Vala, druidess, or prophetess, consulted by the priests, revealed that the Norns had decreed that whoever wielded it would conquer the world and come to his death by it; but in spite of all entreaties she refused to tell who had taken it or where it might be found. Some time after this occurrence a tall and dignified stranger came to Cologne, where Vitellius, the Roman prefect, was feasting, and called him away from his beloved dainties. In the presence of the Roman soldiery he gave him the sword, telling him it would bring him glory and renown, and finally hailed him as emperor. The cry was taken up by the assembled legions, and Vitellius, without making any personal effort to secure the honour, found himself elected Emperor of Rome.

The new ruler, however, was so absorbed in indulging his taste for food and drink that he paid but little heed to the divine weapon. One day while leisurely making his way towards Rome he carelessly left it hanging in the antechamber to his pavilion. A German soldier seized this opportunity to substitute in its stead his own rusty blade, and the besotted emperor did not notice the exchange. When he arrived at Rome, he learned that the Eastern legions had named Vespasian emperor, and that he was even then on his way home to claim the throne.

Searching for the sacred weapon to defend his rights, Vitellius now discovered the theft, and, overcome by superstitious fears, did not even attempt to fight. He crawled away into a dark corner of his palace, whence he was ignominiously dragged by the enraged populace to the foot of the Capitoline Hill. There the prophecy was duly fulfilled, for the German soldier, who had joined the opposite faction, coming along at that moment, cut off Vitellius' head with the sacred sword.

The German soldier now changed from one legion to another, and travelled over many lands; but wherever he and his sword were found, victory was assured. After winning great honour and distinction, this man, having grown old, retired from active service to the banks of the Danube, where he secretly buried his treasured weapon, building his hut over its resting-place to guard it as long as he might live. When he lay on his deathbed he was implored to reveal where he had hidden it, but he persistently refused to do so, saying that it would be found by the man who was destined to conquer the world, but that he would not be able to escape the curse. Years passed by. Wave after wave the tide of barbarian invasion swept over that part of the country, and last of all came the terrible Huns under the leadership of Attila, the "Scourge of God." As he passed along the river, he saw a peasant mournfully examining his cow's foot, which had been wounded by some sharp instrument hidden in the long grass, and when search was made the point of a buried sword was found sticking out of the soil.

Attila, seeing the beautiful workmanship and the fine state of preservation of this weapon, immediately exclaimed that it was Cheru's sword, and brandishing it above his head he announced that he would conquer the world. Battle after battle was fought by the Huns, who, according to the Saga, were everywhere victorious, until Attila, weary of warfare, settled down in Hungary, taking to wife the beautiful Burgundian princess Ildico, whose father he had slain. This princess, resenting the murder of her kin and wishing to avenge it, took advantage of the king's state of intoxication upon his wedding night to secure possession of the divine sword, with which she slew him in his bed, once more fulfilling the prophecy uttered so many years before.

The magic sword again disappeared for a long time, to be unearthed once more, for the last time, by the Duke of Alva, Charles V.'s general, who shortly after won the victory of Mühlberg (1547). The Franks were wont to celebrate yearly martial games in honour of the sword; but it is said that when the heathen gods were renounced in favour of Christianity, the priests transferred many of their attributes to the saints, and that this sword became the property of the Archangel St. Michael, who has wielded it ever since.

Tyr, whose name was synonymous with bravery and wisdom, was also considered by the ancient Northern people to have the white-armed Valkyrs, Odin's attendants, at his command, and they thought that he it was who designated the warriors whom they should transfer to Valhalla to aid the gods on the last day.

## HOW TYR LOST HIS HAND

> *Tyr: I of a hand am wanting,*
> *But thou of honest fame;*
> *Sad is the lack of either.*
> *Nor is the wolf at ease:*
> *He in bonds must abide*
> *Until the gods' destruction.*
> **Benjamin Thorpe, Saemund's Edda**

**T**yr was generally spoken of and represented as one-armed, just as Odin was called one-eyed. Various explanations are offered by different authorities; some claim that it was because he could give the victory only to one side; others, because a sword has but one blade. However this may be, the ancients preferred to account for the fact in the following way:

Loki married secretly at Jötun-heim the hideous giantess Angur-boda (anguish boding), who bore him three monstrous children – the wolf Fenris, Hel, the parti-coloured goddess of death, and Iörmungandr, a terrible serpent. He kept the existence of these monsters secret as long as he could; but they speedily grew so large that they could no longer remain confined in the cave where they had come to light. Odin, from his throne Hlidskialf, soon became aware of their existence, and also of the disquieting rapidity with which they increased in size. Fearful lest the monsters, when they had gained further strength, should invade Asgard and destroy the gods, Allfather determined to get rid of them, and striding off to Jötun-heim, he flung Hel into the depths of Nifl-heim, telling her she could reign over the nine dismal worlds of the dead. He then cast Iörmungandr into the sea, where he attained such immense proportions that at last he encircled the earth and could bite his own tail.

None too well pleased that the serpent should attain such fearful dimensions in his new element, Odin resolved to lead Fenris to Asgard, where he hoped, by kindly treatment, to make him gentle and tractable. But the gods one and all shrank in dismay when they saw the wolf, and none dared approach to give him food except Tyr, whom nothing daunted. Seeing that Fenris daily increased in size, strength, voracity, and fierceness, the gods assembled in council to deliberate how they might best dispose of him. They

unanimously decided that as it would desecrate their peace-
steads to slay him, they would bind him fast so that he could
work them no harm.

With that purpose in view, they obtained a strong chain
named Laeding, and then playfully proposed to Fenris to bind
this about him as a test of his vaunted strength. Confident in
his ability to release himself, Fenris patiently allowed them to
bind him fast, and when all stood aside, with a mighty effort
he stretched himself and easily burst the chain asunder.

Concealing their chagrin, the gods were loud in praise of
his strength, but they next produced a much stronger fetter,
Droma, which, after some persuasion, the wolf allowed
them to fasten around him as before. Again a short, sharp
struggle sufficed to burst this bond, and it is proverbial in
the North to use the figurative expressions, "to get loose out
of Laeding," and "to dash out of Droma," whenever great
difficulties have to be surmounted.

The gods, perceiving now that ordinary bonds, however
strong, would never prevail against the Fenris wolf's great
strength, bade Skirnir, Frey's servant, go down to Svart-alfa-heim
and bid the dwarfs fashion a bond which nothing could sever.

By magic arts the dark elves manufactured a slender
silken rope from such impalpable materials as the sound of
a cat's footsteps, a woman's beard, the roots of a mountain,
the longings of the bear, the voice of fishes, and the spittle
of birds, and when it was finished they gave it to Skirnir,
assuring him that no strength would avail to break it, and
that the more it was strained the stronger it would become.

Armed with this bond, called Gleipnir, the gods went
with Fenris to the Island of Lyngvi, in the middle of Lake

Amsvartnir, and again proposed to test his strength. But although Fenris had grown still stronger, he mistrusted the bond which looked so slight. He therefore refused to allow himself to be bound, unless one of the Aesir would consent to put his hand in his mouth, and leave it there, as a pledge of good faith, and that no magic arts were to be used against him.

The gods heard the decision with dismay, and all drew back except Tyr, who, seeing that the others would not venture to comply with this condition, boldly stepped forward and thrust his hand between the monster's jaws. The gods now fastened Gleipnir securely around Fenris's neck and paws, and when they saw that his utmost efforts to free himself were fruitless, they shouted and laughed with glee. Tyr, however, could not share their joy, for the wolf, finding himself captive, bit off the god's hand at the wrist, which since then has been known as the wolf's joint.

Deprived of his right hand, Tyr was now forced to use the maimed arm for his shield, and to wield his sword with his left hand; but such was his dexterity that he slew his enemies as before.

The gods, in spite of the wolf's struggles, drew the end of the fetter Gelgia through the rock Gioll, and fastened it to the boulder Thviti, which was sunk deep in the ground. Opening wide his fearful jaws, Fenris uttered such terrible howls that the gods, to silence him, thrust a sword into his mouth, the hilt resting upon his lower jaw and the point against his palate. The blood then began to pour out in such streams that it formed a great river, called Von. The wolf was destined to remain thus chained fast until the last day, when he would burst his bonds and would be free to avenge his wrongs.

While some mythologists see in this myth an emblem of crime restrained and made innocuous by the power of the law, others see the underground fire, which kept within bounds can injure no one, but which unfettered fills the world with destruction and woe. Just as Odin's second eye is said to rest in Mimir's well, so Tyr's second hand (sword) is found in Fenris's jaws. He has no more use for two weapons than the sky for two suns.

The worship of Tyr is commemorated in sundry places (such as Tübingen, in Germany), which bear more or less modified forms of his name. The name has also been given to the aconite, a plant known in Northern countries as "Tyr's helm."

## THE NORNS' WEB

*Thence come the maids*
*Who much do know;*
*Three from the hall*
*Beneath the tree;*
*One they named Was,*
*And Being next,*
*The third Shall be.*
**Ebenezer Henderson, The Voluspa**

**The Northern goddesses of fate**, who were called Norns, were in nowise subject to the other gods, who might neither question nor influence their decrees. They were three sisters, probably descendants of the giant Norvi, from whom sprang Nott (night). As soon as the Golden Age was ended, and sin began to steal even into the heavenly homes of Asgard, the Norns made their appearance under the great ash Yggdrasil, and took up their abode near the Urdar fountain. According to some mythologists, their mission was to warn the gods of future evil, to bid them make good use of the present, and to teach them wholesome lessons from the past.

These three sisters, whose names were Urd, Verdandi, and Skuld, were personifications of the past, present, and future. Their principal occupations were to weave the web of fate, to sprinkle daily the sacred tree with water from the Urdar fountain, and to put fresh clay around its roots, that it might remain fresh and ever green.

Some authorities further state that the Norns kept watch over the golden apples which hung on the branches of the tree of life, experience, and knowledge, allowing none but Idunn to pick the fruit, which was that with which the gods renewed their youth.

The Norns also fed and tenderly cared for two swans which swam over the mirror-like surface of the Urdar fountain, and from this pair of birds all the swans on earth are supposed to be descended. At times, it is said, the Norns clothed themselves with swan plumage to visit the earth, or sported like mermaids along the coast and in various lakes and rivers, appearing to mortals, from time to time, to foretell the future or give them sage advice.

The Norns sometimes wove webs so large that while one of the weavers stood on a high mountain in the extreme east, another waded far out into the western sea. The threads of their woof resembled cords, and varied greatly in hue, according to the nature of the events about to occur, and a black thread, tending from north to south, was invariably considered an omen of death. As these sisters flashed the shuttle to and fro, they chanted a solemn song. They did not seem to weave according to their own wishes, but blindly, as if reluctantly executing the wishes of Orlog, the eternal law of the universe, an older and superior power, who apparently had neither beginning nor end.

Two of the Norns, Urd and Verdandi, were considered to be very beneficent indeed, while the third, it is said, relentlessly undid their work, and often, when nearly finished, tore it angrily to shreds, scattering the remnants to the winds of heaven. As personifications of time, the Norns were represented as sisters of different ages and characters, Urd (Wurd, weird) appearing very old and decrepit, continually looking backward, as if absorbed in contemplating past events and people; Verdandi, the second sister, young, active, and fearless, looked straight before her, while Skuld, the type of the future, was generally represented as closely veiled, with head turned in the direction opposite to where Urd was gazing, and holding a book or scroll which had not yet been opened or unrolled.

These Norns were visited daily by the gods, who loved to consult them; and even Odin himself frequently rode down to the Urdar fountain to bespeak their aid, for they generally answered his questions, maintaining silence only about his own fate and that of his fellow gods.

## THE STORY OF NORNAGESTA

*In the mansion it was night:*
*The Norns came,*
*Who should the prince's*
*Life determine.*
**Benjamin Thorpe, Saemund's Edda**

On one occasion the three sisters visited Denmark, and entered the dwelling of a nobleman as his first child came into the world. Entering the apartment where the mother lay, the first Norn promised that the child should be handsome and brave, and the second that he should be prosperous and a great scald – predictions which filled the parents' hearts with joy. Meantime news of what was taking place had gone abroad, and the neighbours came thronging the apartment to such a degree that the pressure of the curious crowd caused the third Norn to be pushed rudely from her chair.

Angry at this insult, Skuld proudly rose and declared that her sister's gifts should be of no avail, since she would decree that the child should live only as long as the taper then burning near the bedside. These ominous words filled the mother's heart with terror, and she tremblingly clasped her babe closer to her breast, for the taper was nearly burned out and its extinction could not be very long delayed. The eldest Norn, however, had no intention of seeing her prediction thus set at naught; but as she could not force her sister to retract her words, she quickly seized the taper, put out the light, and giving the smoking stump to the child's mother, bade her carefully treasure it, and never light it again until her son was weary of life.

The boy was named Nornagesta, in honour of the Norns, and grew up to be as beautiful, brave, and talented as any mother could wish. When he was old enough to comprehend the gravity of the trust his mother told him the story of the Norns' visit, and placed in his hands the candle end, which he treasured for many a year, placing it for safe-keeping inside the frame of his harp. When his parents were dead, Nornagesta wandered from place to place, taking part and distinguishing himself in every battle, singing his heroic lays wherever he went. As he was of an enthusiastic and poetic temperament, he did not soon weary of life, and while other heroes grew wrinkled and old, he remained young at heart and vigorous in frame. He therefore witnessed the stirring deeds of the heroic ages, was the boon companion of the ancient warriors, and after living three hundred years, saw the belief in the old heathen gods gradually supplanted by the teachings of Christian missionaries. Finally Nornagesta came to the court of King Olaf Tryggvesson, who, according to his usual custom, converted him almost by force, and compelled him to receive baptism. Then, wishing to convince his people that the time for superstition was past, the king forced the aged scald to produce and light the taper which he had so carefully guarded for more than three centuries.

In spite of his recent conversion, Nornagesta anxiously watched the flame as it flickered, and when, finally, it went out, he sank lifeless to the ground, thus proving that in spite of the baptism just received, he still believed in the prediction of the Norns.

In the middle ages, and even later, the Norns figure in many a story or myth, appearing as fairies or witches, as, for instance, in the tale of "the Sleeping Beauty," and Shakespeare's tragedy of Macbeth.

Sometimes the Norns bore the name of Vala, or prophetesses, for they had the power of divination – a power which was held in great honour by all the Northern races, who believed that it was restricted to the female sex. The predictions of the Vala were never questioned, and it is said that the Roman general Drusus was so terrified by the appearance of Veleda, one of these prophetesses, who warned him not to cross the Elbe, that he actually beat a retreat. She foretold his approaching death, which indeed happened shortly after through a fall from his steed.

These prophetesses, who were also known as Idises, Dises, or Hagedises, officiated at the forest shrines and in the sacred groves, and always accompanied invading armies. Riding ahead, or in the midst of the host, they would vehemently urge the warriors on to victory, and when the battle was over they would often cut the bloody-eagle upon the bodies of the captives. The blood was collected into great tubs, wherein the Dises plunged their naked arms up to the shoulders, previous to joining in the wild dance with which the ceremony ended.

It is not to be wondered at that these women were greatly feared. Sacrifices were offered to propitiate them, and it was only in later times that they were degraded to the rank of witches, and sent to join the demon host on the Brocken, or Blocksberg, on Valpurgisnacht.

Besides the Norns or Dises, who were also regarded as protective deities, the Northmen ascribed to each human being a guardian spirit named Fylgie, which attended him through life, either in human or brute shape, and was invisible except at the moment of death by all except the initiated few.

The allegorical meaning of the Norns and of their web of fate is too patent to need explanation; still some mythologists have made them demons of the air, and state that their web was the woof of clouds, and that the bands of mists which they strung from rock to tree, and from mountain to mountain, were ruthlessly torn apart by the suddenly rising wind. Some authorities, moreover, declare that Skuld, the third Norn, was at times a Valkyr, and at others personated the goddess of death, the terrible Hel.

## HERMOD

*But there was one, the first of all the gods*
*For speed, and Hermod was his name in Heaven;*
*Most fleet he was.*
**Matthew Arnold, Balder Dead**

Another of Odin's sons was Hermod, his special attendant, a bright and beautiful young god, who was gifted with great rapidity of motion and was therefore designated as the swift or nimble god.

On account of this important attribute Hermod was usually employed by the gods as messenger, and at a mere sign from Odin he was always ready to speed to any part of creation. As a special mark of favour, Allfather gave him a magnificent corselet and helmet, which he often donned when he prepared to take part in war, and sometimes Odin entrusted to his care the precious spear Gungnir, bidding him cast it over the heads of combatants about to engage in battle, that their ardour might be kindled into murderous fury.

Hermod delighted in battle, and was often called "the valiant in battle," and confounded with the god of the universe, Irmin. It is said that he sometimes accompanied the Valkyrs on their ride to earth, and frequently escorted the warriors to Valhalla, wherefore he was considered the leader of the heroic dead.

Hermod's distinctive attribute, besides his corselet and helm, was a wand or staff called Gambantein, the emblem of his office, which he carried with him wherever he went.

Once, oppressed by shadowy fears for the future, and unable to obtain from the Norns satisfactory answers to his questions, Odin bade Hermod don his armour and saddle Sleipnir, which he alone, besides Odin, was allowed to ride, and hasten off to the land of the Finns. This people, who lived in the frozen regions of the pole, besides being able to call up the cold storms which swept down from the North, bringing much ice and snow in their train, were supposed to have great occult powers.

The most noted of these Finnish magicians was Rossthiof (the horse thief) who was wont to entice travellers into his realm by magic arts, that he might rob and slay them; and he had power to predict the future, although he was always very reluctant to do so.

Hermod, "the swift," rode rapidly northward, with directions to seek this Finn, and instead of his own wand, he carried Odin's runic staff, which Allfather had given him for the purpose of dispelling any obstacles that Rossthiof might conjure up to hinder his advance. In spite, therefore, of phantom-like monsters and of invisible snares and pitfalls, Hermod was enabled safely to reach the magician's abode, and upon the giant attacking him, he was able to master him with ease, and he bound him hand and foot, declaring that he would not set him free until he promised to reveal all that he wished to know.

Rossthiof, seeing that there was no hope of escape, pledged himself to do as his captor wished, and upon being set at liberty, he began forthwith to mutter incantations, at the mere sound of which the sun hid behind the clouds, the earth trembled and quivered, and the storm winds howled like a pack of hungry wolves.

Pointing to the horizon, the magician bade Hermod look, and the swift god saw in the distance a great stream of blood reddening the ground. While he gazed wonderingly at this stream, a beautiful woman suddenly appeared, and a moment later a little boy stood beside her. To the god's amazement, this child grew with such marvellous rapidity that he soon attained his full growth, and Hermod further noticed that he fiercely brandished a bow and arrows.

Rossthiof now began to explain the omens which his art had conjured up, and he declared that the stream of blood portended the murder of one of Odin's sons, but that if the father of the gods should woo and win Rinda, in the land of the Ruthenes (Russia), she would bear him a son who would attain his full growth in a few hours and would avenge his brother's death.

Hermod listened attentively to the words of Rossthiof and upon his return to Asgard he reported all he had seen and heard to Odin, whose fears were confirmed and who thus definitely ascertained that he was doomed to lose a son by violent death. He consoled himself, however, with the thought that another of his descendants would avenge the crime and thereby obtain the satisfaction which a true Northman ever required.

# VIDAR

*There sits Odin's*
*Son on the horse's back;*
*He will avenge his father.*
**R.B. Anderson, Norse Mythology**

It is related that Odin once loved the beautiful giantess Grid, who dwelt in a cave in the desert, and that, wooing her, he prevailed upon her to become his wife. The offspring of this union between Odin (mind) and Grid (matter) was Vidar, a son as strong as he was taciturn, whom the ancients considered a personification of the primaeval forest or of the imperishable forces of Nature.

As the gods, through Heimdall, were intimately connected with the sea, they were also bound by close ties to the forests and Nature in general through Vidar, surnamed "the silent," who was destined to survive their destruction and rule over a regenerated earth. This god had his habitation in Landvidi (the wide land), a palace decorated with green boughs and fresh flowers, situated in the midst of an impenetrable primaeval forest where reigned the deep silence and solitude which he loved.

This old Scandinavian conception of the silent Vidar is indeed very grand and poetical, and was inspired by the rugged Northern scenery. "Who has ever wandered through such forests, in a length of many miles, in a boundless expanse, without a path, without a goal, amid their monstrous shadows, their sacred gloom, without being filled with deep reverence for the sublime greatness of Nature above all human agency, without feeling the grandeur of the idea which forms the basis of Vidar's essence?"

Vidar is depicted as tall, well-made, and handsome, clad in armour, girded with a broad-bladed sword, and shod with a great iron or leather shoe. According to some mythologists, he owed this peculiar footgear to his mother Grid, who, knowing that he would be called upon to fight against fire on the last day, designed it as a protection against the fiery element, as her iron gauntlet had shielded Thor in his encounter with Geirrod. But other authorities state that this shoe was made of the leather scraps which Northern cobblers had either given or thrown away. As it was essential that the shoe should be large and strong enough to resist the Fenris wolf's sharp teeth at the last day, it was a matter of religious observance among Northern shoemakers to give away as many odds and ends of leather as possible.

When Vidar joined his peers in Valhalla, they welcomed him gaily, for they knew that his great strength would serve them well in their time of need. After they had lovingly regaled him with the golden mead, Allfather bade him follow to the Urdar fountain, where the Norns were ever busy weaving their web. Questioned by Odin concerning his future and Vidar's destiny, the three sisters answered oracularly; each uttering a sentence:

*"Early begun."*
*"Further spun."*
*"One day done."*

To these their mother, Wyrd, the primitive goddess of fate, added: "With joy once more won." These mysterious answers would have remained totally unintelligible had the goddess not gone on to explain that time progresses, that all must change, but that even if the father fell in the last battle, his son Vidar would be his avenger, and would live to rule over a regenerated world, after having conquered all his enemies.

As Wyrd spoke, the leaves of the world tree fluttered as if agitated by a breeze, the eagle on its topmost bough flapped its wings, and the serpent Nidhug for a moment suspended its work of destruction at the roots of the tree. Grid, joining the father and son, rejoiced with Odin when she heard that their son was destined to survive the older gods and to rule over the new heaven and earth.

Vidar, however, uttered not a word, but slowly wended his way back to his palace Landvidi, in the heart of the primaeval forest, and there, sitting upon his throne, he pondered long about eternity, futurity, and infinity. If he fathomed their secrets he never revealed them, for the ancients averred that he was "as silent as the grave" – a silence which indicated that no man knows what awaits him in the life to come.

Vidar was not only a personification of the imperish-ability of Nature, but he was also a symbol of resurrection and renewal, exhibiting the eternal truth that new shoots and blossoms will spring forth to replace those which have fallen into decay.

The shoe he wore was to be his defence against the wolf Fenris, who, having destroyed Odin, would direct his wrath against him, and open wide his terrible jaws to devour him. But the old Northmen declared that Vidar would brace the foot thus protected against the monster's lower jaw, and, seizing the upper, would struggle with him until he had rent him in twain.

As one shoe only is mentioned in the Vidar myths, some mythologists suppose that he had but one leg, and was the personification of a waterspout, which would rise suddenly on the last day to quench the wild fire personified by the terrible wolf Fenris.

# VALI

*But, see! th' avenger, Vali, come,*
*Sprung from the west, in Rinda's womb,*
*True son of Odin! one day's birth!*

*He shall not stop nor stay on earth*
*His locks to comb, his hands to lave,*
*His frame to rest, should rest it crave,*
*Until his mission be complete,*
*And Balder's death find vengeance meet.*
**J.C. Jones, Valhalla**

**B**illing, king of the Ruthenes, was sorely dismayed when he heard that a great force was about to invade his kingdom, for he was too old to fight as of yore, and his only child, a daughter named Rinda, although she was of marriageable age, obstinately refused to choose a husband from among her many suitors, and thus give her father the help which he so sadly needed.

While Billing was musing disconsolately in his hall, a stranger suddenly entered his palace. Looking up, the king beheld a middle-aged man wrapped in a wide cloak, with a broad-brimmed hat drawn down over his forehead to conceal the fact that he had but one eye. The stranger courteously enquired the cause of his evident depression, and as there was that in his bearing that compelled confidence, the king told him all, and at the end of the relation he volunteered to command the army of the Ruthenes against their foe.

His services being joyfully accepted, it was not long ere Odin – for it was he – won a signal victory, and, returning in triumph, he asked permission to woo the king's daughter Rinda for his wife. Despite the suitor's advancing years, Billing hoped that his daughter would lend a favourable ear to a wooer who appeared to be very distinguished, and he immediately signified his consent. So Odin, still unknown, presented himself before the princess, but she scornfully rejected his proposal, and rudely boxed his ears when he attempted to kiss her.

Forced to withdraw, Odin nevertheless did not relinquish his purpose to make Rinda his wife, for he knew, thanks to Rossthiof's prophecy, that none but she could bring forth the destined avenger of his murdered son. His next step, therefore, was to assume the form of a smith, in which guise he came back to Billing's hall, and fashioning costly ornaments of silver and gold, he so artfully multiplied these precious trinkets that the king joyfully acquiesced when he inquired whether he might pay his addresses to the princess. The smith, Rosterus as he announced himself, was, however, as unceremoniously dismissed by Rinda as the successful general had been; but although his ear once again tingled with the force of her blow, he was more determined than ever to make her his wife.

The next time Odin presented himself before the capricious damsel, he was disguised as a dashing warrior, for, thought he, a young soldier might perchance touch the maiden's heart; but when he again attempted to kiss her, she pushed him back so suddenly that he stumbled and fell upon one knee.

This third insult so enraged Odin that he drew his magic rune stick out of his breast, pointed it at Rinda, and uttered such a terrible spell that she fell back into the arms of her attendants rigid and apparently lifeless.

When the princess came to life again, her suitor had disappeared, but the king discovered with great dismay that she had entirely lost her senses and was melancholy mad. In vain all the physicians were summoned and all their simples tried; the maiden remained passive and sad, and her distracted father had well-nigh abandoned hope when an old woman, who announced herself as Vecha, or Vak, appeared and offered to undertake the cure of the princess. The seeming old woman, who was Odin in disguise, first prescribed a foot-bath for the patient; but as this did not appear to have any very marked effect, she proposed to try a more drastic treatment. For this, Vecha declared, the patient must be entrusted to her exclusive care, securely bound so that she could not offer the least resistance. Billing, anxious to save his child, was ready to assent to anything; and having thus gained full power over Rinda, Odin compelled her to wed him, releasing her from bonds and spell only when she had faithfully promised to be his wife.

The prophecy of Rossthiof was now fulfilled, for Rinda duly bore a son named Vali (Ali, Bous, or Beav), a personification of the lengthening days, who grew with such marvellous rapidity that in the course of a single day he attained his full stature. Without waiting even to wash his face or comb his hair, this young god hastened to Asgard, bow and arrow in hand, to avenge the death of Balder upon his murderer, Hodur, the blind god of darkness.

In this myth, Rinda, a personification of the hard-frozen rind of the earth, resists the warm wooing of the sun, Odin, who vainly points out that spring is the time for warlike exploits, and offers the adornments of golden summer. She only yields when, after a shower (the footbath), a thaw sets in. Conquered then by the sun's irresistible might, the earth yields to his embrace, is freed from the spell (ice) which made her hard and cold, and brings forth Vali the nourisher, or Bous the peasant, who emerges from his dark hut when the pleasant days have come. The slaying of Hodur by Vali is therefore emblematical of "the breaking forth of new light after wintry darkness."

Vali, who ranked as one of the twelve deities occupying seats in the great hall of Glads-heim, shared with his father the dwelling called Valaskialf, and was destined, even before birth, to survive the last battle and twilight of the gods, and to reign with Vidar over the regenerated earth.

# FORSETI

*Glitner is the tenth;*
*It is on gold sustained,*
*And also with silver decked.*
*There Forseti dwells*
*Throughout all time,*
*And every strife allays.*
**Benjamin Thorpe, Saemund's Edda**

**Son of Balder,** god of light, and of Nanna, goddess of immaculate purity, Forseti was the wisest, most eloquent, and most gentle of all the gods. When his presence in Asgard became known, the gods awarded him a seat in the council hall, decreed that he should be patron of justice and righteousness, and gave him as abode the radiant palace Glitnir. This dwelling had a silver roof, supported on pillars of gold, and it shone so brightly that it could be seen from a great distance.

Here, upon an exalted throne, Forseti, the lawgiver, sat day after day, settling the differences of gods and men, patiently listening to both sides of every question, and finally pronouncing sentences so equitable that none ever found fault with his decrees. Such were this god's eloquence and power of persuasion that he always succeeded in touching his hearers' hearts, and never failed to reconcile even the most bitter foes. All who left his presence were thereafter sure to live in peace, for none dared break a vow once made to him, lest they should incur his just anger and be smitten immediately unto death.

As god of justice and eternal law, Forseti was supposed to preside over every judicial assembly; he was invariably appealed to by all who were about to undergo a trial, and it was said that he rarely failed to help the deserving.

In order to facilitate the administration of justice throughout their land it is related that the Frisians commissioned twelve of their wisest men, the Asegeir, or elders, to collect the laws of the various families and tribes composing their nation, and to compile from them a code which should be the basis of uniform laws. The elders, having painstakingly finished their task of collecting this miscellaneous information, embarked upon a small vessel, to seek some secluded spot where they might conduct their deliberations in peace. But no sooner had they pushed away from shore than a tempest arose, which drove their vessel far out to sea, first on this course and then on that, until they entirely lost their bearings. In their distress the twelve jurists called upon Forseti, begging him to help them to reach land once again, and the prayer was scarcely ended when they perceived, to their utter surprise, that the vessel contained a thirteenth passenger.

Seizing the rudder, the newcomer silently brought the vessel round, steering it towards the place where the waves dashed highest, and in an incredibly short space of time they came to an island, where the steersman motioned them to disembark. In awestruck silence the twelve men obeyed; and their surprise was further excited when they saw the stranger fling his battle-axe, and a limpid spring gush forth from the spot on the greensward where it fell. Imitating the stranger, all drank of this water without a word; then they sat down in a circle, marvelling because the newcomer resembled each one of them in some particular, but yet was very different from any one of them in general aspect and mien.

Suddenly the silence was broken, and the stranger began to speak in low tones, which grew firmer and louder as he proceeded to expound a code of laws which combined all the good points of the various existing regulations which the Asegeir had collected. His speech being finished, the speaker vanished as suddenly and mysteriously as he had appeared, and the twelve jurists, recovering power of speech, simultaneously exclaimed that Forseti himself had been among them, and had delivered the code of laws by which the Frisians should henceforth be judged. In commemoration of the god's appearance they declared the island upon which they stood to be holy, and they pronounced a solemn curse upon any who might dare to desecrate its sanctity by quarrel or bloodshed. Accordingly this island, known as Forseti's land or Heligoland (holy land), was greatly respected by all the Northern nations, and even the boldest vikings refrained from raiding its shores, lest they should suffer shipwreck or meet a shameful death in punishment for their crime.

Solemn judicial assemblies were frequently held upon this sacred isle, the jurists always drawing water and drinking it in silence, in memory of Forseti's visit. The waters of his spring were, moreover, considered to be so holy that all who drank of them were held to be sacred, and even the cattle who had tasted of them might not be slain. As Forseti was said to hold his assizes in spring, summer, and autumn, but never in winter, it became customary, in all the Northern countries, to dispense justice in those seasons, the people declaring that it was only when the light shone clearly in the heavens that right could become apparent to all, and that it would be utterly impossible to render an equitable verdict during the dark winter season. Forseti is seldom mentioned except in connection with Balder. He apparently had no share in the closing battle in which all the other gods played such prominent parts.

# ULLER

*Ydalir it is called,*
*Where Ullr has*
*Himself a dwelling made.*
**Benjamin Thorpe, Saemund's Edda**

Uller, the winter-god, was the son of Sif, and the stepson of Thor. His father, who is never mentioned in the Northern sagas, must have been one of the dreaded frost giants, for Uller loved the cold and delighted in travelling over the country on his broad snowshoes or glittering skates. This god also delighted in the chase, and pursued his game through the Northern forests, caring but little for ice and snow, against which he was well protected by the thick furs in which he was always clad.

As god of hunting and archery, he is represented with a quiver full of arrows and a huge bow, and as the yew furnishes the best wood for the manufacture of these weapons, it is said to have been his favourite tree. To have a supply of suitable wood ever at hand ready for use, Uller took up his abode at Ydalir, the vale of yews, where it was always very damp.

As winter-god, Uller, or Oller, as he was also called, was considered second only to Odin, whose place he usurped during his absence in the winter months of the year. During this period he exercised full sway over Asgard and Midgard, and even, according to some authorities, took possession of Frigga, Odin's wife, as related in the myth of Vili and Ve. But as Uller was very parsimonious, and never bestowed any gifts upon mankind, they gladly hailed the return of Odin, who drove his supplanter away, forcing him to take refuge either in the frozen North or on the tops of the Alps. Here, if we are to believe the poets, he had built a summer house into which he retreated until, knowing Odin had departed once more, he again dared appear in the valleys.

Uller was also considered god of death, and was supposed to ride in the Wild Hunt, and at times even to lead it. He is specially noted for his rapidity of motion, and as the snowshoes used in Northern regions are sometimes made of bone, and turned up in front like the prow of a ship, it was commonly reported that Uller had spoken magic runes over a piece of bone, changing it into a vessel, which bore him over land or sea at will.

As snowshoes are shaped like a shield, and as the ice with which he yearly enveloped the earth acts as a shield to protect it from harm during the winter, Uller was surnamed the shield-god, and he was specially invoked by all persons about to engage in a duel or in a desperate fight.

In Christian times, his place in popular worship was taken by St. Hubert, the hunter, who, also, was made patron of the first month of the year, which began on November 22, and was dedicated to him as the sun passed through the constellation of Sagittarius, the bowman.

In Anglo-Saxon, Uller was known as Vulder; but in some parts of Germany he was called Holler and considered to be the husband of the fair goddess Holda, whose fields he covered with a thick mantle of snow, to make them more fruitful when the spring came.

By the Scandinavians, Uller was said to have married Skadi, Niörd's divorced wife, the female personification of winter and cold, and their tastes were so congenial that they lived in perfect harmony together.

Numerous temples were dedicated to Uller in the North, and on his altars, as well as on those of all the other gods, lay a sacred ring upon which oaths were sworn. This ring was said to have the power of shrinking so violently as to sever the finger of any premeditated perjurer. The people visited Uller's shrine, especially during the months of November and December, to entreat him to send a thick covering of snow over their lands, as earnest of a good harvest; and as he was supposed to send out the glorious flashes of the aurora borealis, which illumine the Northern sky during its long night, he was considered nearly akin to Balder, the personification of light.

According to other authorities, Uller was Balder's special friend, principally because he too spent part of the year in the dismal depths of Nifl-heim, with Hel, the goddess of death. Uller was supposed to endure a yearly banishment thither, during the summer months, when he was forced to resign his sway over the earth to Odin, the summer god, and there Balder came to join him at Midsummer, the date of his disappearance from Asgard, for then the days began to grow shorter, and the rule of light (Balder) gradually yielded to the ever encroaching power of darkness (Hodur).

# GIANTS, DWARFS AND ELVES

*Master Olof rode forth ere dawn of the day*
*And came where the Elf-folk were dancing away.*
*The dance is so merry,*
*So merry in the greenwood.*
**W. and M. Howitt, Master Olof at the Elfin Dance**

As well as men and Gods, the Norse universe was also populated by such creatures as giants, dwarfs and elves. Dwarfs and elves in particular were occasionally interchangeable with each other, with dwarfs being seen as 'black elves' as opposed to the light or white elves, but on the whole throughout the different stories we can trace three different races. The Gods often found themselves in opposition to the giants in particular – and therefore they were represented as paragons of evil to be overcome. However they also played an integral part in the lives of the Gods, for example the dwarfs made many magic items which the Gods come to obtain.

## THE GIANTS

*Miserable Senjemand – ugly and grey!*
*Thou win the maid of Kvedfiord!*
*No – a churl thou art and shalt ever remain.*
**Charles Loring Brace, Ballad**

As we have already seen, the Northern races imagined that the giants were the first creatures who came to life among the icebergs which filled the vast abyss of Ginnunga-gap. These giants were from the very beginning the opponents and rivals of the gods, and as the latter were the personifications of all that is good and lovely, the former were representative of all that was ugly and evil.

When Ymir, the first giant, fell lifeless on the ice, slain by the gods, his progeny were drowned in his blood. One couple only, Bergelmir and his wife, effected their escape to Jötun-heim, where they took up their abode and became the parents of all the giant race. In the North the giants were called by various names, each having a particular meaning. Jötun, for instance, meant "the great eater," for the giants were noted for their enormous appetites as well as for their uncommon size. They were fond of drinking as well as of eating, wherefore they were also called Thurses, a word which some writers claim had the same meaning as thirst; but others think they owed this name to the high towers ("turseis") which they were supposed to have built. As the giants were antagonistic to the gods, the latter always strove to force them to remain in Jötun-heim, which was situated in the cold regions of the Pole. The giants were almost invariably worsted in their encounters with the gods, for they were heavy and slow-witted, and had nothing but stone weapons to oppose to the Aesir's bronze. In spite of this inequality, however, they were sometimes greatly envied by the gods, for they were thoroughly conversant with all knowledge relating to the past. Even Odin was envious of this attribute, and no sooner had he secured it by a draught from Mimir's spring than he hastened to Jötun-heim to measure himself against Vafthrudnir, the most learned of the giant brood. But he might never have succeeded in defeating his antagonist in this strange encounter had he not ceased inquiring about the past and propounded a question relating to the future.

Of all the gods Thor was most feared by the Jötuns, for he was continually waging war against the frost and mountain giants, who would fain have bound the earth for ever in their rigid bands, thus preventing men from tilling the soil. In fighting against them, Thor, as we have already seen, generally had recourse to his terrible hammer Miolnir.

According to German legends the uneven surface of the earth was due to the giants, who marred its smoothness by treading upon it while it was still soft and newly created, while streams were formed from the copious tears shed by the giantesses upon seeing the valleys made by their husbands' huge footprints. As such was the Teutonic belief, the people imagined that the giants, who personified the mountains to them, were huge uncouth creatures, who could only move about in the darkness or fog, and were petrified as soon as the first rays of sunlight pierced through the gloom or scattered the clouds.

This belief led them to name one of their principal mountain chains the Riesengebirge (giant mountains). The Scandinavians also shared this belief, and to this day the Icelanders designate their highest mountain peaks by the name of Jokul, a modification of the word "Jötun." In Switzerland, where the everlasting snows rest upon the lofty mountain tops, the people still relate old stories of the time when the giants roamed abroad; and when an avalanche came crashing down the mountain side, they say the giants have restlessly shaken off part of the icy burden from their brows and shoulders.

As the giants were also personifications of snow, ice, cold, stone, and subterranean fire, they were said to be descended from the primitive Fornjotnr, whom some authorities identify with Ymir. According to this version of the myth, Fornjotnr had three sons: Hler, the sea; Kari, the air; and Loki, fire. These three divinities, the first gods, formed the oldest trinity, and their respective descendants were the sea giants Mimir, Gymir, and Grendel, the storm giants Thiassi, Thrym, and Beli, and the giants of fire and death, such as the Fenris wolf and Hel.

As all the royal dynasties claimed descent from some mythical being, the Merovingians asserted that their first progenitor was a sea giant, who rose out of the waves in the form of an ox, and surprised the queen while she was walking alone on the seashore, compelling her to become his wife. She gave birth to a son named Meroveus, the founder of the first dynasty of Frankish kings.

Many stories have already been told about the most important giants. They reappear in many of the later myths

and fairy-tales, and manifest, after the introduction of
Christianity, a peculiar dislike to the sound of church bells
and the singing of monks and nuns.

The Scandinavians relate, in this connection, that in the
days of Olaf the Saint a giant called Senjemand, dwelt on the
Island of Senjen, and he was greatly incensed because a nun
on the Island of Grypto daily sang her morning hymn. This
giant fell in love with a beautiful maiden called Juterna-
jesta, and it was long ere he could find courage to propose
to her. When at last he made his halting request, the fair
damsel scornfully rejected him, declaring that he was far too
old and ugly for her taste.

In his anger at being thus scornfully refused, the giant
swore vengeance, and soon after he shot a great flint arrow
from his bow at the maiden, who dwelt eighty miles away.
Another lover, Torge, also a giant, seeing her peril and
wishing to protect her, flung his hat at the speeding arrow.
This hat was a thousand feet high and proportionately broad
and thick, nevertheless the arrow pierced the headgear,
falling short, however, of its aim. Senjemand, seeing that
he had failed, and fearing the wrath of Torge, mounted his
steed and prepared to ride off as quickly as possible; but the
sun, rising just then above the horizon, turned him into
stone, together with the arrow and Torge's hat, the huge
pile being known as the Torghatten mountain. The people
still point to an obelisk which they say is the stone arrow;
to a hole in the mountain, 289 feet high and 88 feet wide,
which they say is the aperture made by the arrow in its flight
through the hat; and to the horseman on Senjen Island,
apparently riding a colossal steed and drawing the folds of

his wide cavalry cloak closely about him. As for the nun whose singing had so disturbed Senjemand, she was petrified too, and never troubled any one with her psalmody again.

Another legend relates that one of the mountain giants, annoyed by the ringing of church bells more than fifty miles away, once caught up a huge rock, which he hurled at the sacred building. Fortunately it fell short and broke in two. Ever since then, the peasants say that the trolls come on Christmas Eve to raise the largest piece of stone upon golden pillars, and to dance and feast beneath it. A lady, wishing to know whether this tale were true, once sent her groom to the place. The trolls came forward and hospitably offered him a drink from a horn mounted in gold and ornamented with runes. Seizing the horn, the groom flung its contents away and dashed off with it at a mad gallop, closely pursued by the trolls, from whom he escaped only by passing through a stubble field and over running water. Some of their number visited the lady on the morrow to claim this horn, and when she refused to part with it they laid a curse upon her, declaring that her castle would be burned down every time the horn should be removed. The prediction has thrice been fulfilled, and now the family guard the relic with superstitious care. A similar drinking vessel, obtained in much the same fashion by the Oldenburg family, is exhibited in the collection of the King of Denmark.

The giants were not supposed to remain stationary, but were said to move about in the darkness, sometimes transporting masses of earth and sand, which they dropped here and there. The sandhills in northern Germany and Denmark were supposed to have been thus formed.

A North Frisian tradition relates that the giants possessed a colossal ship, called Mannigful, which constantly cruised about in the Atlantic Ocean. Such was the size of this vessel that the captain was said to patrol the deck on horseback, while the rigging was so extensive and the masts so high that the sailors who went up as youths came down as gray-haired men, having rested and refreshed themselves in rooms fashioned and provisioned for that purpose in the huge blocks and pulleys.

By some mischance it happened that the pilot once directed the immense vessel into the North Sea, and wishing to return to the Atlantic as soon as possible, yet not daring to turn in such a small space, he steered into the English Channel. Imagine the dismay of all on board when they saw the passage growing narrower and narrower the farther they advanced. When they came to the narrowest spot, between Calais and Dover, it seemed barely possible that the vessel, drifting along with the current, could force its way through. The captain, with laudable presence of mind, promptly bade his men soap the sides of the ship, and to lay an extra-thick layer on the starboard, where the rugged cliffs of Dover rose threateningly. These orders were no sooner carried out than the vessel entered the narrow space, and, thanks to the captain's precaution, it slipped safely through. The rocks of Dover scraped off so much soap, however, that ever since they have been particularly white, and the waves dashing against them still have an unusually foamy appearance.

This exciting experience was not the only one through which the Mannigful passed, for we are told that it once, nobody knows how, penetrated into the Baltic Sea, where, the water not being deep enough to keep the vessel afloat, the captain ordered all the ballast to be thrown overboard. The material thus cast on either side of the vessel into the sea formed the two islands of Bornholm and Christiansoë.

In Thuringia and in the Black Forest the stories of the giants are legion, and one of the favourites with the peasants is that about Ilse, the lovely daughter of the giant of the Ilsenstein. She was so charming that far and wide she was known as the Beautiful Princess Ilse, and was wooed by many knights, of whom she preferred the Lord of Westerburg. But her father did not at all approve of her consorting with a mere mortal, and forbade her to see her lover. Princess Ilse was wilful, however, and in spite of her sire's prohibition she daily visited her lover. The giant, exasperated by her persistency and disobedience, finally stretched out his huge hands and, seizing the rocks, tore a great gap between the height where he dwelt and the castle of Westerburg. Upon this, Princess Ilse, going to the cleft which parted her from her lover, recklessly flung herself over the precipice into the raging flood beneath, and was there changed into a bewitching undine. She dwelt in the limpid waters for many a year, appearing from time to time to exercise her fascinations upon mortals, and even, it is said, captivating the affections of the Emperor Henry, who paid frequent visits to her cascade. Her last appearance, according to popular belief, was at Pentecost, a hundred years ago; and the natives have not yet ceased to look for the beautiful princess, who is said still to haunt the stream and to wave her white arms to entice travellers into the cool spray of the waterfall.

The giants inhabited all the earth before it was given to mankind, and it was only with reluctance that they made way for the human race, and retreated into the waste and barren parts of the country, where they brought up their families in strict seclusion. Such was the ignorance of their offspring, that a young giantess, straying from home, once came to an inhabited valley, where for the first time in her life she saw a farmer ploughing on the hillside. Deeming him a pretty plaything, she caught him up with his team, and thrusting them into her apron, she gleefully carried them home to exhibit to her father. But the giant immediately bade her carry peasant and horses back to the place where she had found them, and when she had done so he sadly explained that the creatures whom she took for mere playthings, would eventually drive the giant folk away, and become masters of the earth.

## THE DWARFS

*You are the grey, grey Troll,*
*With the great green eyes,*
*But I love you, grey, grey Troll –*
*You are so wise!*
**Robert Buchanan, The Legend of the Little Fay**

**E**arlier we saw how the black elves, dwarfs, or Svart-alfar, were bred like maggots in the flesh of the slain giant Ymir. The gods, perceiving these tiny, unformed creatures creeping in and out, gave them form and features, and they became known as dark elves, on account of their swarthy complexions. These small beings were so homely, with their dark skin, green eyes, large heads, short legs, and crow's feet, that they were enjoined to hide underground, being commanded never to show themselves during the daytime lest they should be turned into stone. Although less powerful than the gods, they were far more intelligent than men, and as their knowledge was boundless and extended even to the future, gods and men were equally anxious to question them.

The dwarfs were also known as trolls, kobolds, brownies, goblins, pucks, or Huldra folk, according to the country where they dwelt.

These little beings could transport themselves with marvellous celerity from one place to another, and they loved to conceal themselves behind rocks, when they would mischievously repeat the last words of conversations overheard from such hiding-places. Owing to this well-known trick, the echoes were called dwarfs' talk, and people fancied that the reason why the makers of such sounds were never seen was because each dwarf was the proud possessor of a tiny red cap which made the wearer invisible. This cap was called Tarnkappe, and without it the dwarfs dared not appear above the surface of the earth after sunrise for fear of being petrified. When wearing it they were safe from this peril.

Helva, daughter of the Lord of Nesvek, was loved by Esbern Snare, whose suit, however, was rejected by the proud father with the scornful words: "When thou shalt build at Kallundborg a stately church, then will I give thee Helva to wife."

Now Esbern, although of low estate, was proud of heart, even as the lord, and he determined, come what might, to find a way to win his coveted bride. So off he strode to a troll in Ullshoi Hill, and effected a bargain whereby the troll undertook to build a fine church, on completion of which Esbern was to tell the builder's name or forfeit his eyes and heart.

Night and day the troll wrought on, and as the building took shape, sadder grew Esbern Snare. He listened at the crevices of the hill by night; he watched during the day; he wore himself to a shadow by anxious thought; he besought the elves to aid him. All to no purpose. Not a sound did he hear, not a thing did he see, to suggest the name of the builder.

Meantime, rumour was busy, and the fair Helva, hearing of the evil compact, prayed for the soul of the unhappy man.

Time passed until one day the church lacked only one pillar, and worn out by black despair, Esbern sank exhausted upon a bank, whence he heard the troll hammering the last stone in the quarry underground. "Fool that I am," he said bitterly, "I have builded my tomb."

Just then he heard a light footstep, and looking up, he beheld his beloved. "Would that I might die in thy stead," said she, through her tears, and with that Esbern confessed how that for love of her he had imperilled eyes and heart and soul.

Then fast as the troll hammered underground, Helva prayed beside her lover, and the prayers of the maiden prevailed over the spell of the troll, for suddenly Esbern caught the sound of a troll-wife singing to her infant, bidding it be comforted, for that, on the morrow, Father Fine would return bringing a mortal's eyes and heart.

Sure of his victim, the troll hurried to Kallundborg with the last stone. "Too late, Fine!" quoth Esbern, and at the word, the troll vanished with his stone, and it is said that the peasants heard at night the sobbing of a woman underground, and the voice of the troll loud with blame.

The dwarfs, as well as the elves, were ruled by a king, who, in various countries of northern Europe, was known as Andvari, Alberich, Elbegast, Gondemar, Laurin, or Oberon. He dwelt in a magnificent subterranean palace, studded with the gems which his subjects had mined from the bosom of the earth, and, besides untold riches and the Tarnkappe, he owned a magic ring, an invincible sword, and a belt of strength. At his command the little men, who were very clever smiths, would fashion marvellous jewels or weapons, which their ruler would bestow upon favourite mortals.

We have already seen how the dwarfs fashioned Sif's golden hair, the ship Skidbladnir, the point of Odin's spear Gungnir, the ring Draupnir, the golden-bristled boar Gullin-bursti, the hammer Miolnir, and Freyia's golden necklace Brisinga-men. They are also said to have made the magic girdle which Spenser describes in his poem of the "Faerie Queene," – a girdle which was said to have the power of revealing whether its wearer were virtuous or a hypocrite.

The dwarfs also manufactured the mythical sword Tyrfing, which could cut through iron and stone, and which they gave to Angantyr. This sword, like Frey's, fought of its own accord, and could not be sheathed, after it was once drawn, until it had tasted blood. Angantyr was so proud of this weapon that he had it buried with him; but his daughter Hervor visited his tomb at midnight, recited magic spells, and forced him to rise from his grave to give her the precious blade. She wielded it bravely, and it eventually became the property of another of the Northern heroes.

Another famous weapon, which according to tradition was forged by the dwarfs in Eastern lands, was the sword Angurvadel which Frithiof received as a portion of his inheritance from his fathers. Its hilt was of hammered gold, and the blade was inscribed with runes which were dull until it was brandished in war, when they flamed red as the comb of the fighting-cock.

The dwarfs were generally kind and helpful; sometimes they kneaded bread, ground flour, brewed beer, performed countless household tasks, and harvested and threshed the grain for the farmers. If ill-treated, however, or turned to ridicule, these little creatures would forsake the house and never come back again. When the old gods ceased to be worshipped in the Northlands, the dwarfs withdrew entirely from the country, and a ferryman related how he had been hired by a mysterious personage to ply his boat back and forth across the river one night, and at every trip his vessel was so heavily laden with invisible passengers that it nearly sank. When his night's work was over, he received a rich reward, and his employer informed him that he had carried the dwarfs across the river, as they were leaving the country for ever in consequence of the unbelief of the people.

According to popular superstition, the dwarfs, in envy of man's taller stature, often tried to improve their race by winning human wives or by stealing unbaptized children, and substituting their own offspring for the human mother to nurse. These dwarf babies were known as changelings, and were recognisable by their puny and wizened forms. To recover possession of her own babe, and to rid herself of the changeling, a woman was obliged either to brew beer in egg-shells or to grease the soles of the child's feet and hold them so near the flames that, attracted by their offspring's distressed cries, the dwarf parents would hasten to claim their own and return the stolen child.

The troll women were said to have the power of changing themselves into Maras or nightmares, and of tormenting any one they pleased; but if the victim succeeded in stopping up the hole through which a Mara made her ingress into his room, she was entirely at his mercy, and he could even force her to wed him if he chose to do so. A wife thus obtained was sure to remain as long as the opening through which she had entered the house was closed, but if the plug were removed, either by accident or design, she immediately effected her escape and never returned.

Naturally, traditions of the little folk abound everywhere throughout the North, and many places are associated with their memory. The well-known Peaks of the Trolls (Trold-Tindterne) in Norway are said to be the scene of a conflict between two bands of trolls, who in the eagerness of combat omitted to note the approach of sunrise, with the result that they were changed into the small points of rock which stand up noticeably upon the crests of the mountain.

Some writers have ventured a conjecture that the dwarfs so often mentioned in the ancient sagas and fairy-tales were real beings, probably the Phœnician miners, who, working the coal, iron, copper, gold, and tin mines of England, Norway, Sweden, etc., took advantage of the simplicity and credulity of the early inhabitants to make them believe that they belonged to a supernatural race and always dwelt underground, in a region which was called Svart-alfa-heim, or the home of the black elves.

## THE ELVES

*Every elf and fairy sprite*
*Hop as light as bird from brier;*
*And this ditty after me*
*Sing, and dance it trippingly.*
**William Shakespeare, A Midsummer Night's Dream**

**Besides the dwarfs** there was another numerous class of tiny creatures called Lios-alfar, light or white elves, who inhabited the realms of air between heaven and earth, and were gently governed by the genial god Frey from his palace in Alf-heim. They were lovely, beneficent beings, so pure and innocent that, according to some authorities, their name was derived from the same root as the Latin word "white" (albus), which, in a modified form, was given to the snow-covered Alps, and to Albion (England), because of her white chalk cliffs which could be seen afar.

The elves were so small that they could flit about unseen while they tended the flowers, birds, and butterflies; and as they were passionately fond of dancing, they often glided down to earth on a moonbeam, to dance on the green. Holding one another by the hand, they would dance in circles, thereby making the "fairy rings," which were to be discerned by the deeper green and greater luxuriance of the grass which their little feet had pressed.

If any mortal stood in the middle of one of these fairy rings he could, according to popular belief in England, see the fairies and enjoy their favour; but the Scandinavians and Teutons vowed that the unhappy man must die. In illustration of this superstition, a story is told of how Sir Olaf, riding off to his wedding, was enticed by the fairies into their ring. On the morrow, instead of a merry marriage, his friends witnessed a triple funeral, for his mother and bride also died when they beheld his lifeless corpse.

These elves, who in England were called fairies or fays, were also enthusiastic musicians, and delighted especially in a certain air known as the elf-dance, which was so irresistible that no one who heard it could refrain from dancing. If a mortal, overhearing the air, ventured to reproduce it, he suddenly found himself incapable of stopping and was forced to play on and on until he died of exhaustion, unless he were deft enough to play the tune backwards, or some one charitably cut the strings of his violin. His hearers, who were forced to dance as long as the tones continued, could only stop when they ceased.

In medieval times, the will-o'-the-wisps were known in the North as elf lights, for these tiny sprites were supposed to mislead travellers; and popular superstition held that the Jack-o'-lanterns were the restless spirits of murderers forced against their will to return to the scene of their crimes. As they nightly walked thither, it is said that they doggedly repeated with every step, "It is right;" but as they returned they sadly reiterated, "It is wrong."

In Scandinavia and Germany sacrifices were offered to the elves to make them propitious. These sacrifices consisted of some small animal, or of a bowl of honey and milk, and were known as Alf-blot. They were quite common until the missionaries taught the people that the elves were mere demons, when they were transferred to the angels, who were long entreated to befriend mortals, and propitiated by the same gifts.

Many of the elves were supposed to live and die with the trees and plants which they tended, but these moss, wood, or tree maidens, while remarkably beautiful when seen in front, were hollow like a trough when viewed from behind. They appear in many of the popular tales, but almost always as benevolent and helpful spirits, for they were anxious to do good to mortals and to cultivate friendly relations with them.

No discussion of the elves is complete without a few words about Oberon. There are stories told far and wide of the fairy king Oberon, and his delicate queen Titiania. Oberon was so exquisitely handsome, that mortals were drawn into his fairy world after just one glance at his elegant profile. In every country across the world, there was a sense of unease on the eve of Midsummer, for this is when the fairies congregate around Oberon and Titiana and dance. Fairy dances are a magical thing, and their music is so compelling that all who hear it find it irresistible. But once a human, or indeed a

god, succumbs to the fairy music, and begins to dance, he
will be damned to do so until the end of his days, when he
will die of an exhaustion like none other.

Oberon was also very powerful, and his tricks above
ground became legend throughout many lands. With the
passing of the dwarfs, humankind had no help with their
work, and the little folk were no longer considered to be a
blessed addition to a household. Many believe that Oberon
harnessed the powers of Frey when he fell, and used them
beneath the earth to set up a kingdom of fairies which
was a complex and commanding as Asgard had once been.
With his strength, and his overwhelming beauty, he was
considered by man to be nothing more than a demon.

In Scandinavia the elves, both light and dark, were
worshipped as household divinities, and their images were
carved on the doorposts. The Norsemen, who were driven
from home by the tyranny of Harald Harfager in 874, took
their carved doorposts with them upon their ships. Similar
carvings, including images of the gods and heroes, decorated
the pillars of their high seats which they also carried away.
The exiles showed their trust in their gods by throwing these
wooden images overboard when they neared the Icelandic
shores and settling where the waves carried the posts, even
if the spot scarcely seemed the most desirable. "Thus they
carried with them the religion, the poetry, and the laws
of their race, and on this desolate volcanic island they
kept these records unchanged for hundreds of years, while
other Teutonic nations gradually became affected by their
intercourse with Roman and Byzantine Christianity." These
records, carefully collected by Saemund the learned, form

the Elder Edda, the most precious relic of ancient Northern literature, without which we should know comparatively little of the religion of our forefathers.

The sagas relate that the first settlements in Greenland and Vinland were made in the same way, – the Norsemen piously landing wherever their household gods drifted ashore.

# THE SIGURD SAGA

*There was a dwelling of Kings ere the world was waxen old;*
*Dukes were the door-wards there, and the*
*roofs were thatched with gold:*
*Earls were the wrights that wrought it,*
*and silver nailed its doors;*
*Earls' wives were the weaving-women,*
*queens' daughters strewed its floors,*
*And the masters of its song-craft were*
*the mightiest men that cast*
*The sails of the storm of battle adown the bickering blast.*
**William Morris, The Story of Sigurd the Volsung**

While the first part of the *Elder Edda* consists of a collection of alliterative poems describing the creation of the world, the adventures of the gods, their eventual downfall, and gives a complete exposition of the Northern code of ethics, the second part comprises a series of heroic lays describing the exploits of the Volsung family, and especially of their chief representative, Sigurd, the favourite hero of the North.

These lays form the basis of the great Scandinavian epic, the *Volsunga Saga*, and have supplied not only the materials for the

*Nibelungenlied*, the German epic, and for countless folk tales, but also for Wagner's celebrated operas, *The Rhinegold*, *Valkyr*, *Siegfried*, and *The Dusk of the Gods*. In England, William Morris has given them the form which they will probably retain in our literature, and it is from his great epic poem that almost all the quotations in this section are taken in preference to extracts from the *Edda*.

## THE SWORD IN THE BRANSTOCK

*So sweet his speaking sounded, so wise his words did seem,*
  *That moveless all men sat there, as in a happy dream*
  *We stir not lest we waken; but there his speech had end*
  *And slowly down the hall-floor, and outward did he wend;*
  *And none would cast him a question or follow on his ways,*
    *For they knew that the gift was Odin's,*
    *a sword for the world to praise.*
**William Morris, The Story of Sigurd the Volsung**

The story of the Volsungs begins with Sigi, a son of Odin, a powerful man, and generally respected, until he killed a man from motives of jealousy, the latter having slain more game when they were out hunting together. In consequence of this crime, Sigi was driven from his own land and declared an outlaw. But it seems that he had not entirely forfeited Odin's favour, for the god now provided him with a well-equipped vessel, together with a number of brave followers, and promised that victory should ever attend him.

Thus aided by Odin, the raids of Sigi became a terror to
his foes, and in the end he won the glorious empire of the
Huns and for many years reigned as a powerful monarch.
But in extreme old age his fortune changed, Odin forsook
him, his wife's kindred fell upon him, and he was slain in a
treacherous encounter.

His death was soon avenged, however, for Rerir, his
son, returning from an expedition upon which he had
been absent from the land at the time, put the murderers
to death as his first act upon mounting the throne. The
rule of Rerir was marked by every sign of prosperity,
but his dearest wish, a son to succeed him, remained
unfulfilled for many a year. Finally, however, Frigga
decided to grant his constant prayer, and to vouchsafe
the heir he longed for. She accordingly despatched her
swift messenger Gna, or Liod, with a miraculous apple,
which she dropped into his lap as he was sitting alone
on the hillside. Glancing upward, Rerir recognised the
emissary of the goddess, and joyfully hastened home to
partake of the apple with his wife. The child who in
due time was born under these favourable auspices was a
handsome little lad. His parents called him Volsung, and
while he was still a mere infant they both died, and the
child became ruler of the land.

Years passed and Volsung's wealth and power ever
increased. He was the boldest leader, and rallied many
brave warriors around him. Full oft did they drink his mead
underneath the Branstock, a mighty oak, which, rising in
the middle of his hall, pierced the roof and overshadowed
the whole house.

Ten stalwart sons were born to Volsung, and one daughter, Signy, came to brighten his home. So lovely was this maiden that when she reached marriageable age many suitors asked for her hand, among whom was Siggeir, King of the Goths, who finally obtained Volsung's consent, although Signy had never seen him.

When the wedding-day came, and the bride beheld her destined husband she shrank in dismay, for his puny form and lowering glances contrasted sadly with her brothers' sturdy frames and open faces. But it was too late to withdraw – the family honour was at stake – and Signy so successfully concealed her dislike that none save her twin brother Sigmund suspected with what reluctance she became Siggeir's wife.

While the wedding feast was in progress, and when the merry-making was at its height, the entrance to the hall was suddenly darkened by the tall form of a one-eyed man, closely enveloped in a mantle of cloudy blue. Without vouchsafing word or glance to any in the assembly, the stranger strode to the Branstock and thrust a glittering sword up to the hilt in its great bole. Then, turning slowly round, he faced the awe-struck and silent assembly, and declared that the weapon would be for the warrior who could pull it out of its oaken sheath, and that it would assure him victory in every battle. The words ended, he then passed out as he had entered, and disappeared, leaving a conviction in the minds of all that Odin, king of the gods, had been in their midst.

Volsung was the first to recover the power of speech, and, waiving his own right first to essay the feat, he invited Siggeir to make the first attempt to draw the divine weapon out of the tree-trunk. The bridegroom anxiously tugged and strained, but the sword remained firmly embedded in the oak and he resumed his seat, with an air of chagrin. Then Volsung tried, with the same result. The weapon was evidently not intended for either of them, and the young Volsung princes were next invited to try their strength.

The nine eldest sons were equally unsuccessful; but when Sigmund, the tenth and youngest, laid his firm young hand upon the hilt, the sword yielded easily to his touch, and he triumphantly drew it out as though it had merely been sheathed in its scabbard.

Nearly all present were gratified at the success of the young prince; but Siggeir's heart was filled with envy, and he coveted possession of the weapon. He offered to purchase it from his young brother-in-law, but Sigmund refused to part with it at any price, declaring that it was clear that the weapon had been intended for him to wear. This refusal so offended Siggeir that he secretly resolved to exterminate the proud Volsungs, and to secure the divine sword at the same time that he indulged his hatred towards his new kinsmen.

Concealing his chagrin, however, he turned to Volsung and cordially invited him to visit his court a month later, together with his sons and kinsmen. The invitation was immediately accepted, and although Signy, suspecting evil, secretly sought her father while her husband slept, and implored him to retract his promise and stay at home, he would not consent to withdraw his plighted word and so exhibit fear.

## SIGGEIR'S TREACHERY

*And men say that Signy wept*
*When she left that last of her kindred:*
*yet wept she never more*
*Amid the earls of Siggeir, and as lovely as before*
*Was her face to all men's deeming: nor*
*aught it changed for ruth,*
*Nor for fear nor any longing; and no man said for sooth*
*That she ever laughed thereafter till the*
*day of her death was come.*
**William Morris, The Story of Sigurd the Volsung**

**A** few weeks after the return of the bridal couple, therefore, Volsung's well-manned vessels arrived within sight of Siggeir's shores. Signy had been keeping anxious watch, and when she perceived them she hastened down to the beach to implore her kinsmen not to land, warning them that her husband had treacherously planned an ambush, whence they could not escape alive. But Volsung and his sons, whom no peril could daunt, calmly bade her return to her husband's palace, and donning their arms they boldly set foot ashore.

It befell as Signy had said, for on their way to the palace the brave little troop fell into Siggeir's ambush, and, although they fought with heroic courage, they were so borne down by the superior number of their foes that Volsung was slain and all his sons were made captive. The young men were led bound into the presence of the cowardly

Siggeir, who had taken no part in the fight, and Sigmund was forced to relinquish his precious sword, after which he and his brothers were condemned to death.

Signy, hearing the cruel sentence, vainly interceded for her brothers: all she could obtain by her prayers and entreaties was that they should be chained to a fallen oak in the forest, to perish of hunger and thirst if the wild beasts should spare them. Then, lest she should visit and succour her brothers, Siggeir confined his wife in the palace, where she was closely guarded night and day.

Every morning early Siggeir himself sent a messenger into the forest to see whether the Volsungs were still living, and every morning the man returned saying a monster had come during the night and had devoured one of the princes, leaving nothing but his bones. At last, when none but Sigmund remained alive, Signy thought of a plan, and she prevailed on one of her servants to carry some honey into the forest and smear it over her brother's face and mouth.

When the wild beast came that night, attracted by the smell of the honey, it licked Sigmund's face, and even thrust its tongue into his mouth. Clinching his teeth upon it, Sigmund, weak and wounded as he was, held on to the animal, and in its frantic struggles his bonds gave way, and he succeeded in slaying the prowling beast who had devoured his brothers. Then he vanished into the forest, where he remained concealed until the king's messenger had come as usual, and until Signy, released from captivity, came speeding to the forest to weep over her kinsmen's remains.

Seeing her intense grief, and knowing that she had not participated in Siggeir's cruelty, Sigmund stole out of his place of concealment and comforted her as best he could. Together they then buried the whitening bones, and Sigmund registered a solemn oath to avenge his family's wrongs. This vow was fully approved by Signy, who, however, bade her brother bide a favourable time, promising to send him aid. Then the brother and sister sadly parted, she to return to her distasteful palace home, and he to a remote part of the forest, where he built a tiny hut and plied the craft of a smith.

Siggeir now took possession of the Volsung kingdom, and during the next few years he proudly watched the growth of his eldest son, whom Signy secretly sent to her brother when he was ten years of age, that Sigmund might train up the child to help him to obtain vengeance if he should prove worthy. Sigmund reluctantly accepted the charge; but as soon as he had tested the boy he found him deficient in physical courage, so he either sent him back to his mother, or, as some versions relate, slew him.

Some time after this Signy's second son was sent into the forest for the same purpose, but Sigmund found him equally lacking in courage. Evidently none but a pure-blooded Volsung would avail for the grim work of revenge, and Signy, realising this, resolved to commit a crime.

Her resolution taken, she summoned a beautiful young witch, and exchanging forms with her, she sought the depths of the dark forest and took shelter in Sigmund's hut. The Volsung did not penetrate his sister's disguise. He deemed her nought but the gypsy she seemed, and being soon won by her coquetry, he made her his wife. Three days later she disappeared from the hut, and, returning to the palace, she resumed her own form, and when she next gave birth to a son, she rejoiced to see in his bold glance and strong frame the promise of a true Volsung hero.

## THE STORY OF SINFIOTLI

*For here, the tale of the elders doth men a marvel to wit,*
*That such was the shaping of Sigmund*
*among all earthly kings,*
*That unhurt he handled adders and other deadly things,*
*And might drink unscathed of venom:*
*but Sinfiotli was so wrought*
*That no sting of creeping creatures*
*would harm his body aught.*
**William Morris, The Story of Sigurd the Volsung**

**W**hen Sinfiotli, as the child was called, was ten years of age, she herself made a preliminary test of his courage by sewing his garment to his skin, and then suddenly snatching it off, and as the brave boy did not so much as wince, but laughed aloud, she confidently sent him to the forest hut. Sigmund speedily prepared his usual test, and ere leaving the hut one day he bade Sinfiotli take meal from a certain sack, and knead it and bake some bread. On returning home, Sigmund asked whether his orders had been carried out. The lad replied by showing the bread, and when closely questioned he artlessly confessed that he had been obliged to knead into the loaf a great adder which was hidden in the meal. Pleased to see that the boy, for whom he felt a strange affection, had successfully stood the test which had daunted his brothers, Sigmund bade him refrain from eating of the loaf, for although he was proof against the bite of a reptile, he could not, like his mentor, taste poison unharmed.

Sigmund now began patiently to teach Sinfiotli all that a warrior of the North should know, and the two soon became inseparable companions. One day while ranging the forest together they came to a hut, where they found two men sound asleep. Near by hung two wolf-skins, which suggested immediately that the strangers were werewolves, whom a cruel spell prevented from bearing their natural form save for a short space at a time. Prompted by curiosity, Sigmund and Sinfiotli donned the wolf-skins, and they were soon, in the guise of wolves, rushing through the forest, slaying and devouring all that came in their way.

Such were their wolfish passions that soon they attacked each other, and after a fierce struggle Sinfiotli, the younger and weaker, fell dead. This catastrophe brought Sigmund to his senses, and he hung over his murdered companion in despair.

While thus engaged he saw two weasels come out of the forest and attack each other fiercely until one lay dead. The victor then sprang into the thicket, to return with a leaf, which it laid upon its companion's breast. Then was seen a marvellous thing, for at the touch of the magic herb the dead beast came back to life. A moment later a raven flying overhead dropped a similar leaf at Sigmund's feet, and he, understanding that the gods wished to help him, laid it upon Sinfiotli, who was at once restored to life.

In dire fear lest they might work each other further mischief, Sigmund and Sinfiotli now crept home and patiently waited until the time of their release should come. To their great relief the skins dropped off on the ninth night, and they hastily flung them into the fire, where they were entirely consumed, and the spell was broken for ever.

Sigmund now confided the story of his wrongs to Sinfiotli, who swore that, although Siggeir was his father (for neither he nor Sigmund knew the secret of his birth), he would aid him in his revenge. At nightfall, therefore, he accompanied Sigmund to the king's hall, and they entered unseen, concealing themselves in the cellar, behind the huge vats of beer. Here they were discovered by Signy's two youngest children, who, while playing with golden rings, which rolled into the cellar, came suddenly upon the men in ambush.

They loudly proclaimed their discovery to their father and his guests, but, before Siggeir and his men could take up arms, Signy took both children, and dragging them into the cellar bade her brother slay the little traitors. This Sigmund utterly refused to do, but Sinfiotli struck off their heads ere he turned to fight against the assailants, who were now closing in upon them.

In spite of all efforts Sigmund and his brave young companion soon fell into the hands of the Goths, whereupon Siggeir sentenced them to be buried alive in the same mound, with a stone partition between them so that they could neither see nor touch each other. The prisoners were accordingly confined in their living grave, and their foes were about to place the last stones on the roof, when

Signy drew near, bearing a bundle of straw, which she was allowed to throw at Sinfiotli's feet, for the Goths fancied that it contained only a few provisions which would prolong his agony without helping him to escape.

When all was still, Sinfiotli undid the sheaf, and great was his joy when he found instead of bread the sword which Odin had given to Sigmund. Knowing that nothing could dull or break the keen edge of this fine weapon, Sinfiotli thrust it through the stone partition, and, aided by Sigmund, he succeeded in cutting an opening, and in the end both effected their escape through the roof.

As soon as they were free, Sigmund and Sinfiotli returned to the king's hall, and piling combustible materials around it, they set fire to the mass. Then stationing themselves on either side of the entrance, they prevented all but the women from passing through. They loudly adjured Signy to escape ere it was too late, but she did not desire to live, and so coming to the entrance for a last embrace she found opportunity to whisper the secret of Sinfiotli's birth, after which she sprang back into the flames and perished with the rest.

The long-planned vengeance for the slaughter of the Volsungs having thus been carried out, Sigmund, feeling that nothing now detained him in the land of the Goths, set sail with Sinfiotli and returned to Hunaland, where he was warmly welcomed to the seat of power under the shade of his ancestral tree, the mighty Branstock. When his authority was fully established, Sigmund married Borghild, a beautiful princess, who bore him two sons, Hamond and Helgi. The latter was visited by the Norns as he lay in his cradle, and they promised him sumptuous entertainment in Valhalla when his earthly career should be ended.

Northern kings generally entrusted their sons' upbringing to a stranger, for they thought that so they would be treated with less indulgence than at home. Accordingly Helgi was fostered by Hagal, and under his care the young prince became so fearless that at the age of fifteen he ventured alone into the hall of Hunding, with whose race his family was at feud. Passing through the hall unmolested and unrecognised, he left an insolent message, which so angered Hunding that he immediately set out in pursuit of the bold young prince, whom he followed to the dwelling of Hagal. Helgi would then have been secured but that meanwhile he had disguised himself as a servant-maid, and was busy grinding corn as if this were his wonted occupation. The invaders marvelled somewhat at the maid's tall stature and brawny arms, nevertheless they departed without suspecting that they had been so near the hero whom they sought.

Having thus cleverly escaped, Helgi joined Sinfiotli, and collecting an army, the two young men marched boldly against the Hundings, with whom they fought a great battle, over which the Valkyrs hovered, waiting to convey the slain to Valhalla. Gudrun, one of the battle-maidens, was so struck by the courage which Helgi displayed, that she openly sought him and promised to be his wife. Only one of the Hunding race, Dag, remained alive, and he was allowed to go free after promising not to endeavour to avenge his kinsmen's death. This promise was not kept, however, and Dag, having obtained possession of Odin's spear Gungnir, treacherously slew Helgi with it. Gudrun, who in the meantime had fulfilled her promise to become his wife, wept many tears at his death, and laid a solemn curse upon his murderer; then, hearing from one of her maids that her slain husband kept calling for her from the depths of the tomb, she fearlessly entered the mound at night and tenderly inquired why he called and why his wounds continued to bleed after death. Helgi answered that he could not rest happy because of her grief, and declared that for every tear she shed a drop of his blood must flow.

To appease the spirit of her beloved husband, Gudrun from that time ceased to weep, but they did not long remain separated; for soon after the spirit of Helgi had ridden over Bifrost and entered Valhalla, to become leader of the Einheriar, he was joined by Gudrun who, as a Valkyr once more, resumed her loving tendance of him. When at Odin's command she left his side for scenes of human strife, it was to seek new recruits for the army which her lord was to lead into battle when Ragnarok, the twilight of the gods, should come.

Sinfiotli, Sigmund's eldest son, also met an early death; for, having slain in a quarrel the brother of Borghild, she determined to poison him. Twice Sinfiotli detected the attempt and told his father that there was poison in his cup. Twice Sigmund, whom no venom could injure, drained the bowl; and when Borghild made a third attempt, he bade Sinfiotli let the wine flow through his beard. Mistaking the meaning of his father's words, Sinfiotli forthwith drained the cup, and fell lifeless to the ground, for the poison was of the most deadly kind.

Speechless with grief, Sigmund tenderly raised his son's body in his arms, and strode out of the hall and down to the shore, where he deposited his precious burden in a skiff which an old one-eyed boatman brought at his call. He would fain have stepped aboard also, but ere he could do so the boatman pushed off and the frail craft was soon lost to sight. The bereaved father then slowly wended his way home, taking comfort from the thought that Odin himself had come to claim the young hero and had rowed away with him "out into the west."

## THE BIRTH OF SIGURD

*'I have wrought for the Volsungs truly,*
*and yet have I known full well*
*That a better one than I am shall bear the tale to tell:*
*And for him shall these shards be smithied:*
*and he shall be my son,*
*To remember what I have forgotten*
*and to do what I left undone.'*
**William Morris, The Story of Sigurd the Volsung**

**S**igmund deposed Borghild as his wife and queen in punishment for this crime, and when he was very old he sued for the hand of Hiordis, a fair young princess, daughter of Eglimi, King of the Islands. This young maiden had many suitors, among others King Lygni of Hunding's race, but so great was Sigmund's fame that she gladly accepted him and became his wife. Lygni, the discarded suitor, was so angry at this decision, that he immediately collected a great army and marched against his successful rival, who, though overpowered by superior numbers, fought with the courage of despair.

From the depths of a thicket which commanded the field of battle, Hiordis and her maid anxiously watched the progress of the strife. They saw Sigmund pile the dead around him, for none could stand against him, until at last a tall, one-eyed warrior suddenly appeared, and the press of battle gave way before the terror of his presence.

Without a moment's pause the new champion aimed a fierce blow at Sigmund, which the old hero parried with his sword. The shock shattered the matchless blade, and although the strange assailant vanished as he had come, Sigmund was left defenceless and was soon wounded unto death by his foes.

As the battle was now won, and the Volsung family all slain, Lygni hastened from the battlefield to take possession of the kingdom and force the fair Hiordis to become his wife. As soon as he had gone, however, the beautiful young queen crept from her hiding-place in the thicket, and sought the spot where Sigmund lay all but dead. She caught the stricken hero to her breast in a last passionate embrace, and then listened tearfully while he bade her gather the fragments of his sword and carefully treasure them for their son whom he foretold was soon to be born, and who was destined to avenge his father's death and to be far greater than he.

While Hiordis was mourning over Sigmund's lifeless body, her handmaiden suddenly warned her of the approach of a band of vikings. Retreating into the thicket once more, the two women exchanged garments, after which Hiordis bade the maid walk first and personate the queen, and they went thus to meet the viking Elf (Helfrat or Helferich). Elf received the women graciously, and their story of the battle so excited his admiration for Sigmund that he caused the remains of the slain hero to be reverentially removed to a suitable spot, where they were interred with all due ceremony. He then offered the queen and her maid a safe asylum in his hall, and they gladly accompanied him over the seas.

As he had doubted their relative positions from the first, Elf took the first opportunity after arriving in his kingdom to ask a seemingly idle question in order to ascertain the truth. He asked the pretended queen how she knew the hour had come for rising when the winter days were short and there was no light to announce the coming of morn, and she replied that, as she was in the habit of drinking milk ere she fed the cows, she always awoke thirsty. When the same question was put to the real Hiordis, she answered, with as little reflection, that she knew it was morning because at that hour the golden ring which her father had given her grew cold on her hand.

The suspicions of Elf having thus been confirmed, he offered marriage to the pretended handmaiden, Hiordis, promising to cherish her infant son, a promise which he nobly kept. When the child was born Elf himself sprinkled him with water – a ceremony which our pagan ancestors scrupulously observed – and bestowed upon him the name of Sigurd. As he grew up he was treated as the king's own son, and his education was entrusted to Regin, the wisest of men, who knew all things, his own fate not even excepted, for it had been revealed to him that he would fall by the hand of a youth.

Under this tutor Sigurd grew daily in wisdom until few could surpass him. He mastered the smith's craft, and the art of carving all manner of runes; he learned languages, music, and eloquence; and, last but not least, he became a doughty warrior whom none could subdue. When he had reached manhood Regin prompted him to ask the king for a war-horse, a request which was immediately granted, and Gripir, the stud-keeper, was bidden to allow him to choose from the royal stables the steed which he most fancied.

On his way to the meadow where the horses were at pasture, Sigurd met a one-eyed stranger, clad in grey and blue, who accosted the young man and bade him drive the horses into the river and select the one which could breast the tide with least difficulty.

Sigurd received the advice gladly, and upon reaching the meadow he drove the horses into the stream which flowed on one side. One of the number, after crossing, raced round the opposite meadow; and, plunging again into the river, returned to his former pasture without showing any signs of fatigue. Sigurd therefore did not hesitate to select this horse, and he gave him the name of Grane or Greyfell. The steed was a descendant of Odin's eight-footed horse Sleipnir, and besides being unusually strong and indefatigable, was as fearless as his master.

One winter day while Regin and his pupil were sitting by the fire, the old man struck his harp, and, after the manner of the Northern scalds, sang or recited in the following tale, the story of his life.

## THE TREASURE OF THE DWARF KING

*That gold*
*Which the dwarf possessed*
*Shall to two brothers*
*Be cause of death,*
*And to eight princes,*
*Of dissension.*
*From my wealth no one*
*Shall good derive.*

**Benjamin Thorpe, Saemund's Edda**

**H**reidmar, king of the dwarf folk, was the father of three sons. Fafnir, the eldest, was gifted with a fearless soul and a powerful arm; Otter, the second, with snare and net, and the power of changing his form at will; and Regin, the youngest, with all wisdom and deftness of hand. To please the avaricious Hreidmar, this youngest son fashioned for him a house lined with glittering gold and flashing gems, and this was guarded by Fafnir, whose fierce glances and Aegis helmet none dared encounter.

Now it came to pass that Odin, Hoenir, and Loki once came in human guise, upon one of their wonted expeditions to test the hearts of men, unto the land where Hreidmar dwelt.

As the gods came near to Hreidmar's dwelling, Loki perceived an otter basking in the sun. This was none other than the dwarf king's second son, Otter, who now succumbed to Loki's usual love of destruction. Killing the unfortunate creature he flung its lifeless body over his shoulders, thinking it would furnish a good dish when meal time came.

Loki then hastened after his companions, and entering Hreidmar's house with them, he flung his burden down upon the floor. The moment the dwarf king's glance fell upon the seeming otter, he flew into a towering rage, and ere they could offer effective resistance the gods found themselves lying bound, and they heard Hreidmar declare that never should they recover their liberty until they could satisfy his thirst for gold by giving him of that precious substance enough to cover the skin of the otter inside and out.

As the otter-skin developed the property of stretching itself to a fabulous size, no ordinary treasure could suffice to cover it, and the plight of the gods, therefore, was a very bad one. The case, however, became a little more hopeful when Hreidmar consented to liberate one of their number. The emissary selected was Loki, who lost no time in setting off to the waterfall where the dwarf Andvari dwelt, in order that he might secure the treasure there amassed.

In spite of diligent search, however, Loki could not find the dwarf, until, perceiving a salmon sporting in the foaming waters, it occurred to him that the dwarf might have assumed this shape. Borrowing Ran's net he soon caught the fish, and learned, as he had suspected, that it was Andvari. Finding that there was nothing else for it, the dwarf now reluctantly brought forth his mighty treasure and surrendered it all, including the Helmet of Dread and a hauberk of gold, reserving only a ring which was gifted with miraculous powers, and which, like a magnet, attracted the precious ore. But the greedy Loki, catching sight of it, wrenched it from off the dwarf's finger and departed laughing, while his victim hurled angry curses after him, declaring that the ring would ever prove its possessor's bane and would cause the death of many.

On arriving at Hreidmar's house, Loki found the mighty treasure none too great, for the skin became larger with every object placed upon it, and he was forced to throw in the ring Andvaranaut (Andvari's loom), which he had intended to retain, in order to secure the release of himself and his companions. Andvari's curse of the gold soon began to operate. Fafnir and Regin both coveted a share, while Hriedmar gloated over his treasure night and day, and would not part with an item of it. Fafnir the invincible, seeing at last that he could not otherwise gratify his lust, slew his father, and seized the whole of the treasure, then, when Regin came to claim a share he drove him scornfully away and bade him earn his own living.

Thus exiled, Regin took refuge among men, to whom he taught the arts of sowing and reaping. He showed them how to work metals, sail the seas, tame horses, yoke beasts of burden, build houses, spin, weave, and sew – in short, all the industries of civilised life, which had hitherto been unknown. Years elapsed, and Regin patiently bided his time, hoping that some day he would find a hero strong enough to avenge his wrongs upon Fafnir, whom years of gloating over his treasure had changed into a horrible dragon, the terror of Gnîtaheid (Glittering Heath), where he had taken up his abode.

His story finished, Regin turned suddenly to the attentive Sigurd, saying he knew that the young man could slay the dragon if he wished, and inquiring whether he were ready to aid him to avenge his wrongs.

Sigurd immediately assented, on the condition, however, that the curse should be assumed by Regin, who, also, in order to fitly equip the young man for the coming fight, should forge him a sword, which no blow could break. Twice Regin fashioned a marvellous weapon, but twice Sigurd broke it to pieces on the anvil. Then Sigurd bethought him of the broken fragments of Sigmund's weapon which were treasured by his mother, and going to Hiordis he begged these from her; and either he or Regin forged from them a blade so strong that it divided the great anvil in two without being dinted, and whose temper was such that it neatly severed some wool floating gently upon the stream.

## THE FIGHT WITH THE DRAGON

*Then all sank into silence, and the son of Sigmund stood*
*On the torn and furrowed desert by*
*the pool of Fafnir's blood,*
*And the Serpent lay before him, dead, chilly, dull, and grey;*
*And over the Glittering Heath fair shone the sun and the day*
**William Morris, The Story of Sigurd the Volsung**

**Sigurd now went upon a farewell visit** to Gripir, who, knowing the future, foretold every event in his coming career; after which he took leave of his mother, and accompanied by Regin set sail for the land of his fathers, vowing to slay the dragon when he had fulfilled his first duty, which was to avenge the death of Sigmund.

On his way to the land of the Volsungs a most marvellous sight was seen, for there came a man walking on the waters. Sigurd straightway took him on board his dragon ship, and the stranger, who gave his name as Feng or Fiöllnir, promised favourable winds. Also he taught Sigurd how to distinguish auspicious omens. In reality the old man was Odin or Hnikar, the wave-stiller, but Sigurd did not suspect his identity.

Sigurd was entirely successful in his descent upon Lygni, whom he slew, together with many of his followers. He then departed from his reconquered kingdom and returned with Regin to slay Fafnir. Together they rode through the mountains, which ever rose higher and higher before them, until they came to a great tract of desert which Regin said was the haunt of Fafnir. Sigurd now rode on alone until he met a one-eyed stranger, who bade him dig trenches in the middle of the track along which the dragon daily dragged his slimy length to the river to quench his thirst, and to lie in wait in one of these until the monster passed over him, when he could thrust his sword straight into its heart.

Sigurd gratefully followed this counsel, and was rewarded with complete success, for as the monster's loathsome folds rolled overhead, he thrust his sword upward into its left breast, and as he sprang out of the trench the dragon lay gasping in the throes of death.

Regin had prudently remained at a distance until all danger was past, but seeing that his foe was slain, he now came up. He was fearful lest the young hero should claim a reward, so he began to accuse him of having murdered his kin, but, with feigned magnanimity, he declared that instead of requiring life for life, in accordance with the custom of the North, he would consider it sufficient atonement if Sigurd would cut out the monster's heart and roast it for him on a spit.

Sigurd was aware that a true warrior never refused satisfaction of some kind to the kindred of the slain, so he agreed to the seemingly small proposal, and immediately prepared to act as cook, while Regin dozed until the meat was ready. After an interval Sigurd touched the roast to ascertain whether it were tender, but burning his fingers severely, he instinctively thrust them into his mouth to allay the smart. No sooner had Fafnir's blood thus touched his lips than he discovered, to his utter surprise, that he could understand the songs of the birds, many of which were already gathering round the carrion. Listening attentively, he found that they were telling how Regin meditated mischief against him, and how he ought to slay the old man and take the gold, which was his by right of conquest, after which he ought to partake of the heart and blood of the dragon. As this coincided with his own wishes, he slew the evil old man with a thrust of his sword and proceeded to eat and drink as the birds had suggested, reserving a small portion of Fafnir's heart for future consumption. He then wandered off in search of the mighty hoard, and, after donning the Helmet of Dread, the hauberk of gold, and the ring Andvaranaut, and loading Greyfell with as much gold as he could carry, he sprang to the saddle and sat listening eagerly to the birds' songs to know what his future course should be.

## THE SLEEPING WARRIOR MAIDEN

*On the fell I know*
*A warrior maid to sleep;*
*Over her waves*
*The linden's bane:*
*Ygg whilom stuck*
*A sleep-thorn in the robe*
*Of the maid who*
*Would heroes choose.*
**Benjamin Thorpe, Lay of Fafnir**

Soon he heard of a warrior maiden fast asleep on a mountain and surrounded by a glittering barrier of flames, through which only the bravest of men could pass to arouse her.

This adventure was the very thing for Sigurd, and he set off at once. The way lay through trackless regions, and the journey was long and cheerless, but at length he came to the Hindarfiall in Frankland, a tall mountain whose cloud-wreathed summit seemed circled by fiery flames.

Sigurd rode up the mountain side, and the light grew more and more vivid as he proceeded, until when he had neared the summit a barrier of lurid flames stood before him. The fire burned with a roar which would have daunted the heart of any other, but Sigurd remembered the words of the birds, and without a moment's hesitation he plunged bravely into its very midst.

The threatening flames having now died away, Sigurd pursued his journey over a broad tract of white ashes, directing his course to a great castle, with shield-hung walls. The great gates stood wide open, and Sigurd rode through them unchallenged by warders or men at arms. Proceeding cautiously, for he feared some snare, he at last came to the centre of the courtyard, where he saw a recumbent form cased in armour. Sigurd dismounted from his steed and eagerly removed the helmet, when he started with surprise to behold, instead of a warrior, the face of a most beautiful maiden.

All his efforts to awaken the sleeper were vain, however, until he had removed her armour, and she lay before him in pure-white linen garments, her long hair falling in golden waves around her. Then as the last fastening of her armour gave way, she opened wide her beautiful eyes, which met the rising sun, and first greeting with rapture the glorious spectacle, she turned to her deliverer, and the young hero and the maiden loved each other at first sight.

The maiden now proceeded to tell Sigurd her story. Her name was Brunhild, and according to some authorities she was the daughter of an earthly king whom Odin had raised to the rank of a Valkyr. She had served him faithfully for a long while, but once had ventured to set her own wishes above his, giving to a younger and therefore more attractive opponent the victory which Odin had commanded for another.

In punishment for this act of disobedience, she had been deprived of her office and banished to earth, where Allfather decreed she should wed like any other member of her sex. This sentence filled Brunhild's heart with dismay, for she greatly feared lest it might be her fate to mate with a coward, whom she would despise. To quiet these apprehensions,

Odin took her to Hindarfiall or Hindfell, and touching her with the Thorn of Sleep, that she might await in unchanged youth and beauty the coming of her destined husband, he surrounded her with a barrier of flame which none but a hero would venture through.

From the top of Hindarfiall, Brunhild now pointed out to Sigurd her former home, at Lymdale or Hunaland, telling him he would find her there whenever he chose to come and claim her as his wife; and then, while they stood on the lonely mountain top together, Sigurd placed the ring Andvaranaut upon her finger, in token of betrothal, swearing to love her alone as long as life endured.

According to some authorities, the lovers parted after thus plighting their troth; but others say that Sigurd soon sought out and wedded Brunhild, with whom he lived for a while in perfect happiness until forced to leave her and his infant daughter Aslaug. This child, left orphaned at three years of age, was fostered by Brunhild's father, who, driven away from home, concealed her in a cunningly fashioned harp, until reaching a distant land he was murdered by a peasant couple for the sake of the gold they supposed it to contain. Their surprise and disappointment were great indeed when, on breaking the instrument open, they found a beautiful little girl, whom they deemed mute, as she would not speak a word. Time passed, and the child, whom they had trained as a drudge, grew to be a beautiful maiden, and she won the affection of a passing viking, Ragnar Lodbrog, King of the Danes, to whom she told her tale. The viking sailed away to other lands to fulfil the purposes of his voyage, but when a year had passed, during which time he won much glory, he came back and carried away Aslaug as his bride.

In continuation of the story of Sigurd and Brunhild, however, we are told that the young man went to seek adventures in the great world, where he had vowed, as a true hero, to right the wrong and defend the fatherless and oppressed.

## THE NIBLUNGS

> *But the heart was changed in Sigurd;*
> *as though it ne'er had been*
> *His love of Brynhild perished as he*
> *gazed on the Niblung Queen:*
> *Brynhild's beloved body was e'en as a wasted hearth,*
> *No more for bale or blessing, for plenty or for dearth*
> **William Morris, The Story of Sigurd the Volsung**

In the course of his wanderings, Sigurd came to the land of the Niblungs, the land of continual mist, where Giuki and Grimhild were king and queen. The latter was specially to be feared, as she was well versed in magic lore, and could weave spells and concoct marvellous potions which had power to steep the drinker in temporary forgetfulness and compel him to yield to her will.

The king and queen had three sons, Gunnar, Högni, and Guttorm, who were brave young men, and one daughter, Gudrun, the gentlest as well as the most beautiful of maidens.

All welcomed Sigurd most warmly, and Giuki invited him to tarry awhile. The invitation was very agreeable after his long wanderings, and Sigurd was glad to stay and share the pleasures and occupations of the Niblungs. He accompanied them to war, and so distinguished himself by his valour, that he won the admiration of Grimhild and she resolved to secure him as her daughter's husband. One day, therefore, she brewed one of her magic potions, and when he had partaken of it at the hand of Gudrun, he utterly forgot Brunhild and his plighted troth, and all his love was diverted unto the queen's daughter.

Although there was not wanting a vague fear that he had forgotten some event in the past which should rule his conduct, Sigurd asked for and obtained Gudrun's hand, and their wedding was celebrated amid the rejoicings of the people, who loved the young hero very dearly. Sigurd gave his bride some of Fafnir's heart to eat, and the moment she had tasted it her nature was changed, and she began to grow cold and silent to all except him. To further cement his alliance with the two eldest Giukings (as the sons of Giuki were called) Sigurd entered the "doom ring" with them, and the three young men cut a sod which was placed upon a shield, beneath which they stood while they bared and slightly cut their right arms, allowing their blood to mingle in the fresh earth. Then, when they had sworn eternal friendship, the sod was replaced.

But although Sigurd loved his wife and felt a true fraternal affection for her brothers, he could not lose his haunting sense of oppression, and was seldom seen to smile as radiantly as of old. Giuki had now died, and his eldest son, Gunnar, ruled in his stead. As the young king was unwedded, Grimhild, his mother, besought him to take a wife, suggesting that none seemed more worthy to become Queen of the Niblungs than Brunhild, who, it was reported, sat in a golden hall surrounded by flames, whence she had declared she would issue only to marry the warrior who would dare brave the fire for her sake.

Gunnar immediately prepared to seek this maiden, and strengthened by one of his mother's magic potions, and encouraged by Sigurd, who accompanied him, he felt confident of success. But when on reaching the summit of the mountain he would have ridden into the fire, his steed drew back affrighted and he could not induce him to advance a step. Seeing that his companion's steed did not show signs of fear, he asked him of Sigurd; but although Greyfell allowed Gunnar to mount, he would not stir because his master was not on his back.

Now as Sigurd carried the Helmet of Dread, and Grimhild had given Gunnar a magic potion in case it should be needed, it was possible for the companions to exchange their forms and features, and seeing that Gunnar could not penetrate the flaming wall Sigurd proposed to assume the appearance of Gunnar and woo the bride for him. The king was greatly disappointed, but as no alternative offered he dismounted, and the necessary exchange was soon effected. Then Sigurd mounted Greyfell in the semblance of his companion, and this time the steed showed not the least hesitation, but leaped into the flames at the first touch on his bridle, and soon brought his rider to the castle, where, in the great hall, sat Brunhild. Neither recognised the other:

Sigurd because of the magic spell cast over him by Grimhild; Brunhild because of the altered appearance of her lover.

The maiden shrank in disappointment from the dark-haired intruder, for she had deemed it impossible for any but Sigurd to ride through the flaming circle. But she advanced reluctantly to meet her visitor, and when he declared that he had come to woo her, she permitted him to take a husband's place at her side, for she was bound by solemn injunction to accept as her spouse him who should thus seek her through the flames.

Three days did Sigurd remain with Brunhild, and his bright sword lay bared between him and his bride. This singular behaviour aroused the curiosity of the maiden, wherefore Sigurd told her that the gods had bidden him celebrate his wedding thus.

When the fourth morning dawned, Sigurd drew the ring Andvaranaut from Brunhild's hand, and, replacing it by another, he received her solemn promise that in ten days' time she would appear at the Niblung court to take up her duties as queen and faithful wife.

The promise given, Sigurd again passed out of the palace, through the ashes, and joined Gunnar, with whom, after he had reported the success of his venture, he hastened to exchange forms once more. The warriors then turned their steeds homeward, and only to Gudrun did Sigurd reveal the secret of her brother's wooing, and he gave her the fatal ring, little suspecting the many woes which it was destined to occasion.

True to her promise, Brunhild appeared ten days later, and solemnly blessing the house she was about to enter, she greeted Gunnar kindly, and allowed him to conduct her to the great hall, where sat Sigurd beside Gudrun. The Volsung looked up at that moment and as he encountered Brunhild's reproachful eyes Grimhild's spell was broken and the past came back in a flood of bitter recollection. It was too late, however: both were in honour bound, he to Gudrun and she to Gunnar, whom she passively followed to the high seat, to sit beside him as the scalds entertained the royal couple with the ancient lays of their land.

The days passed, and Brunhild remained apparently indifferent, but her heart was hot with anger, and often did she steal out of her husband's palace to the forest, where she could give vent to her grief in solitude.

Meanwhile, Gunnar perceived the cold indifference of his wife to his protestations of affection, and began to have jealous suspicions, wondering whether Sigurd had honestly told the true story of the wooing, and fearing lest he had taken advantage of his position to win Brunhild's love. Sigurd alone continued the even tenor of his way, striving against none but tyrants and oppressors, and cheering all by his kindly words and smile.

On a day the queens went down together to the Rhine to bathe, and as they were entering the water Gudrun claimed precedence by right of her husband's courage. Brunhild refused to yield what she deemed her right, and a quarrel ensued, in the course of which Gudrun accused her sister-in-law of not having kept her faith, producing the ring Andvaranaut in support of her charge. The sight of the fatal ring in the hand of her rival crushed Brunhild, and she fled homeward, and lay in speechless grief day after day, until all thought she must die. In vain did Gunnar and the members of the royal family seek her in turn and implore her to speak; she would not utter a word until Sigurd came and inquired the cause of her unutterable grief. Then, like a long-pent-up stream, her love and anger burst forth, and she overwhelmed the hero with reproaches, until his heart so swelled with grief for her sorrow that the tight bands of his strong armour gave way.

Words had no power to mend that woeful situation, and Brunhild refused to heed when Sigurd offered to repudiate Gudrun, saying, as she dismissed him, that she would not be faithless to Gunnar. The thought that two living men had called her wife was unendurable to her pride, and the next time her husband sought her presence she implored him to put Sigurd to death, thus increasing his jealousy and suspicion.

He refused to deal violently with Sigurd, however, because of their oath of good fellowship, and so she turned to Högni for aid. He, too, did not wish to violate his oath, but he induced Guttorm, by means of much persuasion and one of Grimhild's potions, to undertake the dastardly deed.

## THE DEATH OF SIGURD

'Mourn not, O Gudrun, this stroke is the last of ill;
Fear leaveth the House of the Niblungs
on this breaking of the morn;
Mayst thou live, O woman beloved, unforsaken, unforlorn!'
**William Morris, The Story of Sigurd the Volsung**

**A**ccordingly, in the dead of night, Guttorm stole into Sigurd's chamber, weapon in hand; but as he bent over the bed he saw Sigurd's bright eyes fixed upon him, and fled precipitately. Later on he returned and the scene was repeated; but towards morning, stealing in for the third time, he found the hero asleep, and traitorously drove his spear through his back.

Although wounded unto death, Sigurd raised himself in bed, and seizing his renowned sword which hung beside him, he flung it with all his remaining strength at the flying murderer, cutting him in two as he reached the door. Then, with a last whispered farewell to the terrified Gudrun, Sigurd sank back and breathed his last.

Sigurd's infant son was slain at the same time, and poor Gudrun mourned over her dead in silent, tearless grief; while Brunhild laughed aloud, thereby incurring the wrath of Gunnar, who repented, too late, that he had not taken measures to avert the dastardly crime.

The grief of the Niblungs found expression in the public funeral celebration which was shortly held. A mighty pyre was erected, to which were brought precious hangings, fresh flowers, and glittering arms, as was the custom for the burial of a prince; and as these sad preparations took shape, Gudrun was the object of tender solicitude from the women, who, fearing lest her heart would break, tried to open the flood-gate of her tears by recounting the bitterest sorrows they had known, one telling of how she too had lost all she held dear. But these attempts to make her weep were utterly vain, until at length they laid her husband's head in her lap, bidding her kiss him as if he were still alive; then her tears began to flow in torrents.

The reaction soon set in for Brunhild also; her resentment was all forgotten when she saw the body of Sigurd laid on the pyre, arrayed as if for battle in burnished armour, with the Helmet of Dread at his head, and accompanied by his steed, which was to be burned with him, together with several of his faithful servants who would not survive his loss. She withdrew to her apartment, and after distributing her possessions among her handmaidens, she donned her richest array, and stabbed herself as she lay stretched upon her bed.

The tidings soon reached Gunnar, who came with all haste to his wife and just in time to receive her dying injunction to lay her beside the hero she loved, with the glittering, unsheathed sword between them, as it had lain when he had wooed her by proxy. When she had breathed her last, these wishes were faithfully executed, and her body was burned with Sigurd's amid the lamentations of all the Niblungs.

In Richard Wagner's story of "The Ring" Brunhild's end is more picturesque. Mounted on her steed, as when she led the battle-maidens at the command of Odin, she rode into the flames which leaped to heaven from the great funeral pyre, and passed for ever from the sight of men.

The death scene of Sigurd (Siegfried) is far more powerful in the Nibelungenlied. In the Teutonic version his treacherous assailant lures him from a hunting party in the forest to quench his thirst at a brook, where he thrusts him through the back with a spear. His body was thence borne home by the hunters and laid at his wife's feet.

Gudrun, still inconsolable, and loathing the kindred who had treacherously robbed her of all joy in life, fled from her father's house and took refuge with Elf, Sigurd's foster father, who, after the death of Hiordis, had married Thora, the daughter of King Hakon. The two women became great friends, and here Gudrun tarried several years, employing herself in embroidering upon tapestry the great deeds of Sigurd, and watching over her little daughter Swanhild, whose bright eyes reminded her vividly of the husband whom she had lost.

## ATLI, KING OF THE HUNS

'And now, O mighty Atli, I have seen the Niblung's wreck,
And the feet of the faint-heart dastard
have trodden Gunnar's neck;
And if all be little enough, and the Gods begrudge me rest,
Let me see the heart of Högni cut
quick from his living breast,
And laid on the dish before me: and
then shall I tell of the Gold,
And become thy servant, Atli, and
my life at thy pleasure hold.'
**William Morris, The Story of Sigurd the Volsung**

In the meantime, Atli, Brunhild's brother, who was now King of the Huns, had sent to Gunnar to demand atonement for his sister's death; and to satisfy his claims Gunnar had promised that when her years of widowhood had been accomplished he would give him Gudrun's hand in marriage. Time passed, and Atli clamoured for the fulfilment of his promise, wherefore the Niblung brothers, with their mother Grimhild, went to seek the long-absent princess, and by the aid of the magic potion administered by Grimhild they succeeded in persuading Gudrun to leave little Swanhild in Denmark and to become Atli's wife in the land of the Huns.

Nevertheless, Gudrun secretly detested her husband, whose avaricious tendencies were extremely repugnant to her; and even the birth of two sons, Erp and Eitel, did not console her for the death of her loved ones and the absence of Swanhild. Her thoughts were continually of the past, and she often spoke of it, little suspecting that her descriptions of the wealth of the Niblungs had excited Atli's greed, and that he was secretly planning some pretext for seizing it.

Atli at last decided to send Knefrud or Wingi, one of his servants, to invite the Niblung princes to visit his court, intending to slay them when he should have them in his power; but Gudrun, fathoming this design, sent a rune message to her brothers, together with the ring Andvaranaut, around which she had twined a wolf's hair. On the way, however, the messenger partly effaced the runes, thus changing their meaning; and when he appeared before the Niblungs, Gunnar accepted the invitation, in spite of Högni's and Grimhild's warnings, and an ominous dream of Glaumvor, his second wife.

Before departing, however, Gunnar was prevailed upon to bury secretly the great Niblung hoard in the Rhine, and he sank it in a deep hole in the bed of the river, the position of which was known to the royal brothers only, who took a solemn oath never to reveal it.

In martial array the royal band then rode out of the city of the Niblungs, which they were never again to see, and after many adventures they entered the land of the Huns, and arrived at Atli's hall, where, finding that they had been foully entrapped, they slew the traitor Knefrud, and prepared to sell their lives as dearly as possible.

Gudrun hastened to meet them with tender embraces, and, seeing that they must fight, she grasped a weapon and loyally aided them in the terrible massacre which ensued. After the first onslaught, Gunnar kept up the spirits of his followers by playing on his harp, which he laid aside only when the assaults were renewed. Thrice the brave Niblungs resisted the assault of the Huns, until all save Gunnar and Högni had perished, and the king and his brother, wounded, faint, and weary, fell into the hands of their foes, who cast them, securely bound, into a dungeon to await death.

Atli had prudently abstained from taking any active part in the fight, and he now had his brothers-in-law brought in turn before him, promising them freedom if they would reveal the hiding-place of the golden hoard; but they proudly kept silence, and it was only after much torture that Gunnar spake, saying that he had sworn a solemn oath never to reveal the secret as long as Högni lived. At the same time he declared that he would believe his brother dead only when his heart was brought to him on a platter.

Urged by greed, Atli gave immediate orders that Högni's heart should be brought; but his servants, fearing to lay hands on such a grim warrior, slew the cowardly scullion

Hialli. The trembling heart of this poor wretch called forth contemptuous words from Gunnar, who declared that such a timorous organ could never have belonged to his fearless brother. Atli again issued angry commands, and this time the unquivering heart of Högni was produced, whereupon Gunnar, turning to the monarch, solemnly swore that since the secret now rested with him alone it would never be revealed.

Livid with anger, the king bade his servants throw Gunnar, with hands bound, into a den of venomous snakes; but this did not daunt the reckless Niblung, and, his harp having been flung after him in derision, he calmly sat in the pit, harping with his toes, and lulling to sleep all the reptiles save one only. It was said that Atli's mother had taken the form of this snake, and that she it was who now bit him in the side, and silenced his triumphant song for ever.

To celebrate his triumph, Atli now ordered a great feast, commanding Gudrun to be present to wait upon him. At this banquet he ate and drank heartily, little suspecting that his wife had slain both his sons, and had served up their roasted hearts and their blood mixed with wine in cups made of their skulls. After a time the king and his guests became intoxicated, when Gudrun, according to one version of the story, set fire to the palace, and as the drunken men were aroused, too late to escape, she revealed what she had done, and first stabbing her husband, she calmly perished in the flames with the Huns. Another version relates, however, that she murdered Atli with Sigurd's sword, and having placed his body on a ship, which she sent adrift, she cast herself into the sea and was drowned.

According to a third and very different version, Gudrun was not drowned, but was borne by the waves to the land where Jonakur was king. There she became his wife, and the mother of three sons, Sörli, Hamdir, and Erp. She recovered possession, moreover, of her beloved daughter Swanhild, who, in the meantime, had grown into a beautiful maiden of marriageable age.

Swanhild became affianced to Ermenrich, King of Gothland, who sent his son, Randwer, and one of his servants, Sibich, to escort the bride to his kingdom. Sibich was a traitor, and as part of a plan to compass the death of the royal family that he might claim the kingdom, he accused Randwer of having tried to win his young stepmother's affections. This accusation so roused the anger of Ermenrich that he ordered his son to be hanged, and Swanhild to be trampled to death under the feet of wild horses. The beauty of this daughter of Sigurd and Gudrun was such, however, that even the wild steeds could not be induced to harm her until she had been hidden from their sight under a great blanket, when they trod her to death under their cruel hoofs.

Upon learning the fate of her beloved daughter, Gudrun called her three sons to her side, and girding them with armour and weapons against which nothing but stone could prevail, she bade them depart and avenge their murdered sister, after which she died of grief, and was burned on a great pyre.

The three youths, Sörli, Hamdir, and Erp, proceeded to Ermenrich's kingdom, but ere they met their foes, the two eldest, deeming Erp too young to assist them, taunted him with his small size, and finally slew him. Sörli and Hamdir then attacked Ermenrich, cut off his hands and feet, and would have slain him but for a one-eyed stranger who suddenly appeared and bade the bystanders throw stones at the young men. His orders were immediately carried out, and Sörli and Hamdir soon fell slain under the shower of stones, which, as we have seen, alone had power to injure them.

## INTERPRETATION OF THE SAGA

*Ye have heard of Sigurd aforetime,*
*how the foes of God he slew;*
*How forth from the darksome desert the*
*Gold of the Waters he drew;*
*How he wakened Love on the Mountain,*
*and wakened Brynhild the Bright,*
*And dwelt upon Earth for a season*
*and shone in all men's sight.*
*Ye have heard of the Cloudy People,*
*and the dimming of the day,*
*And the latter world's confusion, and Sigurd gone away.*
**William Morris, The Story of Sigurd the Volsung**

This story of the Volsungs is supposed by some authorities to be a series of sun myths, in which Sigi, Rerir, Volsung, Sigmund, and Sigurd in turn personify the glowing orb of day. They are all armed with invincible swords, the sunbeams, and all travel through the world fighting against their foes, the demons of cold and darkness. Sigurd, like

Balder, is beloved of all; he marries Brunhild, the dawn maiden, whom he finds in the midst of flames, the flush of morn, and parts from her only to find her again when his career is ended. His body is burned on the funeral pyre, which, like Balder's, represents either the setting sun or the last gleam of summer, of which he too is a type. The slaying of Fafnir symbolises the destruction of the demon of cold or darkness, who has stolen the golden hoard of summer or the yellow rays of the sun.

According to other authorities, this Saga is based upon history. Atli is the cruel Attila, the "Scourge of God," while Gunnar is Gundicarius, a Burgundian monarch, whose kingdom was destroyed by the Huns, and who was slain with his brothers in 451. Gudrun is the Burgundian princess Ildico, who slew her husband on her wedding-night, as has already been related, using the glittering blade which had once belonged to the sun-god to avenge her murdered kinsmen.

# THE STORY OF FRITHIOF

*Jocund they grew, in guileless glee;*
*Young Frithiof was the sapling tree;*
*In budding beauty by his side,*
*Sweet Ingeborg, the garden's pride.*
**Henry Wadsworth Longfellow, Frithiof Saga**

**P**robably no writer of the nineteenth century did so much to awaken interest in the literary treasures of Scandinavia as Bishop Esaias Tegnér, whom a Swedish author characterised as, "that mighty Genie who organises even disorder."

Tegnér's "Frithiof Saga" has been translated once at least into every European tongue, and some twenty times into English and German. Goethe spoke of the work with the greatest enthusiasm, and the tale, which gives a matchless picture of the life of our heathen ancestors in the North, drew similar praise from Longfellow, who considered it to be one of the most remarkable productions of his century.

Although Tegnér has chosen for his theme the Frithiof saga only, we find that that tale is the sequel to the older but less interesting Thorsten saga, of which we give here a very brief outline, merely to enable the reader to understand clearly every allusion in the more modern poem.

As is so frequently the case with these ancient tales, the story begins with Haloge (Loki), who came north with Odin, and began to reign over northern Norway, which from him was called Halogaland. According to Northern mythology, this god had two lovely daughters. They were carried off by bold suitors, who, banished from the mainland by Haloge's curses and magic spells, took refuge with their newly won wives upon neighbouring islands.

## THE BIRTH OF VIKING

*Then the Scald took his harp and sang,*
*And loud through the music rang*
*The sound of that shining word;*
*And the harp-strings a clangour made,*
*As if they were struck with the blade*
*Of a sword.*

**Henry Wadsworth Longfellow, Saga of King Olaf**

**T**hus it happened that Haloge's grandson, Viking, was born upon the island of Bornholm, in the Baltic Sea, where he dwelt until he was fifteen, and where he became the biggest and strongest man of his time. Rumours of his valour finally reached Hunvor, a Swedish princess, who was oppressed by the attentions of a gigantic suitor whom none dared drive away, and she sent for Viking to deliver her.

Thus summoned, the youth departed, after having received from his father a magic sword named Angurvadel, whose blows would prove fatal even to a giant like the suitor of Hunvor. A "holmgang," as a duel was termed in the North, ensued as soon as the hero arrived upon the scene, and Viking, having slain his antagonist, could have married the princess had it not been considered disgraceful for a Northman to marry before he was twenty.

To beguile the time of waiting for his promised bride, Viking set out in a well-manned dragon ship; and cruising about the Northern and Southern seas, he met with countless adventures. During this time he was particularly persecuted by the kindred of the giant he had slain, who were adepts in magic, and they brought upon him innumerable perils by land and sea.

Aided and abetted by his bosom friend, Halfdan, Viking escaped every danger, slew many of his foes, and, after rescuing Hunvor, whom, in the meantime, the enemy had carried off to India, he settled down in Sweden. His friend, faithful in peace as well as in war, settled near him, and married also, choosing for wife Ingeborg, Hunvor's attendant.

The saga now describes the long, peaceful winters, when the warriors feasted and listened to the tales of scalds, rousing themselves to energetic efforts only when returning spring again permitted them to launch their dragon ships and set out once more upon their piratical expeditions.

In the old story the scalds relate with great gusto every phase of attack and defence during cruise and raid, and describe every blow given and received, dwelling with satisfaction upon the carnage and lurid flames which envelop both enemies and ships in common ruin. A fierce fight is often an earnest of future friendship, however, and we are told that Halfdan and Viking, having failed to conquer Njorfe, a foeman of mettle, sheathed their swords after a most obstinate struggle, and accepted their enemy as a third link in their close bond of friendship.

On returning home from one of these customary raids, Viking lost his beloved wife; and, entrusting her child, Ring, to the care of a foster father, after undergoing a short period of mourning, the brave warrior married again. This time his marital bliss was more lasting, for the saga tells that his second wife bore him nine stalwart sons.

Njorfe, King of Uplands, in Norway, also rejoiced in a family of nine brave sons. Now, although their fathers were united in bonds of the closest friendship, having sworn blood brotherhood according to the true Northern rites, the young men were jealous of one another, and greatly inclined to quarrel.

Notwithstanding this smouldering animosity, the youths often met; and the saga relates that they used to play ball together, and gives a description of the earliest ball game on record in the Northern annals. Viking's sons, as tall and strong as he, were inclined to be rather reckless of their opponents' welfare, and, judging from the following account, translated from the old saga, the players were often left in as sorry a condition as after a modern game.

"The next morning the brothers went to the games, and generally had the ball during the day; they pushed men and let them fall roughly, and beat others. At night three men had their arms broken, and many were bruised or maimed."

The game between Njorfe's and Viking's sons culminated in a disagreement, and one of Njorfe's sons struck one of his opponents a dangerous and treacherous blow. Prevented from taking his revenge then and there by the interference of the spectators, the injured man made a trivial excuse to return to the ground alone; and, meeting his assailant there, he slew him.

When Viking heard that one of his sons had slain one of his friend's children, he was very indignant, and mindful of his oath to avenge all Njorfe's wrongs, he banished the young murderer. The other brothers, on hearing this sentence, vowed that they would accompany the exile, and so Viking sorrowfully bade them farewell, giving his sword Angurvadel to Thorsten, the eldest, and cautioning him to remain quietly on an island in Lake Wener until all danger of retaliation on the part of Njorfe's remaining sons should be over.

The young men obeyed; but Njorfe's sons were determined to avenge their brother, and although they had no boats to convey them over the lake, they made use of a conjurer's art to bring about a great frost. Accompanied by many armed men, they then stole noiselessly over the ice to attack Thorsten and his brothers, and a terrible carnage ensued. Only two of the attacking party managed to escape, but they left, as they fancied, all their foes among the dead.

Then came Viking to bury his sons, and he found that two of them, Thorsten and Thorer, were still alive; whereupon he secretly conveyed them to a cellar beneath his dwelling, and in due time they recovered from their wounds.

Njorfe's two surviving sons soon discovered by magic arts that their opponents were not dead, and they made a second desperate but vain attempt to kill them. Viking saw that the quarrel would be incessantly renewed if his sons remained at home; so he now sent them to Halfdan, whose court they reached after a series of adventures which in many points resemble those of Theseus on his way to Athens.

When spring came round Thorsten embarked on a piratical excursion, in the course of which he encountered Jokul, Njorfe's eldest son, who, meanwhile, had taken forcible possession of the kingdom of Sogn, having killed the king, banished his heir, Belé, and changed his beautiful daughter, Ingeborg, into the similitude of an old witch.

Throughout the story Jokul is represented as somewhat of a coward, for he resorted by preference to magic when he wished to injure Viking's sons. Thus he stirred up great tempests, and Thorsten, after twice suffering shipwreck, was only saved from the waves by the seeming witch, whom he promised to marry in gratitude for her good offices. Thorsten, advised by Ingeborg, now went in search of Belé, whom he found and replaced upon his hereditary throne, having sworn eternal friendship with him. After this, the baleful spell was removed, and Ingeborg, now revealed in her native beauty, was united to Thorsten, and dwelt with him at Framnäs.

## FRITHIOF'S LOVE FOR INGEBORG

*But close behind them Frithiof goes,*
*Wrapp'd in his mantle blue;*
*His height a whole head taller rose*
*Than that of both the two.*
**G. Stephens, Frithiof Saga**

Every spring Thorsten and Belé set out together in their ships; and, upon one of these expeditions, they joined forces with Angantyr, a foe whose mettle they had duly tested, and proceeded to recover possession of a priceless treasure, a magic dragon ship named Ellida, which Aegir, god of the sea, had once given to Viking in reward for hospitable treatment, and which had been stolen from him.

The next season, Thorsten, Belé, and Angantyr conquered the Orkney Islands, which were given as a kingdom to the latter, he voluntarily pledging himself to pay a yearly tribute to Belé. Next Thorsten and Belé went in quest of a magic ring, or armlet, once forged by Völund, the smith, and stolen by Soté, a famous pirate.

This bold robber was so afraid lest some one should gain possession of the magic ring, that he had buried himself alive with it in a mound in Bretland. Here his ghost was said to keep constant watch over it, and when Thorsten entered his tomb, Belé, who waited outside, heard the sound of frightful blows given and returned, and saw lurid gleams of supernatural fire.

When Thorsten finally staggered out of the mound, pale and bloody, but triumphant, he refused to speak of the horrors he had encountered to win the coveted treasure, but often would he say, as he showed it, "I trembled but once in my life, and 'twas when I seized it!"

Thus owner of the three greatest treasures of the North, Thorsten returned home to Framnäs, where Ingeborg bore him a fine boy, Frithiof, while two sons, Halfdan and Helgé, were born to Belé. The lads played together, and were already well grown when Ingeborg, Belé's little daughter, was born, and some time later the child was entrusted to the care of Hilding, who was already Frithiof's foster father, as Thorsten's frequent absences made it difficult for him to undertake the training of his boy.

Frithiof soon became hardy and fearless under his foster father's training, and Ingeborg rapidly developed the sweetest traits of character and loveliness. Both were happiest when together; and as they grew older their childish affection daily became deeper and more intense, until Hilding, perceiving this state of affairs, bade the youth remember that he was a subject of the king, and therefore no mate for his only daughter.

These wise admonitions came too late, however, and Frithiof vehemently declared that he would win the fair Ingeborg for his bride in spite of all obstacles and his more humble origin.

Shortly after this Belé and Thorsten met for the last time, near the magnificent shrine of Balder, where the king, feeling that his end was near, had convened a solemn assembly, or Thing, of all his principal subjects, in order to present his sons Helgé and Halfdan to the people as his chosen successors. The young heirs were very coldly received on this occasion, for Helgé was of a sombre and taciturn disposition, and inclined to the life of a priest, and Halfdan was of a weak, effeminate nature, and noted for his love of pleasure rather than of war and the chase. Frithiof, who was present, and stood beside them, was the object of many admiring glances from the throng.

After giving his last instructions and counsel to his sons, and speaking kindly to Frithiof, for whom he entertained a warm regard, the old king turned to his lifelong companion, Thorsten, to take leave of him, but the old warrior declared that they would not long be parted. Belé then spoke again to his sons, and bade them erect his howe, or funeral mound, within sight of that of Thorsten, that their spirits might commune over the waters of the narrow firth which would flow between them, that so they might not be sundered even in death.

These instructions were piously carried out when, shortly after, the aged companions breathed their last; and the great barrows having been erected, the brothers, Helgé and Halfdan, began to rule their kingdom, while Frithiof, their former playmate, withdrew to his own place at Framnäs, a fertile homestead, lying in a snug valley enclosed by the towering mountains and the waters of the ever-changing firth.

But although surrounded by faithful retainers, and blessed with much wealth and the possession of the famous treasures of his hero sire, the sword Angurvadel, the Völund ring, and the matchless dragon ship Ellida, Frithiof was unhappy, because he could no longer see the fair Ingeborg daily. All his former spirits revived, however, when in the spring, at his invitation, both kings came to visit him, together with their fair sister, and once again they spent long hours in cheerful companionship. As they were thus constantly thrown together, Frithiof found opportunity to make known to Ingeborg his deep affection, and he received in return an avowal of her love.

When the visit was ended and the guests had departed, Frithiof informed his confidant and chief companion,

Björn, of his determination to follow them and openly ask for Ingeborg's hand. His ship was set free from its moorings and it swooped like an eagle over to the shore near Balder's shrine, where the royal brothers were seated in state on Belé's tomb to listen to the petitions of their subjects. Straightway Frithiof presented himself before them, and manfully made his request, adding that the old king had always loved him and would surely have granted his prayer.

Then he went on to promise lifelong fealty and the service of his strong right arm in exchange for the boon he craved.

As Frithiof ceased King Helgé rose, and regarding the young man scornfully, he said: "Our sister is not for a peasant's son; proud chiefs of the Northland may dispute for her hand, but not thou. As for thy arrogant proffer, know that I can protect my kingdom. Yet if thou wouldst be my man, place in my household mayst thou have."

Enraged at the insult thus publicly offered, Frithiof drew his invincible sword; but, remembering that he stood on a consecrated spot, he struck only at the royal shield, which fell in two pieces clashing to the ground. Then striding back to his ship in sullen silence, he embarked and sailed away angrily.

## SIGURD RING, A SUITOR

*In Balder's fane, griefs loveliest prey,*
*Sweet Ing'borg weeps the livelong day:*
*Say, can her tears unheeded fall,*
*Nor call her champion to her side?*
**Henry Wadsworth Longfellow, Frithiof Saga**

**A**fter his departure came messengers from Sigurd Ring, the aged King of Ringric, in Norway, who, having lost his wife, sent to Helgé and Halfdan to ask Ingeborg's hand in marriage. Before returning answer to this royal suitor, Helgé consulted the Vala, or prophetess, and the priests, who all declared that the omens were not in favour of the marriage. Upon this Helgé assembled his people to hear the word which the messengers were to carry to their master, but unfortunately King Halfdan gave way to his waggish humour, and made scoffing reference to the advanced age of the royal suitor. These impolitic words were reported to King Ring, and so offended him that he immediately collected an army and prepared to march against the Kings of Sogn to avenge the insult with his sword. When the rumour of his approach reached the cowardly brothers they were terrified, and fearing to encounter the foe unaided, they sent Hilding to Frithiof to implore his help.

Hilding found Frithiof playing chess with Björn, and immediately made known his errand.

While the old man was speaking Frithiof continued to play, ever and anon interjecting an enigmatical reference to the game, until at this point he said:

*"Björn; thou in vain my queen pursuest,*
*She from childhood dearest, truest!*
*She's my game's most darling piece, and*
*Come what will – I'll save my queen!"*

Hilding did not understand such mode of answering, and at length rebuked Frithiof for his indifference. Then Frithiof rose, and pressing kindly the old man's hand, he bade him tell the kings that he was too deeply offended to listen to their appeal.

Helgé and Halfdan, thus forced to fight without their bravest leader, preferred to make a treaty with Sigurd Ring, and they agreed to give him not only their sister Ingeborg, but also a yearly tribute.

While they were thus engaged at Sogn Sound, Frithiof hastened to Balder's temple, to which Ingeborg had been sent for security, and where, as Hilding had declared, he found her a prey to grief. Now although it was considered a sacrilege for man and woman to exchange a word in the sacred building, Frithiof could not forbear to console her; and, forgetting all else, he spoke to her and comforted her, quieting all her apprehensions of the gods' anger by assuring her that Balder, the good, must view their innocent passion with approving eyes, for love so pure as theirs could defile no sanctuary; and they ended by plighting their troth before the shrine of Balder.

Reassured by this reasoning, which received added strength from the voice which spoke loudly from her own heart, Ingeborg could not refuse to see and converse with Frithiof. During the kings' absence the young lovers met every day, and they exchanged love-tokens, Frithiof giving to Ingeborg Völund's arm-ring, which she solemnly promised to send back to her lover should she be compelled to break her promise to live for him alone. Frithiof lingered at Framnäs until the kings' return, when, yielding to the fond entreaties of Ingeborg the Fair, he again appeared before them, and pledged himself to free them from their thraldom to Sigurd Ring if they would only reconsider their decision and promise him their sister's hand.

## FRITHIOF BANISHED

> *Helgé on the strand*
> *Chants his wizard-spell,*
> *Potent to command*
> *Fiends of earth or hell.*
> *Gathering darkness shrouds the sky;*
> *Hark, the thunder's distant roll!*
> *Lurid lightnings, as they fly,*
> *Streak with blood the sable pole*

**Henry Wadsworth Longfellow, Frithiof Saga**

**B**ut although this offer was received with acclamation by the assembled warriors, Helgé scornfully demanded of Frithiof whether he had spoken with Ingeborg and so defiled the temple of Balder.

A shout of "Say nay, Frithiof! say nay!" broke from the ring of warriors, but he proudly answered: "I would not lie to gain Valhalla. I have spoken to thy sister, Helgé, yet have I not broken Balder's peace."

A murmur of horror passed through the ranks at this avowal, and when the harsh voice of Helgé was raised in judgment, none was there to gainsay the justice of the sentence.

This apparently was not a harsh one, but Helgé well knew that it meant death, and he so intended it.

Far westward lay the Orkney Islands, ruled by Jarl Angantyr, whose yearly tribute to Belé was withheld now that the old king lay in his cairn. Hard-fisted he was said to be, and heavy of hand, and to Frithiof was given the task of demanding the tribute face to face.

Before he sailed upon the judgment-quest, however, he once more sought Ingeborg, and implored her to elope with him to a home in the sunny South, where her happiness should be his law, and where she should rule over his subjects as his honoured wife. But Ingeborg sorrowfully refused to accompany him, saying that, since her father was no more, she was in duty bound to obey her brothers implicitly, and could not marry without their consent.

The fiery spirit of Frithiof was at first impatient under this disappointment of his hopes, but in the end his noble nature conquered, and after a heartrending parting scene, he embarked upon Ellida, and sorrowfully sailed out of the harbour, while Ingeborg, through a mist of tears, watched the sail as it faded and disappeared in the distance.

The vessel was barely out of sight when Helgé sent for two witches named Heid and Ham, bidding them by incantations to stir up a tempest at sea in which it would be impossible for even the god-given vessel Ellida to live, that so all on board should perish. The witches immediately complied; and with Helgé's aid they soon stirred up a storm the fury of which is unparalleled in history.

Unfrighted by tossing waves and whistling blasts, Frithiof sang a cheery song to reassure his terrified crew; but when the peril grew so great that his exhausted followers gave themselves up for lost, he bethought him of tribute to the goddess Ran, who ever requires gold of them who would rest in peace under the ocean wave. Taking his armlet, he hewed it with his sword and made fair division among his men.

He then bade Björn hold the rudder, and himself climbed to the mast-top to view the horizon. While perched there he descried a whale, upon which the two witches were riding the storm. Speaking to his good ship, which was gifted with power of understanding and could obey his commands, he now ran down both whale and witches, and the sea was reddened with their blood. At the same instant the wind fell, the waves ceased to threaten, and fair weather soon smiled again upon the seas.

Exhausted by their previous superhuman efforts and by the labour of baling their water-logged vessel, the men were too weak to land when they at last reached the Orkney Islands, and had to be carried ashore by Björn and Frithiof, who gently laid them down on the sand, bidding them rest and refresh themselves after all the hardships they had endured.

The arrival of Frithiof and his men, and their mode of landing, had been noted by the watchman of Angantyr, who immediately informed his master of all he had seen. The jarl exclaimed that the ship which had weathered such a gale could be none but Ellida, and that its captain was doubtless Frithiof, Thorsten's gallant son. At these words one of his Berserkers, Atlé, caught up his weapons and strode from the hall, vowing that he would challenge Frithiof, and thus satisfy himself concerning the veracity of the tales he had heard of the young hero's courage.

Although still greatly exhausted, Frithiof immediately accepted Atlé's challenge, and, after a sharp encounter with swords, in which Angurvadel was triumphant, the two champions grappled in deadly embrace. Widely is that wrestling-match renowned in the North, and well matched were the heroes, but in the end Frithiof threw his antagonist, whom he would have slain then and there had his sword been within reach. Atlé saw his intention, and bade him go in search of the weapon, promising to remain motionless during his absence. Frithiof, knowing that such a warrior's promise was inviolable, immediately obeyed; but when he returned with his sword, and found his antagonist calmly awaiting death, he relented, and bade Atlé rise and live.

Together the appeased warriors now wended their way to Angantyr's hall, which Frithiof found to be far different from the rude dwellings of his native land. The walls were covered with leather richly decorated with gilt designs. The chimney-piece was of marble, and glass panes were in the window-frames. A soft light was diffused from many candles burning in silver branches, and the tables groaned under the most luxurious fare.

High in a silver chair sat the jarl, clad in a coat of golden mail, over which was flung a rich mantle bordered with ermine, but when Frithiof entered he strode from his seat with cordial hand outstretched. "Full many a horn have I emptied with my old friend Thorsten," said he, "and his brave son is equally welcome at my board."

Nothing loth, Frithiof seated himself beside his host, and after he had eaten and drunk he recounted his adventures upon land and sea.

At last, however, Frithiof made known his errand, whereupon Angantyr said that he owed no tribute to

Helgé, and would pay him none; but that he would give the required sum as a free gift to his old friend's son, leaving him at liberty to dispose of it as he pleased. Meantime, since the season was unpropitious for the return journey, and storms continually swept the sea, the king invited Frithiof to tarry with him over the winter; and it was only when the gentle spring breezes were blowing once more that he at last allowed him to depart.

## FRITHIOF'S HOMECOMING

> *All, all's lost! From half-burned hall*
> *Th' fire-red cock up-swingeth! —*
> *Sits on the roof, and, with shrilly call*
> *Flutt'ring, his free course wingeth*
> **G. Stephens, Frithiof Saga**

Taking leave of his kind host, Frithiof set sail, and wafted by favourable winds, the hero, after six days, came in sight of Framnäs, and found that his home had been reduced to a shapeless heap of ashes by Helgé's orders. Sadly Frithiof strode over the ravaged site of his childhood's home, and as he viewed the desolate scene his heart burned within him. The ruins were not entirely deserted, however, and suddenly Frithiof felt the cold nozzle of his hound thrust into his hand. A few moments later his favourite steed bounded to his master's side, and the faithful creatures were well-nigh frantic with delight. Then came Hilding to greet him with the information that Ingeborg was now the wife of Sigurd Ring. When Frithiof heard this he flew into a Berserker rage, and bade his men scuttle the vessels in the harbour, while he strode to the temple in search of Helgé.

The king stood crowned amid a circle of priests, some of whom brandished flaming pine-knots, while all grasped a sacrificial flint knife. Suddenly there was a clatter of arms and in burst Frithiof, his brow dark as autumn storms. Helgé's face went pale as he confronted the angry hero, for he knew what his coming presaged. "Take thy tribute, King," said Frithiof, and with the words, he took the purse from his girdle and flung it in Helgé's face with such force that blood gushed from his mouth and he fell swooning at Balder's feet.

The silver-bearded priests advanced to the scene of violence, but Frithiof motioned them back, and his looks were so threatening that they durst not disobey.

Then his eye fell upon the arm-ring which he had given to Ingeborg and which Helgé had placed upon the arm of Balder, and striding up to the wooden image he said: "Pardon, great Balder, not for thee was the ring wrested from Völund's tomb!" Then he seized the ring, but strongly as he tugged it would not come apart. At last he put forth all his strength, and with a sudden jerk he recovered the ring, and at the same time the image of the god fell prone across the altar fire. The next moment it was enveloped in flames, and before aught could be done the whole temple was wreathed in fire and smoke.

Frithiof, horror-stricken at the sacrilege which he had involuntarily occasioned, vainly tried to extinguish the flames and save the costly sanctuary, but finding his efforts unavailing he escaped to his ship and resolved upon the weary life of an outcast and exile.

Helgé started in pursuit with ten great dragon-ships, but these had barely got under way when they began to sink, and Björn said with a laugh, "What Ran enfolds I trust she will keep." Even King Helgé was with difficulty got ashore, and the survivors were forced to stand in helpless inactivity while Ellida's great sails slowly sank beneath the horizon. It was thus that Frithiof sadly saw his native land vanish from sight; and as it disappeared he breathed a tender farewell to the beloved country which he never expected to see again.

After thus parting from his native land, Frithiof roved the sea as a pirate, or viking. His code was never to settle anywhere, to sleep on his shield, to fight and neither give nor take quarter, to protect the ships which paid him tribute and to plunder the others, and to distribute all the booty to his men, reserving for himself nothing but the glory of the enterprise. Sailing and fighting thus, Frithiof visited many lands, and came at last to the sunny isles of Greece, whither he would fain have carried Ingeborg as his bride; and the sights called up such a flood of sad memories that he was well-nigh overwhelmed with longing for his beloved and for his native land.

## AT THE COURT OF SIGURD RING

*Then threw Frithiof down his mantle,*
*and upon the greensward spread,*
*And the ancient king so trustful laid*

*on Frithiof's knee his head;*
*Slept, as calmly as the hero sleepeth after war's alarms*
*On his shield, calm as an infant sleepeth in its mother's arms*
**Henry Wadsworth Longfellow, Frithiof Saga**

**T**hree years had passed away and Frithiof determined to return northward and visit Sigurd Ring's court. When he announced his purpose to Björn, his faithful companion reproached him for his rashness in thinking to journey alone, but Frithiof would not be turned from his purpose, saying: "I am never alone while Angurvadel hangs at my side." Steering Ellida up the Vik (the main part of the Christiania Fiord), he entrusted her to Björn's care, and, enveloped in a bear-hide, which he wore as a disguise, he set out on foot alone for the court of Sigurd Ring, arriving there as the Yuletide festivities were in progress. As if nothing more than an aged beggar, Frithiof sat down upon the bench near the door, where he quickly became the butt of the courtiers' rough jokes. When one of his tormentors, however, approached too closely, the seeming beggar caught him in a powerful grasp and swung him high above his head.

Terrified by this exhibition of superhuman strength, the courtiers quickly withdrew from the dangerous vicinity, while Sigurd Ring, whose attention was attracted by the commotion, sternly bade the stranger-guest approach and tell who thus dared to break the peace in his royal hall.

Frithiof answered evasively that he was fostered in penitence, that he inherited want, and that he came from the wolf; as to his name, this did not matter. The king, as was the courteous custom, did not press him further, but invited him to take a seat beside him and the queen, and to share his good cheer. "But first," said he, "let fall the clumsy covering which veils, if I mistake not, a proper form."

Frithiof gladly accepted the invitation thus cordially given, and when the hairy hide fell from off his head and shoulders, he stood disclosed in the pride of youth, much to the surprise of the assembled warriors.

But although his appearance marked him as of no common race, none of the courtiers recognised him. It was different, however, with Ingeborg. Had any curious eye been upon her at that moment her changing colour and the quick heaving of her breast would have revealed her deep emotion.

Frithiof had barely taken his seat at the board when with flourish of trumpets a great boar was brought in and placed before the king. In accordance with the Yule-tide custom of those days the old monarch rose, and touching the head of the animal, he uttered a vow that with the help of Frey, Odin, and Thor, he would conquer the bold champion Frithiof. The next moment Frithiof, too, was upon his feet, and dashing his sword upon the great wooden bench he declared that Frithiof was his kinsman and he also would vow that though all the world withstood, no harm should reach the hero while he had power to wield his sword.

At this unexpected interruption the warriors had risen quickly from the oaken benches, but Sigurd Ring smiled indulgently at the young man's vehemence and said: "Friend, thy words are overbold, but never yet was guest restrained from uttering his thoughts in this kingly hall." Then he turned to Ingeborg and bade her fill to the brim with her choicest mead a huge horn, richly decorated, which stood in front of her, and present it to the guest. The queen obeyed with downcast eyes, and the trembling of her hand caused the liquid to overflow. Two ordinary men could hardly have drained the mighty draught, but Frithiof raised it to his lips, and when he removed the horn not one drop of the mead remained.

Ere the banquet was ended Sigurd Ring invited the youthful stranger to remain at his court until the return of spring, and accepting the proffered hospitality, Frithiof became the constant companion of the royal couple, whom he accompanied upon all occasions.

One day Sigurd Ring set out to a banquet with Ingeborg. They travelled in a sleigh, while Frithiof, with steel-shod feet, sped gracefully by their side, cutting many mystic characters in the ice. Their way lay over a dangerous portion of the frozen surface, and Frithiof warned the king that it would be prudent to avoid this. He would not listen to the counsel, however, and suddenly the sleigh sank in a deep fissure, which threatened to engulph it with the king and queen. But like falcon descending upon its quarry, Frithiof was at their side in a moment, and without apparent effort he dragged the steed and its burden on to the firm ice. "In good sooth," said Ring, "Frithiof himself could not have done better."

The long winter came to an end, and in the early spring the king and queen arranged a hunting-party in which all the court were to take part. During the progress of the chase the advancing years of Sigurd Ring made it impossible for him to keep up with the eager hunt, and thus it happened that he dropped behind, until at length he was left with Frithiof as his sole companion. They rode slowly together until they reached a pleasant dell which invited the weary king to repose, and he declared that he would lie down for a season to rest.

While the aged king was thus reposing, a bird sang to Frithiof from a tree near by, bidding him take advantage of his host's powerlessness to slay him, and recover the bride of whom he had been unfairly deprived. But although Frithiof's hot young heart clamoured for his beloved, he utterly refused to entertain the dastardly suggestion, but, fearing lest he should be overcome by temptation, despite his horror at the thought, he impulsively flung his sword far from him into a neighbouring thicket.

A few moments later Sigurd Ring opened his eyes, and informed Frithiof that he had only feigned sleep; he told him also that having recognised him from the first, he had tested him in many ways, and had found his honour equal to his courage. Old age had now overtaken him and he felt that death was drawing nigh. In but a short time, therefore, Frithiof might hope to realise his dearest hope, and Sigurd Ring told him that he would die happy if he would stay by him until the end.

A revulsion of feeling had, however, overtaken Frithiof, and he told the aged king that he felt that Ingeborg could never be his, because of the wrath of Balder. Too long had he stayed; he would now go once more upon the sea and would seek death in the fray, that so he might appease the offended gods.

Full of his resolve, he quickly made preparations to depart, but when he returned to the court to bid farewell to his royal hosts he found that Sigurd Ring was at the point of death. The old warrior bethought him that "a straw death" would not win the favour of Odin, and in the presence of Frithiof and his court he slashed bravely the death runes on his arm and breast. Then clasping Ingeborg with one hand, he raised the other in blessing over Frithiof and his youthful son, and so passed in peace to the halls of the blessed.

## BETROTHAL OF FRITHIOF AND INGEBORG

*Then sudden, o'er the western waters pendent,*
*An Image comes, with gold and flames resplendent,*
*O'er Balder's grove it hovers, night's clouds under,*
*Like gold crown resting on a bed of green.*
*At last to a temple settling, firm 'tis grounded*
*Where Balder stood, another temple's founded*
**G. Stephens, Frithiof Saga**

**T**he warriors of the nation now assembled in solemn Thing to choose a successor to the throne. Frithiof had won the people's enthusiastic admiration, and they would fain have elected him king; but he raised Sigurd Ring's little son high on his shield when he heard the shout which acclaimed his name, and presented the boy to the assembly as their future king, publicly swearing to uphold him until he was of age to defend the realm. The lad, weary of his cramped position, boldly sprang to the ground as soon as Frithiof's speech was ended, and alighted upon his feet. This act of agile daring in one so young appealed to the rude Northmen, and a loud shout arose, "We choose thee, shield-borne child!"

According to some accounts, Frithiof now made war against Ingeborg's brothers, and after conquering them, allowed them to retain their kingdom on condition that they paid him a yearly tribute. Then he and Ingeborg remained in Ringric until the young king was able to assume the government, when they repaired to Hordaland, a kingdom Frithiof had obtained by conquest, and which he left to his sons Gungthiof and Hunthiof.

Bishop Tegnér's conclusion, however, differs very considerably, and if it appears less true to the rude temper of the rugged days of the sea-rovers, its superior spiritual qualities make it more attractive. According to Tegnér's poem, Frithiof was urged by the people of Sigurd Ring to espouse Ingeborg and remain amongst them as guardian of the realm. But he answered that this might not be, since the wrath of Balder still burned against him, and none else could bestow his cherished bride. He told the people that he would fare over the seas and seek forgiveness of the god, and soon after, his farewells were spoken, and once more his vessel was speeding before the wind.

Frithiof's first visit was paid to his father's burial mound, where, plunged in melancholy at the desolation around, he poured out his soul to the outraged god. He reminded him that it was the custom of the Northmen to exact blood-fines for kinsmen slain, and surely the blessed gods would not be less forgiving than the earth-born. Passionately he adjured Balder to show him how he could make reparation for his unpremeditated fault, and suddenly, an answer was vouchsafed, and Frithiof beheld in the clouds a vision of a new temple.

The hero immediately understood that the gods had thus indicated a means of atonement, and he grudged neither wealth nor pains until a glorious temple and grove, which far exceeded the splendour of the old shrine, rose out of the ruins.

Meantime, while the timbers were being hewed, King Helgé was absent upon a foray amongst the Finnish mountains. One day it chanced that his band passed by a crag where stood the lonely shrine of some forgotten god, and King Helgé scaled the rocky summit with intent to raze the ruined walls. The lock held fast, and, as Helgé tugged fiercely at the mouldered gate, suddenly a sculptured image of the deity, rudely summoned from his ancient sleep, started from his niche above.

Heavily he fell upon the head of the intruder, and Helgé stretched his length upon the rocky floor, nor stirred again.

When the temple was duly consecrated to Balder's service, Frithiof stood by the altar to await the coming of his expected bride. But Halfdan first crossed the threshold, his faltering gait showing plainly that he feared an unfriendly reception. Seeing this, Frithiof unbuckled his sword and strode frankly to Halfdan with hand outstretched, whereupon the king, blushing deeply, grasped heartily the proffered hand, and from that moment all their differences were forgotten. The next moment Ingeborg approached and the renewed amity of the long-sundered friends was ratified with the hand of the bride, which Halfdan placed in that of his new brother.

# THE END OF
# THE WORLD

*We shall see emerge*
*From the bright Ocean at our feet an earth*
*More fresh, more verdant than the last, with fruits*
*Self-springing, and a seed of man preserved,*
*Who then shall live in peace, as then in war.*
**Matthew Arnold, Balder Dead**

**Balder was pure of heart**, and he represented goodness in every form. His life in Asgard was one of kindness and generosity, and while he lived the force of his righteousness would allow everyone in Asgard to enjoy peace from evil. But evil comes in many forms and not even the gods could be protected from its sinister influence forever. In Asgard, Loki was the evil that would burst the bauble of their happiness, and it was Loki who would bring about the end to the eternal conflict between virtue and corruption. It was an end that had been predicted since the earth was created, and its reality was as frightening as every prediction had suggested. Ragnarok would rid the world of evil, and leave a trail of ashes that blotted out the sun and all that had once glowed in their gilded world. But it is from ashes that new life springs, and the world of the Viking gods was no exception.

## THE DEATH OF BALDER

*So on the floor lay Balder dead; and round*
*Lay thickly strewn swords, axes, darts, and spears,*
*Which all the Gods in sport had idly thrown*
*At Balder, whom no weapon pierced or clove;*
*But in his breast stood fixed the fatal bough*
*Of mistletoe, which Lok, the Accuser, gave*
*To Hoder, and unwitting Hoder threw –*
*'Gainst that alone had Balder's life no charm.*

**Matthew Arnold, Balder Dead**

To Odin and Frigga, we are told, were born twin sons as dissimilar in character and physical appearance as it was possible for two children to be. Hodur, god of darkness, was sombre, taciturn, and blind, like the obscurity of sin, which he was supposed to symbolise, while his brother Balder, the beautiful, was worshipped as the pure and radiant god of innocence and light. From his snowy brow and golden locks seemed to radiate beams of sunshine which gladdened the hearts of gods and men, by whom he was equally beloved. Each life that he touched glowed with goodness, and he was loved by all who knew him. Balder tended to his twin brother Hodur with every kindness and consideration. Hodur worshipped Balder, and would do nothing in his power to harm him.

The youthful Balder attained his full growth with marvellous rapidity, and was early admitted to the council of the gods. He took up his abode in the palace of Breidablik, whose silver roof rested upon golden pillars, and whose purity was such that nothing common or unclean was ever allowed within its precincts, and here he lived in perfect unity with his young wife Nanna (blossom), the daughter of Nip (bud), a beautiful and charming goddess.

The god of light was well versed in the science of runes, which were carved on his tongue; he knew the various virtues of simples, one of which, the camomile, was called "Balder's brow," because its flower was as immaculately pure as his forehead. The only thing hidden from Balder's radiant eyes was the perception of his own ultimate fate.

There came a morning when Balder woke with the dawn, his face tightened with fear and foresight. He had dreamed of his own death and he lay there petrified, aware, somehow, that the strength of this dream forecasted sinister things to come. So Balder travelled to see Odin, who listened carefully, and knew at once that the fears of his son were justified – for in his shining eyes there was no longer simply innocence; there was knowledge as well. Odin went at once to his throne at the top of Yggdrasill, and he prayed there for a vision to come to him. At once he saw the head of Vala the Seer come to him, and he knew he must travel to Hel's kingdom, to visit Vala's grave. Only then would he learn the truth of his favourite son's fate.

It was many long days before Odin reached the innermost graves on Hel's estate. He moved quietly so that Hel would not know of his coming, and he was disregarded by most of the workers in her lands, for they were intent on some celebrations, and were preparing the hall for the arrival of an esteemed guest. At last the mound of Vala's grave appeared, and he sat there on it, keeping his head low so that the prophetess would not catch a glimpse of his face. Vala was a seer of all things future, and all things past; there was nothing that escaped her bright eyes, and she could be called upon only by the magic of the runes to tell of her knowledge.

The grave was wreathed in shadows, and a mist hung uneasily over the tombstone. There was silence as Odin whispered to Vala to come forth, and then, at once, there was a grating and steaming that poured forth an odour that caused even the all-powerful Odin to gag and spit.

'Who disturbs me from my sleep,' said Vala with venom. Odin thought carefully before replying. He did not wish her to know that he was Odin, king of gods and men, for she may not wish to tell him of a future that would touch on his own. And so he responded:

'I am Vegtam, son of Valtam, and I wish to learn of the fate of Balder.'

'Balder's brother will slay him,' said Vala, and with that she withdrew into her grave.

Odin leapt up and cried out, 'With the power of the runes, you must tell me more. Tell me, Vala, which esteemed guest does Hel prepare for?'

'Balder,' she muttered from the depths of her grave, 'and I will say no more.'

Odin shook his head with concern. He could not see how it could be possible that Balder's brother would take his life; Balder and Hodur were the closest of brothers, and shared the same thoughts and indeed speech for much of the time. He returned to Asgard with his concerns still intact, and he discussed them there with Frigga, who listened carefully.

'I have a plan,' she announced, 'and I am certain you will agree that this is the best course of action for us all. I plan to travel through all nine lands, and I will seek the pledge of every living creature, every plant, every metal and stone, not to harm Balder.'

And Frigga was as good as her word, for on the morrow she set out and travelled far and wide, everywhere she went extracting with ease the promise of every living creature, and inanimate object, to love Balder, and to see that he was not injured in any way.

And so it was that Balder was immune to injury of any kind, and it became a game among the children of Asgard to aim their spears and arrows at him, and laugh as they bounced off, leaving him unharmed. Balder was adored throughout the worlds, and there was no one who did not smile when he spied him.

No one, that is except Loki, whose jealousy of Balder had reached an unbearable pitch. Each night he ruminated over the ways in which he could murder Balder, but he could think of none. Frigga had taken care to involve all possible dangers in her oath, and there was nothing now that would hurt him. But the scheming Loki was not unwise, and he soon came up with a plan. Transforming himself into a beggarwoman, he knocked on Frigga's door and requested a meal. Frigga was pleased to offer her hospitality, and she sat down to keep the beggar company as she ate.

Loki, in his disguise, chattered on about the handsome Balder, who he'd seen in the hall, and he mentioned his fears that Balder would be killed by one of the spears and arrows he had seen hurled at him. Frigga laughed, and explained that Balder was now invincible.

'Did everything swear an oath to you then?' asked Loki slyly.

'Oh, yes,' said Frigga, but then she paused, 'all, that is, except for a funny little plant which was growing at the base of the oak tree at Valhalla. Why I'd never before set eyes on such a little shoot of greenery and it was far too immature to swear to anything so important as my oath.'

'What's it called?' asked Loki again.

'Hmmm,' said Frigga, still unaware of the dangers her information might invoke, 'mistletoe. Yes, mistletoe.'

Loki thanked Frigga hastily for his meal, and left her palace, transforming at once into his mischievous self, and travelling to Valhalla as quickly as his feet would take him. He carefully plucked the budding mistletoe, and returned to Odin's hall, where Balder played with the younger gods and goddesses, as they shot him unsuccessfully with arms of every shape and size.

Hodur was standing frowning in the corner, and Loki whispered for him to come over.

'What is it, Hodur,' he asked.

'Nothing, really, just that I cannot join their games,' said Hodur quietly.

'Come with me,' said Loki, 'for I can help.' And leading Hodur to a position close to Balder, he placed in his hands a bow and arrow fashioned from the fleetest of fabrics. To the end of the arrow, he tied a small leaf of mistletoe, and topped the razor-sharp tip with a plump white berry. 'Now, shoot now,' he cried to Hodur, who pulled back the bow and let the arrow soar towards its target.

There was a sharp gasp, and then there was silence. Hodur shook his head with surprise – where were the happy shouts, where was the laughter telling him that his own arrow had hit its mark and failed to harm the victim? The silence spoke volumes, for Balder lay dead in a circle of admirers as pale and frightened as if they had seen Hel herself.

The agony spread across Asgard like a great wave. When it was discovered who had shot the fatal blow, Hodur was sent far from his family, and left alone in the wilderness. He had not yet had a moment to utter the name of the god who had encouraged him to perpetrate this grave crime, and his misery kept him silent.

Frigga was disconsolate with grief. She begged Hermod, the swiftest of her sons, to set out at once for Filheim, to beg Hel to release Balder to them all. And so he climbed upon Odin's finest steed, Sleipnir, and set out for the nine worlds of Hel, a task so fearsome that he shook uncontrollably.

In Asgard, Frigga and Odin carried their son's body to the sea, where a funeral pyre was created and lit. Nanna, Balder's wife, could bear it no longer, and before the pyre was set out on the tempestuous sea, she threw herself on the flames, and perished there with her only love. As a token of their great affection and esteem, the gods offered, one by one, their most prized possessions and laid them on the pyre as it set out for the wild seas. Odin produced his magic ring Draupnir, and the greatest gods of Asgard gathered to see the passing of Balder.

And so the blazing ship left the shore, will full sail set. And then darkness swallowed it, and Balder had gone.

Throughout this time, Hermod had been travelling at great speed towards Hel. He rode for nine days and nine nights, and never took a moment to sleep. He galloped on and on, bribing the watchman of each gate to let him past, and invoking the name of Balder as the reason for his journey. At last, he reached the hall of Hel, where he found Balder sitting easily with Nanna, in great comfort and looking quite content. Hel stood by his side, keeping a close watch on her newest visitor. She looked up at Hermod with disdain, for everyone knew that once a spirit had reached Hel it could not be released. But Hermod fell on one knee and begged the icy mistress to reconsider her hold over Balder.

'Please, Queen Hel, without Balder we cannot survive. There can be no future for Asgard without his presence,' he cried.

But Hel would not be moved. She held out for three days and three nights, while Hermod stayed right by her side, begging and pleading and offering every conceivable reason why Balder should be released. And finally the Queen of darkness gave in.

'Return at once to Asgard,' she said harshly, 'and if what you say is true, if everything – living and inanimate – in Asgard loves Balder and cannot live without him, then he will be released. But if there is even one dissenter, if there is even one stone in your land who does not mourn the passing of Balder, then he shall remain here with me.'

Hermod was gladdened by this news, for he knew that everyone – including Hodur who had sent the fatal arrow flying through the air – loved Balder. He agreed to these terms at once, and set off for Asgard, relaying himself and his news with speed that astonished all who saw him arrive.

Immediately, Odin sent messengers to all corners of the universe, asking for tears to be shed for Balder. And as they travelled, everyone and everything began to weep, until a torrent of water rushed across the tree of life. And after everyone had been approached, and each had shed his tears, the messengers made their way back to Odin's palace with glee. Balder would be released, there could be no doubt!

But it was not to be, for as the last messenger travelled back to the palace, he noticed the form of an old beggarwoman, hidden in the darkness of a cave. He approached her then, and bid her to cry for Balder, but she did not. Her eyes remained dry. The uproar was carried across to the palace, and Odin himself came to see 'dry eyes', whose inability to shed tears would cost him the life of his son. He stared into those eyes and he saw then what the messenger had failed to see, what Frigga had failed to see, and what had truly caused the death of Balder. For those eyes belonged to none other than Loki, and it was he who had murdered Balder as surely as if the arrow had left his own hands.

The sacred code of Asgard had been broken, for blood had been spilled by one of their own, in their own land. The end of the world was nigh – but first, Loki would be punished once and for all.

## THE REVENGE OF THE GODS

*Thee, on a rock's point,*
*With the entrails of thy ice-cold son,*
*The god will bind.*
**Benjamin Thorpe, Saemund's Edda**

**T**he wrath of the gods was so great that Asgard shuddered and shook. As Odin looked down upon Loki in the form of the beggarwoman, and made the decision to punish him, Loki transformed himself into a fly and disappeared.

Although he was crafty, even his most supreme efforts to save himself were as nothing in the face of Odin's determination to trace him.

Loki travelled to far distant mountains, and on the peak of the most isolated of them all, he built a cabin, with windows and doors on all sides so that he could see the enemy approaching, and flee from any side before they reached him. By day, he haunted a pool by a rushing waterfall, taking the shape of a salmon. His life was uncomplicated, and although he was forced to live by his wits, and the fear of the god's revenge was great, Loki was not unhappy.

From his throne above the worlds, Odin watched, and waited. And when he saw that Loki had grown complacent, and no longer looked with quite such care from his many windows, he struck.

It was one particular evening that Loki sat weaving. He had just invented what we today call a fish net, and as he worked he hummed to himself, glancing every now and then from his great windows, and then back at his work. The gods were almost upon him when he first noticed them, and they were led by Kvasir, who was known amongst all gods for his wisdom and ability to unravel the tricks of even the most seasoned trickster. And as he saw them arriving, Loki fled from the back door, and transformed himself into a salmon, and leapt into the pond.

The gods stood in the doorway, surveying the room. Kvasir walked over to the fishing net and examined it closely. His keen eyes caught a glimmer of fish scales on the floor, and he nodded sagely.

'It is my assessment,' he said, 'that our Loki has become a fish. And,' he held up the fishing net, 'we will catch him with his own web.'

The gods made their way to the stream, and the pond which lay at the bottom of the waterfall. Throwing the net into the water, they waited for daybreak, when Loki the salmon would enter the waters and be caught in their net. Of course, Loki was too clever to be trapped so easily, and he swam beneath the net and far away from the part of the pond where the gods were fishing. Kvasir soon realized their mistake, and he ordered that rocks be placed at the bottom of the net, so that none could swim beneath it. And they waited.

Loki looked with amusement at the god's trap, and gracefully soared through the air above the net, his eyes glinting in the early morning light. And as his fins were just inches from the water, and when he was so close to escape that he had begun to plan his celebrations, two firm hands were thrust out, and he was lifted into the air.

He hardly dared look at his captor, and he began to tremble when he saw that it was none other than Thor who had moved so swiftly to catch him.

'I command you to take your own form, Loki,' he shouted, holding tight to the smooth scales of the salmon.

Loki knew he was beaten. Quietly he transformed himself once again into Loki, only to find himself hung by the heels over the rippling waters. And as Thor raised his great hammer to beat Loki to death, a hand reached out and stopped him. It was Odin, and he spoke gently, and with enormous purpose.

'Death is too good for this rodent,' he whispered. 'Take him at once to the Hel's worlds and tie him there for good.'

And so it was that Loki was taken to Filheim, where Thor grabbed three massive rocks and formed a platform for the hapless trickster. Then, Loki's two sons, Vali and Nari, were brought forth, and an enchantment was laid upon Vali so that he took the form of a wolf and attacked his brother Nari, tearing him to pieces in front of his anguished father. Gathering up Nari's entrails, which were now endowed with magic properties, he tied Loki's limbs so that he lay across the three rocks, unable to move. The entrails would tighten with every effort he made to escape, and to ensure that he could not use trickery to free himself, Thor placed the rocks on a precipice. One false move and he would be sent crashing to his death in the canyon below.

Finally, Skadi caught a poisonous snake, and trapped it by its tail so that it hung over Loki's face, dripping venom into his mouth so that he screamed with pain and terror. He began to convulse and was such a terrible sight that his wife Sigyn rushed forward and begged to be allowed to stay beside him, holding a bowl with which to collect the poison.

The work of the gods was done. They turned then and left, and Sigyn remained with her husband, ever true to her wedding vows. Every day or so she moved from her position at his side in order to empty her bowl, and Loki's convulsions brought an earthquake to Asgard that lasted just as long as it took her to return with her bowl. They would remain there until the end of time – for the gods, that is. The end of time was nigh, and it was Ragnarok.

## RAGNAROK

> *Brothers slay brothers;*
> *Sisters' children*
> *Shed each other's blood.*
> *Hard is the world;*
> *Sensual sin grows huge.*
> *There are sword-ages, axe-ages;*
> *Shields are cleft in twain;*
> *Storm-ages, murder-ages;*
> *Till the world falls dead,*
> *And men no longer spare*
> *Or pity one another.*
> **R.B. Anderson, Norse Mythology**

**T**he end of the world had been prophesied from its beginning, and everyone across the world knew what to expect when Ragnarok fell upon them. For Ragnarok was the twilight of the gods, an end to the golden years of Asgard, an end to the palaces of delight, an end to the timeless world where nothing could interfere. It was the death of Balder that set the stage for the end of the world, and it was Loki's crimes which laid in place the main characters. And when the action had begun, there was no stopping it.

When evil entered Asgard, it tainted all nine worlds. Sol and Mani, high in the sky, paled with fright, and their chariots slowed as they moved with effort across the sky. They knew that the wolves would be soon upon them and that it would be only a matter of time before eternal darkness would fall once again. And when Sol and Mani had been devoured, there was no light to shine on the earth, and the terrible cold crept into the warm reaches of summer and drew from the soil what was growing there. Snow began to drift down upon the freezing land, and soon it snowed a little faster, and a little harder, until the earth was covered once again in a dark layer of ice.

Winter was upon them, and it did not cease. For three long, frozen seasons, it was winter, and then, after a thaw that melted only one single layer of ice, it was back for three more. With the cold and the darkness came evil, which rooted itself in the hearts of men. Soon crime was rampant, and all shreds of human kindness disappeared with the spring. At last, the stars were flung from the skies, causing the earth to tremble and shake. Loki and Fenris were freed from their manacles, and together they moved forward to wreak their revenge on the gods and men who had bound them so cruelly.

At the bottom of Yggdrasill, there was a groan that emanated the entire length of the tree, for at that moment, Nithog had gnawed through the root of the world tree, which quivered and shook from bottom to top. Fialar, the red cock who made his home above Valhalla shrieked out his cry, and then flew away from the tree as his call was echoed by Gullinkambi, the rooster in Midgard.

Heimdall knew at once what was upon them, and raising his mighty horn to his lips he blew the call that filled the hearts of all gods and mankind with terror. Ragnarok. The gods sprang from their beds, and thrust aside the finery that hung in their bed chambers. They armed themselves and mounted their horses, ready for the war that had been expected since the beginning of time. They moved quickly over the rainbow bridge and then they reached the field of Vigrid, where the last battle would be fought.

The turmoil on earth caused the seas to toss and twist with waves, and soon the world serpent Jormungander was woken from his deep sleep. The movement of the seas yanked his tail from his mouth, and it lashed around, sending waves crashing in every direction. And as he crawled out upon land for the first time, a tidal wave swelled across the earth, and set afloat Nagilfar, the ship of the dead, which had been constructed from the nails of the dead whose relatives had failed in their duties, and had neglected to pare the nails of the deceased when they were laid to rest. As the wind caught the blackened sail, Loki leapt aboard, and took her wheel – the ship of the undead captained by the personification of all evil. Loki called upon the fire-gods from Muspell, and they arrived in a conflagration of terrible glory.

Another ship had set out for Vigrid, and this was steered by Hrym and crewed by the frost-giants who had waited many centuries for this battle. Across the raging sea, both vessels made for the battlefield.

As they travelled, Hel, crept from her underground estate, bringing with her Nithog, and the hellhound Garm. From up above, there was a great crack, and Surtr, with sword blazing, leapt with his sons to the Bifrost bridge, and with one swoop they felled it, and sent the shimmering rainbow crashing to the depths below. Quickly, Odin escaped from the battlefield, and slipped one last time to the Urdar fountain, where the Norns sat quietly, accepting their fate. He leant over Mimir, and requested her wisdom, but for once the head would not talk to him, and he remounted Sleipnir and returned to the field, frightened and aware that he had no powers left with which to defend his people.

The opposing armies lined themselves on Vigrid field. On one side were the Aesir, the Vanir and the Einheriear – on the other, were the fire-giants led by Surtr, the frost-giants, the undead with Hel, and Loki with his children – Fenris and Jormungander. The air was filled with poison and the stench of evil from the opposing army, yet the gods held up their heads and prepared for a battle to end all time.

And so it was that the ancient enemies came to blows. Odin first met with the evil Fenris, and as he charged towards the fierce wolf, Fenris's massive jaws stretched open and Odin was flung deep into the red throat. Thor stopped in his tracks, the death of his father burning deep in his breast, and with renewed fury he lunged at the world serpent, engaging in a combat that would last for many hours. His hammer laid blow after blow on the serpent, and at last there was silence. Thor sat back in exhaustion, Jormungander dying at his side. But as Thor made to move forward, to carry on and support his kin in further battles, the massive serpent exhaled one last time, in a cloud of poison so vile that Thor fell at once, lifeless in the mist of the serpent's breath.

Tyr fought bravely with just one arm, but he, like his father, was swallowed whole, by the hellhound Garm, but as he passed through the gullet of the hound he struck out one last blow with his sword and pierced the heart of his enemy, dying in the knowledge that he had obtained his life's ambition.

Heimdall met Loki hand to hand, and the forces of good and evil engaged in the battle that had been raging for all time. Their flames engulfed one another; there was a flash of light. And then there was nothing.

The silent Vidar came rushing from a distant part of the plain to avenge the death of Odin, and he laid upon the jaw of Fenris a shoe which had been created for this day. With his arms and legs in motion he tore the wolf's head from his body, and then lay back in a pool of blood. Of all the gods, only Frey was left fighting. He battled valiantly, and as he laid down giant after giant, he felt a warmth on the back of his neck that meant only one thing. The heat burned and sizzled his skin, and as he turned he found himself face to face with Surtr. With a cry of rage that howled through the torn land, and shook the massive stem of the world ash, Yggdrasill, Surtr flung down bolts of fire that engulfed the golden palaces of the gods, and each of the worlds which lay beneath it. The heat caused the seas to bubble and to boil, and there came at once a wreath of smoke that blotted out the fire, and then, the world.

At last all was as it had been in the beginning. There was blackness. There was chaos. There was a nothingness that stretched as far as there was space.

## THE END OF THE WORLD

*All evil*
*Dies there an endless death, while goodness riseth*
*From that great world-fire, purified at last,*
*to a life far higher, better, nobler than the past.*
**R.B. Anderson, Viking Tales of the North**

The earth was purged by the fire and there was at once a new beginning. The sun rose in the sky, mounted on a chariot driven by the daughter of Sol, born before the wolf had eaten her father and her mother. Fresh green grass sprung up in the crevices, and flowers and fruits burst forth. Two new humans, Lif, a woman, and Lifthrasir, a man, emerged from Mimir's forest, where they had been reincarnated at the end of the world. Vali and Vidar, the forces of nature had survived the fiery battle, and they returned to the plan to be greeted by Thor's sons, Modi and Magni, who carried with them their father's hammer.

Hoenir had escaped from the Vanir, who had vanished forever, and from the deepest depths of the earth came Balder, renewed and as pure as he had ever been. Hodur rose with him, and the two brothers embraced, and greeted the new day. And so this small group of gods turned to face the scenes of destruction and devastation, and to witness the new life that was already curling up from the cloak of death and darkness. The land had become a refuge for the good. They looked up – they all looked way up – and there in front of them, stronger than ever was the world ash, Yggdrasill, which had trembled but not fallen.

There was a civilization to be created, and a small band of gods with whom it could be done. The gods had returned in a blaze of white light – a light as pure and virtuous as the new inhabitants of the earth – and in that light they brought forth our own world.

# GREEK AND NORTHERN
# MYTHOLOGIES

**H**aving read many of the Norse myths, we now turn to a comparison of Norse and Greek mythologies to see what we can divine about the origins and nature of the stories told above. During the past fifty years learned men of many nations have investigated philology and comparative mythology so thoroughly that they have ascertained beyond the possibility of doubt "that English, together with all the Teutonic dialects of the Continent, belongs to that large family of speech which comprises, besides the Teutonic, Latin, Greek, Slavonic, and Celtic, the Oriental languages of India and Persia."

"It has also been proved that the various tribes who started from the central home to discover Europe in the north, and India in the south, carried away with them, not only a common language, but a common faith and a common mythology. These are facts which may be ignored but cannot be disputed, and the two sciences of comparative grammar and comparative mythology, though but of recent origin, rest on a foundation as sound and safe as that of any of the inductive sciences."

"For more than a thousand years the Scandinavian inhabitants of Norway have been separated in language from their Teutonic brethren on the Continent, and yet both have not only preserved the same stock of popular stories, but they tell them, in several instances, in almost the same words."

## COMPARATIVE MYTHOLOGY

This resemblance, so strong in the early literature of nations inhabiting countries which present much the same physical aspect and have nearly the same climate, is not so marked when we compare the Northern myths with those of the genial South. Still, notwithstanding the contrast between Northern and Southern Europe, where these myths gradually ripened and attained their full growth, there is an analogy between the two mythologies which shows that the seeds from whence both sprang were originally the same.

In the foregoing chapters the Northern system of mythology has been outlined as clearly as possible, and the physical significance of the myths has been explained. Now we shall endeavour to set forth the resemblance of Northern mythology to that of the other Aryan nations, by comparing it with the Greek, which, however, it does not resemble as closely as it does the Oriental.

It is, of course, impossible in a work of this character to do more than mention the main points of resemblance in the stories forming the basis of these religions; but that will be sufficient to demonstrate, even to the most sceptical, that they must have been identical at a period too remote to indicate now with any certainty.

The Northern nations, like the Greeks, imagined that the world rose out of chaos; and while the latter described it as a vapoury, formless mass, the former, influenced by their immediate surroundings, depicted it as a chaos of fire and ice – a combination which is only too comprehensible to any one who has visited Iceland and seen the wild, peculiar contrast between its volcanic soil, spouting geysers, and the great icebergs which hedge it round during the long, dark winter season.

From these opposing elements, fire and ice, were born the first divinities, who, like the first gods of the Greeks, were gigantic in stature and uncouth in appearance. Ymir, the huge ice giant, and his descendants, are comparable to the Titans, who were also elemental forces of Nature, personifications of subterranean fire; and both, having held full sway for a time, were obliged to yield to greater perfection. After a fierce struggle for supremacy, they all found themselves defeated and banished to the respective remote regions of Tartarus and Jötun-heim.

The triad, Odin, Vili, and Ve, of the Northern myth is the exact counterpart of Jupiter, Neptune, and Pluto, who, superior to the Titan forces, rule supreme over the world in their turn. In the Greek mythology, the gods, who are also all related to one another, betake themselves to Olympus, where they build golden palaces for their use; and in the Northern mythology the divine conquerors repair to Asgard, and there construct similar dwellings.

Northern cosmogony was not unlike the Greek, for the people imagined that the earth, Mana-heim, was entirely surrounded by the sea, at the bottom of which lay coiled the huge Midgard snake, biting its own tail; and it was perfectly natural that, viewing the storm-lashed waves which beat against their shores, they should imagine these to be caused by his convulsive writhing. The Greeks, who also fancied the earth was round and compassed by a mighty river called Oceanus, described it as flowing with "a steady, equable current," for they generally gazed out upon calm and sunlit seas. Nifl-heim, the Northern region of perpetual cold and mist, had its exact counterpart in the land north of the Hyperboreans, where feathers (snow) continually hovered in the air, and where Hercules drove the Ceryneian stag into a snowdrift ere he could seize and bind it fast.

Like the Greeks, the Northern races believed that the earth was created first, and that the vaulted heavens were made afterwards to overshadow it entirely. They also imagined that the sun and moon were daily driven across the sky in chariots drawn by fiery steeds. Sol, the sun maiden, therefore corresponded to Helios, Hyperion, Phœbus, or Apollo, while Mani, the Moon (owing to a peculiarity of Northern grammar, which makes the sun feminine and the moon masculine), was the exact counterpart of Phœbe, Diana, or Cynthia.

The Northern scalds, who thought that they descried the prancing forms of white-maned steeds in the flying clouds, and the glitter of spears in the flashing light of the aurora borealis, said that the Valkyrs, or battle maidens, galloped across the sky, while the Greeks saw in the same natural phenomena the white flocks of Apollo guarded by Phaetusa and Lampetia.

As the dew fell from the clouds, the Northern poets declared that it dropped from the manes of the Valkyrs' steeds, while the Greeks, who observed that it generally sparkled longest in the thickets, identified it with Daphne and Procris, whose names are derived from the Sanskrit word which means "to sprinkle," and who are slain by their lovers, Apollo and Cephalus, personifications of the sun.

The earth was considered in the North as well as in the South as a female divinity, the fostering mother of all things; and it was owing to climatic difference only that the mythology of the North, where people were daily obliged to conquer the right to live by a hand-to-hand struggle with Nature, should represent her as hard and frozen like Rinda, while the Greeks embodied her in the genial goddess Ceres. The Greeks believed that the cold winter winds swept down from the North, and the Northern races, in addition, added that they were produced by the winnowing of the wings of the great eagle Hrae-svelgr.

The dwarfs, or dark elves, bred in Ymir's flesh, were like Pluto's servants in that they never left their underground realm, where they, too, sought the precious metals, which they moulded into delicate ornaments such as Vulcan bestowed upon the gods, and into weapons which no one could either dint or mar. As for the light elves, who lived above ground and cared for plants, trees, and streams, they were evidently the Northern equivalents to the nymphs, dryads, oreades, and hamadryads, which peopled the woods, valleys, and fountains of ancient Greece.

## JUPITER AND ODIN

Jupiter, like Odin, was the father of the gods, the god of victory, and a personification of the universe. Hlidskialf, Allfather's lofty throne, was no less exalted than Olympus or Ida, whence the Thunderer could observe all that was taking place; and Odin's invincible spear Gungnir was as terror-inspiring as the thunderbolts brandished by his Greek prototype. The Northern deities feasted continually upon mead and boar's flesh, the drink and meat most suitable to the inhabitants of a Northern climate, while the gods of Olympus preferred the nectar and ambrosia which formed their only sustenance.

Twelve Aesir sat in Odin's council hall to deliberate over the wisest measures for the government of the world and men, and an equal number of gods assembled on the cloudy peak of Mount Olympus for a similar purpose. The Golden Age in Greece was a period of idyllic happiness, amid ever-flowering groves and under balmy skies, while the Northern age of bliss was also a time when peace and innocence flourished on the earth, and when evil was as yet entirely unknown.

Using the materials near at hand, the Greeks modelled their first images out of clay; hence they naturally imagined that Prometheus had made man out of that substance when called upon to fashion a creature inferior to the gods only. As the Northern statues were hewn out of wood, the Northern races inferred, as a matter of course, that Odin, Vili, and Ve (who here correspond to Prometheus, Epimetheus, and Minerva, the three Greek creators of man) made the first human couple, Ask and Embla, out of blocks of wood.

The goat Heidrun, which supplied the heavenly mead, is like Amalthea, Jupiter's first nurse, and the busy, tell-tale Ratatosk is equivalent to the snow-white crow in the story of Coronis, which was turned black in punishment for its tattling. Jupiter's eagle has its counterpart in the ravens Hugin and Munin, or in the wolves Geri and Freki, which are ever crouching at Odin's feet.

## NORNS AND FATES

The close resemblance between the Northern Orlog and the Greek Destiny, goddesses whose decrees the gods themselves were obliged to respect, and the equally powerful Norns and Mœrae, is too obvious to need pointing out, while the Vanas are counterparts of Neptune and the other ocean divinities. The great quarrel between the Vanas and the Aesir is merely another version of the dispute between Jupiter and Neptune for the supremacy of the world. Just as Jupiter forces his brother to yield to his authority, so the Aesir remain masters of all, but do not refuse to continue to share their power with their conquered foes, who thus become their allies and friends.

Like Jupiter, Odin is always described as majestic and middle-aged, and both gods are regarded as the divine progenitors of royal races, for while the Heraclidae claimed Jupiter as their father, the Inglings, Skioldings, etc., held that Odin was the founder of their families. The most solemn oaths were sworn by Odin's spear as well as by Jupiter's footstool, and both gods rejoice in a multitude of names, all descriptive of the various phases of their nature and worship.

Odin, like Jupiter, frequently visited the earth in disguise, to judge of the hospitable intentions of mankind, as in the story of Geirrod and Agnar, which resembles that of Philemon and Baucis. The aim was to encourage hospitality; therefore, in both stories, those who showed themselves humanely inclined are richly rewarded, and in the Northern myth the lesson is enforced by the punishment inflicted upon Geirrod, as the scalds believed in poetic justice and saw that it was carefully meted out.

The contest of wit between Odin and Vafthrudnir has its parallel in the musical rivalry of Apollo and Marsyas, or in the test of skill between Minerva and Arachne. Odin further resembled Apollo in that he, too, was god of eloquence and poetry, and could win all hearts by means of his divine voice; he was like Mercury in that he taught mortals the use of runes, while the Greek god introduced the alphabet.

## MYTHS OF THE SEASONS

The disappearance of Odin, the sun or summer, and the consequent desolation of Frigga, the earth, is merely a different version of the myths of Proserpine and Adonis. When Proserpine and Adonis have gone, the earth (Ceres or Venus) bitterly mourns their absence, and refuses all consolation. It is only when they return from their exile that she casts off her mourning garments and gloom, and again decks herself in all her jewels. So Frigga and Freyia bewail the absence of their husbands Odin and Odur, and remain hard and cold until their return. Odin's wife, Saga, the goddess of history, who lingered by Sokvabek, "the stream of time and events," taking note of all she saw, is like Clio, the muse of history, whom Apollo sought by the inspiring fount of Helicon.

Just as, according to Euhemerus, there was an historical Zeus, buried in Crete, where his grave can still be seen, so there was an historical Odin, whose mound rises near Upsala, where the greatest Northern temple once stood, and where there was a mighty oak which rivalled the famous tree of Dodona.

## FRIGGA AND JUNO

Frigga, like Juno, was a personification of the atmosphere, the patroness of marriage, of connubial and motherly love, and the goddess of childbirth. She, too, is represented as a beautiful, stately woman, rejoicing in her adornments; and her special attendant, Gna, rivals Iris in the rapidity with which she executes her mistress's behests. Juno has full control over the clouds, which she can brush away with a motion of her hand, and Frigga is supposed to weave them out of the thread she has spun on her jewelled spinning wheel.

In Greek mythology we find many examples of the way in which Juno seeks to outwit Jupiter. Similar tales are not lacking in the Northern myths. Juno obtains possession of

Io, in spite of her husband's reluctance to part with her, and Frigga artfully secures the victory for the Winilers in the Langobarden Saga. Odin's wrath at Frigga's theft of the gold from his statue is equivalent to Jupiter's marital displeasure at Juno's jealousy and interference during the war of Troy. In the story of Gefjon, and the clever way in which she procured land from Gylfi to form her kingdom of Seeland, we have a reproduction of the story of Dido, who obtained by stratagem the land upon which she founded her city of Carthage. In both accounts oxen come into play, for while in the Northern myth these sturdy beasts draw the piece of land far out to sea, in the other an ox hide, cut into strips, serves to enclose the queen's grant.

## MUSICAL MYTHS

The **Pied Piper of Hamelin**, who could attract all living creatures by his music, is like Orpheus or Amphion, whose lyres had the same power; and Odin, as leader of the dead, is the counterpart of Mercury Psychopompus, both being personifications of the wind, on whose wings disembodied souls were thought to be wafted from this mortal sphere.

The trusty Eckhardt, who would fain save Tannhäuser and prevent his returning to expose himself to the enchantments of the sorceress, in the Hörselberg, is like the Greek Mentor, who not only accompanied Telemachus, but gave him good advice and wise instructions, and would have rescued Ulysses from the hands of Calypso.

## THOR, TYR AND BRAGI

**T**hor, the Northern thunder-god, also has many points of resemblance with Jupiter. He bears the hammer Miolnir, the Northern emblem of the deadly thunderbolt, and, like Jupiter, uses it freely when warring against the giants. In his rapid growth Thor resembles Mercury, for while the former playfully tosses about several loads of ox hides a few hours after his birth, the latter steals Apollo's oxen before he is one day old. In physical strength Thor resembles Hercules, who also gave early proofs of uncommon vigour by strangling the serpents sent to slay him in his cradle, and who delighted, later on, in attacking and conquering giants and monsters. Hercules became a woman and took to spinning to please Omphale, the Lydian queen, and Thor assumed a woman's apparel to visit Thrym and recover his hammer, which had been buried nine rasts underground. The hammer, his principal attribute, was used for many sacred purposes. It consecrated the funeral pyre and the marriage rite, and boundary stakes driven in by a hammer were considered as sacred among Northern nations as the Hermae or statues of Mercury, removal of which was punishable by death.

Thor's wife, Sif, with her luxuriant golden hair, is, as we have already stated, an emblem of the earth, and her hair of its rich vegetation. Loki's theft of these tresses is equivalent to Pluto's rape of Proserpine. To recover the golden locks, Loki must visit the dwarfs (Pluto's servants), crouching in the low passages of the underground world; so Mercury must seek Proserpine in Hades.

The gadfly which hinders Jupiter from recovering possession of Io, after Mercury has slain Argus, reappears in the Northern myth to sting Brock and to endeavour to prevent the manufacture of the magic ring Draupnir, which is merely a counterpart of Sif's tresses, as it also represents the fruits of the earth. The fly continues to torment the dwarf during the manufacture of Frey's golden-bristled boar, a prototype of Apollo's golden sun chariot, and it prevents the perfect formation of the handle of Thor's hammer.

The magic ship Skidbladnir, also made by the dwarfs, is like the swift-sailing Argo, which was a personification of the clouds sailing overhead; and just as the former was said to be large enough to accommodate all the gods, so the latter bore all the Greek heroes off to the distant land of Colchis.

The Germans, wishing to name the days of the week after their gods, as the Romans had done, gave the name of Thor to Jove's day, and thus made it the present Thursday.

Thor's struggle against Hrungnir is a parallel to the fight between Hercules and Cacus or Antaeus; while Groa is evidently Ceres, for she, too, mourns for her absent child Orvandil (Proserpine), and breaks out into a song of joy when she hears that it will return.

Magni, Thor's son, who when only three hours old exhibits his marvellous strength by lifting Hrungnir's leg off his recumbent father, also reminds us of the infant Hercules; and Thor's voracious appetite at Thrym's wedding feast has its parallel in Mercury's first meal, which consisted of two whole oxen.

The crossing of the swollen tide of Veimer by Thor reminds us of Jason's feat when he waded across the torrent on his way to visit the tyrant Pelias and recover possession of his father's throne.

The marvellous necklace worn by Frigga and Freyia to enhance their charms is like the cestus or girdle of Venus, which Juno borrowed to subjugate her lord, and is, like Sif's tresses and the ring Draupnir, an emblem of luxuriant vegetation or a type of the stars which shine in the firmament.

The Northern sword-god Tyr is, of course, the Greek war-god Ares, whom he so closely resembles that his name was given to the day of the week held sacred to Ares, which is even now known as Tuesday or Tiu's day. Like Ares, Tyr was noisy and courageous; he delighted in the din of battle, and was fearless at all times. He alone dared to brave the Fenris wolf; and the Southern proverb concerning Scylla and Charybdis has its counterpart in the Northern adage, "to get loose out of Laeding and to dash out of Droma." The Fenris wolf, also a personification of subterranean fire, is bound, like his prototypes the Titans, in Tartarus.

The similarity between the gentle, music-loving Bragi, with his harp, and Apollo or Orpheus, is very great; so is the resemblance between the magic draught Od-hroerir and the waters of Helicon, both of which were supposed to serve as inspiration to mortal as well as to immortal poets. Odin dons eagle plumes to bear away this precious mead, and Jupiter assumes a similar guise to secure his cupbearer Ganymede.

Idunn, like Adonis and Proserpine, or still more like Eurydice, is also a fair personification of spring. She is borne away by the cruel ice giant Thiassi, who represents the boar which slew Adonis, the kidnapper of Proserpine, or the poisonous serpent which bit Eurydice. Idunn is detained for a long time in Jötun-heim (Hades), where she forgets all her merry, playful ways, and becomes mournful and pale. She cannot return alone to Asgard, and it is only when Loki (now an emblem of the south wind) comes to bear her away in the shape of a nut or a swallow that she can effect her escape. She reminds us of Proserpine and Adonis escorted back to earth by Mercury (god of the wind), or of Eurydice lured out of Hades by the sweet sounds of Orpheus's harp, which were also symbolical of the soughing of the winds.

## IDUNN AND EURYDICE

The myth of Idunn's fall from Yggdrasil into the darkest depths of Nifl-heim, while subject to the same explanation and comparison as the above story, is still more closely related to the tale of Orpheus and Eurydice, for the former, like Bragi, cannot exist without the latter, whom he follows even into the dark realm of death; without her his songs are entirely silenced. The wolf-skin in which Idunn is enveloped is typical of the heavy snows in Northern regions, which preserve the tender roots from the blighting influence of the extreme winter cold.

## SKADI AND DIANA

The Van Niord, who is god of the sunny summer seas, has his counterpart in Neptune and more especially in Nereus, the personification of the calm and pleasant aspect of the mighty deep. Niord's wife, Skadi, is the Northern huntress; she therefore resembles Diana. Like her, she bears a quiver full of arrows, and a bow which she handles with consummate skill. Her short gown permits the utmost freedom of motion, also, and she, too, is generally accompanied by a hound.

The story of the transference of Thiassi's eyes to the firmament, where they glow like brilliant stars, reminds us of many Greek star myths, and especially of Argus's eyes ever on the watch, of Orion and his jewelled girdle, and of his dog Sirius, all changed into stars by the gods to appease angry goddesses. Loki's antics to win a smile from the irate Skadi are considered akin to the quivering flashes of sheet-lightning which he personified in the North, while Steropes, the Cyclops, typified it for the Greeks.

## FREY AND APOLLO

The Northern god of sunshine and summer showers, the genial Frey, has many traits in common with Apollo, for, like him, he is beautiful and young, rides the golden-bristled boar which was the Northern conception of the sunbeams, or drives across the sky in a golden car, which reminds us of Apollo's glittering chariot.

Frey has some of the gentle Zephyrus's characteristics besides, for he, too, scatters flowers along his way. His horse Blodug-hofi is not unlike Pegasus, Apollo's favourite steed, for it can pass through fire and water with equal ease and velocity.

Fro, like Odin and Jupiter, is also identified with a human king, and his mound lies beside Odin's near Upsala. His reign was so happy that it was called the Golden Age, and he therefore reminds us of Saturn, who, exiled to earth, ruled over the people of Italy, and granted them similar prosperity.

## FREYIA AND VENUS

**G**erda, the beautiful maiden, is like Venus, and also like Atalanta; she is hard to woo and hard to win, like the fleet-footed maiden, but, like her, she yields at last and becomes a happy wife. The golden apples with which Skirnir tries to bribe her remind us of the golden fruit which Hippomenes cast in Atalanta's way, and which made her lose the race.

Freyia, the goddess of youth, love, and beauty, like Venus, sprang from the sea, for she is a daughter of the sea-god Niord. Venus bestowed her best affections upon the god of war and upon the martial Anchises, while Freyia often assumes the garb of a Valkyr, and rides rapidly to earth to take part in mortal strife and bear away the heroic slain to feast in her halls. Like Venus, she delights in offerings of fruits and flowers, and lends a gracious ear to the petitions of lovers. Freyia also resembles Minerva, for, like her, she wears a helmet and breastplate, and, like her, also, she is noted for her beautiful blue eyes.

## ODUR AND ADONIS

Odur, Freyia's husband, is like Adonis, and when he leaves her, she, too, sheds countless tears, which, in her case, are turned to gold, while Venus's tears are changed into anemones, and those of the Heliades, mourning for Phaeton, harden to amber, which resembles gold in colour and in consistency. Just as Venus rejoices at Adonis's return, and all Nature blooms in sympathy with her joy, so Freyia becomes lighthearted once more when she has found her husband beneath the flowering myrtles of the South. Venus's car is drawn by fluttering doves, and Freyia's is swiftly carried along by cats, which are emblems of sensual love, as the doves were considered types of tenderest love. Freyia is appreciative of beauty and angrily refuses to marry Thrym, while Venus scorns and finally deserts Vulcan, whom she has been forced to marry against her will.

The Greeks represented Justice as a goddess blindfolded, with scales in one hand and a sword in the other, to indicate the impartiality and the fixity of her decrees. The corresponding deity of the North was Forseti, who patiently listened to both sides of a question ere he, too, promulgated his impartial and irrevocable sentence.

Uller, the winter-god, resembles Apollo and Orion only in his love for the chase, which he pursues with ardour under all circumstances. He is the Northern bowman, and his skill is quite as unerring as theirs.

Heimdall, like Argus, was gifted with marvellous keenness of sight, which enabled him to see a hundred miles off as plainly by night as by day. His Giallar-horn, which could be heard throughout all the world, proclaiming the gods' passage to and fro over the quivering bridge Bifrost, was like the trumpet of the goddess Renown. As he was related to the water deities on his mother's side, he could, like Proteus, assume any form at will, and he made good use of this power on the occasion when he frustrated Loki's attempt to steal the necklace Brisinga-men.

Hermod, the quick or nimble, resembles Mercury not only in his marvellous celerity of motion. He, too, was the messenger of the gods, and, like the Greek divinity, flashed hither and thither, aided not by winged cap and sandals, but by Odin's steed Sleipnir, whom he alone was allowed to bestride. Instead of the Caduceus, he bore the wand Gambantein. He questioned the Norns and the magician Rossthiof, through whom he learned that Vali would come to avenge his brother Balder and to supplant his father Odin. Instances of similar consultations are found in Greek mythology, where Jupiter would fain have married Thetis, yet desisted when the Fates foretold that if he did so she would be the mother of a son who would surpass his father in glory and renown.

The Northern god of silence, Vidar, has some resemblance to Hercules, for while the latter has nothing but a club with which to defend himself against the Nemean lion, whom he tears asunder, the former is enabled to rend the Fenris wolf at Ragnarok by the possession of one large shoe.

## RINDA AND DANAE

Odin's courtship of Rinda reminds us of Jupiter's wooing of Danae, who is also a symbol of the earth; and while the shower of gold in the Greek tale is intended to represent the fertilising sunbeams, the footbath in the Northern story typifies the spring thaw which sets in when the sun has overcome the resistance of the frozen earth. Perseus, the child of this union, has many points of resemblance with Vali, for he, too, is an avenger, and slays his mother's enemies just as surely as Vali destroys Hodur, the murderer of Balder.

The Fates were supposed to preside over birth in Greece, and to foretell a child's future, as did the Norns; and the story of Meleager has its unmistakable parallel in that of Nornagesta. Althaea preserves the half-consumed brand in a chest, Nornagesta conceals the candle-end in his harp; and while the Greek mother brings about her son's death by casting the brand into the fire, Nornagesta, compelled to light his candle-end at Olaf's command, dies as it sputters and burns out.

Hebe and the Valkyrs were the cupbearers of Olympus and Asgard. They were all personifications of youth; and while Hebe married the great hero and demigod Hercules when she ceased to fulfil her office, the Valkyrs were relieved from their duties when united to heroes like Helgi, Hakon, Völund, or Sigurd.

The Cretan labyrinth has its counterpart in the Icelandic Völundarhaus, and Völund and Daedalus both effect their escape from a maze by a cleverly devised pair of wings, which enable them to fly in safety over land and sea and escape from the tyranny of their respective masters, Nidud and Minos. Völund resembles Vulcan, also, in that he is a clever smith and makes use of his talents to work out his revenge.

Vulcan, lamed by a fall from Olympus, and neglected by Juno, whom he had tried to befriend, sends her a golden throne, which is provided with cunning springs to seize and hold her fast. Völund, hamstrung by the suggestion of Nidud's queen, secretly murders her sons, and out of their eyes fashions marvellous jewels, which she unsuspectingly wears upon her breast until he reveals their origin.

## MYTHS OF THE SEA AND THE DEAD

**Just as the Greeks fancied** that the tempests were the effect of Neptune's wrath, so the Northern races attributed them either to the writhings of Iörmungandr, the Midgard snake, or to the anger of Aegir, who, crowned with seaweed like Neptune, often sent his children, the wave maidens (the counterpart of the Nereides and Oceanides), to play on the tossing billows. Neptune had his dwelling in the coral caves near the Island of Eubœa, while Aegir lived in a similar palace near the Cattegat. Here he was surrounded by the nixies, undines, and mermaids, the counterpart of the Greek water nymphs, and by the river-gods of the Rhine, Elbe, and Neckar, who remind us of Alpheus and Peneus, the river-gods of the Greeks.

The frequency of shipwrecks on the Northern coasts made the people think of Ran (the equivalent of the Greek sea-goddess Amphitrite) as greedy and avaricious, and they described her as armed with a strong net, with which she drew all things down into the deep. The Greek Sirens had their parallel in the Northern Lorelei, who possessed the same gift of song, and also lured mariners to their death; while Princess Ilse, who was turned into a fountain, reminds us of the nymph Arethusa, who underwent a similar transformation.

In the Northern conception of Nifl-heim we have an almost exact counterpart of the Greek Hades. Mödgud, the guardian of the Giallar-bridge (the bridge of death), over which all the spirits of the dead must pass, exacts a tribute of blood as rigorously as Charon demands an obolus from every soul he ferries over Acheron, the river of death. The fierce dog Garm, cowering in the Gnipa hole, and keeping guard at Hel's gate, is like the three-headed monster Cerberus; and the nine worlds of Nifl-heim are not unlike the divisions of Hades, Nastrond being an adequate substitute for Tartarus, where the wicked were punished with equal severity.

The custom of burning dead heroes with their arms, and of slaying victims, such as horses and dogs, upon their pyre, was much the same in the North as in the South; and while Mors or Thanatos, the Greek Death, was represented with a sharp scythe, Hel was depicted with a broom or rake, which she used as ruthlessly, and with which she did as much execution.

## BALDER AND APOLLO

Balder, the radiant god of sunshine, reminds us not only of Apollo and Orpheus, but of all the other heroes of sun myths. His wife Nanna is like Flora, and still more like Proserpine, for she, too, goes down into the underworld, where she tarries for a while. Balder's golden hall of Breidablik is like Apollo's palace in the east; he, also, delights in flowers; all things smile at his approach, and willingly pledge themselves not to injure him. As Achilles was vulnerable only in the heel, so Balder could be slain only by the harmless mistletoe, and his death is occasioned by Loki's jealousy just as Hercules was slain by that of Deianeira. Balder's funeral pyre on Ringhorn reminds us of Hercules's death on Mount Œta, the flames and reddish glow of both fires serving to typify the setting sun. The Northern god of sun and summer could only be released from Nifl-heim if all animate and inanimate objects shed tears; so Proserpine could issue from Hades only upon condition that she had partaken of no food. The trifling refusal of Thok to shed a single tear is like the pomegranate seeds which Proserpine ate, and the result is equally disastrous in both cases, as it detains Balder and Proserpine underground, and the earth (Frigga or Ceres) must continue to mourn their absence.

Through Loki evil entered into the Northern world; Prometheus's gift of fire brought the same curse upon the Greeks. The punishment inflicted by the gods upon the culprits is not unlike, for while Loki is bound with adamantine chains underground, and tortured by the continuous dropping of venom from the fangs of a snake fastened above his head, Prometheus is similarly fettered to Caucasus, and a ravenous vulture continually preys upon his liver. Loki's punishment has another counterpart in that of Tityus, bound in Hades, and in that of Enceladus, chained beneath Mount Aetna, where his writhing produced earthquakes, and his imprecations caused sudden eruptions of the volcano. Loki, further, resembles

Neptune in that he, too, assumed an equine form and was the parent of a wonderful steed, for Sleipnir rivals Arion both in speed and endurance.

The Fimbul-winter has been compared to the long preliminary fight under the walls of Troy, and Ragnarok, the grand closing drama of Northern mythology, to the burning of that famous city. "Thor is Hector; the Fenris wolf, Pyrrhus, son of Achilles, who slew Priam (Odin); and Vidar, who survives in Ragnarok, is Aeneas." The destruction of Priam's palace is the type of the ruin of the gods' golden halls; and the devouring wolves Hati, Sköll, and Managarm, the fiends of darkness, are prototypes of Paris and all the other demons of darkness, who bear away or devour the sun-maiden Helen.

According to another interpretation, however, Ragnarok and the consequent submersion of the world is but a Northern version of the Deluge. The survivors, Lif and Lifthrasir, like Deucalion and Pyrrha, were destined to repeople the world; and just as the shrine of Delphi alone resisted the destructive power of the great cataclysm, so Gimli stood radiant to receive the surviving gods.

## GIANTS AND TITANS

We have already seen how closely the Northern giants resembled the Titans. It only remains to mention that while the Greeks imagined that Atlas was changed into a mountain, so the Northmen believed that the Riesengebirge, in Germany, were formed from giants, and that the avalanches which descended from their lofty heights were the burdens of snow which these giants impatiently shook from their crests as they changed their cramped positions. The apparition, in the shape of a bull, of one of the water giants, who came to woo the queen of the Franks, has its parallel in the story of Jupiter's wooing of Europa, and Meroveus is evidently the exact counterpart of Sarpedon. A faint resemblance can be traced between the giant ship Mannigfual and the Argo, for while the one is supposed to have cruised through the Aegean and Euxine Seas, and to have made many places memorable by the dangers it encountered there, so the Northern vessel sailed about the North and Baltic Seas, and is mentioned in connection with the Island of Bornholm and the cliffs of Dover.

While the Greeks imagined that Nightmares were the evil dreams which escaped from the Cave of Somnus, the Northern race fancied they were female dwarfs or trolls, who crept out of the dark recesses of the earth to torment them. All magic weapons in the North were said to be the work of the dwarfs, the underground smiths, while those of the Greeks were manufactured by Vulcan and the Cyclopes, under Mount Aetna, or on the Island of Lemnos.

## THE VOLSUNG SAGA

In the Sigurd myth we find Odin one-eyed like the Cyclopes, who, like him, are personifications of the sun. Sigurd is instructed by Gripir, the horse-trainer, who is reminiscent of Chiron, the centaur. He is not only able to teach a young hero all he need know, and to give him good advice concerning his future conduct, but is also possessed of the gift of prophecy.

The marvellous sword which becomes the property of Sigmund and of Sigurd as soon as they prove themselves worthy to wield it, and the sword Angurvadel which Frithiof inherits from his sire, remind us of the weapon which Aegeus concealed beneath the rock, and which Theseus secured as soon as he had become a man. Sigurd, like Theseus, Perseus, and Jason, seeks to avenge his father's wrongs ere he sets out in search of the golden hoard, the exact counterpart of the golden fleece, which is also guarded by a dragon, and is very hard to secure. Like all the Greek sun-gods and heroes, Sigurd has golden hair and bright blue eyes. His struggle with Fafnir reminds us of Apollo's fight with Python, while the ring Andvaranaut can be likened to Venus's cestus, and the curse attached to its possessor is like the tragedy of Helen, who brought endless bloodshed upon all connected with her.

Sigurd could not have conquered Fafnir without the magic sword, just as the Greeks failed to take Troy without the arrows of Philoctetes, which are also emblems of the all-conquering rays of the sun. The recovery of the stolen treasure is like Menelaus's recovery of Helen, and it apparently brings as little happiness to Sigurd as his recreant wife did to the Spartan king.

## BRUNHILD

Brunhild resembles Minerva in her martial tastes, physical appearance, and wisdom; but her anger and resentment when Sigurd forgets her for Gudrun is like the wrath of Œnone, whom Paris deserts to woo Helen. Brunhild's anger continues to accompany Sigurd through life, and she even seeks to compass his death, while Œnone, called to cure her wounded lover, refuses to do so and permits him to die. Œnone and Brunhild are both overcome by the same remorseful feelings when their lovers have breathed their last, and both insist upon sharing their funeral pyres, and end their lives by the side of those whom they had loved.

## SUN MYTHS

Containing, as it does, a whole series of sun myths, the Volsunga Saga repeats itself in every phase; and just as Ariadne, forsaken by the sun-hero Theseus, finally marries Bacchus, so Gudrun, when Sigurd has departed, marries Atli, the King of the Huns. He, too, ends his life amid the flames of his burning palace or ship. Gunnar, like Orpheus or Amphion, plays such marvellous strains upon his harp that even the serpents are lulled to sleep. According to some interpretations, Atli is like Fafnir, and covets the possession of the gold. Both are therefore probably personifications "of the winter cloud which broods over and keeps from mortals the gold of the sun's light and heat, till in the spring the bright orb overcomes the powers of darkness and tempests, and scatters his gold over the face of the earth."

Swanhild, Sigurd's daughter, is another personification of the sun, as is seen in her blue eyes and golden hair; and her death under the hoofs of black steeds represents the blotting out of the sun by clouds of storm or of darkness.

Just as Castor and Pollux hasten to rescue their sister Helen when she has been borne away by Theseus, so Swanhild's brothers, Erp, Hamdir, and Sörli, hasten off to avenge her death.

Such are the main points of resemblance between the mythologies of the North and South, and the analogy goes far to prove that they were originally formed from the same materials, the principal differences being due to the local colouring imparted unconsciously by the different races.

# A GENERAL GLOSSARY OF MYTHOLOGICAL TERMS

**Aaru**  Heavenly paradise where the blessed went after death.

**Ab**  Heart or mind.

**Absál**  Nurse to Salámán, who died after their brief love affair.

**Achilles**  The son of Peleus and the sea-nymph Thetis, who distinguished himself in the Trojan War. He was made almost immortal by his mother, who dipped him in the River Styx, and he was invincible except for a portion of his heel which remained out of the water.

**Acropolis**  Citadel in a Greek city.

**Adad-Ea**  Ferryman to Ut-Napishtim, who carried Gilgamesh to visit his ancestor.

**Adapa**  Son of Ea and a wise sage.

**Adar**  God of the sun, who is worshipped primarily in Nippur.

**Aditi**  Sky goddess and mother of the gods.

**Adityas**  Vishnu, children of Aditi, including Indra, Mitra, Rudra, Tvashtar, Varuna and Vishnu.

**Aeneas**  The son of Anchises and the goddess Aphrodite, reared by a nymph. He led the Dardanian troops in the Trojan War According to legend, he became the founder of Rome.

**Aengus Óg**  Son of Dagda and Boann (a woman said to have given the Boyne river its name), Aengus is the Irish god of love whose stronghold is reputed to have been at New Grange. The famous tale Dream of Aengus tells of how he fell in love with a maiden he had dreamt of. He eventually discovered that she was to be found at the Lake of the Dragon's Mouth in Co. Tipperary, but that she lived every alternate year in the form of a swan. Aengus pursues the woman of his dreams and plunges into the lake transforming himself also into the shape of a swan. Then the two fly back together to his palace on the Boyne where they live out their days as guardians of would-be lovers.

**Aesir** Northern gods who made their home in Asgard; there are twelve in number.

**Afrásiyáb** Son of Poshang, king of Túrán, who led an army against Nauder. Afrásiyáb became ruler of Persia on defeating Nauder.

**Afterlife** Life after death or paradise, reached only by the process of preserving the body from decay through embalming and preparing it for reincarnation.

**Agamemnon** A famous King of Mycenae. He married Helen of Sparta's sister Clytemnestra. When Paris abducted Helen, beginning the Trojan War, Menelaus called on Agamemnon to raise the Greek troops. He had to sacrifice his daughter Iphigenia in order to get a fair wind to travel to Troy.

**Agastya** A rishi (sage). Leads hermits to Rama.

**Agemo** (Yoruba) A chameleon who aided Olorun in outwitting Olokun, who was angry at him for letting Obatala create life on her lands without her permission. Agemo outwitted Olokun by changing colour, letting her think that he and Olorun were better cloth dyers than she was. She admitted defeat and there was peace between the gods once again.

**Aghasur** A dragon sent by Kans to destroy Krishna.

**Aghríras** Son of Poshang and brother of Afrásiyáb, who was killed by his brother.

**Agni** The god of fire.

**Agora** Greek marketplace.

**Ahura-Mazda** Supreme god of the Persians, god of the sky. Similar to the Hindu god Varuna.

**Ajax** Ajax of Locris was another warrior at Troy. When Troy was captured, he committed the ultimate sacrilege by seizing Cassandra from her sanctuary with the Palladium.

**Ajax**  Ajax the Greater was the bravest, after Achilles, of all warriors at Troy, fighting Hector in single combat and distinguishing himself in the Battle of the Ships. He was not chosen as the bravest warrior and eventually went mad.

**Aje**  (Igbo) Goddess of the earth and the underworld.

**Aje**  (Yoruba) Goddess of the River Niger, daughter of Yemoja.

**Akhet**  Season of the year when the River Nile traditionally flooded.

**Akkadian**  Person of the first Mesopotamian empire, centred in Akkad.

**Akwán Diw**  An evil spirit who appeared as a wild ass in the court of Kai-khosráu. Rustem fought and defeated the demon, presenting its head to Kai-khosráu.

**Alberich**  King of the dwarfs.

**Alcinous**  King of the Phaeacians.

**Alf-heim**  Home of the elves, ruled by Frey.

**All Hallowmass**  All Saints' Day.

**Allfather**  Another name for Odin; Yggdrasill was created by Allfather.

**Alsvider**  Steed of the moon (Mani) chariot.

**Alsvin**  Steed of the sun (Sol) chariot.

**Amado**  Outer panelling of a dwelling, usually made of wood.

**Ama-no-uzume**  Goddess of the dawn, meditation and the arts, who showed courage when faced with a giant who scared the other deities, including Ninigi. Also known as Uzume.

**Amaterasu**  Goddess of the sun and daughter of Izanagi after Izanami's death; she became ruler of the High Plains of Heaven on her father's withdrawal from the world. Sister of Tsuki-yomi and Susanoo.

**Ambalika**  Daughter of the king of Benares.

**Ambika**  Daughter of the king of Benares.

**Ambrosia**  Food of the gods.

**Amemet**  Eater of the dead, monster who devoured the souls of the unworthy.

**Amen**  Original creator deity.

**Amen-Ra**  A being created from the fusion of Ra and Osiris. He champions the poor and those in trouble. Similar to the Greek god Zeus.

**Ananda**  Disciple of Buddha.

**Anansi**  One of the most popular African animal myths, Anansi the spider is a clever and shrewd character who outwits his fellow animals to get his own way. He is an entertaining but morally dubious character. Many African countries tell Anansi stories.

**Ananta**  Thousand-headed snake that sprang from Balarama's mouth, Vishnu's attendant, serpent of infinite time.

**Andhrímnir**  Cook at Valhalla.

**Andvaranaut**  Ring of Andvari, the King of the dwarfs.

**Angada**  Son of Vali, one of the monkey host.

**Anger-Chamber**  Room designated for an angry queen.

**Angurboda**  Loki's first wife, and the mother of Hel, Fenris and Jormungander.

**Aniruddha**  Son of Pradyumna.

**Anjana**  Mother of Hanuman.

**Anunnaki**  Great spirits or gods of Earth.

**Ansar**  God of the sky and father of Ea and Anu. Brother-husband to Kishar. Also known as Anshar or Asshur.

**Anshumat**  A mighty chariot fighter.

**Anu**  God of the sky and lord of heaven, son of Ansar and Kishar.

**Anubis**  Guider of souls and ruler of the underworld before Osiris.; he was one of the divinities who brought Osiris back to life. He is portrayed as a canid, African wolf or jackal.

**Apep**  Serpent and emblem of chaos.

**Apollo**  One of the twelve Olympian gods, son of Zeus and Leto. He is attributed with being the god of plague, music, song and prophecy.

**Apsu**  Primeval domain of fresh water, originally part of Tiawath with whom he mated to have Mummu. The term is also used for the abyss from which creation came.

**Aquila**  The divine eagle.

**Arachne**  A Lydian woman with great skill in weaving. She was challenged in a competition by the jealous Athene who destroyed her work and when she killed herself, turned her into a spider destined to weave until eternity.

**Aralu**  Goddess of the underworld, also known as Eres-ki-Gal. Married to Nergal.

**Ares**  God of War, 'gold-changer of corpses', and the son of Zeus and Hera.

**Argonauts**  Heroes who sailed with Jason on the ship Argo to fetch the golden fleece from Colchis.

**Ariki**  A high chief, a leader, a master, a lord.

**Arjuna**  The third of the Pandavas.

**Aroha**  Affection, love.

**Artemis**  The virgin goddess of the chase, attributed with being the moon goddess and the primitive mother-goddess. She was daughter of Zeus and Leto.

**Arundhati**  The Northern Crown.

**Asamanja**  Son of Sagara.

**Asclepius**  God of healing who often took the form of a snake. He is the son of Apollo by Coronis.

**Asgard**  Home of the gods, at one root of Yggdrasill.

**Ashvatthaman**  Son of Drona.

**Ashvins** Twin horsemen, sons of the sun, benevolent gods and related to the divine.

**Ashwapati** Uncle of Bharata and Satrughna.

**Asipû** Wizard.

**Asopus** The god of the River Asopus.

**Apsaras** Dancing girls of Indra's court and heavenly nymphs.

**Astrolabe** Instrument for making astronomical measurements.

**Asuras** Titans, demons, and enemies of the gods possessing magical powers.

**Atef crown** White crown made up of the Hedjet, the white crown of Upper Egypt, and red feathers.

**Atem** The first creator-deity, he is also thought to be the finisher of the world. Also known as Tem.

**Athene** Virgin warrior-goddess, born from the forehead of Zeus when he swallowed his wife Metis. Plays a key role in the travels of Odysseus, and Perseus.

**Atlatl** Spear-thrower.

**Atua** A supernatural being, a god.

**Atua-toko** A small carved stick, the symbol of the god whom it represents. It was stuck in the ground whilst holding incantations to its presiding god.

**Augeas** King of Elis, one of the Argonauts.

**Augsburg** Tyr's city.

**Avalon** Legendary island where Excalibur was created and where Arthur went to recover from his wounds. It is said he will return from Avalon one day to reclaim his kingdom.

**Ba** Dead person or soul. Also known as ka.

**Bairn** Little child, also called bairnie.

**Balarama** Brother of Krishna.

**Balder** Son of Frigga; his murder causes Ragnarok.

**Bali** Brother of Sugriva and one of the five great monkeys in the Ramayana.

**Balor** The evil, one-eyed King of the Fomorians and also grandfather of Lugh of the Long Arm. It was prophesied that Balor would one day be slain by his own grandson so he locked his daughter away on a remote island where he intended that she would never fall pregnant. But Cian, father of Lugh, managed to reach the island disguised as a woman, and Balor's daughter eventually bore him a child. During the second battle of Mag Tured (or Moytura), Balor was killed by Lugh who slung a stone into his giant eye.

**Ban** King of Benwick, father of Lancelot and brother of King Bors.

**Bannock** Oat or barley cake.

**Barû** Seer.

**Basswood** Any of several North American linden trees with a soft light-coloured wood.

**Bastet** Goddess of love, fertility and sex and a solar deity. She is often portrayed with the head of a cat.

**Bateta** (Yoruba) The first human, created alongside Hanna by the Toad and reshaped into human form by the Moon.

**Bau** Goddess of humankind and the sick, and known as the 'divine physician'. Daughter of Anu.

**Beaver** Largest rodent in the United States of America, held in high esteem by the native American people. Although a land mammal, it spends a great deal of time in water and has a dense waterproof fur coat to protect it from harsh weather conditions.

**Behula** Daughter of Saha.

**Bel** Name for the god En-lil, the word is also used as a title meaning 'lord'.

**Belus** Deity who helped form the heavens and earth and created animals and celestial beings. Similar to Zeus in Greek mythology.

**Benten** Goddess of the sea and one of the Seven Divinities of Luck. Also referred to as the goddess of love, beauty and eloquence and as being the personification of wisdom.

**Bere** Barley.

**Berossus** Priest of Bel who wrote a history of Babylon.

**Bestla** Giant mother of Aesir's mortal element.

**Bhadra** A mighty elephant.

**Bhagavati** Shiva's wife, also known as Parvati.

**Bhagiratha** Son of Dilipa.

**Bharadhwaja** Father of Drona and a hermit.

**Bharata** One of Dasharatha's four sons.

**Bhaumasur** A demon, slain by Krishna.

**Bhima** The second of the Pandavas.

**Bhimasha** King of Rajagriha and disciple of Buddha.

**Bier** Frame on which a coffin or dead body is placed before being carried to the grave.

**Bifrost** Rainbow bridge presided over by Heimdall.

**Big-Belly** One of Ravana's monsters.

**Bilskirnir** Thor's palace.

**Bodach** The term means 'old man'. The Highlanders believed that the Bodach crept down chimneys in order to steal naughty children. In other territories, he was a spirit who warned of death.

**Boer** Person of Dutch origin who settled in southern Africa in the late seventeenth century. The term means 'farmer'. Boer people are often called Afrikaners.

**Book of the Dead** Book for the dead, thought to be written by Thoth, texts from which were written on papyrus and buried with the dead, or carved on the walls of tombs, pyramids or sarcophagi.

**Bors** King of Gaul and brother of King Ban.

**Brahma** Creator of the world, mythical origin of colour (caste).

**Brahmadatta** King of Benares.

**Brahman** Member of the highest Hindu caste, traditionally a priest.

**Bran** In Scottish legend, Bran is the great hunting hound of Fionn Mac Chumail. In Irish mythology, he is a great hero.

**Branstock** Giant oak tree in the Volsung's hall; Odin placed a sword in it and challenged the guests of a wedding to withdraw it.

**Brave** Young warrior of native American descent, sometimes also referred to as a 'buck'.

**Breidablik** Balder's palace.

**Brigit** Scottish saint or spirit associated with the coming of spring.

**Brisingamen** Freyia's necklace.

**Britomartis** A Cretan goddess, also known as Dictynna.

**Brocéliande** Legendary enchanted forest and the supposed burial place of Merlin.

**Brokki** Dwarf who makes a deal with Loki, and who makes Miolnir, Draupnir and Gulinbursti.

**Brollachan** A shapeless spirit of unknown origin. One of the most frightening in Scottish mythology, it spoke only two words, 'Myself' and 'Thyself', taking the shape of whatever it sat upon.

**Brownie** A household spirit or creature which took the form of a small man (usually hideously ugly) who undertakes household chores, and mill or farm work, in exchange for a bowl of milk.

**Brunhilde** A Valkyrie found by Sigurd.

**Buddha** Founder of buddhism, Gautama, avatar of Vishnu in Hinduism.

**Buddhism** Buddhism arrived in China in the first century BC via the silk trading route from India and Central Asia. Its founder was

Guatama Siddhartha (the Buddha), a religious teacher in northern India. Buddhist doctrine declared that by destroying the causes of all suffering, mankind could attain perfect enlightenment. The religion encouraged a new respect for all living things and brought with it the idea of reincarnation; i.e. that the soul returns to the earth after death in another form, dictated by the individual's behaviour in his previous life. By the fourth century, Buddhism was the dominant religion in China, retaining its powerful influence over the nation until the mid-ninth century.

**Buffalo** A type of wild ox, once widely scattered over the Great Plains of North America. Also known as a 'bison', the buffalo was an important food source for the Indian tribes and its hide was also used in the construction of tepees and to make clothing. The buffalo was also sometimes revered as a totem animal, i.e. venerated as a direct ancestor of the tribesmen, and its skull used in ceremonial fashion.

**Bull of Apis** Sacred bull, thought to be the son of Hathor.

**Bulu** Sacrificial rite.

**Bundles, sacred** These bundles contained various venerated objects of the tribe, believed to have supernatural powers. Custody or ownership of the bundle was never lightly entered upon, but involved the learning of endless songs and ritual dances.

**Bushel** Unit of measurement, usually used for agricultural products or food.

**Bushi** Warrior.

**Byrny** Coat of mail.

**Cacique** King or prince.

**Cailleach Bheur** A witch with a blue face who represents winter. When she is reborn each autumn, snow falls. She is mother of the god of youth (Angus mac Og).

**Calchas** The seer of Mycenae who accompanied the Greek fleet to Troy. It was his prophecy which stated that Troy would never be taken without the aid of Achilles.

**Calpulli** Village house, or group or clan of families.

**Calumet** Ceremonial pipe used by the north American Indians.

**Calypso** A nymph who lived on the island of Ogygia.

**Camaxtli** Tlascalan god of war and the chase, similar to Huitzilopochtli.

**Camelot** King Arthur's castle and centre of his realm.

**Caoineag** A banshee.

**Caravanserai** Traveller's inn, traditionally found in Asia or North Africa.

**Cat** A black cat has great mythological significance, is often the bearer of bad luck, a symbol of black magic, and the familiar of a witch. Cats were also the totem for many tribes.

**Cath Sith** A fairy cat who was believed to be a witch transformed.

**Cazi** Magical person or influence.

**Ceasg** A Scottish mermaid with the body of a maiden and the tail of a salmon.

**Ceilidh** Party.

**Cerberus** The three-headed dog who guarded the entrance to the Underworld.

**Chalchiuhtlicue** Goddess of water and the sick or newborn, and wife of Tlaloc. She is often symbolized as a small frog.

**Channa** Guatama's charioteer.

**Chaos** A state from which the universe was created – caused by fire and ice meeting.

**Charon** The ferryman of the dead who carries souls across the River Styx to Hades.

**Charybdis** *See* Scylla and Charybdis.

**Chicomecohuatl** Chief goddess of maize and one of a group of deities called Centeotl, who care for all aspects of agriculture.

**Chicomoztoc** Legendary mountain and place of origin of the Aztecs. The name means 'seven caves'.

**Chinawezi** Primordial serpent.

**Chinvat Bridge** Bridge of the Gatherer, which the souls of the righteous cross to reach Mount Alborz or the world of the dead. Unworthy beings who try to cross Chinvat Bridge fall or are dragged into a place of eternal punishment.

**Chitambaram** Sacred city of Shiva's dance.

**Chrysaor** Son of Poseidon and Medusa, born from the severed neck of Medusa when Perseus beheaded her.

**Chryseis** Daughter of Chryses who was taken by Agamemnon in the battle of Troy.

**Chullasubhadda** Wife of Buddha-elect (Sumedha).

**Chunda** A good smith who entertains Buddha.

**Churl** Mean or unkind person.

**Circe** An enchantress and the daughter of Helius. She lived on the island of Aeaea with the power to change men to beasts.

**Citlalpol** The Mexican name for Venus, or the Great Star, and one of the only stars they worshipped. Also known as Tlauizcalpantecutli, or Lord of the Dawn.

**Cleobis and Biton** Two men of Argos who dragged the wagon carrying their mother, priestess of Hera, from Argos to the sanctuary.

**Clio** Muse of history and prophecy.

**Clytemnestra** Daughter of Tyndareus, sister of Helen, who married Agamemnon but deserted him when he sacrificed Iphigenia, their daughter, at the beginning of the Trojan War.

**Coatepetl** Mythical mountain, known as the 'serpent mountain'.

**Coatl** Serpent.

**Coatlicue** Earth mother and celestial goddess, she gave birth to Huitzilopochtli and his sister, Coyolxauhqui, and the moon and stars.

**Codex** Ancient book, often a list with pages folded into a zigzag pattern.

**Confucius (Kong Fuzi)** Regarded as China's greatest sage and ethical teacher, Confucius (551–479 BC) was not especially revered during his lifetime and had a small following of some three thousand people. After the Burning of the Books in 213 BC, interest in his philosophies became widespread. Confucius believed that mankind was essentially good, but argued for a highly structured society, presided over by a strong central government which would set the highest moral standards. The individual's sense of duty and obligation, he argued, would play a vital role in maintaining a well-run state.

**Coyolxauhqui** Goddess of the moon and sister to Huitzilopochtli, she was decapitated by her brother after trying to kill their mother.

**Crodhmara** Fairy cattle.

**Crow** Usually associated with battle and death, but many mythological figures take this form.

**Cu Sith** A great fairy dog, usually green and oversized.

**Cutty** Girl.

**Cyclopes** One-eyed giants who were imprisoned in Tartarus by Uranus and Cronus, but released by Zeus, for whom they made thunderbolts. Also a tribe of pastoralists who live without laws, and on, whenever possible, human flesh.

**Daedalus** Descendant of the Athenian King Erechtheus and son of Eupalamus. He killed his nephew and apprentice. Famed for constructing the labyrinth to house the Minotaur, in which he was later imprisoned. He constructed wings for himself and his son to make their escape.

**Dagda** One of the principal gods of the Tuatha De Danann, the father and chief, the Celtic equivalent of Zeus. He was the god reputed to have led the People of Dana in their successful conquest of the Fir Bolg.

**Dagon** God of fish and fertility; he is sometimes described as a sea-monster or chthonic god.

**Daikoku** God of wealth and one of the gods of luck.

**Daimyō** Powerful lord or magnate.

**Daksha** The chief Prajapati.

**Dana** Also known as Danu, a goddess worshipped from antiquity by the Celts and considered to be the ancestor of the Tuatha De Danann.

**Danae** Daughter of Acrisius, King of Argos. Acrisius trapped her in a cave when he was warned that his grandson would be the cause of his ultimate death. Zeus came to her and Perseus was born.

**Danaids** The fifty daughters of Danaus of Argos, by ten mothers.

**Daoine Sidhe** The people of the Hollow Hills, or Otherworld.

**Dardanus** Son of Zeus and Electra, daughter of Atlas.

**Dasharatha** A Manu amongst men, King of Koshala, father of Santa.

**Deianeira** Daughter of Oeneus, who married Heracles after he won her in a battle with the River Achelous.

**Demeter** Goddess of agriculture and nutrition, whose name means earth mother. She is the mother of Persephone.

**Demophoon** Son of King Celeus of Eleusis, who was nursed by Demeter and then dropped in the fire when she tried to make him immortal.

**Dervish** Member of a religious order, often Sufi, known for their wild dancing and whirling.

**Desire** The god of love.

**Deva** A god other than the supreme God.

**Devadatta** Buddha's cousin, plots evil against Buddha.

**Dhrishtadyumna** Twin brother of Draupadi, slays Drona.

**Dibarra** God of plague. Also a demonic character or evil spirit.

**Dik-dik** Dwarf antelope native to eastern and southern Africa.

**Dilipa** Son of Anshumat, father of Bhagiratha.

**Dionysus** The god of wine, vegetation and the life force, and of ecstasy. He was considered to be outside the Greek pantheon, and generally thought to have begun life as a mortal.

**Dioscuri** Castor and Polydeuces, the twin sons of Zeus and Leda, who are important deities.

**Divan** Privy council.

**Divots** Turfs.

**Dog** The dog is a symbol of humanity, and usually has a role helping the hero of the myth or legend. Fionn's Bran and Grey Dog are two examples of wild beasts transformed to become invaluable servants.

**Dōshin** Government official.

**Dossal** Ornamental altar cloth.

**Doughty** Persistent and brave person.

**Dragon** Important animal in Japanese culture, symbolizing power, wealth, luck and success.

**Draupadi** Daughter of Drupada.

**Draupnir** Odin's famous ring, fashioned by Brokki.

**Drona** A Brahma, son of the great sage Bharadwaja.

**Druid** An ancient order of Celtic priests held in high esteem who flourished in the pre-Christian era. The word 'druid' is derived from an ancient Celtic one meaning 'very knowledgeable'. These individuals were believed to have mystical powers and in ancient Irish literature possess the ability to conjure up magical charms, to create tempests, to curse and debilitate their enemies and to perform as soothsayers to the royal courts.

**Drupada** King of the Panchalas.

**Dryads** Nymphs of the trees.

**Dun** A stronghold or royal abode surrounded by an earthen wall.

**Durga** Goddess, wife of Shiva.

**Durk** Knife.

**Duryodhana** One of Drona's pupils.

**Dvalin** Dwarf visited by Loki; also the name for the stag on Yggdrasill.

**Dwarfs** Fairies and black elves are called dwarfs.

**Dwarkanath** The Lord of Dwaraka; Krishna.

**Dyumatsena** King of the Shalwas and father of Satyavan.

**Ea** God of water, light and wisdom, and one of the creator deities. He brought arts and civilization to humankind. Also known as Oannes and Nudimmud.

**Eabani** Hero originally created by Aruru to defeat Gilgamesh, the two became friends and destroyed Khumbaba together. He personifies the natural world.

**Each Uisge** The mythical water-horse which haunts lochs and appears in various forms.

**Ebisu** One of the gods of luck. He is also the god of labour and fishermen.

**Echo** A nymph who was punished by Hera for her endless stories told to distract Hera from Zeus's infidelity.

**Ector** King Arthur's foster father, who raised Arthur to protect him.

**Edda** Collection of prose and poetic myths and stories from the Norsemen.

**Eight Immortals** Three of these are reputed to be historical: Han Chung-li, born in Shaanxi, who rose to become a Marshal of the Empire in 21 BC. Chang Kuo-Lao, who lived in the seventh to eighth century AD, and Lü Tung-pin, who was born in AD 755.

**Einheriear** Odin's guests at Valhalla.

**Eisa** Loki' daughter.

**Ekalavya** Son of the king of the Nishadas.

**Electra** Daughter of Agamemnon and Clytemnestra.

**Eleusis** A town in which the cult of Demeter is centred.

**Elf** Sigmund is buried by an elf; there are light and dark elves (the latter called dwarfs).

**Elokos** (Central African) Imps of dwarf-demons who eat human flesh.

**Elpenor** The youngest of Odysseus's crew who fell from the roof of Circe's house on Aeaea and visited with Odysseus at Hades.

**Elysium** The home of the blessed dead.

**Emain Macha** The capital of ancient Ulster.

**Emma Dai-o** King of hell and judge of the dead.

**En-lil** God of the lower world, storms and mist, who held sway over the ghostly animistic spirits, which at his bidding might pose as the friends or enemies of men. Also known as Bel.

**Eos** Goddess of the dawn and sister of the sun and moon.

**Erichthonius** A child born of the semen spilled when Hephaestus tried to rape Athene on the Acropolis.

**Eridu** The home of Ea and one of the two major cities of Babylonian civilization.

**Erirogho** Magical mixture made from the ashes of the dead.

**Eros** God of Love, the son of Aphrodite.

**Erpa** Hereditary chief.

**Erysichthon** A Thessalian who cut down a grove sacred to Demeter, who punished him with eternal hunger.

**Eshu** (Yoruba) God of mischief. He also tests people's characters and controls law enforcement.

**Eteocles** Son of Oedipus.

**Eumaeus** Swineherd of Odysseus's family at Ithaca.

**Euphemus** A son of Poseidon who could walk on water. He sailed with the Argonauts.

**Europa** Daughter of King Agenor of Tyre, who was taken by Zeus to Crete.

**Eurydice** A Thracian nymph married to Orpheus.

**Excalibur** The magical sword given to Arthur by the Lady of the Lake. In some versions of the myths, Excalibur is also the sword that the young Arthur pulls from the stone to become king.

**Fabulist** Person who composes or tells fables.

**Fafnir** Shape-changer who kills his father and becomes a dragon to guard the family jewels. Slain by Sigurd.

**Fairy** The word is derived from 'Fays' which means Fates. They are immortal, with the gift of prophecy and of music, and their role changes according to the origin of the myth. They were often considered to be little people, with enormous propensity for mischief, but they are central to many myths and legends, with important powers.

**Faro** (Mali, Guinea) God of the sky.

**Fates** In Greek mythology, daughters of Zeus and Themis, who spin the thread of a mortal's life and cut it when his time is due. Called Norns in Viking mythology.

**Fenris** A wild wolf, who is the son of Loki. He roams the earth after Ragnarok.

**Ferhad** Sculptor who fell in love with Shireen, the wife of Khosru, and undertook a seemingly impossible task to clear a passage through the mountain of Beysitoun and join the rivers in return for winning Shireen's hand.

**Fialar** Red cock of Valhalla.

**Fianna/Fenians** The word 'fianna' was used in early times to describe young warrior-hunters. These youths evolved under the leadership of Finn Mac Cumaill as a highly skilled band of military men who took up service with various kings throughout Ireland.

**Filheim** Land of mist, at the end of one of Yggdrasill's roots.

**Fingal** Another name for Fionn Mac Chumail, used after MacPherson's Ossian in the eighteenth century.

**Fionn Mac Chumail** Irish and Scottish warrior, with great powers of fairness and wisdom. He is known not for physical strength but for knowledge, sense of justice, generosity and canny instinct. He had two hounds, which were later discovered to be his nephews transformed. He became head of the Fianna, or Féinn, fighting the enemies of Ireland and Scotland. He was the father of Oisin (also called Ossian, or other derivatives), and father or grandfather of Osgar.

**Fir Bolg** One of the ancient, pre-Gaelic peoples of Ireland who were reputed to have worshipped the god Bulga, meaning god of lighting. They are thought to have colonized Ireland around 1970 BC, after the death of Nemed and to have reigned for a short period of thirty-seven years before their defeat by the Tuatha De Danann.

**Fir Chlis** Nimble men or merry dancers, who are the souls of fallen angels.

**Folkvang** Freyia's palace.

**Fomorians** A race of monstrous beings, popularly conceived as sea-pirates with some supernatural characteristics who opposed the earliest settlers in Ireland, including the Nemedians and the Tuatha De Danann.

**Frey** Comes to Asgard with Freyia as a hostage following the war between the Aesir and the Vanir.

**Freyia** Comes to Asgard with Frey as a hostage following the war between the Aesir and the Vanir. Goddess of beauty and love.

**Frigga** Odin's wife and mother of gods; she is goddess of the earth.

**Fuath** Evil spirits which lived in or near the water.

**Fulla** Frigga's maidservant.

**Furies** Creatures born from the blood of Cronus, guarding the greatest sinners of the Underworld. Their power lay in their ability to drive mortals mad. Snakes writhed in their hair and around their waists.

**Furoshiki** Cloths used to wrap things.

**Gae Bolg** Cuchulainn alone learned the use of this weapon from the woman-warrior, Scathach and with it he slew his own son Connla and his closest friend, Ferdia. Gae Bolg translates as 'harpoon-like javelin' and the deadly weapon was reported to have been created by Bulga, the god of lighting.

**Gaea** Goddess of Earth, born from Chaos, and the mother of Uranus and Pontus. Also spelled as Gaia.

**Gage** Object of value presented to a challenger to symbolize good faith.

**Galahad**  Knight of the Round Table, who took up the search for the Holy Grail. Son of Lancelot, Galahad is considered the purest and most perfect knight.

**Galatea**  Daughter of Nereus and Doris, a sea-nymph loved by Polyphemus, the Cyclops.

**Gandhari**  Mother of Duryodhana.

**Gandharvas**  Demi-gods and musicians.

**Gandjharva**  Musical ministrants of the upper air.

**Ganesha**  Elephant-headed god of scribes and son of Shiva.

**Ganges**  Sacred river personified by the goddess Ganga, wife of Shiva and daughter of the mount Himalaya.

**Gareth of Orkney**  King Arthur's nephew and knight of the Round Table.

**Garm**  Hel's hound.

**Garuda**  King of the birds and mount Vishnu, the divine bird, attendant of Narayana.

**Gautama**  Son of Suddhodana and also known as Siddhartha.

**Gawain**  Nephew of King Arthur and knight of the Round Table, he is best known for his adventure with the Green Knight, who challenges one of Arthur's knights to cut off his head, but only if he agrees to be beheaded in turn in a year and a day, if the Green Knight survives. Gawain beheads the Green Knight, who simply replaces his head. At the appointed time, they meet, and the Green Knight swings his axe but merely nicks Gawain's skin instead of beheading him.

**Geisha**  Performance artist or entertainer, usually female.

**Geri**  Odin's wolf.

**Giallar**  Bridge in Filheim.

**Giallarhorn**  Heimdall's trumpet – the final call signifies Ragnarok.

**Giants**  In Greek mythology, a race of beings born from Gaea, grown from the blood that dropped from the castrated Uranus. Usually represent evil in Viking mythology.

**Gilgamesh**  King of Erech known as a half-human, half-god hero similar to the Greek Heracles, and often listed with the gods. He is the personification of the sun and is protected by the god Shamash, who in some texts is described as his father. He is also portrayed as an evil tyrant at times.

**Gladheim**  Where the twelve deities of Asgard hold their thrones. Also called Gladsheim.

**Golden Fleece**  Fleece of the ram sent by Poseidon to substitute for Phrixus when his father was going to sacrifice him. The Argonauts went in search of the fleece.

**Goodman**  Man of the house.

**Goodwife**  Woman of the house.

**Gopis**  Lovers of the young Krishna and milkmaids.

**Gorgon**  One of the three sisters, including Medusa, whose frightening looks could turn mortals to stone.

**Graces**  Daughters of Aphrodite by Zeus.

**Gramercy**  Expression of surprise or strong feeling.

**Great Head**  The Iroquois Indians believed in the existence of a curious being known as Great Head, a creature with an enormous head poised on slender legs.

**Great Spirit**  The name given to the Creator of all life, as well as the term used to describe the omnipotent force of the Creator existing in every living thing.

**Great-Flank**  One of Ravana's monsters.

**Green Knight**  A knight dressed all in green and with green hair and skin who challenged one of Arthur's knights to strike him a blow with an axe and that, if he survived, he would return to behead the knight in a year and a day. He turned out to be Lord

Bertilak and was under an enchantment cast by Morgan le Fay to test Arthur's knights.

**Gruagach** A kind of brownie, usually dressed in red or green as opposed to the traditional brown. He has great power to enchant the hapless, or to help mortals who are worthy (usually heroes). He often appears to challenge a boy-hero, during his period of education.

**Gudea** High priest of Lagash, known to be a patron of the arts and a writer himself.

**Guebre** Religion founded by Zoroaster, the Persian prophet.

**Gugumatz** Creator god who, with Huracan, formed the sky, earth and everything on it.

**Guha** King of Nishadha.

**Guidewife** Woman.

**Guinevere** Wife of King Arthur; she is often portrayed as a virtuous lady and wife, but is perhaps best known for having a love affair with Lancelot, one of Arthur's friends and knights of the Round Table. Her name is also spelled Guenever.

**Gulistan** *Rose Garden*, written by the poet Sa'di

**Gungnir** Odin's spear, made of Yggdrasill wood, and the tip fashioned by Dvalin.

**Gylfi** A wandering king to whom the Eddas are narrated.

**Haab** Mayan solar calendar that consisted of eighteen twenty-day months.

**Hades** One of the three sons of Cronus; brother of Poseidon and Zeus. Hades is King of the Underworld, which is also known as the House of Hades.

**Haere-mai** Maori phrase meaning 'come here, welcome.'

**Haere-mai-ra, me o tatou mate** Maori phrase meaning 'come here, that I may sorrow with you.'

**Haere-ra**  Maori phrase meaning 'goodbye, go, farewell.'

**Haji**  Muslim pilgrim who has been to Mecca.

**Hakama**  Traditional Japanese clothing, worn on the bottom half of the body.

**Hanuman**  General of the monkey people.

**Harakiri**  Suicide, usually by cutting or stabbing the abdomen. Also known as seppuku.

**Hari-Hara**  Shiva and Vishnu as one god.

**Harmonia**  Daughter of Ares and Aphrodite, wife of Cadmus.

**Hatamoto**  High-ranking samurai.

**Hathor**  Great cosmic mother and patroness of lovers. She is portrayed as a cow.

**Hati**  The wolf who pursues the sun and moon.

**Hatshepsut**  Second female pharaoh.

**Hauberk**  Armour to protect the neck and shoulders, sometimes a full-length coat of mail.

**Hector**  Eldest son of King Priam who defended Troy from the Greeks. He was killed by Achilles.

**Hecuba**  The second wife of Priam, King of Troy. She was turned into a dog after Troy was lost.

**Heimdall**  White god who guards the Bifrost bridge.

**Hel**  Goddess of death and Loki's daughter.

**Helen**  Daughter of Leda and Tyndareus, King of Sparta, and the most beautiful woman in the world. She was responsible for starting the Trojan War.

**Heliopolis**  City in modern-day Cairo, known as the City of the Sun and the central place of worship of Ra. Also known as Anu.

**Helius**  The sun, son of Hyperion and Theia.

**Henwife**  Witch.

**Hephaestus** or **Hephaistos**  The Smith of Heaven.

**Hera**  A Mycenaean palace goddess, married to Zeus.

**Heracles**  An important Greek hero, the son of Zeus and Alcmena. His name means 'Glory of Hera'. He performed twelve labours for King Eurystheus, and later became a god.

**Hermes**  The conductor of souls of the dead to Hades, and god of trickery and of trade. He acts as messenger to the gods.

**Hermod**  Son of Frigga and Odin who travelled to see Hel in order to reclaim Balder for Asgard.

**Hero and Leander**  Hero was a priestess of Aphrodite, loved by Leander, a young man of Abydos. He drowned trying to see her.

**Hestia**  Goddess of the hearth, daughter of Cronus and Rhea.

**Hieroglyphs**  Type of writing that combines symbols and pictures, usually cut into tombs or rocks, or written on papyrus.

**Himalaya**  Great mountain and range, father of Parvati.

**Hiordis**  Wife of Sigmund and mother of Sigurd.

**Hoderi**  A fisher and son of Okuninushi.

**Hodur**  Balder's blind twin; known as the personification of darkness.

**Hoenir**  Also called Vili; produced the first humans with Odin and Loki, and was one of the triad responsible for the creation of the world.

**Hōichi the Earless**  A *biwa hōshi*, a blind storyteller who played the biwa or lute. Also a priest.

**Homayi**  Phoenix.

**Hoori**  A hunter and son of Okuninushi.

**Horus**  God of the sky and kinship, son of Isis and Osiris. He captained the boat that carried Ra across the sky. He is depicted with the head of a falcon.

**Hotei**  One of the gods of luck. He also personifies humour and contentment.

**Houlet**  Owl.

**Houri**  Beautiful virgin from paradise.

**Hrim-faxi**  Steed of the night.

**Hubris**  Presumptuous behaviour which causes the wrath of the gods to be brought on to mortals.

**Hueytozoztli**  Festival dedicated to Tlaloc and, at times, Chicomecohuatl or other deities. Also the fourth month of the Aztec calendar.

**Hugin**  Odin's raven.

**Huitzilopochtli**  God of war and the sun, also connected with the summer and crops; one of the principal Aztec deities. He was born a full-grown adult to save his mother, Coatlicue, from the jealousy of his sister, Coyolxauhqui, who tried to kill Coatlicue. The Mars of the Aztec gods. In some origin stories he is one of four offspring of Ometeotl and Omecihuatl.

**Hurley**  A traditional Irish game played with sticks and balls, quite similar to hockey.

**Hurons**  A tribe of Iroquois stock, originally one people with the Iroquois.

**Huveane**  (Pedi, Venda) Creator of humankind, who made a baby from clay into which he breathed life. He is known as the High God or Great God. He is also known as a trickster god.

**Hymir**  Giant who fishes with Thor and is drowned by him.

**Iambe**  Daughter of Pan and Echo, servant to King Celeus of Eleusis and Metaeira.

**Icarus**  Son of Daedalus, who plunged to his death after escaping from the labyrinth.

**Ichneumon**  Mongoose.

**Idunn**  Guardian of the youth-giving apples.

**Ifa**  (Yoruba) God of wisdom and divination. Also the term for a Yoruban religion.

**Ife**  (Yoruba) The place Obatala first arrived on Earth and took for his home.

**Igigi**  Great spirits or gods of Heaven and the sky.

**Igraine**  Wife of the duke of Tintagel, enemy of Uther Pendragon, who marries Uther when her first husband dies. She is King Arthur's mother.

**Ile**  (Yoruba) Goddess of the earth.

**Imhetep**  High priest and wise sage. He is sometimes thought to be the son of Ptah.

**Imam**  Person who leads prayers in a mosque.

**In**  The male principle who, joined with Yo, the female side, brought about creation and the first gods. In and Yo correspond to the Chinese Yang and Yin.

**Inari**  God of rice, fertility, agriculture and, later, the fox god. Inari has both good and evil attributes but is often presented as an evil trickster.

**Indra**  The King of Heaven.

**Indrajit**  Son of Ravana.

**Indrasen**  Daughter of Nala and Damayanti.

**Indrasena**  Son of Nala and Damayanti.

**Inundation**  Annual flooding of the River Nile.

**Iphigenia**  The eldest daughter of Agamemnon and Clytemnestra who was sacrificed to appease Artemis and obtain a fair wind for Troy.

**Iris**  Messenger of the gods who took the form of a rainbow.

**Iseult**  Princess of Ireland and niece of the Morholt. She falls in love with Tristan after consuming a love potion but is forced to marry King Mark of Cornwall.

**Ishtar** Goddess of love, beauty, justice and war, especially in Ninevah, and earth mother who symbolizes fertility. Married to Tammuz, she is similar to the Greek goddess Aphrodite. Ishtar is sometimes known as Innana or Irnina.

**Isis** Goddess of the Nile and the moon, sister-wife of Osiris. She and her son, Horus, are sometimes thought of in a similar way to Mary and Jesus. She was one of the most worshipped female Egyptian deities and was instrumental in returning Osiris to life after he was killed by his brother, Set.

**Istakbál** Deputation of warriors.

**Izanagi** Deity and brother-husband to Izanami, who together created the Japanese islands from the Floating Bridge of Heaven. Their offspring populated Japan.

**Izanami** Deity and sister-wife of Izanagi, creator of Japan. Their children include Amaterasu, Tsuki-yomi and Susanoo.

**Jade** It was believed that jade emerged from the mountains as a liquid which then solidified after ten thousand years to become a precious hard stone, green in colour. If the correct herbs were added to it, it could return to its liquid state and when swallowed increase the individual's chances of immortality.

**Jambavan** A noble monkey.

**Jason** Son of Aeson, King of Iolcus and leader of the voyage of the Argonauts.

**Jatayu** King of all the eagle-tribes.

**Jesseraunt** Flexible coat of armour or mail.

**Jimmo** Legendary first emperor of Japan. He is thought to be descended from Hoori, while other tales claim him to be descended from Amaterasu through her grandson, Ninigi.

**Jizo** God of little children and the god who calms the troubled sea.

**Jord** Daughter of Nott; wife of Odin.

**Jormungander** The world serpent; son of Loki. Legends tell that when his tail is removed from his mouth, Ragnarok has arrived.

**Jorō** Geisha who also worked as a prostitute.

**Jotunheim** Home of the giants.

**Ju Ju tree** Deciduous tree that produces edible fruit.

**Jurasindhu** A rakshasa, father-in-law of Kans.

**Jyeshtha** Goddess of bad luck.

**Ka** Life power or soul. Also known as ba.

**Kai-káús** Son of Kai-kobád. He led an army to invade Mázinderán, home of the demon-sorcerers, after being persuaded by a demon. Known for his ambitious schemes, he later tried to reach Heaven by trapping eagles to fly him there on his throne.

**Kaikeyi** Mother of Bharata, one of Dasharatha's three wives.

**Kai-khosrau** Son of Saiawúsh, who killed Afrásiyáb in revenge for the death of his father.

**Kai-kobád** Descendant of Feridún, he was selected by Zál to lead an army against Afrásiyáb. Their powerful army, led by Zál and Rustem, drove back Afrásiyáb's army, who then agreed to peace.

**Kali** The Black, wife of Shiva.

**Kalindi** Daughter of the sun, wife of Krishna.

**Kaliya** A poisonous hydra that lived in the jamna.

**Kalki** Incarnation of Vishnu yet to come.

**Kalnagini** Serpent who kills Lakshmindara.

**Kal-Purush** The Time-man, Bengali name for Orion.

**Kaluda** A disciple of Buddha.

**Kalunga-ngombe** (Mbundu) Death, also depicted as the king of the netherworld.

**Kama** God of desire.

**Kamadeva** Desire, the god of love.

**Kami** Spirits, deities or forces of nature.

**Kamund** Lasso.

**Kans** King of Mathura, son of Ugrasena and Pavandrekha.

**Kanva** Father of Shakuntala.

**Kappa** River goblin with the body of a tortoise and the head of an ape. Kappa love to challenge human beings to single combat.

**Karakia** Invocation, ceremony, prayer.

**Karna** Pupil of Drona.

**Kasbu** A period of twenty-four hours.

**Kashyapa** One of Dasharatha's counsellors.

**Kauravas or Kurus** Sons of Dhritarashtra, pupils of Drona.

**Kaushalya** Mother of Rama, one of Dasharatha's three wives.

**Kay** Son of Ector and adopted brother to King Arthur, he becomes one of Arthur's knights of the Round Table.

**Keb** God of the earth and father of Osiris and Isis, married to Nut. Keb is identified with Kronos, the Greek god of time.

**Kehua** Spirit, ghost.

**Kelpie** Another word for each uisge, the water-horse.

**Ken** Know.

**Keres** Black-winged demons or daughters of the night.

**Keshini** Wife of Sagara.

**Khalif** Leader.

**Khara** Younger brother of Ravana.

**Khepera** God who represents the rising sun. He is portrayed as a scarab. Also known as Nebertcher.

**Kher-heb** Priest and magician who officiated over rituals and ceremonies.

**Khnemu** God of the source of the Nile and one of the original Egyptian deities. He is thought to be the creator of children and of other gods. He is portrayed as a ram.

**Khosru** King and husband to Shireen, daughter of Maurice, the Greek Emperor. He was murdered by his own son, who wanted his kingdom and his wife.

**Khumbaba** Monster and guardian of the goddess Irnina, a form of the goddess Ishtar. Khumbaba is likened to the Greek gorgon.

**Kia-ora** Welcome, good luck. A greeting.

**Kiboko** Hippopotamus.

**Kikinu** Soul.

**Kimbanda** (Mbundu) Doctor.

**Kimono** Traditional Japanese clothing, similar to a robe.

**King Arthur** Legendary king of Britain who plucked the magical sword from the stone, marking him as the heir of Uther Pendragon and 'true king' of Britain. He and his knights of the Round Table defended Britain from the Saxons and had many adventures, including searching for the Holy Grail. Finally wounded in battle, he left Britain for the mythical Avalon, vowing to one day return to reclaim his kingdom.

**Kingu** Tiawath's husband, a god and warrior who she promised would rule Heaven once he helped her defeat the 'gods of light'. He was killed by Merodach who used his blood to make clay, from which he formed the first humans. In some tales, Kingu is Tiawath's son as well as her consort.

**Kinnaras** Human birds with musical instruments under their wings.

**Kinyamkela** (Zaramo) Ghost of a child.

**Kis** Solar deity, usually depicted as an eagle.

**Kishar** Earth mother and sister-wife to Anshar.

**Kitamba** (Mbundu) Chief who made his whole village go into mourning when his head-wife, Queen Muhongo, died. He also pledged that no one should speak or eat until she was returned to him.

**Knowe** Knoll or hillock.

**Kojiki** One of two myth-histories of Japan, along with the *Nihon Shoki*.

**Ko-no-Hana** Goddess of Mount Fuji, princess and wife of Ninigi.

**Kore** 'Maiden', another name for Persephone.

**Kraal** Traditional rural African village, usually consisting of huts surrounded by a fence or wall. Also an animal enclosure.

**Krishna** The Dark one, worshipped as an incarnation of Vishnu.

**Kui-see** Edible root.

**Kumara** Son of Shiva and Paravati, slays demon Taraka.

**Kumbha-karna** Ravana's brother.

**Kunti** Mother of the Pandavas.

**Kura** Red. The sacred colour of the Maori.

**Kusha or Kusi** One of Sita's two sons.

**Kvasir** Clever warrior and colleague of Odin. He was responsible for finally outwitting Loki.

**Kwannon** Goddess of mercy.

**Labyrinth** A prison built at Knossos for the Minotaur by Daedalus.

**Lady of the Lake** Enchantress who presents Arthur with Excalibur.

**Laertes** King of Ithaca and father of Odysseus.

**Laestrygonians** Savage giants encountered by Odysseus on his travels.

**Laili** In love with Majnun but unable to marry him, she was given to the prince, Ibn Salam, to marry. When he died, she escaped and found Majnun, but they could not be legally married. The couple died of grief and were buried together. Also known as Laila.

**Lakshmana** Brother of Rama and his companion in exile.

**Lakshmi** Consort of Vishnu and a goddess of beauty and good fortune.

**Lakshmindara**  Son of Chand resurrected by Manasa Devi.

**Lancelot**  Knight of the Round Table. Lancelot was raised by the Lady of the Lake. While he went on many quests, he is perhaps best known for his affair with Guinevere, King Arthur's wife.

**Land of Light**  One of the names for the realm of the fairies. If a piece of metal welded by human hands is put in the doorway to their land, the door cannot close. The door to this realm is only open at night, and usually at a full moon.

**Lang syne**  The days of old.

**Lao Tzu (Laozi)**  The ancient Taoist philosopher thought to have been born in 571 BC a contemporary of Confucius with whom, it is said, he discussed the tenets of Tao. Lao Tzu was an advocate of simple rural existence and looked to the Yellow Emperor and Shun as models of efficient government. His philosophies were recorded in the Tao Te Ching. Legends surrounding his birth suggest that he emerged from the left-hand side of his mother's body, with white hair and a long white beard, after a confinement lasting eighty years.

**Laocoon**  A Trojan wiseman who predicted that the wooden horse contained Greek soldiers.

**Laomedon**  The King of Troy who hired Apollo and Poseidon to build the impregnable walls of Troy.

**Lava**  Son of Sita.

**Leda**  Daughter of the King of Aetolia, who married Tyndareus. Helen and Clytemnestra were her daughters.

**Legba**  (Dahomey) Youngest offspring of Mawu-Lisa. He was given the gift of all languages. It was through him that humans could converse with the gods.

**Leman**  Lover.

**Lethe** One of the four rivers of the Underworld, also called the River of Forgetfulness.

**Lif** The female survivor of Ragnarok.

**Lifthrasir** The male survivor of Ragnarok.

**Lil** Demon.

**Lofty mountain** Home of Ahura-Mazda.

**Logi** Utgard-loki's cook.

**Loki** God of fire and mischief-maker of Asgard; he eventually brings about Ragnarok.

**Lotus-Eaters** A race of people who live a dazed, drugged existence, the result of eating the lotus flower.

**Ma'at** State of order meaning truth, order or justice. Personified by the goddess Ma'at, who was Thoth's consort.

**Macha** There are thought to be several different Machas who appear in quite a number of ancient Irish stories. For the purposes of this book, however, the Macha referred to is the wife of Crunnchu. The story unfolds that after her husband had boasted of her great athletic ability to the King, she was subsequently forced to run against his horses in spite of the fact that she was heavily pregnant. Macha died giving birth to her twin babies and with her dying breath she cursed Ulster for nine generations, proclaiming that it would suffer the weakness of a woman in childbirth in times of great stress. This curse had its most disastrous effect when Medb of Connacht invaded Ulster with her great army.

**Machi-bugyō** Senior official or magistrate, usually samurai.

**Macuilxochitl** God of art, dance and games, and the patron of luck in gaming. His name means 'source of flowers' or 'prince of flowers'. Also known as Xochipilli, meaning 'five-flower'.

**Madake** Weapon used for whipping, made of bamboo.

**Maduma** Taro tuber.

**Mag Muirthemne** Cuchulainn's inheritance. A plain extending from River Boyne to the mountain range of Cualgne, close to Emain Macha in Ulster.

**Magni** Thor's son.

**Mahaparshwa** One of Ravana's generals.

**Maharaksha** Son of Khara, slain at Lanka.

**Mahasubhadda** Wife of Buddha-select (Sumedha).

**Majnun** Son of a chief, who fell in love with Laili and followed her tribe through the desert, becoming mad with love until they were briefly reunited before dying.

**Makaras** Mythical fish-reptiles of the sea.

**Mana** Power, authority, prestige, influence, sanctity, luck.

**Manasa Devi** Goddess of snakes, daughter of Shiva by a mortal woman.

**Manasha** Goddess of snakes.

**Mandavya** Daughter of Kushadhwaja.

**Man-Devourer** One of Ravana's monsters.

**Mandodari** Wife of Ravana.

**Mani** The moon.

**Manitto** Broad term used to describe the supernatural or a potent spirit among the Algonquins, the Iroquois and the Sioux.

**Man-Slayer** One of Ravana's counsellors.

**Manthara** Kaikeyi's evil nurse, who plots Rama's ruin.

**Mantle** Cloak or shawl.

**Manu** Lawgiver.

**Manu** Mythical mountain on which the sun sets.

**Mara** The evil one, tempts Gautama.

**Markandeya** One of Dasharatha's counsellors.

**Mashu** Mountain of the Sunset, which lies between Earth and the underworld. Guarded by scorpion-men.

**Matali** Sakra's charioteer.

**Mawu-Lisa** (Dahomey) Twin offspring of Nana Baluka. Mawu (female) and Lisa (male) are often joined to form one being. Their own offspring populated the world.

**Mbai** (Igbo) Person of great intelligence, also known as Ekake (Ibani), which means 'tortoise'.

**Medea** Witch and priestess of Hecate, daughter of Aeetes and sister of Circe. She helped Jason in his quest for the Golden Fleece.

**Medusa** One of the three Gorgons whose head had the power to turn onlookers to stone.

**Melpomene** One of the muses, and mother of the Sirens.

**Menaka** One of the most beautiful dancers in Heaven.

**Menat** Amulet, usually worn for protection.

**Mendicant** Beggar.

**Menelaus** King of Sparta, brother of Agamemnon. Married Helen and called war against Troy when she eloped with Paris.

**Menthu** Lord of Thebes and god of war. He is portrayed as a hawk or falcon.

**Mere-pounamu** A native weapon made of a rare green stone.

**Merlin** Wizard and advisor to King Arthur. He is thought to be the son of a human female and an incubus (male demon). He brought about Arthur's birth and ascension to king, then acted as his mentor.

**Merodach** God who battled Tiawath and defeated her by cutting out her heart and dividing her corpse into two pieces. He used these pieces to divide the upper and lower waters once controlled by Tiawath, making a dwelling for the gods of light. He also created humankind. Also known as Marduk.

**Metaneira** Wife of Celeus, King of Eleusis, who hired Demeter in disguise as her nurse.

**Metztli** Goddess of the moon, her name means 'lady of the night'. Also known as Yohualtictl.

**Michabo** Also known as Manobozho, or the Great Hare, the principal deity of the Algonquins, maker and preserver of the earth, sun and moon.

**Mictlan** God of the dead and ruler of the underworld. He was married to Mictecaciuatl and is often represented as a bat. He is also the Aztec lord of Hades. Also known as Mictlantecutli. Mictlan is also the name for the underworld.

**Midgard** Dwelling place of humans (Earth).

**Midsummer** A time when fairies dance and claim human victims.

**Mihrab** Father of Rúdábeh and descendant of Zohák, the serpent-king.

**Milesians** A group of iron-age invaders led by the sons of Mil, who arrived in Ireland from Spain around 500 BC and overcame the Tuatha De Danann.

**Mimir** God of the ocean. His head guards a well; reincarnated after Ragnarok.

**Minos** King of Crete, son of Zeus and Europa. He was considered to have been the ruler of a sea empire.

**Minotaur** A creature born of the union between Pasiphae and a Cretan Bull.

**Minúchihr** King who lives to be one hundred and twenty years old. Father of Nauder.

**Miolnir** Thor's hammer.

**Mithra** God of the sun and light in Iran, protector of truth and guardian of pastures and cattle. Also known as Mitra in Hindu mythology and Mithras in Roman mythology.

**Mixcoatl** God of the chase or the hunt. Sometimes depicted as the god of air and thunder, he introduced fire to humankind. His name means 'cloud serpent'.

**Mnoatia** Forest spirits.

**Moccasins** One-piece shoes made of soft leather, especially deerskin.

**Modi** Thor's son.

**Moly** A magical plant given to Odysseus by Hermes as protection against Circe's powers.

**Montezuma** Great emperor who consolidated the Aztec Empire.

**Mordred** Bastard son of King Arthur and Morgawse, Queen of Orkney, who, unknown to Arthur, was his half-sister. Mordred becomes one of King Arthur's knights of the Round Table before betraying and fatally wounding Arthur, causing him to leave Britain for Avalon.

**Morgan le Fay** Enchantress and half-sister to King Arthur, Morgan was an apprentice of Merlin's. She is generally depicted as benevolent, yet did pit herself against Arthur and his knights on occasion. She escorts Arthur on his final journey to Avalon. Also known as Morgain le Fay.

**Morholt, the** Knight sent to Cornwall to force King Mark to pay tribute to Ireland. He is killed by Tristan.

**Morongoe the brave** (Lesotho) Man who was turned into a snake by evil spirits because Tau was jealous that he had married the beautiful Mokete, the chief's daughter. Morongoe was returned to human form after his son, Tsietse, returned him to their family.

**Mosima** (Bapedi) The underworld or abyss.

**Mount Fuji** Highest mountain in Japan, on the island of Honshū.

**Mount Kunlun** This mountain features in many Chinese legends as the home of the great emperors on Earth. It is written in the *Shanghaijing* (*The Classic of Mountains and Seas*) that this towering structure measured no less than 3300 miles in circumference and 4000 miles in height. It acted both as a central pillar to support the heavens, and as a gateway between Heaven and Earth.

**Moving Finger** Expression for taking responsibility for one's life and actions, which cannot be undone.

**Moytura** Translated as the 'Plain of Weeping', Mag Tured, or Moytura, was where the Tuatha De Danann fought two of their most significant battles.

**Mua** An old-time Polynesian god.

**Muezzin** Person who performs the Muslim call to prayer.

**Mugalana** A disciple of Buddha.

**Muilearteach** The Cailleach Bheur of the water, who appears as a witch or a sea-serpent. On land she grew larger and stronger by fire.

**Mul-lil** God of Nippur, who took the form of a gazelle.

**Muloyi** Sorcerer, also called mulaki, murozi, ndozi or ndoki.

**Mummu** Son of Tiawath and Apsu. He formed a trinity with them to battle the gods. Also known as Moumis. In some tales, Mummu is also Merodach, who eventually destroyed Tiawath.

**Munin** Odin's raven.

**Murile** (Chaga) Man who dug up a taro tuber that resembled his baby brother, which turned into a living boy. His mother killed the baby when she saw Murile was starving himself to feed it.

**Muses** Goddesses of poetry and song, daughters of Zeus and Mnemosyne.

**Muskrat** North American beaver-like, amphibious rodent.

**Muspell** Home of fire, and the fire-giants.

**Mwidzilo** Taboo which, if broken, can cause death.

**Nabu** God of writing and wisdom. Also known as Nebo. Thought to be the son of Merodach.

**Nahua** Ancient Mexicans.

**Nakula**  Pandava twin skilled in horsemanship.

**Nala**  One of the monkey host, son of Vishvakarma.

**Nana Baluka**  (Dahomey) Mother of all creation. She gave birth to an androgynous being with two faces. The female face was Mawu, who controlled the night and lands to the west. The male face was Lisa and he controlled the day and the east.

**Nanahuatl**  Also known as Nanauatzin. Presided over skin diseases and known as Leprous, which in Nahua meant 'divine'.

**Nandi**  Shiva's bull.

**Nanna**  Balder's wife.

**Nannar**  God of the moon and patron of the city of Ur.

**Naram-Sin**  Son or ancestor of Sargon and king of the Four Zones or Quarters of Babylon.

**Narcissus**  Son of the River Cephisus. He fell in love with himself and died as a result.

**Narve**  Son of Loki.

**Nataraja**  Manifestation of Shiva, Lord of the Dance.

**Natron**  Preservative used in embalming, mined from the Natron Valley in Egypt.

**Nauder**  Son of Minúchihr, who became king on his death and was tyrannical and hated until Sám begged him to follow in the footsteps of his ancestors.

**Nausicaa**  Daughter of Alcinous, King of Phaeacia, who fell in love with Odysseus.

**Nebuchadnezzar**  Famous king of Babylon. Also known as Nebuchadrezzar.

**Necromancy**  Communicating with the dead.

**Nectar**  Drink of the gods.

**Neith**  Goddess of hunting, fate and war. Neith is sometimes known as the creator of the universe.

**Nemesis** Goddess of retribution and daughter of night.

**Neoptolemus** Son of Achilles and Deidameia, he came to Troy at the end of the war to wear his father's armour. He sacrificed Polyxena at the tomb of Achilles.

**Nephthys** Goddess of the air, night and the dead. Sister of Isis and sister-wife to Seth, she is also the mother of Anubis.

**Nereids** Sea-nymphs who are the daughters of Nereus and Doris. Thetis, mother of Achilles, was a Nereid.

**Nergal** God of death and patron god of Cuthah, which was often known as a burial place. He is also known as the god of fire. Married to Aralu, the goddess of the underworld.

**Nestor** Wise King of Pylus, who led the ships to Troy with Agamemnon and Menelaus.

**Neta** Daughter of Shiva, friend of Manasa.

**Ngaka** (Lesotho) Witch doctor.

**Night** Daughter of Norvi.

**Nikumbha** One of Ravana's generals.

**Nila** One of the monkey host, son of Agni.

**Nin-Girsu** God of fertility and war, patron god of Girsu. Also known as Shul-gur.

**Ninigi** Grandson of Amaterasu, Ninigi came to Earth bringing rice and order to found the Imperial family. He is known as the August Grandchild.

**Niord** God of the sea; marries Skadi.

**Nippur** The home of En-lil and one of the two major cities of Babylonian civilization.

**Nirig** God of war and storms, and son of Bel. Also known as Enu-Restu.

**Nirvana** Transcendent state and the final goal of Buddhism.

**Noatun** Niord's home.

**Noisy-Throat** One of Ravana's counsellors.

**Norns** The fates and protectors of Yggdrasill. Many believe them to be the same as the Valkyries.

**Norvi** Father of the night.

**Nott** Goddess of night.

**Nsasak bird** Small bird who became chief of all small birds after winning a competition to go without food for seven days. The Nsasak bird beat the Odudu bird by sneaking out of his home to feed.

**Nü Wa** The Goddess Nü Wa, who in some versions of the Creation myths is the sole creator of mankind, and in other tales is associated with the God Fu Xi, also a great benefactor of the human race. Some accounts represent Fu Xi as the brother of Nü Wa, but others describe the pair as lovers who lie together to create the very first human beings. Fu Xi is also considered to be the first of the Chinese emperors of mythical times who reigned from 2953 to 2838 BC.

**Nuada** The first king of the Tuatha De Danann in Ireland, who lost an arm in the first battle of Moytura against the Fomorians. He became known as 'Nuada of the Silver Hand' when Diancecht, the great physician of the Tuatha De Danann, replaced his hand with a silver one after the battle.

**Nunda** (Swahili, East Africa) Slayer that took the form of a cat and grew so big that it consumed everyone in the town except the sultan's wife, who locked herself away. Her son, Mohammed, killed Nunda and cut open its leg, setting free everyone Nunda had eaten.

**Nut** Goddess of the sky, stars and astronomy. Sister-wife of Keb and mother of Osiris, Isis, Set and Nephthys.

**Nyame** (Ashanti) God of the sky, who sees and knows everything.

**Nymphs** Minor female deities associated with particular parts of the land and sea.

**Obatala** (Yoruba) Creator of humankind. He climbed down a golden chain from the sky to the earth, then a watery abyss, and formed land and humankind. When Olorun heard of his success, he created the sun for Obatala and his creations.

**Oberon** Fairy king.

**Odin** Allfather and king of all gods, he is known for travelling the nine worlds in disguise and recognized only by his single eye; dies at Ragnarok.

**Odur** Freyia's husband.

**Odysseus** Greek hero, son of Laertes and Anticleia, who was renowned for his cunning, the master behind the victory at Troy, and known for his long voyage home.

**Oedipus** Son of Leius, King of Thebes and Jocasta. Became King of Thebes and married his mother.

**Ogdoad** Group of eight deities who were formed into four male-female couples who joined to create the gods and the world.

**Ogham** One of the earliest known forms of Irish writing, originally used to inscribe upright pillar stones.

**Oiran** Courtesan.

**Oisin** Also called Ossian (particularly by James Macpherson who wrote a set of Gaelic Romances about this character, supposedly garnered from oral tradition). Ossian was the son of Fionn and Sadbh, and had various brothers, according to different legends. He was a man of great wisdom, became immortal for many centuries, but in the end he became mad.

**Ojibwe** Another name for the Chippewa, a tribe of Algonquin stock.

**Okuninushi** Deity and descendant of Susanoo, who married Suseri-hime, Susanoo's daughter, without his consent.

Susanoo tried to kill him many times but did not succeed and eventually forgave Okuninushi. He is sometimes thought to be the son or grandson of Susanoo.

**Olokun** (Yoruba) Most powerful goddess who ruled the seas and marshes. When Obatala created Earth in her domain, other gods began to divide it up between them. Angered at their presumption, she caused a great flood to destroy the land.

**Olorun** (Yoruba) Supreme god and ruler of the sky. He sees and controls everything, but others, such as Obatala, carry out the work for him. Also known as Olodumare.

**Olympia** Zeus's home in Elis.

**Olympus** The highest mountain in Greece and the ancient home of the gods.

**Omecihuatl** Female half of the first being, combined with Ometeotl. Together they are the lords of duality or lords of the two sexes. Also known as Ometecutli and Omeciuatl or Tonacatecutli and Tonacaciuatl. Their offspring were Xipe Totec, Huitzilopochtli, Quetzalcoatl and Tezcatlipoca.

**Ometeotl** Male half of the first being, combined with Omecihuatl.

**Ometochtli** Collective name for the pulque-gods or drink-gods. These gods were often associated with rabbits as they were thought to be senseless creatures.

**Onygate** Anyway.

**Opening the Mouth** Ceremony in which mummies or statues were prayed over and anointed with incense before their mouths were opened, allowing them to eat and drink in the afterlife.

**Oracle** The response of a god or priest to a request for advice – also a prophecy; the place where such advice was sought; the person or thing from whom such advice was sought.

**Orestes** Son of Agamemnon and Clytemnestra who escaped following Agamemnon's murder to King Strophius. He later returned to Argos to murder his mother and avenge the death of his father.

**Orpheus** Thracian singer and poet, son of Oeagrus and a Muse. Married Eurydice and when she died tried to retrieve her from the Underworld.

**Orunmila** (Yoruba) Eldest son of Olorun, he helped Obatala create land and humanity, which he then rescued after Olokun flooded the lands. He has the power to see the future.

**Osiris** God of fertility, the afterlife and death. Thought to be the first of the pharaohs. He was murdered by his brother, Set, after which he was conjured back to life by Isis, Anubis and others before becoming lord of the afterworld. Married to Isis, who was also his sister.

**Otherworld** The world of deities and spirits, also known as the Land of Promise, or the Land of Eternal Youth, a place of everlasting life where all earthly dreams come to be fulfilled.

**Owuo** (Krachi, West Africa) Giant who personifies death. He causes a person to die every time he blinks his eye.

**Palamedes** Hero of Nauplia, believed to have created part of the ancient Greek alphabet. He tricked Odysseus into joining the fleet setting out for Troy by placing the infant Telemachus in the path of his plough.

**Palermo Stone** Stone carved with hieroglyphs, which came from the Royal Annals of ancient Egypt and contains a list of the kings of Egypt from the first to the early fifth dynasties.

**Palfrey** Docile and light horse, often used by women.

**Palladium** Wooden image of Athene, created by her as a monument to her friend Pallas who she accidentally killed. While in Troy it protected the city from invaders.

**Pallas** Athene's best friend, whom she killed.

**Pan** God of Arcadia, half-goat and half-man. Son of Hermes. He is connected with fertility, masturbation and sexual drive. He is also associated with music, particularly his pipes, and with laughter.

**Pan Gu** Some ancient writers suggest that this God is the offspring of the opposing forces of nature, the yin and the yang. The yin (female) is associated with the cold and darkness of the earth, while the yang (male) is associated with the sun and the warmth of the heavens. 'Pan' means 'shell of an egg' and 'Gu' means 'to secure' or 'to achieve'. Pan Gu came into existence so that he might create order from chaos.

**Pandareus** Cretan King killed by the gods for stealing the shrine of Zeus.

**Pandavas** Alternative name for sons of Pandu, pupils of Drona.

**Pandora** The first woman, created by the gods, to punish man for Prometheus's theft of fire. Her dowry was a box full of powerful evil.

**Papyrus** Paper-like material made from the pith of the papyrus plant, first manufactured in Egypt. Used as a type of paper as well as for making mats, rope and sandals.

**Paramahamsa** The supreme swan.

**Parashurama** Human incarnation of Vishnu, 'Rama with an axe'.

**Paris** Handsome son of Priam and Hecuba of Troy, who was left for dead on Mount Ida but raised by shepherds. Was reclaimed by his family, then brought them shame and caused the Trojan War by eloping with Helen.

**Parsa** Holy man. Also known as a zahid.

**Parvati** Consort of Shiva and daughter of Himalaya.

**Passion** Wife of desire.

**Pavanarekha**  Wife of Ugrasena, mother of Kans.

**Pegasus**  The winged horse born from the severed neck of Medusa.

**Peleus**  Father of Achilles. He married Antigone, caused her death, and then became King of Phthia. Saved from death himself by Jason and the Argonauts. Married Thetis, a sea nymph.

**Penelope**  The long-suffering but equally clever wife of Odysseus who managed to keep at bay suitors who longed for Ithaca while Odysseus was at the Trojan War and on his ten-year voyage home.

**Pentangle**  Pentagram or five-pointed star.

**Pentecost**  Christian festival held on the seventh Sunday after Easter. It celebrates the holy spirit descending on the disciples after Jesus's ascension.

**Percivale**  Knight of the Round Table and original seeker of the Holy Grail.

**Persephone**  Daughter of Zeus and Demeter who was raped by Hades and forced to live in the Underworld as his queen for three months of every year.

**Perseus**  Son of Danae, who was made pregnant by Zeus. He fought the Gorgons and brought home the head of Medusa. He eventually founded the city of Mycenae and married Andromeda.

**Pesh Kef**  Spooned blade used in the Opening the Mouth ceremony.

**Phaeacia**  The Kingdom of Alcinous on which Odysseus landed after a shipwreck which claimed the last of his men as he left Calypso's island.

**Pharaoh**  King or ruler of Egypt.

**Philoctetes**  Malian hero, son of Poeas, received Heracles's bow and arrows as a gift when he lit the great hero's pyre on Mount Oeta. He was involved in the last part of the Trojan War, killing Paris.

**Philtre**  Magic potion, usually a love potion.

**Pibroch**  Bagpipe music.

**Pintura**  Native manuscript or painting.

**Pipiltin**  Noble class of the Aztecs.

**Pismire**  Ant.

**Piu-piu**  Short mat made from flax leaves and neatly decorated.

**Po**  Gloom, darkness, the lower world.

**Polyphemus**  A Cyclops, but a son of Poseidon. He fell in love with Galatea, but she spurned him. He was blinded by Odysseus.

**Polyxena**  Daughter of Priam and Hecuba of Troy. She was sacrificed on the grave of Achilles by Neoptolemus.

**Popol Vuh**  Sacred 'book of counsel' of the Quiché or K'iche' Maya people.

**Poseidon**  God of the sea, and of sweet waters. Also the god of earthquakes. His is brother to Zeus and Hades, who divided the earth between them.

**Pradyumna**  Son of Krishna and Rukmini.

**Prahasta (Long-Hand)**  One of Ravana's generals.

**Prajapati**  Creator of the universe, father of the gods, demons and all creatures, later known as Brahma.

**Priam**  King of Troy, married to Hecuba, who bore him Hector, Paris, Helenus, Cassandra, Polyxena, Deiphobus and Troilus. He was murdered by Neoptolemus.

**Pritha**  Mother of Karna and of the Pandavas.

**Prithivi**  Consort of Dyaus and goddess of the earth.

**Proetus**  King of Argos, son of Abas.

**Prometheus**  A Titan, son of Iapetus and Themus. He was champion of mortal men, which he created from clay. He stole fire from the gods and was universally hated by them.

**Proteus**  The old man of the sea who watched Poseidon's seals.

**Psyche**  A beautiful nymph who was the secret wife of Eros, against the wishes of his mother Aphrodite, who sent Psyche to perform many tasks in hope of causing her death. She eventually married Eros and was allowed to become partly immortal.

**Ptah**  Creator god and deity of Memphis who was married to Sekhmet. Ptah built the boats to carry the souls of the dead to the afterlife.

**Puddock**  Frog.

**Pulque**  Alcoholic drink made from fermented agave.

**Purusha**  The cosmic man, he was sacrificed and his dismembered body became all the parts of the cosmos, including the four classes of society.

**Purvey**  To provide or supply.

**Pushkara**  Nala's brother.

**Pushpaka**  Rama's chariot.

**Putana**  A rakshasi.

**Pygmalion**  A sculptor who was so lonely he carved a statue of a beautiful woman, and eventually fell in love with it. Aphrodite brought the image to life.

**Quauhtli**  Eagle.

**Quetzalcoatl**  Deity and god of wind. He is represented as a feathered or plumed serpent and is usually a wise and benevolent god. Offspring of Ometeotl and Omecihuatl, he is also known as Kukulkan.

**Ra**  God of the sun, ruling male deity of Egypt whose name means 'sole creator'.

**Radha**  The principal mistress of Krishna.

**Ragnarok**  The end of the world.

**Rahula**  Son of Siddhartha and Yashodhara.

**Raiden**  God of thunder. He traditionally has a fierce and demonic appearance.

**Rakshasas**  Demons and devils.

**Ram of Mendes**  Sacred symbol of fatherhood and fertility.

**Rama** or **Ramachandra**  A prince and hero of the Ramayana, worshipped as an incarnation of Vishnu.

**Ra-Molo**  (Lesotho) Father of fire, a chief who ruled by fear. When trying to kill his brother, Tau the lion, he was turned into a monster with the head of a sheep and the body of a snake.

**Rangatira**  Chief, warrior, gentleman.

**Regin**  A blacksmith who educated Sigurd.

**Reinga**  The spirit land, the home of the dead.

**Reservations**  Tracts of land allocated to the native American people by the United States Government with the purpose of bringing the many separate tribes under state control.

**Rewati**  Daughter of Raja, marries Balarama.

**Rhadha**  Wife of Adiratha, a gopi of Brindaban and lover of Krishna.

**Rhea**  Mother of the Olympian gods. Cronus ate each of her children, but she concealed Zeus and gave Cronus a swaddled rock in his place.

**Rill**  Small stream.

**Rishis**  Sacrificial priests associated with the devas in Swarga.

**Rituparna**  King of Ayodhya.

**Rohini**  The wife of Vasudeva, mother of Balarama and Subhadra, and carer of the young Krishna. Another Rohini is a goddess and consort of Chandra.

**Rōnin**  Samurai whose master had died or fallen out of favour.

**Rubáiyát**  Collection of poems written by Omar Khayyám.

**Rúdábeh**  Wife of Zál and mother of Rustem.

**Rudra**  Lord of Beasts and disease, later evolved into Shiva.

**Rukma**  Rukmini's eldest brother.

**Rustem** Son of Zál and Rúdábeh, he was a brave and mighty warrior who undertook seven labours to travel to Mázinderán to rescue Kai-káús. Once there, he defeated the White Demon and rescued Kai-káús. He rode the fabled stallion Rakhsh and is also known as Rustam.

**Ryō** Traditional gold currency.

**Sabdh** Mother of Ossian, or Oisin.

**Sabitu** Goddess of the sea.

**Sagara** King of Ayodhya.

**Sahadeva** Pandava twin skilled in swordsmanship.

**Sahib diwan** Lord high treasurer or chief royal executive.

**Saiawúsh** Son of Kai-káús, who was put through trial by fire when Sudaveh, Kai-káús's wife, told him that Saiawúsh had taken advantage of her. His innocence was proven when the fire did not harm him. He was eventually killed by Afrásiyáb.

**Saithe** Blessed.

**Sajara** (Mali) God of rainbows. He takes the form of a multi-coloured serpent.

**Sake** Japanese rice wine.

**Sakuni** Cousin of Duryodhana.

**Salam** Greeting or salutation.

**Saláman** Son of the Shah of Yunan, who fell in love with Absál, his nurse. She died after they had a brief love affair and he returned to his father.

**Salmali tree** Cotton tree.

**Salmon** A symbol of great wisdom, around which many Scottish legends revolve.

**Sám** Mighty warrior who fought and won many battles. Father of Zál and grandfather to Rustem.

**Sambu** Son of Krishna.

**Sampati** Elder brother of Jatayu.

**Samurai** Noblemen who were part of the military in medieval Japan.

**Sanehat** Member of the royal bodyguard.

**Sangu** (Mozambique) Goddess who protects pregnant women, depicted as a hippopotamus.

**Santa** Daughter of Dasharatha.

**Sarapis** Composite deity of Apis and Osiris, sometimes known as Serapis. Thought to be created to unify Greek and Egyptian citizens under the Greek pharaoh Ptolemy.

**Sarasvati** The tongue of Rama.

**Sarcophagus** Stone coffin.

**Sargon of Akkad** Raised by Akki, a husbandman, after being hidden at birth. Sargon became King of Assyria and a great hero. He founded the first library in Babylon. Similar to King Arthur or Perseus.

**Sarsar** Harsh, whistling wind.

**Sasabonsam** (Ashanti) Forest ogre.

**Sati** Daughter of Daksha and Prasuti, first wife of Shiva.

**Satrughna** One of Dasharatha's four sons.

**Satyavan** Truth speaker, husband of Savitri.

**Satyavati** A fisher-maid, wife of Bhishma's father, Shamtanu.

**Satyrs** Elemental spirits which took great pleasure in chasing nymphs. They had horns, a hairy body and cloven hooves.

**Saumanasa** A mighty elephant.

**Scamander** River running across the Trojan plain, and father of Teucer.

**Scarab** Dung beetle, often used as a symbol of the immortal human soul and regeneration.

**Scylla and Charybdis** Scylla was a monster who lived on a rock of the same name in the Straits of Messina, devouring sailors.

Charybdis was a whirlpool in the Straits which was supposedly inhabited by the hateful daughter of Poseidon.

**Seal** Often believed that seals were fallen angels. Many families are descended from seals, some of which had webbed hands or feet. Some seals were the children of sea-kings who had become enchanted (selkies).

**Seelie-Court** The court of the Fairies, who travelled around their realm. They were usually fair to humans, doling out punishment that was morally sound, but they were quick to avenge insults to fairies.

**Segu** (Swahili, East Africa) Guide who informs humans where honey can be found.

**Sekhmet** Solar deity who led the pharaohs in war. She is goddess of healing and was sent by Ra to destroy humanity when people turned against the sun god. She is portrayed with the head of a lion.

**Selene** Moon-goddess, daughter of Hyperion and Theia. She was seduced by Pan, but loved Endymion.

**Selkie** Seals with the capacity to become humans, leaving their seal-skins to take human form.

**Seneschal** Steward of a royal or noble household.

**Sensei** Teacher.

**Seriyut** A disciple of Buddha.

**Sessrymnir** Freyia's home.

**Set** God of chaos and evil, brother of Osiris, who killed him by tricking him into getting into a chest, which he then threw in the Nile, before cutting Osiris's body into fourteen separate pieces. Also known as Seth.

**Sgeulachd** Stories.

**Shah Nameh** *The Book of Kings* written by Ferdowski, one of the world's longest epic poems, which describes the mythology and history of the Persian Empire.

**Shaikh** Respected religious man.

**Shaivas or Shaivites** Worshippers of Shiva.

**Shakti** Power or wife of a god and Shiva's consort as his feminine aspect.

**Shaman** Also known as the 'Medicine Men' of Indian tribes, it was the shaman's role to cultivate communication with the spirit world. They were endowed with knowledge of all healing herbs, and learned to diagnose and cure disease. They could foretell the future, find lost property and had power over animals, plants and stones.

**Shamash** God of the sun and protector of Gilgamesh, the great Babylonian hero. Known as the son of Sin, the moon god, he is also portrayed as a judge of good and evil.

**Shamtanu** Father of Bhishma.

**Shankara** A great magician, friend of Chand Sadagar.

**Shashti** The Sixth, goddess who protects children and women in childbirth.

**Shesh** A serpent that takes human birth through Devaki.

**Shi-en** Fairy dwelling.

**Shinto** Indigenous religion of Japan, from the pre-sixth century to the present day.

**Shireen** Married to Khosru. Her beauty meant that she was desired by many, including Khosru's own son by his previous marriage. She killed herself rather than give in to her stepson.

**Shitala** The Cool One and goddess of smallpox.

**Shiva** One of the two great gods of post-Vedic Hinduism with Vishnu.

**Shogun** Military ruler or overlord.

**Shoji** Sliding door, usually a lattice screen of paper.

**Shu** God of the air and half of the first divine couple created by Atem. Brother and husband to Tefnut, father to Keb and Nut.

**Shubistán** Household.

**Shudra** One of the four fundamental colours (caste).

**Siddhas** Musical ministrants of the upper air.

**Sif** Thor's wife; known for her beautiful hair.

**Sigi** Son of Odin.

**Sigmund** Warrior able to pull the sword from Branstock in the Volsung's hall.

**Signy** Volsung's daughter.

**Sigurd** Son of Sigmund, and bearer of his sword. Slays Fafnir the dragon.

**Sigyn** Loki's faithful wife.

**Símúrgh** Griffin, an animal with the body of a lion and the head and wings of an eagle. Known to hold great wisdom. Also called a symurgh.

**Sin** God of the moon, worshipped primarily in Ur.

**Sindri** Dwarf who worked with Brokki to fashion gifts for the gods; commissioned by Loki.

**Sirens** Sea nymphs who are half-bird, half-woman, whose song lures hapless sailors to their death.

**Sisyphus** King of Ephrya and a trickster who outwitted Autolycus. He was one of the greatest sinners in Hades.

**Sita** Daughter of the earth, adopted by Janaka, wife of Rama.

**Skadi** Goddess of winter and the wife of Niord for a short time.

**Skanda** Six-headed son of Shiva and a warrior god.

**Skrymir** Giant who battled against Thor.

**Sleipnir** Odin's steed.

**Sluagh** The host of the dead, seen fighting in the sky and heard by mortals.

**Smote** Struck with a heavy blow.

**Sohráb** Son of Rustem and Tahmineh, Sohráb was slain in battle by his own father, who killed him by mistake.

**Sol** The sun-maiden.

**Soma** A god and a drug, the elixir of life.

**Somerled** Lord of the Isles, and legendary ancestor of the Clan MacDonald.

**Squaw** North American Indian married woman.

**Squint-Eye** One of Ramana's monsters.

**Squire** Shield- or armour-bearer of a knight.

**Srutakirti** Daughter of Kushadhwaja.

**Stone Giants** A malignant race of stone beings whom the Iroquois believed invaded Indian territory, threatening the Confederation of the Five Nations. These fierce and hostile creatures lived off human flesh and were intent on exterminating the human race.

**Stoorworm** A great water monster which frequented lochs. When it thrust its great body from the sea, it could engulf islands and whole ships. Its appearance prophesied devastation.

**Styx** River in Arcadia and one of the four rivers in the Underworld. Charon ferried dead souls across it into Hades, and Achilles was dipped into it to make him immortal.

**Subrahmanian** Son of Shiva, a mountain deity.

**Sugriva** The chief of the five great monkeys in the Ramayana.

**Sukanya** The wife of Chyavana.

**Suman** Son of Asamanja.

**Sumantra** A noble Brahman.

**Sumati** Wife of Sagara.

**Sumedha** A righteous Brahman who dwelt in the city of Amara.

**Sumitra** One of Dasharatha's three wives, mother of Lakshmana and Satrughna.

**Suniti** Mother of Dhruva.

**Suparshwa** One of Ravana's counsellors.

**Supranakha** A rakshasi, sister of Ravana.

**Surabhi** The wish-bestowing cow.

**Surcoat** Loose robe, traditionally worn over armour.

**Surtr** Fire-giant who eventually destroys the world at Ragnarok.

**Surya** God of the sun.

**Susanoo** God of the storm. He is depicted as a contradictory character with both good and bad characteristics. He was banished from Heaven after trying to kill his sister, Amaterasu.

**Sushena** A monkey chief.

**Svasud** Father of summer.

**Swarga** An Olympian paradise, where all wishes and desires are gratified.

**Sweating** A ritual customarily associated with spiritual purification and prayer practised by most tribes throughout North America prior to sacred ceremonies or vision quests. Steam was produced within a 'sweat lodge', a low, dome-shaped hut, by sprinkling water on heated stones.

**Syrinx** An Arcadian nymph who was the object of Pan's love.

**Tablet of Destinies** Cuneiform clay tablet on which the fates were written. Tiawath had given this to Kingu, but it was taken by Merodach when he defeated them. The storm god Zu later stole it for himself.

**Taiaha** A weapon made of wood.

**Tailtiu** One of the most famous royal residences of ancient Ireland.

**Tall** One of Ravana's counsellors.

**Tammuz** Solar deity of Eridu who, with Gishzida, guards the gates of Heaven. Protector of Anu.

**Tamsil** Example or guidance.

**Tangi** Funeral, dirge. Assembly to cry over the dead.

**Taniwha** Sea monster, water spirit.

**Tantalus** Son of Zeus who told the secrets of the gods to mortals and stole their nectar and ambrosia. He was condemned to eternal torture in Hades, where he was tempted by food and water but allowed to partake of neither.

**Taoism** Taoism (or Daoism) came into being at roughly the same time as Confucianism, although its tenets were radically different and were largely founded on the philosophies of Lao Tzu (Laozi). While Confucius argued for a system of state discipline, Taoism strongly favoured self-discipline and looked upon nature as the architect of essential laws. A newer form of Taoism evolved after the Burning of the Books, placing great emphasis on spirit worship and pacification of the gods.

**Tapu** Sacred, supernatural possession of power. Involves spiritual rules and restrictions.

**Tara** Also known as Temair, the Hill of Tara was the popular seat of the ancient High-Kings of Ireland from the earliest times to the sixth century. Located in Co. Meath, it was also the place where great noblemen and chieftains congregated during wartime, or for significant events.

**Tara** Sugriva's wife.

**Tartarus** Dark region, below Hades.

**Tau** (Lesotho) Brother to Ra-Molo, depicted as a lion.

**Taua** War party.

**Tefnut** Goddess of water and rain. Married to Shu, who was also her brother. She, like Sekhmet, is portrayed with the head of a lion. Also known as Tefenet.

**Telegonus** Son of Odysseus and Circe. He was allegedly responsible for his father's death.

**Telemachus** Son of Odysseus and Penelope who was aided by Athene in helping his mother to keep away the suitors in Odysseus's absence.

**Temu** The evening form of Ra, the Sun God.

**Tengu** Goblin or gnome, often depicted as bird-like. A powerful fighter with weapons.

**Tenochtitlán** Capital city of the Aztecs, founded around AD 1350 and the site of the 'Great Temple'. Now Mexico City.

**Teo-Amoxtli** Divine book.

**Teocalli** Great temple built in Tenochtitlán, which is now Mexico City.

**Teotleco** Festival of the Coming of the Gods; also the twelfth month of the Aztec calendar.

**Tepee** A conical-shaped dwelling constructed of buffalo hide stretched over lodge-poles. Mostly used by native American tribes living on the plains.

**Tepeyollotl** God of caves, desert places and earthquakes, whose name means 'heart of the mountain'. He is depicted as a jaguar, often leaping at the sun. Also known as Tepeolotlec.

**Tepitoton** Household gods.

**Tereus** King of Daulis who married Procne, daughter of Pandion King of Athens. He fell in love with Philomela, raped her and cut out her tongue.

**Tezcatlipoca** Supreme deity and Lord of the Smoking Mirror. He was also patron of royalty and warriors. Invented human sacrifice to the gods. Offspring of Ometeotl and Omecihuatl, he is known as the Jupiter of the Aztec gods.

**Thalia** Muse of pastoral poetry and comedy.

**Theia** Goddess of many names, and mother of the sun.

**Theseus** Son of King Aegeus of Athens. A cycle of legends has been woven around his travels and life.

**Thetis** Chief of the Nereids loved by both Zeus and Poseidon. They married her to a mortal, Peleus, and their child was Achilles. She tried to make him immortal by dipping him in the River Styx.

**Thialfi** Thor's servant, taken when his peasant father unwittingly harms Thor's goat.

**Thiassi** Giant and father of Skadi, he tricked Loki into bringing Idunn to him. Thrymheim is his kingdom.

**Thomas the Rhymer** Also called 'True Thomas', he was Thomas of Ercledoune, who lived in the thirteenth century. He met with the Queen of Elfland, and visited her country, was given clothes and a tongue that could tell no lie. He was also given the gift of prophecy, and many of his predictions were proven true.

**Thor** God of thunder and of war (with Tyr). Known for his huge size, and red hair and beard. Carries the hammer Miolnir. Slays Jormungander at Ragnarok.

**Thoth** God of the moon. Invented the arts and sciences and regulated the seasons. He is portrayed with the head of an ibis or a baboon.

**Three-Heads** One of Ravana's monsters.

**Thrud** Thor's daughter.

**Thrudheim** Thor's realm. Also called Thrudvang.

**Thunder-Tooth** Leader of the rakshasas at the siege of Lanka.

**Tiawath** Primeval dark ocean or abyss, Tiawath is also a monster and evil deity of the deep. She took the form of a dragon or sea serpent and battled the gods of light for supremacy over all living beings. She was eventually defeated by Merodach, who used her body to create Heaven and Earth.

**Tiglath-Pileser I**  King of Assyria, who made it a leading power for centuries.

**Tiki**  First man created, a figure carved of wood, or other representation of man.

**Tirawa**  The name given to the Great Creator (*see* Great Spirit) by the Pawnee tribe who believed that four direct paths led from his house in the sky to the four semi-cardinal points: north-east, north-west, south-east and south-west.

**Tiresias**  A Theban who was given the gift of prophecy by Zeus. He was blinded for seeing Athene bathing. He continued to use his prophetic talents after his death, advising Odysseus.

**Tisamenus**  Son of Orestes, who inherited the Kingdom of Argos and Sparta.

**Titania**  Queen of the fairies.

**Tlaloc**  God of rain and fertility, so important to the people, because he ensured a good harvest, that the Aztec heaven or paradise was named Tlalocan in his honour.

**Tlazolteotl**  Goddess of ordure, filth and vice. Also known as the earth-goddess or Tlaelquani, meaning 'filth-eater'. She acted as a confessor of sins or wrongdoings.

**Tohu-mate**  Omen of death.

**Tohunga**  A priest; a possessor of supernatural powers.

**Toltec**  Civilization that preceded the Aztecs.

**Tomahawk**  Hatchet with a stone or iron head used in war or hunting.

**Tonalamatl**  Record of the Aztec calendar, which was recorded in books made from bark paper.

**Tonalpohualli**  Aztec calendar composed of twenty thirteen-day weeks called trecenas.

**Totec**  Solar deity known as Our Great Chief.

**Totemism** System of belief in which people share a relationship with a spirit animal or natural being with whom they interact. Examples include Ea, who is represented by a fish.

**Toxilmolpilia** The binding up of the years.

**Tristan** Nephew of King Mark of Cornwall, who travels to Ireland to bring Iseult back to marry his uncle. On the way, he and Iseult consume a love potion and fall madly in love before their story ends tragically.

**Triton** A sea-god, and son of Poseidon and Amphitrite. He led the Argonauts to the sea from Lake Tritonis.

**Trojan War** War waged by the Greeks against Troy, in order to reclaim Menelaus's wife Helen, who had eloped with the Trojan prince Paris. Many important heroes took part, and form the basis of many legends and myths.

**Truage** Tribute or pledge of peace or truth, usually made on payment of a tax.

**Tsuki-yomi** God of the moon, brother of Amaterasu and Susanoo.

**Tuat** The other world or land of the dead.

**Tupuna** Ancestor.

**Tvashtar** Craftsman of the gods.

**Tyndareus** King of Sparta, perhaps the son of Perseus's daughter Grogphone. Expelled from Sparta but restored by Heracles. Married Leda and fathered Helen and Clytemnestra, among others.

**Tyr** Son of Frigga and the god of war (with Thor). Eventually kills Garm at Ragnarok.

**Tzompantli** Pyramid of Skulls.

**Uayeb** The five unlucky days of the Mayan calendar, which were believed to be when demons from the underworld could reach Earth. People would often avoid leaving their houses on uayeb days.

**Ubaaner**  Magician, whose name meant 'splitter of stones', who created a wax crocodile that came to life to swallow up the man who was trying to seduce his wife.

**Uisneach**  A hill formation between Mullingar and Athlone said to mark the centre of Ireland.

**uKqili**  (Zulu) Creator god.

**Uller**  God of winter, whom Skadi eventually marries.

**Unseelie Court**  An unholy court comprising a kind of fairies, antagonistic to humans. They took the form of a kind of Sluagh, and shot humans and animals with elf-shots.

**Urd**  One of the Norns.

**Urien**  King of Gore, husband of Morgan le Fey and father to Yvain.

**Urmila**  Second daughter of Janaka.

**Usha**  Wife of Aniruddha, daughter of Vanasur.

**Ushas**  Goddess of the dawn.

**Utgard-loki**  King of the giants. Tricked Thor.

**Uther Pendragon**  King of England in sub-Roman Britain; father of King Arthur.

**Utixo**  (Hottentot) Creator god.

**Ut-Napishtim**  Ancestor of Gilgamesh, whom Gilgamesh sought out to discover how to prevent death. Similar to Noah in that he was sent a vision warning him of a great deluge. He built an ark in seven days, filling it with his family, possessions and all kinds of animals.

**Uz**  Deity symbolized by a goat.

**Vach**  Goddess of speech.

**Vajrahanu**  One of Ravana's generals.

**Vala**  Another name for Norns.

**Valfreya**  Another name for Freyia.

**Valhalla**  Odin's hall for the celebrated dead warriors chosen by the Valkyries.

**Vali**  The cruel brother of Sugriva, dethroned by Rama.

**Valkyries**  Odin's attendants, led by Freyia. Chose dead warriors to live at Valhalla. Also spelled as Valkyrs.

**Vamadeva**  One of Dasharatha's priests.

**Vanaheim**  Home of the Vanir.

**Vanir**  Race of gods in conflict with the Aesir; they are gods of the sea and wind.

**Varuna**  Ancient god of the sky and cosmos, later, god of the waters.

**Vasishtha**  One of Dasharatha's priests.

**Vassal**  Person under the protection of a feudal lord.

**Vasudev**  Descendant of Yadu, husband of Rohini and Devaki, father of Krishna.

**Vasudeva**  A name of Narayana or Vishnu.

**Vavasor**  Vassal or tenant of a baron or lord who himself has vassals.

**Vedic**  Mantras, hymns.

**Vernandi**  One of the Norns.

**Vichitravirya**  Bhishma's half-brother.

**Vidar**  Slays Fenris.

**Vidura**  Friend of the Pandavas.

**Vigrid**  The plain where the final battle is held.

**Vijaya**  Karna's bow.

**Vikramaditya**  A king identified with Chandragupta II.

**Vintail**  Moveable front of a helmet.

**Virabhadra**  A demon that sprang from Shiva's lock of hair.

**Viradha**  A fierce rakshasa, seizes Sita, slain by Rama.

**Virupaksha**  The elephant who bears the whole world.

**Vishnu**  The Preserver, Vedic sun-god and one of the two great gods of post-Vedic Hinduism.

**Vision Quest**  A sacred ceremony undergone by native Americans to establish communication with the spirit set to direct them in life. The quest lasted up to four days and nights and was preceded by a period of solitary fasting and prayer.

**Vivasvat**  The sun.

**Vizier**  High-ranking official or adviser. Also known as vizir or vazir.

**Volsung**  Family of great warriors about whom a great saga was spun.

**Vrishadarbha**  King of Benares.

**Vrishasena**  Son of Karna, slain by Arjuna.

**Vyasa**  Chief of the royal chaplains.

**Wairua**  Spirit, soul.

**Wanjiru**  (Kikuyu) Maiden who was sacrificed by her village to appease the gods and make it rain after years of drought.

**Weighing of the heart**  Procedure carried out after death to assess whether the deceased was free from sin. If the deceased's heart weighed less than the feather of Ma'at, they would join Osiris in the Fields of Peace.

**Whare**  Hut made of fern stems tied together with flax and vines, and roofed in with raupo (reeds).

**White Demon**  Protector of Mázinderán. He prevented Kai-káús and his army from invading.

**Wolverine**  Large mammal of the musteline family with dark, very thick, water-resistant fur, inhabiting the forests of North America and Eurasia.

**Wroth**  Angry.

**Wyrd**  One of the Norns.

**Xanthus & Balius**  Horses of Achilles, immortal offspring of Zephyrus the west wind. A gift to Achilles's father Peleus.

**Xipe Totec** High priest and son of Ometeotl and Omecihuatl. Also known as the god of the seasons.

**Xiupohualli** Solar year, composed of eighteen twenty-day months.

**Yadu** A prince of the Lunar dynasty.

**Yakshas** Same as rakshasas.

**Yakunin** Government official.

**Yama** God of Death, king of the dead and son of the sun.

**Yamato Take** Legendary warrior and prince. Also known as Yamato Takeru.

**Yashiki** Residence or estate, usually of a daimyō.

**Yasoda** Wife of Nand.

**Yemaya** (Yoruba) Wife of Obatala.

**Yemoja** (Yoruba) Goddess of water and protector of women.

**Yggdrasill** The World Ash, holding up the Nine Worlds. Does not fall at Ragnarok.

**Ymir** Giant created from fire and ice; his body created the world.

**Yo** The female principle who, joined with In, the male side, brought about creation and the first gods. In and Yo correspond to the Chinese Yang and Yin.

**Yomi** The underworld.

**Yudhishthira** The eldest of the Pandavas, a great soldier.

**Yuki-Onna** The Snow-Bride or Lady of the Snow, who represents death.

**Yvain** Son of Morgan le Fay and knight of the Round Table, who goes on chivalric quests with a lion he rescued from a dragon.

**Zahid** Holy man.

**Zál** Son of Sám, who was born with pure white hair. Sám abandoned Zál, who was raised by the Símúrgh, or griffins. Zal became a great warrior, second only to his son, Rustem. Also known as Ním-rúz and Dustán.

**Zephyr** Gentle breeze.

**Zeus** King of gods, god of sky, weather, thunder, lightning, home, hearth and hospitality. He plays an important role as the voice of justice, arbitrator between man and gods, and among them. Married to Hera, but lover of dozens of others.

**Zohák** Serpent-king and figure of evil. Father of Mihrab.

**Zu** God of the storm, who took the form of a huge bird. Similar to the Persian símúrgh.

**Zukin** Head covering.

# COLLECTOR'S EDITIONS

## FLAME TREE

A wide range of new and classic fiction, including short story anthologies, *Collectable Classics*, *Gothic Fantasy* collections and *Epic Tales* of mythology.

•

Available at all good bookstores, and online at *flametreepublishing.com*

## FLAME TREE PUBLISHING